T0369454

the Way Out

The Road, The Sky, The Love, The Journey

Dick Elder

iUniverse LLC
Bloomington

THE WAY OUT
THE ROAD, THE SKY, THE LOVE, THE JOURNEY

This is a work of fiction. All of the characters, names, incidents, organizations, and dialogue in this novel are either the products of the author's imagination or are used fictitiously.

iUniverse books may be ordered through booksellers or by contacting:

iUniverse
1663 Liberty Drive
Bloomington, IN 47403
www.iuniverse.com
1-800-Authors (1-800-288-4677)

Because of the dynamic nature of the Internet, any web addresses or links contained in this book may have changed since publication and may no longer be valid. The views expressed in this work are solely those of the author and do not necessarily reflect the views of the publisher, and the publisher hereby disclaims any responsibility for them.

Any people depicted in stock imagery provided by Thinkstock are models, and such images are being used for illustrative purposes only.

Certain stock imagery © Thinkstock

ISBN: 978-1-4759-9623-4 (sc)
ISBN: 978-1-4759-9625-8 (hc)
ISBN: 978-1-4759-9624-1 (e)

Library of Congress Control Number: 2013911198

Printed in the United States of America

iUniverse rev. date: 6/19/2013

 **acknowledgments**

during the six months it took to write this story, I relied heavily on the comments and suggestions of my nine first-draft readers who reviewed chapters as I completed them. These readers were both male and female and very diverse in terms of background, education, and age. The youngest was twenty-six, the oldest eighty-seven. I would be remiss if I did not acknowledge their contribution to this work. So thank you for your help, Annabelle, Howard, Carmela, Don, Julie, Liz, Chris, Debbie and Lauren.

For technical assistance, I went to Ken Hendrickson who flew for United States Steel for five years in the 1950s, and later for United Airlines until he retired. He's flown dozens of different aircraft and was able to provide practical, first-hand information on a whole range of related topics.

My good friend and motorcycle buddy, Don Turner, was a Naval aviator. His experiences, particularly relating to the type of training he received, were critical to give the main character credibility.

I also want to thank my editor, Elizabeth Testa, who showed me what was wrong and suggested ways to make it right. This is the second novel she has edited for me and you can be sure, if she's willing to put up with me, she will edit my next one.

Dick Elder

 prologue

young lady in cheerful scrubs stepped through the open door into the waiting room and called my name. I put down the magazine I was reading.

"Mr. Richard Elkins?"

I nodded.

"Good morning, sir. I'm Margaret. And how are you feeling today?"

I was going to say "fine," but if I was fine, why the hell would I be at the Mayo Clinic? No, I wasn't fine. Not even close to fine. Basically, I was a goner. But what the heck. She seemed so hopeful.

"Fine," I said.

Margaret smiled sweetly and said, "Well, that's good. Now, if you'll follow me, I'll take you back to meet your cardiologist."

We walked the length of a long, well-lit hallway lined with doors leading to examination rooms. Near the end, Margaret stopped at one, knocked and opened it, motioning me to follow. At a small desk at the back of the room sat the doctor, wearing a white coat, a light blue shirt and a colorful tie with a rather large Windsor knot. The man had gray hair, wore rimless glasses and presented a pleasant, kindly face. I judged him to be in his late sixties or early seventies.

"Doctor Hasfeld," Margaret said. "Richard Elkins." She nodded at us both and withdrew.

Doctor Hasfeld glanced at the chart on his desk. "Do sit down, Mr. Elkins." He gestured graciously.

I took a seat on a small leather couch adjacent to the desk. The doctor scanned what I assumed were notes and reports sent to him from my cardiologist in Los Angeles. Then he swiveled his chair toward me, crossed his legs and smiled. "Now then. Tell me about yourself—what sort of life you've lived, what you've been doing since you found out you have some heart problems—that sort of thing."

I gave the doc a twenty minute bio and mentioned that even at age 83 I still rode my Harley-Davidson motorcycle, a Heritage Softail.

"Sounds to me like you've lived a pretty exciting and interesting life. You're probably still able to ride that motorcycle because you seem to be in darn good shape. In fact, if I hadn't noted your age here," he tapped a forefinger on the paperwork, "I might have taken you to be considerably younger." He considered my face for a moment. "Perhaps early seventies."

I brightened. "I get that all the time. People think I'm a lot younger than I am." My smile faded. "Which can be a problem."

"Really? How so?"

"They expect me to be able to keep up with them. You know, like I was their age or something. Well, I just can't do it anymore." I paused and looked down at my boots. Without emotion I added, "I'm old and I just don't have the get up and go like I used to. Fact is, I never thought I'd even make it to eighty, let alone eighty-three."

Dr. Hasfeld wrote something on a pad. "At what age did your parents die?"

"Both my parents were killed in an auto accident in 1934. I was an only child. My father's sister, my aunt Rose, and my uncle Jack raised me."

The doctor asked me to undress and then gave me a very thorough examination. He spent a lot of time listening to my heart. When he was finished, I put on my clothes and took a seat on the couch.

Returning to his desk, he made some notes on his pad, stared at them for a moment or two, then swiveled his chair to face me again. "Okay, this is what I recommend we do. From the information sent to me by your doctor in LA, you've had some problems with both the aortic and the mitral valves for some time now. Whereas the aortic problem was characterized as moderate and the mitral valve as moderately severe, it appears that there has been further degradation, so that you now have severe mitral regurgitation and a moderately severe aortic condition. So I'd like you to go through a series of tests so we can pin point exactly where you are right now, and then come up with a plan to address these issues."

I didn't say anything, but I did nod my head to indicate that I understood what he'd just said. It wasn't news, exactly, but hearing him say it did set me back a bit.

"After the tests have been completed and evaluated, I'll send you to talk to a cardiac surgeon so you will know what, if any, surgical intervention is indicated. Then I'll see you again and we'll talk about what regimen you wish to follow. I do want to point out that you are always in control." He smiled and added. "It's like being on a carousel. You can get off at any time. It's always your choice."

 chapter one

O nce again, I was sitting on the little couch in Dr. Hasfeld's office. Several weeks had passed. During that time I endured just about every type of test you can think of and quite a few you can't even imagine. When the results of all these tests had been turned over to Dr. Hasfeld, they confirmed that my mitral valve was pretty much shot and the aortic valve wasn't much better. Hasfeld had sent me to see the specialist who explained why I needed a mitral valve replacement and he said that while he had me open he might find that the aortic should be replaced as well.

The surgeon took his time and explained what was involved, how long it would take to recuperate from the surgery and the course of rehabilitation that I'd have to follow before I could expect a complete recovery. This could take a year or more, he said, but he thought that given my otherwise good physical shape, I should expect a good outcome.

Dr. Hasfeld was reading the information on his desk-top computer. After several minutes he said, "A very comprehensive report. You know what the surgeon said about what he thought needed to be done. And after looking over all of your tests and reading this I would certainly agree with his findings. You need to get those valves repaired or replaced." He frowned. "And honestly, I wouldn't wait too long before you have it done."

I thought a moment and smiled. "And what, in your opinion, would be too long?"

The doctor scratched his head, looked back at the computer screen, put a finger to pursed lips and said, "Six months could be too long, although it could be a year. But here's the thing, the longer you wait, the more likely you will become weaker, and thus the surgery will present a greater risk. What I'm saying is, if you decide to get it done, sooner rather than later will provide the best chance for a successful outcome." He gave me a questioning look.

"I'm sure you're right, and I have no doubt that you guys can pull it off successfully, but here's what I've been thinking about these past few weeks."

Dr. Hasfeld gave me an encouraging nod.

"I've come to the conclusion," I said, "that at age eighty-three, plus a year or more to recuperate fully...so I'll be eighty-four, it doesn't make a hell of a lot of sense to go through all the pain and discomfort and time out of any kind of an active lifestyle just to gain a couple more years of life." I leaned forward and looked him in the eye. "I think that by the time I'm back to somewhat normal, assuming the anesthesia doesn't mess up my brain, which I've heard happens sometimes..."

I waited for a comment, but he didn't say anything so I went on. "So, by the time I can actually do anything that would be fun and worth going through all that stuff for, I'd probably have kidney failure or prostate cancer and all sorts of other things that eighty-four year old guys end up with. The bottom line is I'd end up with no life, that is, no life I'd be interested in, if you know what I mean."

He uncrossed his legs, laid his hands on his knees and said,

"So you're saying you would rather not have the operation and just let nature take its course?"

"Yes, that's what I'm saying. Remember, you said I could get off the carousel any time I wanted and I've decided to get off."

"I understand, and it is your decision to make. Frankly, I can't totally disagree with you, although I have to tell you that we've done valve replacements on men older than you and most of them did all right. But you do have time—not a lot of time—during which you may change your mind. And if you do, we are here to take care of you."

I nodded. He held up a hand and continued, "However, remember what I said before. If you wait too long..."

I jumped in, "I know. If I wait too long it may be too late. Well, I don't think I'll change my mind." I paused, not sure if I really wanted to ask the next question, or maybe not wanting to know the answer. Then I plunged in. "So tell me, if you had to take a guess," I circled my hand in the air, "an educated guess, how long do you think I have before I would become an invalid or, you know, in a wheelchair, or something?"

Or die? I couldn't quite bring myself to say it.

He tilted back in his chair, took a long breath through his nose and let it out slowly. He rubbed his lips with the back of his hand while he stared at me, apparently trying to get some inspiration before he spoke.

I returned his stare, widening my eyes and raising my eyebrows to let him know: I wanted an honest answer.

"You know, about the best answer I can give you is I don't really know. But that's not the answer you're looking for. So my best guess, and it's only a guess, is you have around four to six months before you start seriously going downhill, and, oh, I don't know, maybe a year before..." He spread his palms in a gesture of finality. He stood up. "I want to see you in a couple of months, or sooner if you're having problems, okay?"

I shook his outstretched hand. "Okay, I'll keep in touch." I turned to go, but stopped at the door. "And thanks a lot for all your help. By the way, I want to say that everybody, and I mean everybody, here at Mayo has been great. Couldn't have been better."

"Thank you. I'll pass that on. Good bye." He held the door open.

It was a long walk down the hallway that led to the waiting area that led to the parking lot that led to my car. I got in and sat there for a while. Aloud I said, "Okay. I made my decision. Now let's see if I have the guts to stick to it no matter what happens." I turned the key and started the engine. "What the heck, if life gets too tough I can always find a way out."

 chapter two

fter my appointment with Dr. Hasfeld, I slid into my favorite booth at Gallagher's Sports Bar and sat there for a while, sipping a Guinness and thinking about the doctor and his comment after I had told him the abbreviated version of my life. It was true what he'd said—I had led a rather exciting and interesting sort of life. I raised the glass and took a long drink. I glanced at one of the dozens of TV screens and momentarily watched but the college ball game seemed childish and irrelevant. My gaze returned to the dark beer in front of me. An exciting sort of life? Well, maybe so, at least compared to the lives that most men live.

After World War II ended, I decided to stay in the Navy and see if I could get in to the Naval Aviators School at Pensacola, Florida. I had been an aviation radio man during the war after passing up an opportunity to go to the V-12 pilot training program right after boot camp. I sure regretted that decision. But as it turned out, the pilot program was closed so I took the discharge and the $300 that went with it and went back to my aunt and uncle's home in northeast Ohio. Within a month I was in the College of Commerce and Administration at Ohio State University.

It was during my sophomore year that I befriended Ken

Wright, a vet who had been with General Patton's Seventh Army during the invasion of Sicily in 1943. He was older than me by at least twenty years, but in spite of our age difference, we hit it off from the get-go. Ken had purchased a Harley-Davidson Army Signal Corps motorcycle in 1947 when the government sold tons of WWII surplus equipment to civilians. Ken bought a brand new model WLA with a 45 cubic inch engine, for around a hundred bucks. I learned to ride on it and later I was able to buy one just like his–olive drab, with black-out lights, leather rifle scabbard, saddlebags and other Army accessories.

I had some interesting things happen to me back then on my Harley. Unlike the bikes we ride today, it didn't have all the fancy amenities. It had a kick start, with a spark advance and retard on the left handle, and a three-speed transmission with the shifter mounted on the left side the gas tank. The seat was not padded and resembled an old time bicycle seat. It wasn't easy to drive and a lot squirrelier than the bikes we ride now.

I took some bad falls on that bike. After classes, I rode the bike to my night time job at Charlie Barrows' Sohio gas station which was out in the country around 25 miles from the university. Besides gas and all the other filling station stuff, we sold cigars, cigarettes, chewing tobacco, candy bars and pop (also known as sodas in some parts of the country). I had never chewed tobacco, but the idea of it appealed to me.

One evening around midnight before locking up the station, I picked up a pack of Beech Nut chewing tobacco. I put a big chew in my mouth, got on the bike, kicked the starter and took off down Cleveland Avenue. I chewed as I rode along. It tasted real good...kind of sweet. I couldn't spit while moving as it would blow back in my face, so every now and then I'd stop, drain my mouth and continue on. I remember going down the road when suddenly I became very dizzy. The next thing I knew I had jumped the curb and driven up on someone's front lawn. I hit a tree with the left handlebar, which spun the bike around and it fell over on me. I swallowed my chew of Beech Nut! I crawled out from under the bike and immediately threw up all over the tidy little flower bed that surrounded the tree.

I was lying there in the dark retching when the porch light came on and a rather big guy in a plaid robe opened the front door. He stood under the light staring at me. I was still on my hands and knees trying to get rid of the remaining bits of tobacco that clung to the insides of my mouth and lips.

I guess the man couldn't quite believe what he was seeing at first. Then he roared, "What the hell do you think you're doing?"

"I'm real sorry, sir. It was an accident. I must have hit something and lost control of the bike."

The man walked down the steps and came up to me. Gazing down, he observed the mess I had made in his flowers and I'm sure he could smell the pungent fragrance that emanated from it.

"Jesus H. Christ," he growled. "Look at those flowers! And the stink! What did you do, shit your pants?"

He got a water hose and had me spray water on the mess, then he told me he wanted to see me the next day because I was going to straighten up his flower bed. To add insult to injury, I had to ask him to help me pick up the bike and straighten up my handle bars.

Not long afterwards, I was riding to school when it started to snow. I turned left on Neil Avenue and rode between the streetcar tracks heading for the campus entry. I could hear the clang, clang of the streetcar bell behind me so I turned to get out its way but when the front tire hit the steel rail, it somehow whipped around and the next thing I knew I was down on the tracks with the bike on me and the hot cylinders burning my leg. The streetcar was bearing down with the motorman clanging the bell like crazy. I thought, "Geeze, I made it through the war and now a God damn streetcar is going to kill me." Two students walking on the sidewalk saw what was going on and ran over and pulled me out from under the bike. Then—with the streetcar almost on us—we managed to pull the bike clear of the track. I learned a valuable lesson: Sometimes a motorcycle isn't the safest way to get around.

After graduating with a degree in business administration, I had several uninteresting jobs during 1950, and I began to wonder why the hell I'd majored in business when what I really wanted was to become a pilot. So on a cold and windy day in January, 1951, while on my way to get a haircut, I stopped in at a Navy recruiting office. I asked the chief petty officer behind the desk if the Navy was accepting men for their pilot training program.

"Selectively," he said. "You got to have a college degree, or no chance."

I nodded. "I have a bachelor of science degree." Then I told him my history as a Navy veteran having flown as a radioman/ gunner in dive bombers and other aircraft during the war.

That seemed to get his attention and the long and short of it is I enlisted as a cadet, starting my training at the Naval Air Station at Pensacola in the spring of 1951. The Korean War (called a "police action" by our government) had begun in June, 1950 and I think the reason I was able to get into the pilot program was because the war was creating an immediate need for more pilots. Many WWII pilots in the Navy Reserve were called back to serve in that war. I saw *The Bridges at Toko-Ri* a couple years later—the movie depicted the futility of that war and the impact it had on the WWII reservists who were called back to active duty. It sure had an impact on me because after serving as a fighter pilot over Korea, I saw life, and my place in it, in a whole new way. I remember after a particularly rough mission, a guy telling me, "Don't take life too seriously 'cause you're not going to get out of it alive."

chapter three

all the new cadets had to go through something like the basic training I had when I was in boot camp during WWII. Most of these cadets were just out of college and didn't have a clue about, well, anything. They thought life in the Navy's pilot program was going to be similar to college. They had a rude awakening and about half the guys that were in my class flunked out. After three months, I was commissioned an ensign and went on to flight school.

The primary trainer back then was the T-28 and I loved it, all of it—the flying, the courses in navigation, radio, tactics training— the works. I went on to NAS Whiting Field for advanced training in the F4U Corsair, a single engine fighter that saw a lot of action in WWII and was one hell of a hot airplane. The Corsair and I hit it off from the start and even though landing that plane could be tricky, I enjoyed the hell out of flying it. I took "tail hook" training which prepared me for carrier duty. By the time they got done with me and passed me for fleet service, I felt I was ready and could handle it. Was that naive? Probably.

My first posting was to the USS *Oriskany* (CVA-34), a relatively new attack carrier that had been assigned to Task Force 77 in October, 1952. I reported in February, 1953, about the time the ship was starting its fifth tour in the Korean war. Having been trained in the F4U, I was assigned to Squadron VF124. I wasn't the youngest pilot in that squadron but I sure was the greenest. Our CO was Commander Matt Hensen, a thirty-six year old fighter jock who had flown many combat missions in the Pacific during WWII. He was a great guy who not only helped me with advice on flying combat missions but was someone who, after a mission, I could talk to, and who helped me keep my nerves under control.

I'm not afraid to admit it—it could be pretty scary at times. Most of our problems came from ground fire which could be intense when flying low to bomb bridges or rail yards or to strafe trains and truck convoys. Landing in rough seas was no picnic either, especially when the ship was bobbing around like a cork— that could make you sweat a gallon before catching a wire.

I had flown only sixteen missions when I caught a shit pot full of enemy fire while on a bomb run. I was flying wing for Lt. Bill Gorman. He took a bad hit and lost control of his plane. I saw the plane roll to the left and go into a steep dive. My target was dead ahead and I couldn't do anything but go in and drop my bombs. On the pull out, I took another hit. I felt it rip through the plane just under my feet. I was soaked in sweat and, frankly, scared shitless. I could smell the hydraulic fluid but the controls seemed to be responding normally. The squadron joined up minus two aircraft, and headed back to the ship which fortunately wasn't very far. By this time, my nerves had calmed and I concentrated on landing the plane on the first try.

My eyes were glued to the LSO (Landing Signal Officer) as he signaled landing directions. I hit it just right, actually one of the best carrier landings of my career, but the right gear buckled, probably damaged from that last hit. Somehow my tail hook, which had caught the second wire, snapped loose and I went squirreling across the deck. They got me out of the cockpit pretty fast, God bless 'em, but my neck and shoulder took a beating from the harness and I was off the active roster for several weeks. The ship was relieved in late April and sailed back to San Diego, arriving about three weeks later.

Even though I loved flying them, I sure wasn't anxious to get back in a fighter, at least not anywhere near Korea. I asked for and received a transfer to multi-engine training. My goal after I got out was to have a career as a civilian commercial pilot and I knew the training and experience I'd have on larger, multi-engine planes could be my ticket to a job with one of the airlines. I completed the course and flew right seat in an R4D, the same plane the airlines had been using since the mid-1930s—the Douglas DC3. When I moved to the left seat as captain, I was promoted to Lieutenant JG (Junior Grade). A year later, I applied for training in four engine aircraft and ended my Navy tour in 1956 with the rank of Lieutenant, flying left seat in a Douglas R5D, the Navy version of the Douglas DC4.

After my discharge, I got a job flying co-pilot with Frontier Airlines, a young regional outfit that started up in 1950 flying DC3s on short haul routes to forty cities in the Rocky Mountain region. One of my first trips was Denver-Durango with four stops in between. It was fun. About the time you cleaned up (raised the landing gear and retracted flaps) you were over your next stop and doing a landing check list. When we flew the afternoon trip from Denver, we'd overnight in Durango and fly the route back north the next morning.

 chapter four

he DC3 was manned by a crew of three—pilot, co-pilot and stewardess (these days called a flight attendant). The plane held twenty-one passengers. However, very rarely did we have more than a dozen souls on board and sometimes only a couple of passengers. We also carried the mail, which subsidized the operation to a large extent.

It was on one of those afternoon Durango trips with Captain Art Stillman, a former Army Air Corps bomber pilot, that I met Angie Mertz, the stewardess. After our stop in Pueblo, where we picked up a couple of passengers, Angie came up front.

"You boys want some coffee?" she asked.

"Sure," I said. I had control and was scanning gauges and didn't look up. "Got anything to go with it?"

"Some packaged sweet rolls. You want one of those?"

"Yes. Thanks."

"How about you, Captain? You want something?"

Stillman turned around and looked at her for a moment. "Yeah, I'll have the same. Thanks."

Angie withdrew and slid the curtain closed. Stillman shot a look my way. "How about that? That's one very cute gal, don't you think?"

I was flying the aircraft and really hadn't taken notice. "I was a little busy but I'll take a good look when she comes back."

Angie returned with the coffee and rolls. "Here you go."

I turned to accept her offering and took that good look. Yes, she was cute...darn cute. About five foot eight, she had soft blond hair, wonderful blue eyes set wide apart, and a nice figure—at least, what I saw of it at that point. When she smiled, and she smiled a lot, the dimples on either side of her smallish mouth made me want to smile as well...which I did. "Thanks. I'm sorry, I forgot your name."

"It's Angie...Angie Mertz."

Captain Stillman turned back to the windscreen, "Okay, I've got it. There's Gunnison." He eased back on the power, the plane slowed. "Full flaps, drop the gear."

After unloading passengers and cargo at La Plata Field, Durango, we secured the plane and took a cab to town to check in at the Strater Hotel. Stillman and I shared a room, as was the custom with flight crews back then. Naturally, Angie had a separate room.

In the elevator going up to the third floor, Stillman said, "How 'bout we eat at that Chinese place across the street?" He didn't wait for an answer but said to Angie, "We'll meet you in the lobby in half an hour, okay?"

"Sure, that's fine."

The elevator door slid open at the third floor and we walked to our rooms. When we were in and had closed the door, Stillman asked, "So, my boy, what do you think of our little Angie? Was I right?"

"You got it exactly right. That's a real pretty girl with a great personality."

"But I'm too old for her and besides I'm married," he paused, "not that it would be a problem...you know. But you're not married.

So after dinner, I'll go up to the room and you should take her over to the bar and have a drink and see what develops."

I took off my tie and the uniform jacket and pulled a leather jacket from my bag. Shrugging into it, I said, "I'll just take it easy and we'll see what happens. As for the drink, that'll have to be Coke, straight on the rocks. I haven't been with the company long enough to start bending the rules." No alcohol was allowed within twenty-four hours of a flight.

After dinner, Stillman, true to his word, said he was tired and was going to bed. I looked at my watch. "It's only 8:30," I said to Angie. "Do you feel like chatting?"

We walked into the hotel bar and sat at a small table in the back of the room. After we'd each ordered a Coke, Angie looked at me with those amazing eyes. With elbows on the table, she rested her chin on tented fingers.

"So tell me, Richard, what's your story?"

I smiled. I liked the way she got right to the important stuff. I sat back in my chair and just savored the moment...it felt good. "It's a long story but I suppose I could come up with a synopsis. Would that do?"

Her lips blossomed into a large smile. "Sure, a synopsis will do but don't leave out any of the, you know, meaty parts. I want the good and the bad."

"And why would you even be interested? We just met."

Angie took a sip of Coke and set the glass down. "To tell you the truth, I've been hearing things about you from some of the other stews who have crewed with you and they say you're a very nice guy, very thoughtful and considerate and...what else?" She paused and cocked her head to one side, holding me with her unblinking eyes before continuing, "Oh, yes. You *are* a very nice looking man. Okay? That's my story. Now, now let's have yours."

Over the next hour or so I told her about myself—well, the highlights anyway. More than my time in the Navy during two wars, the thing she seemed to latch onto was my love of flying and motorcycles. I told her I had sold my Army surplus bike and bought a used a Harley Panhead.

She leaned in and exclaimed, "My dad has a Panhead. When I was a kid, my dad would put me behind him and take me riding. When I was around fifteen, he got me a little Honda which I loved. Then for my eighteenth birthday I got a Honda street bike—I forget the model."

"Really? That's great. Okay then. Now I know that we have something in common. Do you still have your bike? We could go riding some time."

"No, it's at my folks' house in California." She grinned. "But I wouldn't mind riding the back seat with you. I think, given all the flying and bike riding you've done, I'd be in pretty good hands." Looking at her watch, she said, "It's late, we'd better get to bed." Angie pushed her chair back and stood. "You've got preflight check around six, don't you?"

"Yeah, that's right." We walked to the hotel lobby entrance and over to the elevator. Neither of us spoke in the elevator. I was too busy wondering what she'd meant by saying "*We'd* better get to bed." The door slid open at our floor and I walked her to her room.

She reached in her purse for the room key, found it, pushed it into the lock and opened the door. Then she turned and suddenly reached up and put her arms around my neck, pulled me to her and kissed me on the mouth.

"Thanks for a very nice evening," she whispered. "I hope we will see each other again, I mean, aside from work. Goodnight." She stepped in the room and closed the door before I could utter a word.

I stood there in the dim light of the hallway, a little confused, just staring at the door, before I finally walked the few steps to my room. Stillman was sleeping so I undressed quietly and slipped into my bed, but once there, my mind took off like a gyro spinning out of control. I remember my last thought before falling asleep an hour later: *I'm going to marry that girl.*

 chapter five

i n those days, pilots could fly no more than eighty-five hours a
month so I had quite a lot of free time to ride my Harley and
to take Angie as a passenger. We had fun on and off the bike.
We just enjoyed being together like a couple of buddies—more
than lovers, really good friends. We never seemed to be at a loss
for something to say. It was just so good. I couldn't believe my
amazing fortune in finding someone with whom I could share
my life and love. It wasn't exactly what you call a whirlwind
romance but it was something like that, because a little less than
a year from the time we first met on that Durango trip, we were
married.

I checked out and flew the left seat on DC-3s and made the
grand sum of $850 a month if I got all of my eighty-five hours
in. We loved the Durango area so Angie and I bought a small
home in the rural Animas Valley just north of Durango. I bought
her a nearly new Harley Sportster and whenever we could, we
would ride our bikes all over that country. Sometimes we'd ride
to Silverton, about fifty miles to the north, over several passes
on Route 550, a challenging, twisting two-lane highway. We'd
have lunch there then continue on to Ouray, a charming little
town nestled in the mountains. We'd spend the night making

love and talking—there was always lots of conversation. We both loved those trips and the intimacy they brought.

Frontier Airlines bought a small fleet of Convair aircraft, both the 330 and 440 versions, to replace some of the DC3s. I checked out in the left seat of the 440, which was a nice step up from the DC-3. The plane was considerably faster, had a crew of three, could carry fifty-two passengers, and was equipped with radar and more reliable navigation and radio equipment.

Angie was also assigned to the new planes. The bad part was that in 1961, Durango and the other towns on the Denver-Durango route were still served by the older DC-3s and both of us had to hop on one of them to pick up our flights that originated in Denver. After doing this for better than a year, we decided it was just too much hassle. We agreed to sell our home and buy something in the Denver area, but we'd wait until after Christmas.

Then, a few days before Christmas, Angie was driving from the airport to our home in the Animas Valley. It was getting dark and a light snow was falling. After driving through Durango, she headed north on the two lane highway. Suddenly a car in the southbound lane loaded with a bunch of teenagers drifted over into her lane. She frantically mashed down on the horn then tried to get over as far to her right as she could. Too late. The oncoming car smashed into the driver's door. The front seat passenger in the other car was killed, the driver severely injured as were the two passengers in the back seat. Everyone in that car had been drinking. Angie was killed instantly.

I was home putting a split pine log on the fire when the phone rang. I had been off for the past four days while Angie had to work. I replaced the poker in its stand, walked into the kitchen and picked up the wall phone handset on the fourth ring.

"Hello. Yes, this Richard Elkins. Who did you say this

was? Mercy Hospital? Okay. Angela, yes. She's my wife—wait. Is something wrong? Is she hurt? What accident? When? Okay, Okay, I'll be right down. What? What are you saying? She's dead! No, no. That can't be right. She called me from the airport, she's on her way home...she's on...she's dead?"

The phone slipped from my hand and banged the wall as it swung on its coiled cord. My legs turned to rubber. I remember sliding to the floor where I sat with my back to the wall looking at the table and the bottle of wine I had just opened so it could breathe until Angie got home. I don't remember anything else about that night except looking at that bottle of wine and the two shiny stemmed wine glasses on the oval silver tray. It had been a wedding present.

 chapter six

he funeral was held on December 27. I was still in a semi-
stupor and recall little of what was said except that there
was a huge crowd there, including Angie's parents, Otto and
Marcie, whom I met for the first time. They were as devastated
as I. They just could not believe they were at their only child's
funeral. The three of us sat together in a front pew at the service.
It was pitiful. Afterward, I shook hands and hugged dozens
of people I'd never met before who told me they knew Angie.
Most of them were from Frontier, but other folks came as well.
The president of the company was there, as were many of the
higher ups, along with pilots, agents, baggage handlers and many
stewardesses. Obviously, a lot of people knew and loved my
beautiful wife. How could they not?

My boss, Matt Dumbrowski, a salty old ex-Air Corps bomber
pilot who had flown more than twenty missions over Germany,
placed both his hands on my shoulders and said, "I'm so sorry
about this. Who would ever have imagined such a thing? If that
guy lives, I think I'd kill the bastard when he walked out of the
hospital. You know what I mean. It just ain't right." He dropped
his arms and stepped back. "Anyway, I just want you to take some
time off, as much as you need. Your job's secure so don't worry

about it. And if there's anything I or anyone in the outfit can do to help you through this, just ask, okay?"

"Thanks, Matt. I'll definitely be taking some time—don't think you'd want me flying until I'm thinking straight again. Don't know when that'll be."

He patted my shoulder. "Like I said, don't worry about it. You'll know when you'll be ready to go up again."

I had dinner with my in-laws that evening. We didn't talk very much, although I did tell them some stories of how Angie and I met, our adventures on motorcycles, that sort of thing. They seemed to hang on my every word.

When I dropped them off at their hotel after dinner, Otto said, "I need you to do me a favor, Richard. I want you to take me out to where the accident happened. I just need to see it, you know?"

I told them I'd pick them up in the morning and show them the spot. Actually, I had to drive right by it every time I made the trip to Durango. When we arrived at the site, Otto wanted the details as they were told to me by the first responders. It wasn't easy but I grudgingly complied. Marci kept her hands over her face and sobbed uncontrollably.

That afternoon I drove them to La Plata field for their flight on Frontier Airlines that would take them to Denver and their connecting flight. I walked them to the plane and saw them on board. The two pilots and the stewardess, all of whom knew me and Angie, came out and gave me hugs and condolences.

There was no reason for me to stay in Durango. Just being in our house, conjuring up memories, made me crazy enough. With nothing much to do, I was spending way too much time and money at bars and drinking more than I ever had in my life, even during the wars.

Finally getting my act together, I signed with a realtor and put the house up for sale. I rode my Panhead Harley down to Farmington, New Mexico, to the nearest Harley-Davidson dealer, and traded it for a used 1961 Harley Duo-Glide with only 3,000 miles on it. This was a real nice bike, fast and solid, just what I needed for a long trip. My 1957 Ford F-150 pickup ended up on a used car lot and most of my clothes were disposed of at the Humane Society Thrift Store.

I packed what I could in my saddlebags and in my bedroll which I lashed behind the seat. I had so damn much stuff packed on the bike I couldn't swing my leg over it and had to throw my leg up and over the saddle to get on. Being a pilot, I was always very much aware of the weather and so I waited for a forecast that promised good weather for a couple of days. I got that forecast the last week in January, 1963, and without a second thought, I took off for sunny California.

chapter seven

ngie came along for the ride. I tried not to think about her by concentrating on riding the bike, looking at the scenery, singing songs in my head, but no matter what I did, my thoughts returned to her...to some scene played out together with memories of where we were and what we said...to the laughter, the loving, the.... No use. I finally gave up and let her occupy my mind. What else could I do?

The bike rumbled along. The miles went by and before I knew it, I was at the outskirts of Gallup. I pulled into a gas station and filled up, went to the bathroom, drank a Dr. Pepper and was on my way heading down the I-40. At Flagstaff I took an off-ramp and stopped again for gas It was getting dark and the temperature had become quite cold, around freezing. I noticed a small café across the street and rode over. I took a seat at a booth and looked around. Not many customers but it was only a little after five. A girl came over and handed me a menu. She was young, probably no more than seventeen or eighteen. She was pretty enough but there was something about her that made me think she wasn't healthy.

"Can I git ya sumthin' ta drink?" she asked.

I looked up from the menu and smiled, "Sure. How 'bout some black coffee if it's fresh? Otherwise..." I shrugged dismissively.

"I'll make a fresh pot for ya. No problem," she said eagerly.

"Okay, then. And I'll have the chicken fried steak. By the way, what's your name?"

"It's Elizabeth but most ever'one calls me Bett."

"If you don't mind me asking, how old are you?"

"I jes' turned sixteen las' week. Me and my little girl had birthday cake at Denny's. They give it ta me when they heard it was my birthday."

"You're sixteen? How old's your daughter?"

"She be two in March." She seemed uncomfortable talking to me and quickly stepped back from the table. "I best turn in your order now." She headed for the kitchen.

I couldn't help myself but here I was feeling sorry for this girl who had a baby when she was fourteen years old and trying to support herself with this crappy waitress job.

Bett returned with the coffee. "Here ya go. Fresh from the urn," she said placing a mug and a small coffee carafe in front of me. "Your dinner will up right away."

She turned to leave but I took hold of her thin wrist. "Wait a sec. Can you sit down and talk to me for a minute?"

Bett looked around, then slid in the opposite seat, "What is it ya wanted?" She seemed apprehensive, perhaps thinking I was about to hit on her.

"I'm sorry," I said, leaning across the table. In a lowered voice I asked, "Is this job the only way you make a living? I don't mean to be nosy but you're just a kid yourself and you have a kid and..."

"Naw, it's okay. When my boyfriend was with us it wasn't too bad. He had a pretty good job over at Ratcliff's Garage but one night 'bout six months ago he jest upped an' took off and I ain't seen or heard from him since. I reckon he couldn't stand bein' stuck with me an' the baby. Anyways, besides this job I also clean rooms over at the motel." She turned her head and pointed toward the window. "It's just down the road about a block. The Starlite. It's a purdy good job and the lady treats me real nice and don't charge us much for our room." Bett turned back and she held me with her dark brown, sad eyes. "What's the matter? Did I say somethin' that..."

I waved my hand, cleared my throat and croaked an answer, "No, no." I pulled a napkin from the dispenser and blotted my eyes. "It's just that I'm going through a hard time myself and, well, I just feel bad that a young girl like you has to deal with so much, so much..."

Bett placed her hand on mine and whispered, "Don't you worry none. I'm doin' okay. Ain't no reason fer you ta be sad. I ain't no kin ta you so it's not your problem." She smiled broadly, showing uneven stained teeth, and added, "but I do thank ya for bein' interested in me." The tinkle of a bell brought her head up and she slid out of the booth. "There's your dinner. I'll be right back."

After I finished my meal, I went into the men's room and stepped inside a stall. I slid the door lock, opened my shirt and fished out a $50 bill from my money belt. Returning to the dining room, I saw the check for $3.24 that Bett had left on the table. I put the $50 bill on top of the check, set my coffee cup on top of it and walked out. I had just started the bike when Bett came running over.

"Hey," she yelled breathlessly, "da ya know that was a fifty you left?"

I cut the engine and turned my head. Facing her, I said, "Yes, I know. Use it wisely and good luck. I have to go." I kicked the starter pedal, the engine roared into life and I took off. I watched her for a moment in the mirror. She just stood there looking after me. I rode past the Starlite and pulled in to a motel a little further down the road.

Under a tepid shower, the management's way of saving money, I thought about my encounter with Bett and how silly it was for me to have even engaged her in conversation other than to order a meal. If I got caught up in every down and out person's story, I'd be broke in no time, not to mention the wear and tear on my own emotions, which weren't any too solid right at the moment. I promised myself I'd take care of number one and the other guy could do the same.

It was pretty cold the next morning. I had to choke the hell out of the engine before it would start. I stopped at a different café and had some breakfast before heading for Phoenix. I got there a couple hours later, stopped for gas, traded the heavy jacket for a lighter one. I had planned to spend the day in Phoenix but changed my mind and headed for the I-10. My plan was to go to Quartzsite, then south on Route 95 to Yuma, after which I'd work my way up the California coast on the Coast Highway. That was my plan but it didn't quite work out that way. You might say I got sidetracked.

chapter eight

I stopped for gas in Yuma. The engine had been running rough so I got the plug wrench from my emergency tool kit and cleaned, re-gapped and replaced both spark plugs. I emptied and cleaned the carburetor sediment bowl and tightened the head bolts. After washing up in the men's room, I sat down with a bottle of Coke and studied the road map. I had planned to continue west to Chula Vista then turn north up the Pacific Coast Highway but I saw that Chula Vista wasn't very far from Tijuana, just south of the Mexican border. When I was in the Navy, I had heard some wild things about that town from sailors who had been stationed in San Diego and so I decided to take a little run down there and see what was going on.

I also heard that border security was pretty lax and a guy should be prepared to protect himself, what with bar fights, mobs of thieves and what have you. So I removed the Colt .45 pistol that I kept in my sleeping bag and strapped on the shoulder holster. The model 1911 Colt was the standard automatic pistol Navy and Marine pilots carried when flying over enemy held territory. The last time I wore that piece was when I was flying missions in Korea. I popped a loaded clip into the grip, made sure the safety was on and secured it in the holster.

After repacking my gear and getting it squared away on the

bike, I took off. The engine was running like a champ, so I rolled the throttle and headed on down the road at 85mph. *Look out Tijuana, I'm a bad-ass biker and I'm headed your way!* Just the thought of it made me laugh.

I stopped at a gas station in Chula Vista and pumped three gallons of gas. An old man in dirty bib overalls and glasses halfway down his nose shuffled over and took my dollar bill. He shuffled back into the little building and returned with a quarter.

"Here's your change." Scanning my bike he added, "Looks like you're taking a long trip with all that crap piled on there." He stepped to the back of the bike, squinted and remarked, "That's a Colorado plate. You drive that thing all the way from Colorado?"

"Yep...all the way from Colorado. Nothin' special about that, is there?"

He blew through pursed lips. "I guess not... 'cept, I wouldn't drive that thing from here to Dago."

I laughed. "Why not?"

"Them fuckin' things are way too dangerous to be on a highway with a bunch of cars and semis. A feller used to be a regular customer got one of them motorcycles. Didn't have it a month when some lady drivin' a Studebaker run him off the road. Killed him." The man turned to walk off but stopped and faced me. "Where ya headed now?"

"I thought I'd run on down to Tijuana and check it out."

He raised an eyebrow and gave me a quizzical look. "Ah. Don't think that'd be too smart. Not on that outfit anyways."

"What do you mean? What's wrong with riding a motorcycle down there?"

He rubbed the stubble on his chin, then he held up a finger.

"For one thing, my guess is you'll be comin' back without that machine."

"And why's that?"

"Whadaya think? The first time you leave that outfit ta go inta a bar or somethin', when you come out agin, it'll be long gone. There was this guy who chained his front wheel to a post and when he come back all that was left was the front wheel and the chain." He dropped his chin and looked at me over the top of his glasses. "You savvy? Now, if you was ta go down there with a bunch of them roughhouse bikers, ya know? Guys who knew how to take care of binness, them Mesicans would prob'ly leave ya alone." He spread his hands in front of him, palms up as if to say, "Okay, need I say more?"

"I sure do appreciate your advice. Thanks for telling me about it," I said as I climbed on the bike. I kicked the start pedal, put it in gear, rolled the throttle and headed north. Tijuana would have to wait for another time—a time when maybe I'd have some back up with me.

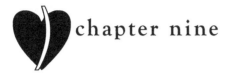 chapter nine

I stopped for the night at a tourist court near Seal Beach. After unloading my gear and putting it in the room, I walked down the street to a café that touted *Tasty Home-Made Meals* in blue neon. After eating what actually turned out to be pretty tasty dinner, including a generous slice of home-made cherry pie which I washed down with two cups of super-strong coffee, I hiked over the sandy beach to the water.

Aaah. The Pacific Ocean. I pulled off my boots and socks, rolled up my Levi's and let the cold water wash over my feet. I looked at the moon rising above the water and flashed back on the times I'd stood on the fantail of the carrier looking at the moon and worrying about the mission in the morning. I never could help wondering if it would it be my last or if I would somehow make it through the mission.

I stepped back a few feet from the water and lay down on the moist sand. It was beautiful and peaceful here. Tijuana would probably have been a disaster. There'd be noise and crowds, nothing like here on the beach. I was glad that old man at the filling station had told me not to go down there.

I let my mind slip into neutral but within seconds Angie returned from the far corners of my brain where she had been lurking all along and then I was overcome with sorrow. Angie should be here with me. We could have made this trip together. It would have been so great, the two of us riding down the highway together, stopping to look over all the new and wonderful sights neither of us had ever seen before. Lying in bed, chatting about the day's events, making love...

I jumped up. Enough. I couldn't handle any more of that. I pulled on my socks and boots and stalked back to my room. I was really tired from riding all day but I had trouble sleeping. I never should have let Angie out of her box.

The next morning I ate a "home-made" breakfast at that same café, packed my stuff on the bike and paid the lady $2.50 for the room. I fired up the bike and was off on the Pacific Coast Highway heading to... I had no idea.

Around noon I pulled in to a filling station in Arroyo Grande. There were around as dozen motorcycles at the pumps or parked off to the side. I waited for a vacant pump, pulled up to it and started filling my tank. An attractive young lady dressed in a black leather biker jacket walked up and watched me hang up the hose and screw the gas cap on the tank. I handed the station attendant a buck, he gave me fifteen cents change. She spoke when I turned my head and looked at her.

"Colorado eh? You're quite a ways from home."

"Yeah, guess so. Just touring around seeing what California is all about."

She stuck out her hand. "My name's Ann but these guys," she swept her arm around taking in the other riders, "call me 'Gunner.'"

We shook hands. "Richard. Call me Rick or Dick or whatever you want," I said through a grin. "I'm from Durango. It's in the southwest corner of Colorado. Ever hear of it?"

"No, can't say as I have. So tell me, where you going?"

I ran my eyes over her which I'm sure she noticed. Her red hair, what I could see of it under her cap, was long, her green eyes were large with little laugh lines emanating from the corners. Her nose was thin, straight, a bit longish and her mouth, devoid of anything other than natural color was, well, I'll just say, inviting.

Gunner, with hands on her hips, laughed. "Are you done taking inventory?"

"I'm sorry. Didn't mean to..."

"Hell, don't be sorry. I'm flattered you even bothered to give me the once over. Now, are you going answer my question? I asked you where you were going with all that kit and caboodle on your bike...it's a Harley, right?"

"Yes. It's their newest model, a '61 Panhead Duo-Glide." I glanced admiringly at the Harley. "It's a real nice machine. Anyway, to answer your question, I don't know where I'm going. Just touring around seeing some country. I haven't a time table, no place I have to be."

Gunner stuck out her lower lip and nodded. "Then I say, good for you." She turned toward the group of riders who were looking our way and grabbed my hand, "C'mon. I'd like you to meet my husband and some of my friends." She moved closer and in a lowered voice said, "I don't know some of these people. I guess they're friends of some of our club members." Still holding my hand, she walked over to an older man with gray hair, bright blue eyes and what I would call a rugged sort of face. He, like Gunner, was wearing a black leather biker jacket and was sitting on a good looking bike—a Triumph.

"Honey," Gunner said, "meet Rick. He rode all the way from Colorado." She dropped my hand and turned to me, "And this is my husband, Royce Silbert."

Royce threw his leg over the back fender, took a step toward me and offered his hand. "Pleased to meet you. So you rode that teeth-jarring Harley from Colorado? Do you live there?"

I shook his hand. "Yes I do, Durango."

"That's a pretty little town. I was there...when was it? Emm, a few years ago. Went hunting for elk in the San Juan Mountains. Beautiful country! Going back there one of these days." He paused, fished a cigarette from his jacket pocket, offered me one, which I declined. Reaching in a side pocket, he pulled out a Zippo lighter and while speaking, lit it. "So, what's"—he paused to puff—"your destination on this trip?"

"As I told your wife, I'm on a..." I thought a moment about how I'd put it. "Vacation from the airline. I just decided to get out of the cold country and come to warm California... have some fun seeing new places riding around on my bike." I was upset with myself for mentioning the airline. They didn't need to know anything about that.

"Oh," Gunner said, "You didn't tell me about being with an airline. Are you a pilot?"

"Yes, but we don't need to talk about that now, do we? I'm on vacation and—"

Royce interrupted, "What airline are you with?"

"It's a regional carrier, Frontier."

Royce nodded. "I flew Frontier from Denver to Durango in an old DC3 when I went hunting up there. Did you ever fly that route?"

"All the time until recently, when I checked out on Convairs."

Gunner piped up with, "Royce was an Army pilot during the war, weren't you, honey?"

Royce smiled at his wife and nodded his head. Turning back to me, he asked, "Did you fly during the war? I mean, we don't need to talk about it...it's not important. All that crap is behind us, right?"

"I guess. But yes, I was a Navy air crewman during the war and later got into pilot training. I flew F4U's in Korea. By the time I got out, I was flying transports which helped me get the job with Frontier." Again I realized I was talking way too much and determined to back off. I pulled back my sleeve and studied my watch. "I have to get moving. Looks like your pals are getting antsy to go. Sure was nice meeting you two." We shook hands, I turned and walked to my bike. I was about to kick the start pedal when Gunner came running over.

"Listen, Rick, would you like to ride with us? We're going up to Morro Bay for lunch. There's a great restaurant there, the Crab Trap. You'll like it and you can meet some of these folks. I'll bet they'd enjoy hearing about your trip."

I hesitated for a moment. "Sure. What the hell, why not?" I fired up the bike and took a position at the back of the group. They were cruising along at around 50, sometimes slower. I had to keep dropping a gear to keep up my RPM's. It got boring so when I had a clear shot, I swung out into the oncoming lane and roared past the line of bikes. When I passed Gunner and Royce, I slowed down and yelled, "I'll see you up there."

I found the Crab Trap, parked the bike, took off my jacket, sat under a tree and waited. They showed up about twenty minutes later.

Gunner came over, unzipped her jacket and asked, "What the hell was that all about?"

I looked up at her. Damn, she was pretty. I shrugged. "What was what about?"

"What?" There went the hands on hips again as she said, "Blowing by us like that. You always ride like a maniac? Geeze, it's a wonder you didn't get yourself killed driving all that way from Colorado."

"Me, a maniac?" I laughed. She didn't. I stood up, brushed off the back of my Levi's. "I've been called a lot of things but maniac...never. I mean, who hires a maniac airline pilot? No, I'm a pretty careful guy. But you guys were going so slow and I had to keep shifting down. That Harley needs at least 2,000 RPMs and that means over 50 miles an hour. I just got a little frustrated back there."

Gunner raised her voice. "You know what? That's the dumbest thing I ever heard, but I'll try to keep a straight face when I explain your fancy maneuver to the group because I'm sure they'll ask."

"Hey, I'll be happy to tell them myself and apologize for being....what? Rude? Bad bike manners?" Suddenly my mood changed. I was angry. I reached out and tapped her shoulder. "I'm sorry. I guess I'm running on a short fuse these days, so it'll be better if I just shove off."

I put out my hand but she by-passed my arm, put her arms around me and delivered a peck on my cheek. I took a step back in surprise.

She stood there in front of me, a hint of a smile crossing her lips. She pulled a small wallet from her breast pocket and handed me a card. "I'd like to see you again, I mean if, you know, if you come back this way. We live near Atascadero. It's not very far from here. My phone number is on the card. Call me."

Royce came out of the restaurant and yelled, "Hey, you guys coming to lunch? We're ready to order."

I scanned her card. *Annette E. Gunther, MA – Financial Planner.* I picked up my jacket, turned back to her and said, "Maybe our paths will cross again and if they do, I'll try and be more sociable." As I walked away I yelled over my shoulder, "Be careful riding that Honda." I glanced toward the restaurant entrance. Royce was watching me as I got on my bike and rode off.

 **chapter ten**

I missed lunch that day but I didn't even think about it. As I sped north I kept wondering why the hell I'd become so irritated with Gunner. I looked down at the speedometer—I was going 90. I slowed down to a respectable 65. Was I mad at her or was I mad at myself for thinking I'd like to get that gal in bed?

Maybe that was it. In some weird way the thought of fooling around with a woman other than my wife caused me to feel ashamed, like I was cheating on my wife. How could I cheat on her? She was gone! I had no wife! *I know, I know,* I kept saying over and over, *but I miss her so much.* She was always in my thoughts. I couldn't get her out of my head. I could just picture it, in bed with...with, okay, Gunner. Why not? In my mind, we're making love and suddenly I'm not looking down at Gunner -it's Angie and then what? Then I'm crying, my tears falling on Gunner's face and... and I'm an idiot! I rolled the throttle and shot up to 95.

Later I spotted a rest stop and pulled in. There was an old Indian motorcycle parked near the toilets. I walked into the ramshackle outhouse and saw an older man in the process of zipping up his pants. I nodded a greeting which he returned with a "How ya doin'?"

When I came out, the man was standing by my bike and giving it the once-over. I said, "It's the new Duo-Glide."

"Yeah. A buddy o' mine has one. Sweet ride. So, ya like it?"

"Sure do. I haven't had it too long but I rode it from Colorado and it's still percolating right along." I glanced at his Indian. "I haven't seen one just like that. What year is it?"

"That be a nineteen and forty-nine Scout. Got a pre-war Indian Chief back at the house but it ain't runnin.' Needs some fixin' up, but parts are hard ta come by."

I walked around his bike again and looked at it closely. When I looked back at him, he was sitting on my Harley. I walked over and said, "You like it?"

He flashed a smile. "Damn tootin' I like it. Would love to have one but don't reckon I ever will." He stepped off and added, "So, where ya off to with that load of stuff?"

"I don't know. Just wherever the road takes me. I was thinking about seeing the Hearst Castle in San Simeon. That's not very far from here, right? Ever been there?"

"Nope, can't say as I have." He laughed. "And I've lived 'round these parts forever. They tell me it's real nice...probably worth takin' a look at." He looked at me for a long moment then stuck out his hand. "My name's Emmett...Emmett Walker."

I shook his hand. "Rick Elkins. Pleased to meet you. If you're heading north, why don't we ride together? If you're in no hurry, this could be your chance to see the Hearst Castle after all these years."

And so he did. We got up there in jig time and took a good look around. It was something to see and we both were glad that we made the trip. The sun was getting low over the ocean and Emmett suggested we go back down to his place near Cambria. "I'm sure Mama wouldn't mind settin' another place for dinner, I mean if ya don't mind that it won't be nothin' fancy. You can bunk at my place if ya want."

I thanked him for the invite and we rode down to his house. He owned a small patch of land in front of and adjacent to a very large vineyard. The house was kind of a rambling frame outfit that needed a coat of paint. I noticed a lot of "junk" lying about the yard. It was, I thought, a regular Johnny Tumbledown outfit. However, once inside I was impressed with how neat and clean everything was. Emmett's wife was named Edna and she was almost as tall and stout as her husband. She had a pleasant face with a quick smile. I remember the supper she laid out–everything was homemade and delicious, especially the buttermilk biscuits. I ate three of them covered with butter and honey.

During the meal the conversation got around to questions about what I did for a living, was I married and so on. At first, I was reluctant to talk about myself but eventually with their gentle prodding, I laid it all out there–Angie dying, being a commercial pilot, even a little of my Navy history. In return, they told me how they had known each other since school days, got married when both were seventeen, and how Emmett had worked for the vineyard for close to forty years when he had a heart attack and was forced to leave work for a while.

"I was sixty-three years old," Emmett explained. "They said I could come back to work but I figured I'd worked long enough and just went ahead and retired."

"He opened a little shop right here on the place and started fixin' motorcycles. Cars, too. Been doin' it ever since," Edna told me.

Emmett patted her hand and said, "If ya like, I'd be happy to tune up that Harley of yours before you head out. That's the thing about Harleys, they need working on all the time ta keep running like they supposed ta."

"Well, thanks. I sure would appreciate you looking at it. It seems to be running okay. I cleaned the plugs a few days ago but it sure wouldn't hurt for you to check it out. I got a long way to go before this trip's over."

Edna asked, "Where ya headed fer next?"

I shook my head. "I don't know. Maybe run up to Frisco. I spent some time there when my ship came back from Korea for re-fitting. Then maybe head north to Alaska."

"Be pretty cold up there this time o' year," Emmett said.

"You're right. Maybe I'll drop down a ways and head over to Nevada. I've never been to Las Vegas. They say that's one wild town with all of those gambling places—"

Edna broke in, "You might get yourself into trouble in that town. I've read where the Eyetalyans run everything there and they ain't a bit bashful about killing people, ya know what I mean? Ya might want ta give that town a wide berth."

Emmett and I laughed. Smiling broadly, I said, "Okay then, I'll pass her up."

Later, after more coffee and conversation, they showed me a small room in the back of the house. The only things in the room were a narrow bed and a rocking chair. I went out to the bike, got my bedroll, threw it on the bed and was asleep in minutes. It was one of the best sleeps I'd had since Angie died.

A little after six the next morning, Edna fixed breakfast, put some biscuits in a paper bag for me to take along, and wished me good luck. I thanked her for the hospitality and the great food and without thinking too much about it, gave her a generous hug. I think she actually blushed a little as she stepped back.

"Oh, you go on now," she said. "Emmett's out there working on your bike."

I picked up my sleeping bag and walked outside.

As I approached, Emmett wiped his hand on a red shop rag and yelled, "There ya are. Got yer outfit ready to roll. Actually, wasn't much it needed but I think you'll notice a little difference. I changed the timing, tightened your front brake, took a little slack outta the clutch an' a couple other things. It's runnin' like it's s'posed to." He stuffed the rag in a pocket and offered his hand, which I heartily shook.

"Edna fix ya somethin' to eat?" he asked.

"You bet she did and plenty of it. Even gave me some of her fine biscuits to take along."

Emmett dropped my hand. "Good, good. Now listen, son, you be careful on that bike. Don't be drivin' too fast. Seventy, seventy-five is 'bout as fast as it's safe 'specially on these highways. You've had enough trouble in yer life so don't make it worse... you unnerstan'?"

"Thanks. I'll be careful and thanks for working on the bike. I sure appreciate it and your hospitality. You folks are great and if I come back this way, you can bet I'll be stopping by."

"The latch string will always be out fer ya."

I got on the bike and fired her up. "See you later then," I yelled as I drove down the dusty drive to the highway. I was heading toward Monterey, about a hundred miles north of Cambria. I planned on eating lunch there and spending a couple of days checking out all the places that John Steinbeck had written about in *Cannery Row*. But about an hour into the trip, I turned around and headed south. For some reason, I had a compelling urge to see Gunner.

chapter eleven

he thing about riding a motorcycle over long distances is that there's not a whole lot you can do other than make sure you don't kill yourself or let somebody do it for you. At the time, there was no such thing as iPods or other devices where you can fill the time listening to music. However, to this day, I never distract myself with these things while I'm riding. For me, now as then, I fill the miles thinking about stuff or maybe hearing songs in my head, and that's what I was doing when I was heading north to Monterey... thinking about stuff.

Stuff, in this case, was pushing back every time thoughts of Angie popped into my consciousness. I was trying to concentrate on my driving and heeding Emmett's advice about not going too fast when without warning, Gunner sprang from the shadows and dominated my thoughts. I tried to push her away, too, but no matter how hard I tried to replace her image with something else, she remained in the forefront.

Gunner. The card she had given me appeared in my mind's eye: *Annette E. Gunther, MA.* Gunther...Gunner. So that's where her nickname came from. Not exactly an epiphany, but something to consider as I rolled along. Then I started wondering about the occupation listed on her card. *Financial Planner.* I couldn't quite see her as a financial anything except that she obviously had planned to marry a guy who was financially pretty damn secure. I laughed thinking about it. Well, that took some planning. But why did she ask me to call her? What kind of planning was behind that? The sound of a horn startled me. What the—? A car went whizzing past me. "What's your problem, you dumb jerk?" I yelled after him. Then I looked in my mirror and saw a line of cars behind me. Apparently, the steady flow of oncoming traffic had kept them from passing. I checked my speed. I was going forty-five miles an hour. No wonder that guy blew his horn. That's what happens when you get too occupied with your thoughts while riding a motorcycle. I kicked her up to seventy-five, much to the delight of the drivers behind me.

I turned left on Route 41 and headed toward Atascadero. Stopping at a filling station, I fished a dime from my pocket, stuck it in the pay phone and called the number on Gunner's card. She picked up on the third ring.

I took a breath and blurted out, "Hi. It's Richard. You asked me to call you if I was ever in the vicinity and I'm in the vicinity."

I could hear the surprise in her voice. "Rick?"

"Yep, it's Rick, the Harley guy. You remember me, right?"

She laughed. "Where are you exactly?"

"I'm at a 76 station on the 41 just outside of Atascadero."

"Okay, I know where that is. Listen, just stay there and I'll come down and guide you to my place. It's a little hard to find. I'll see you in about fifteen minutes, okay?"

"I'll be here." I heard the phone click. I began to wonder if this was such a good idea. She sure seemed anxious to see me. On the other hand, what about her husband? He sure gave me the evil eye when I left them. Did he see Gunner give me that kiss? I was getting nervous.

50

I put some gas in the bike and used the restroom. There was a Coke machine outside. I put in a nickel, opened the lid and slid a bottle out of the rack. Using the bottle opener on the outside of the box, I popped the cap and took a long drink. One more slug and the six ounces were gone. A horn blew. It came from an MG convertible sports coupe. Gunner flung open the door, jumped out and ran over to me. I just stood there flat footed as she threw her arms around me and gave me a wet kiss on the mouth.

"Damn," she squealed. "I didn't think I'd ever see you again. What a surprise!" She kissed me again, dropped her arms and said, "Get on your bike and follow me." She ran over to her car and started the engine.

I followed her for about ten miles where she turned right on a black top driveway. The driveway wandered through a double line of Poplar trees and ended up at a beautiful, rambling ranch house. There was a huge grass lawn with lots of shrubs and small trees in the front of house and as we continued on past the side of the house to the back, I saw some other smaller buildings set back about fifty yards behind the house. Lush landscaping was evident in every direction. They must have a crew of gardeners, I thought.

She pulled up in front of a four car garage, remotely opened the overhead door and drove the MG inside. She got out of the car, opened the adjacent overhead door and motioned for me to drive in. Inside, I saw that the garage was deep enough to hold two cars in line. There were four overhead doors on the far side. A quick scan of the garage revealed an older International pickup, a newer Dodge pickup, a '61 Mercury Cougar, a '59 Cadillac sedan and another car, which I couldn't identify. When I got off the bike, Gunner again put her arms around me. Her green eyes were flashing as she looked into my eyes. I'm sure she saw my astonishment.

"Here we are. Just you and me. I hope you're not too tired from riding today." She paused and pushed back, raising one eyebrow. "Are you?"

As you may have gathered by now, I'm not the kind of guy who gets easily flustered but I've got to tell you, that damn girl had my head spinning. There was no doubt what she was getting at and, by extension, what she expected me to do. I thought, *I'd better jump on my bike and get the hell out of here.*

Instead I stammered, "Ah, what's going on here? I mean..."

Gunner laughed. "Don't be afraid. I'm not the big bad wolf and you're not Little Red Riding Hood. Relax. It's okay." She smiled, took my hand in hers and squeezed. "C'mon. Get your stuff off the bike and follow me."

I did as she requested, following her to one of the smaller cabin-like buildings behind the main house. We stepped into a living room with a stone fireplace where I threw my sleeping bag and saddlebags down on an over-size chair. Before I could take in the rest of the room, she grabbed my hand and pulled me past a bathroom to a large well-furnished bedroom. Someone had spent a lot of money furnishing this place and some high priced decorator no doubt had a hand in it.

"Here's your bedroom. Like it?" she asked.

"Yes, sure, it's real nice but..."

"Relax, I'll lay it all out for you. Don't worry."

Back in the living room, she took off her windbreaker and casually tossed it on a chair. As she crossed the room to the couch, I had a chance to study her. The last time I saw her she'd been wearing jeans, boots and a heavy jacket. Now, in a slim plaid skirt, loafers and a pale blue sweater, she was a vision. Her red hair tumbled down her neck and shoulders, her legs were just exactly the kind of legs you'd want on a girl and...well, let's just say that this gal was a peach.

She took a seat on the couch and motioned for me to sit next to her. "Now listen, I want to explain some things. First of all, don't call me Gunner. It's not a name I really like. My name is Annette. You can call me Ann if you like. Okay. Actually, I'm not married to Royce although people around here think we're married and we just let it go at that since two unmarried people living together is a sin, at least in most people's minds. Right?"

I'm fairly sure my mouth dropped open.

She didn't wait for an answer but hurried on. "A few years ago Royce's company, he's a CPA and financial planner and runs a large accounting firm—offices in LA, San Diego, other cities—anyway, his company sent some people out to recruit employees and they came up to UC Berkley. It was 1956 and I had just finished the Master's program and got an interview. Bottom line, they hired me and I went to work in their LA office. Royce called me in for a chat and we started dating, so to speak. He had recently divorced so I figured what the hell. He's a good looking guy and really rich." She leaned in close and asked, "Are you with me so far?"

"Absolutely." I smiled. "You saw a good thing and you went for it. Why not? The fact that you're not married to the guy doesn't bother me like it would some people. In fact, given what's happened so far today, I'd have to say I'm glad you're single even though you've got some..." I tried to think of just the right word. "Responsibilities. I'm thinking, however, that Royce might not condone what you've done today and what I'm thinking you may do later on. Am I right?"

"Royce won't be back up here for at least a week. And what you're thinking I'd like to do later on is exactly what I intend to do." Ann wrinkled her nose, pursed her lips and added, "That is, if you agree to be a willing participant."

I gazed into those marvelous green pools of light, leaned

toward her and kissed her. Her mouth opened and her tongue searched for mine.

Reluctantly breaking the kiss, I said, "I'm going to take a long, hot shower and then we'll see what happens."

"Sounds good. When you're ready, come up to the house and we'll have a drink or two then I'll show you my workbench. Okay?"

"Perfect."

Ann headed for the door. "Oh, by the way," she said, pausing, "what do you like to drink?"

"Just about anything, but given a choice, I'd go for 100 proof bourbon with a little ginger ale."

Ann smiled, opened the door, "Good choice. It'll be ready when you arrive."

We sat in front of the fireplace on a tapestry upholstered loveseat sipping our drinks, making small talk interspersed with kisses. I was wearing a pair of Chino slacks and a T-shirt. She wore a white silk robe emblazoned on the back with a colorful Chinese dragon and embroidered with some red and blue decorations on the front. A tie made of the same material around her waist kept the robe closed, more or less. I could tell that she was wearing nothing underneath. For that matter, neither was I. When we had dispatched the second drink, she laid her glass on the round table in front of the loveseat, took my almost empty glass from my hand and set it down on the table. She pulled on the tie allowing the front of the robe to part, revealing her modest breasts. She pushed me back until the top half of my body was lying flat then she moved on top of me, her face close to mine, her breathing coming in staccato bursts. As she pressed against me, I could feel her racing heart.

"Do you want me?" she purred.

"Yes, very much." I whispered.

She reached down and felt my building erection. "Yes, I believe you do."

She jumped up, grabbed my hand and, pulling me down a hall to her bedroom, exclaimed, "Come along, Richard. We've got work to do."

I don't know why, but all I could think to say was, "Wilco."

chapter twelve

during the following two hours I must admit that I never once thought of Angie. I never made an invidious comparison between her and Ann. Later on though, I would go through a period of really bad depression thinking that somehow I had betrayed Angie. But that night in bed with Ann, I was too carried away, to into what was happening to have a solitary thought about anything other than what an artist Ann was.

Yes, artist! Satiated at last, we donned robes, there was a bunch of them in the closet, and we moved into the den. Ann poured port from a crystal decanter. We sipped the wine, which was quite good, and smoked cigarettes (which I didn't normally do, the cigarettes that is), and I learned how it was that red-headed stick of dynamite knew what she knew about how to please a man but even more than that, how to send him into sexual heaven.

Ann took a long drag on the king-size Pall Mall, inhaling deeply and then letting the smoke slowly escape from her mouth and nose. I watched with keen interest as she took a puff, drank some wine and exhaled the smoke.

She smiled, cocking her head to one side, and said, "What? What are you gawking at?"

"Just watching you smoke. You do it quite beautifully, you

know. Personally I don't smoke very often, never have but watching you do it, well..."

Ann gave me a dismissive wave. "You're better off if you don't smoke. They're starting to say that smoking may be bad for you." She crushed the cigarette in a crystal ashtray.

I replied, "I don't know much about it but I can't see how it can be good for you." I reached across the table and took her hands in mine. "Listen, I know I've said it tonight about a hundred times but you are amazing. The things you do and, and... Honestly, I've never experienced anything like it. Where did you learn to do all those things?"

Ann rose and came over to me. "Come with me and I'll show you."

"You'll *show* me?" I shook my head. "What are you talking about?"

Ann took my hand and we walked to the end of a long hall. The walls were covered with pictures but I didn't have a chance to really look at them as she hurried me along. We came to a spiral stairway and, letting go of my hand, she said, "This will take us to the projection room."

I followed her up the stairs which emptied into a large room with theater style chairs arranged in three rows facing a screen on the opposite wall. On a raised table behind the seats was a movie projector. Shelves lined the wall in the back of the room; they were filled with an abundance of gray film cans which I guessed held 16 mm movie film. I turned to Ann, my question obvious.

"Yes, there's movie film in every one of those cans," she said. "I'll show you one in a minute, but first, let me explain something to you which will answer the question you asked downstairs." We took seats side by side in the front row.

"Do you know what a 'Key Club' is?" she asked.

My eyes opened wide in disbelief. Was she going to tell me that she played around with other couples? I hesitated for a moment but when she repeated the question, ending with, "Well, do you?" I answered, "Sure I do. It's where couples have a party at someone's house and after they get all liquored up, they put their house keys in a bowl or something and then they shake up the keys, hold the bowl up high and then the guys take turns reaching in the bowl and pulling out a key. Then they go shack up with the lady of that house."

Ann burst out laughing, slapping her thigh with each new guffaw.

I got to laughing, too.

"You got the gist of it all right," she blurted out. "But it's a little more subtle than that in actual practice—at least the way it's played around here." She composed herself and became serious. "When I first starting going out with Royce, I thought he was, you know, an upstanding citizen. When we moved up here he asked if I'd be interested in trying group sex. I told him hell no and what was he thinking about. Later on, he toned it down to just switching partners with one couple. He called it 'swinging.' I wasn't interested in that either, but he kept after me about it and I thought he might dump me if I didn't go along. So that's how it started.

"There was this couple, Carl and Charlotte, who Royce and his former girlfriend had done it with. Royce invited them up to spend the weekend with us. They were really nice and very attractive people, and so, after an evening of some pretty heavy drinking and a lot of conversation with sexual innuendo, Royce and Charlotte walked off together. Carl sat down next to me and we started kissing and then he had his hand inside my blouse and, well, we ended up in bed. He showed me some things that even Royce hadn't done and Royce is pretty damn good at giving

59

a woman what she wants. We fooled around with those two a number of times and I'll admit I found it exciting."

Ann walked her fingers up my arm playfully, and gave me a mock grave look. "I'm not boring you with all this, am I? Or do you find it shocking?"

"Hell no," I lied, catching her hand in mine. "In fact, I'm getting worked up just hearing about it. Go on. So, what happened next?"

Ann took a deep breath and let it out slowly. "We went to a party at Carl's and there were, I don't know, maybe six or eight couples there. They were young, tan, good looking LA types. And, before the night was over, everyone was naked and doing it with everyone else. I think I must have fucked…" Ann stopped and put her hand to her mouth, her face reddening. "Oops. I'm sorry. That just slipped out. Really, it's not a word I ever use."

I laughed and gave her a hug and a long kiss. "It's okay, honey. Believe me—I've heard the word before. So go on, you said you fucked how many guys that night?"

Ann giggled and kissed me back. "Ah, I don't remember… maybe all of them." Her face lit up again. "I know, I'm really bad and I shouldn't even be telling you all this but I'm just trying to explain how I got the sex education that you were the beneficiary of tonight. The truth is, I got to where I was actually enjoying those parties. They called them swinger parties and Royce and I were doing them every weekend. But after partying like that for almost a year, it got a little boring and we backed off.

"Now, about those movies. Royce started taking pictures with his movie camera and showing them at parties. Those swingers loved watching themselves and weren't the least bit bashful about being filmed in the nude or even while screwing around." Ann laughed. "Yeah, there were a lot times when it turned into a full blown orgy with people smoking weed or doing drugs. It got out of hand so we got out of it...the big parties."

"Wow, that's some story but it sure explains your, how can I put it? Your..."

Ann suggested, "Expertise in the sack?"

My mouth spread in a broad smile. "Expertise is exactly the right word." I shook my head and grinned, "You know, I always thought I was a man of the world. I've been around and then some, but truthfully what you have been telling me is a revelation. I've heard about this kind of thing, you know, swinging and key parties, and all that, but to be with a real live player is, I'll have to admit, pretty damn exciting."

Ann walked to one of the packed shelves, selected a film can and set it down next to the projector. "Ready to take a look at one of the movies?" she asked. "Want to see what a 'real live player' does? You can see me and a bunch of other people in action."

I sensed a bit of mockery in her tone so I went to her, put my arms around her and pressed her body to mine. I kissed her neck, stepped back, put my hands on either side of her face and kissed her long and hard. I looked deep into her wide open eyes. I dropped my hands and put them around her again and hugged her. My mouth was touching her ear as I whispered, "No, I don't want to see any movies of you. What I want right now is to go back to bed and just hold you. Can we do that?"

I awoke in the morning to find Ann propped on an elbow staring at me.

She smiled. "Good morning, darling." She glanced at the digital clock on the nightstand. "It's almost ten o'clock. Time to get up, don't you think?"

Yawning, I blinked my eyes, cleared my throat and croaked, "I guess, but we really haven't had that much sleep, you know. It must have been three before we finally stopped fucking." I put my hand to my mouth in mock embarrassment. "Oh, I'm so sorry. I never use that word. It...it just slipped out. Please forgive the lapse in decorum."

Ann laughed. "I forgive you, but," she said, faking seriousness and wagging a finger, "don't ever use that dirty word again." She rolled over on top of me. "Now, come on and fuck me!"

Over breakfast of scrambled eggs and fried ham, Ann told me that yesterday, after I had called her from the gas station, she had called her office and told them that she was going to work at home. However, today she needed to go in and work the rest of the day and tomorrow.

"I've things I have to get done before the weekend," she said. "I might have to work part of Saturday as well just so I'll be ready for Monday." She told me she would be spending the night at her apartment in Beverly Hills but I should make myself at home while she was gone. Royce would not be back so I shouldn't worry about that and she'd see me either Saturday afternoon or Sunday. Meanwhile she would call me here at the house, to make sure I was okay.

I told her not to worry about me. However I didn't feel comfortable staying there when she was gone and that I'd probably ride up to Monterey and spend some time there until she returned. She gave me her office number and said to call her. I promised I would.

Ann showered and dressed. She looked like a million bucks in what I guessed was a very expensive designer suit. We walked out to the garage where she passed up the MG and got in the Cougar. She cranked down the window and said, "Be careful riding up to Monterey and don't forget to call me so we can line things up for when I get back."

I stuck my head in and kissed her. "How 'bout you be careful?

I'm always careful—that's why I'm still alive." I kissed her again and pulled my head out of the car. "See you soon."

Ann started the car, adjusted the mirrors and backed out of the garage. I walked out of the garage as she pressed the remote to close the overhead door. Ann backed around then headed down the drive, sticking her arm out the window and waving. I waved back.

I walked over to the cabin, took a shower and dressed for a bike ride. I started to walk out with what I thought I would need for just the next few days, but for some reason that I can't explain to this day, I returned to the bedroom and picked up my bedroll and the rest of my stuff and walked back to the detached garage. The doors were closed.

"Damn," I said aloud. There was a walk-in door but it was locked. I tried the windows but they were locked as well. "Son of a bitch, what the fu..." I had to laugh. Was I actually ashamed to use the word? I went in the house hoping to find a garage remote. I pulled open drawer after drawer searching but no luck. I tried the office and other rooms but no remote. I went up the spiral staircase to the projection room and gave it a going over without success. I was about to climb back down the stairs when for some perverse reason I found myself in front of the shelves with all of those movies. The cans were labeled with dates and titles such as "Fosters' Party, 7/4/60." I selected "New Year's Eve, 1959," threaded it on the projector and started it. Then I sat down and watched.

There was Ann in the very first scene wearing a very revealing costume. You could see right through the flimsy fabric—she had nothing on underneath. She was laughing and making faces into the camera. A pretty girl came up behind her and began to massage Ann's breasts and laid her head on Ann's shoulder. The girl was laughing and saying something as Ann reached behind her to take hold of the girl. The girl slipped the straps of Ann's dress over Ann's arms and pulled down, exposing Ann's breasts. Ann continued to laugh and talk. A blond man stepped into the scene and began to kiss and lick Ann's nipples. She pushed his head down to her crotch. The movie switches to other couples having intercourse on the floor, girls giving blow jobs. Now Ann appeared again and she was giving a blow job to some guy.

I jumped up and stopped the projector, rewound the film, put it back in the can and placed it where I had found it. I was boiling mad! How could she do that? How could all those people do that? At that moment I was sickened by what I saw. I hurried down the stairs and ran out the door and over to the garage. I found a rock and threw it at a window. I put on my leather jacket and gloves and reached through the broken shards of glass to unlock the window. Then I raised the sash and crawled through, located a door button and opened the overhead door behind my bike. I went back outside, got my stuff, secured it, pushed the bike out of the garage, closed the door and took off.

chapter thirteen

Still fuming, I headed up the coast highway, my thoughts a jumble of disconnected images, some good, but mostly images of Ann in the movie. I couldn't understand why I was so upset with her. After all, she'd told me all about what she had done at those parties. Oh, maybe not as graphically as portrayed in the movies. It's one thing to imagine something but another to actually witness it. And yet, what was it that got me so mad? Maybe I wasn't mad so much as upset, disappointed that the lovely girl, who gave me the most spectacular sexual experience of my entire life, was also doing it with anybody and everybody who asked for it. But the fact remained—it was what she did at those parties with all those different partners that made it possible for her to have the talent she shared with me in bed.

I was going round and round with these thoughts and damn near ran into the back of a car while thinking about it. The shock of coming that close to an accident, maybe one that would kill me, forced me to concentrate on riding the bike. But that didn't last long. Try as I might, I kept coming back to the same old theme. Why was I so upset with Ann? She was open and totally honest with me. I should admire that. Yet those movie scenes played over and over in my mind regardless of how hard I tried to suppress them, and they sickened me.

Angie would be so disappointed in me. Angie? Where did she come from? Now it was Angie that took control. Her sweet face was scowling. I imagined her saying, "What in the world is wrong with you? You're not that kind of man. You always enjoyed making love with me as much I enjoyed you. It was always so very tender and you were so attentive and loving, holding me afterward and whispering words of love in my ear. I loved that. Ann is not your kind of woman." Angie's face turned menacing as she shrieked, "Ann is a whore! Do you want to be with a whore? Is that how you're going to forget me by screwing every dirty girl you can?"

"No, no. Go away. Don't do this to me," I yelled into the onrushing wind. I pulled over to the side of the road, got off, sat in the dirt, put my hands to my face and cried.

I rode into Carmel, a sleepy little town south of Monterey, late in the afternoon. I had something to eat at a sea-side café and sat at a table outside. I looked out at the ocean, beautiful and serene and darn near started to cry again. I couldn't shake that image of Angie scolding me. I needed to get my mind on something else so I walked over to a phone booth and called Arnold Skiff, the realtor who listed my house in Durango. He told me the house had sold about a week before and that after paying off the mortgage, his commission, the title policy and so on, I ended up with $3,426 and change.

"That's great. I didn't think it would sell that quickly."

"I guess we got lucky," Arnold said. "I deposited the money in your account at the First National. Is that okay?"

"Sure, and thanks a lot for all your help,"

"Glad I was able to get the job done for you. I'm holding the settlement sheet and other closing papers here. You can pick them up when you get back. By the way, Richard, when are you coming back?"

I looked out at the ocean for a long moment before answering. "I don't know. Probably never."

"What do you mean? You're not coming back at all? What about your job with Frontier?"

Right there and then I made what turned out to be a life-changing decision. "I mean I'm not coming back to Durango. I plan to quit my job with Frontier and..." I stopped. What did I want to do next? "I'm not sure but I'll probably try to get on with United or American or one of the other airlines here in California with an LA base. Anyway, don't worry about it. I've got plenty of money now so I've got time to get myself squared away. Listen, I've got to go but thanks a lot for getting the house sold. I sure do appreciate it."

"Okay then," he replied. "Take care of yourself and best of luck to you. Goodbye."

"Bye." I hung up, heard the coins drop in the phone box and walked out to the water's edge. Another thought occurred to me; I turned back to the phone booth. I was out of change. I called my lawyer, Bud Schultz, asking the operator to reverse charges.

Bud answered and accepted the charge. "Richard, my boy, I was wondering what happened to you. Where the hell are you and why haven't you called or written to me?"

"I've been on the road. Right now I'm in Carmel, California. I—"

Bud interrupted, "We've got this lawsuit going with the insurance company and I needed to talk with you about it. There are some decisions you need to make so I can proceed."

Suddenly I was again having to deal with the reality of Angie's death. "Okay, what decisions?"

Bud went into a drawn-out monologue, as lawyers usually

do, of what he wanted the insurance company to pay in terms of damages, settlements and so on. The long and short of it was, they wanted to settle for $78,000 and Bud had initiated a lawsuit demanding $150,000.

I said, "I don't know what to tell you. Maybe split the difference, something like that. Would they go for that?"

"Maybe. But I think we should hold out for the one-fifty. What the hell, Richard, the kid was drunk, that's been established and the company is not contesting it. Your wife was killed which robbed you of spousal companionship. In addition, you endured and still endure, I'm sure, pain and suffering beyond what a person should, plus Angie's car was totaled and frankly you deserve every penny we can squeeze out of those bastards."

I mulled over his words for a few seconds. "Okay. Tell you what. You work on it as you think best. But one thing, Bud, let's not stretch it out for, you know, a long time. See if you can wrap it up fairly quickly, okay?"

"All right. You're the boss but I don't want to see you short-changed. You've had a horrific loss and I feel compelled to do the best I can for you, knowing that money, no matter how much, isn't going to—"

I cut in. "Yes, I know and I appreciate what you're doing for me."

"So tell me, what's your plan, for the near future anyway?"

What was my plan? Did I actually have a plan? At this point I was too screwed up mentally to even consider my future and yet that's what I did. Recalling what I had told Arnold, I said, "I'm going to leave Frontier and find a job with one of the major airlines based in LA. That's my plan for now."

Bud didn't respond immediately. "Oh? I wasn't expecting that but I guess it's a plan. With all of your flying hours, you shouldn't have any trouble getting a job." He paused. "Oh, by the way, do you know that your house sold?"

"Yes. I talked to Arnold Skiff a little while ago. I came out all right, better than I thought I would."

"Good for you. Now listen, son, I need you to stay in touch with me. I want you to call me at least once a week in case there's something I need you to do. Will you please do that?"

"Sure, I'll call you. Don't worry." We said our goodbyes.

I stood in the phone booth for a while scanning the far out horizon. I liked what I saw. I thought, I could live in a place like this. Between the house sale and the insurance settlement I wouldn't have to worry about making money for years. If I end up with, let's say, a hundred thousand, why, heck, that would last me for what? Let's see. If I lived on five thousand a year, which would be more than plenty, I'd be good for twenty years. How old would I be in twenty years? I'm thirty-six now so I'd be fifty-six. So at only fifty-six I'd have to get a job. That wasn't going to work.

I walked over to my bike muttering, "Maybe I better go back to work now and retire when I'm fifty-six. Yeah, that's a better idea."

So, it was right there on the beach at Carmel I made up my mind to quit horsing around and get a job flying airplanes because, when I finally faced myself, I saw reality—I really did miss flying.

I was in no hurry to begin my quest for a pilot job, though. I was in quite possibly the most picturesque area in the entire country. So, after spending the night in Carmel, I rode north beside the Pacific Ocean through places like Carmel Woods, Pebble Beach, and Pacific Grove.

I took my time, driving slowly, taking in the sights and sounds, stopping here and there chatting with the colorful and sometimes weird local inhabitants. An old man with a long white beard and unkempt hair half way down his back asked if I'd like to trade my leather jacket for "some really prime shit." As tempting as it was, especially in my current frame of mind, I respectfully declined.

I still had a couple hundred dollars in my money belt which was more than enough to allow me to hang around the area for almost a month. I ate enough seafood on that visit to Monterey to last me a lifetime. It was delicious and cheap as hell.

I'd spend hours on the beach enjoying the warmth of the winter sun in the company of lovely tan and eager young girls. Initially, I think it was seeing the Harley that caught their attention. Seeing the Colorado plate, they'd ask if I had come all the way from Colorado. "Wow," they would coo, "That's awesome." First thing you know, they wanted to know about me and then we'd be on the beach or in the water playing around. It was all very innocent. I suppose I could have easily seduced some of these kids but Angie wouldn't let me.

That's right. She still had a very tight rein on me, letting me know *right* from *wrong*. On more than one occasion, though, when I was wasted from drinking too many shots of Tequila, I seriously thought about calling Ann. Her card was still in my wallet. One time I actually called her and when she answered, I hung up. Another time I was drinking coffee on the patio outside a coffee shop with a couple of local guys I met at a bar the night before. We were all hung over pretty bad. I was sitting with my back to the building looking out toward the street. A green MG with the top down drove by slowly and a girl wearing a cap with red hair peeking out from under it was turning her head right and left as if looking for some address or someone. It was Ann, no doubt about it. Who else had red hair and drove a green MG?

At first, I was too surprised to move. Sure, I now had a heavy beard and hadn't had a haircut in over a month but I jumped up, surprising my table mates, and ran inside the shop. I watched from a window for a good fifteen minutes but I didn't see the MG again. My drinking mates came inside the shop, wondering if I was on a bad trip or just suddenly gone off the deep end. I explained my predicament—I just didn't want to see her.

One of guys exclaimed, "Are you fuckin' nuts? From what I could see of her, that gal was a beaut."

"Yeah, I know but anyway, if she comes poking around, you don't know me...never heard of me, understand?"

Instead of walking up the road to the boarding house where I was staying, I headed to the beach and walked behind the houses and shops. It occurred to me that my bike was parked in front of the house, not too far from the road and if Ann drove past the house, she was bound to recognize it and then my goose would be cooked. I needed to get up there and hide the bike.

I ran up the beach and arrived at the house about five minutes later. Cautiously, I walked from the beach to the back of the house, then worked my way slowly toward the front. I stepped behind a bush and peered out to the street. Too late! There was the MG. I looked around but didn't see Ann. I thought about jumping on the bike and getting the hell out of there but the key was in my room. Damn! Now what? My goose was in the oven and she was about to cook it.

Okay, let's get it over with, I thought. I walked up the steps, crossed the porch and opened the door. Ann was sitting on the couch in the living room talking to Bea, my motherly landlady. They both looked up as I approached.

"Hi," I said, very casually even though my heart was racing so fast I supposed it would jump out of my throat.

Ann jumped up and ran to throw her arms around me so

tightly I could hardly breathe. "Richard! Oh my God, I'm so glad to see you're okay." She kissed me hard on the mouth. "Honestly, I thought you had an accident with your motorcycle and–"

I pushed her back. "Take it easy. As you can see, I'm fine."

Bea cleared her throat, "Looks like you two have a lot to talk about so I'll leave you. You kids can just stay right here as long as you want." Bea left the room. I heard the back door close. We were alone in the house.

Ann returned to the couch and patted the seat beside her. "Come, sit down and tell me what happened. You never did call me. Why?"

I was at a loss. I just stood there like an idiot staring at her. She was beautiful in white slacks, a pale tan short-sleeve sweater and the baseball cap with all of that red hair curling out from under it. I couldn't help myself. I just wanted take her to my room and make love to her all day. But what I did do was nothing.

Ann became anxious. "What's the matter? Why are standing there?" She patted the seat again. "Sit down...please?"

I knew if I sat down beside her, even touched her, I'd be lost. But I sat down anyway.

Ann immediately took both of my hands in hers. Her tone was beseeching as she asked, "What happened, Richard? I get the feeling you were running away from me and weren't coming back. Is that what you did? Is that what you wanted to do...get away from me?" She searched my face for a clue but my face revealed nothing. "But why? What did I do to..." She couldn't hold back the tears and began to sob uncontrollably.

I watched for a few moments, and then I just gave in and took her into my arms. She deserved some answers and at that moment I decided to tell her. Soon her sobs gave way to sniffles. Still holding her, my mouth by her ear I whispered. "I'm sorry, Ann. I guess I'm a coward. I should have called you that afternoon and told you what happened but I was just so, I don't know, angry is not the right word. Humiliated and disgusted, disillusioned, anyway, something like that."

Ann sat back, her face inches from mine. "What are you talking about? Why would you have those feelings? We were fine when I left the house. What happened to..."

"Okay, wait a sec and I'll explain." I stood up and began to pace in front of the couch. Ann, no doubt, wondered what the hell I was doing. I stopped in front of her and, looking down at her tear-streaked face, began recounting the events of the day I took off. I spent an hour describing every emotion, every event, every crazy thought I'd had that day and for days after. Ann listened without uttering a single word. From the look on her face I could tell she was trying to process what I told her although I don't think it was possible for her to do so, at least not just then.

When I finished speaking, she said, "So, at least that explains the broken garage window. That had us stumped since nothing was missing."

Us. That word caught my attention. "Did you tell Royce I had been there?" I asked.

"Yes." She offered nothing further on that subject. "I want to understand all of this because it's so, so unexpected, so crazy I don't even know where to begin."

I sat back down next to her and said, "Begin with my watching you in the movie. How about that?"

"Okay. You said you just watched a little bit of the New Year's Eve movie and saw me doing, well, what I was doing and you became disgusted and couldn't watch anymore." I nodded. "But this is what I can't understand. I told you about the parties and what we did at those parties and I remember you saying that just hearing about it excited you. You certainly didn't get all bent out of joint or condemn me for it, right?"

I nodded again.

She continued, "About that New Year's' Eve party—I remember it very well. It was at our house and it got pretty much out of control. I mean, we were smoking grass, drinking like crazy... just going wild. The only reason I remember what went on that night was because Royce showed me the movie the next day. To tell you the God's honest truth, I was very embarrassed by what I saw and walked out of the room after about five minutes." She paused and gazed directly into my eyes. "I know that drugs were involved at that party, which, by the way, was not typical of the parties we went to. And Royce told me that one of the girls gave me something, although I don't recall that."

"Something? You mean some kind of a drug?"

"I'm not sure what it was but I remember that it made everything seem very bright and colorful and it probably increased my sex drive to where I was doing things I wouldn't normally do. Ever hear of a drug like that?"

"No, can't say as I have but I don't take drugs and don't hang around people that do. You understand? Nobody wants to be in an airplane with a drugged up pilot. But, go on with what you were saying."

Ann sighed. "I guess what I can't begin to understand is why seeing me in that movie set you off like that, especially since I had told you all about what I did and you didn't seem to mind. We went to bed after leaving the projection room and made love half the night." Ann slowly shook her head from side to side. "I'm sorry, Richard, but I just don't get it. Are you sure there wasn't something or maybe *someone* else...that might account for your actions?"

I looked down at the linoleum and thought about it. Was

there something else? What was it that set me off? I was on the bike, fuming that Ann had somehow betrayed me and degraded herself as well…riding along thinking, thinking about it when— bingo! There it was. I looked earnestly at Ann and in a quiet voice I said, "It was Angie."

"What? You told me Angie was killed in an auto accident last year." She wailed, "Was that a lie?"

"No, she did die…she's dead. What I meant was that I'm going down the road with all these convoluted thoughts racing around in my head when without warning there was Angie—in my mind, you understand. And she said that I should be ashamed of myself. That I was a good man, an honest and sincere man, something like that, and that I should be ashamed to be fooling around with a whore. That's what she called you, a whore." I raised my right arm, "I swear to God I heard her distinctly tell me that. And that's when I made up my mind that I must never see you again."

Ann fell back against the cushion behind her. Her face was ashen, all the color drained. I thought she was going to faint. Her mouth was open but she didn't speak. I got nervous. Maybe I told her too much. Maybe she thinks I'm crazy listening to voices in my head. Maybe I am crazy! What if I am crazy? Of course, that could account for my bizarre behavior, my irrational thoughts. I reached for Ann and pulled her to me. She was limp. "Ann, listen. I know that all this must sound like I'm a nut case and maybe I am. I'm sorry, but you did ask and I needed to tell you why I did what I did."

Ann's mouth closed and she inhaled deeply. The color slowly came back to her face and she sat up, taking another breath. Slowly a faint smile crossed her lips. "You really loved your wife, that's obvious and that's why she's always in your thoughts. You miss her and you keep wishing she was with you. I understand.

Believe me, you're not crazy and your wife is right. You are—really are a good man." Ann stood and walked toward the door and said in a voice so low I could barely hear her. "And she's right. I am a whore."

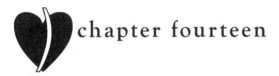 **chapter fourteen**

I stood in the doorway watching as Ann ran to her car. I wasn't sure what to do. What was the right thing to do?

"Wait!" I yelled. I raced to the car and laid my hands on the door, then leaned down and said, "Wait. Just wait a minute, will you, please?"

Ann turned her head and looked up at me, her green eyes glistening with tears. "Richard, this isn't going to work. I can see that now."

"Yes, it can, I–"

"No, it's too soon."

"Too soon? What do you mean?"

"It's too soon for you to become involved with any woman. You suffered a terrible loss and you're grieving. You buried your wife, who you obviously adored, just a few months ago and you need time to mourn and come to terms with the fact that she is gone forever. I understand now what this is all about and I think you do, too. If you and I are going anywhere then we have to wait until you are ready to let go of Angie and let me into your heart."

I was surprised, but not about what she said about Angie. She sure had that right. What took me aback was her apparent willingness to have a serious relationship with me. But what about her relationship with Royce? "You want me to, as you say, let you into my heart? Does that mean..."

Ann took her hands off of the steering wheel and laid them on mine. "It means that you are the first and only man I felt like I could love...be with forever."

"As in *marry?*"

"Yes. Why? Does that sound ridiculous?" Ann was prepared to answer my next question before I even articulated it. "Royce? That's what you're about to ask, right? Royce and I, well it's over. Actually, it's been over for months. We're just figuring out how to make it work. Royce's friends and business associates, even his clients believe Royce and I are married and he's very worried about the business implications of our split. It's complicated but in the end, and the end will be very soon, I'll be moving back to my place and I'm just going to let him worry about the details. I'll probably keep my job with the firm but if not, I'm good at what I do. I can get another job."

I walked around the car and got in. "Drive."

"Where do you want to go?"

I gave her directions to a little cove I had been to. She parked the car and we walked, hand in hand, toward a row of tall cypress trees that lined a little spit of black rocks that jutted out into the water. The gentle waves lapped against the rocks just a few feet below. We sat on a small patch of sand nestled between two large boulders.

"This is beautiful," Ann said. "It's like we're all alone in the world."

"I came across this place by accident. I was riding my bike just checking out the area when I saw it. It's a place where I could just let my mind relax. I often thought about Angie and how wonderful it would be if she could enjoy this place with me and..." I couldn't stem the tears gathering in my eyes and tumbling down my cheeks. I took a deep breath and wiped away the tears with the back of my hand. "I'm sorry, that just popped out."

Ann squeezed my hand. "You see. You're not done with Angie, and so you and I will have to wait until you are. If we try to hurry it along, I don't think it will work. This thing between you and me...We do have a 'thing,' would you agree?"

I reached out with my hand and gently turned her head toward me. We kissed. "We certainly have a thing, more than a thing. I think in time we will use the word, 'love.'"

Ann pushed me back until I was lying flat in the sand. Straddling me, her hands pressing my shoulders into the soft sand, her face very close to mine, green eyes flashing, her red hair cascading over me, she murmured, "I could love you at this moment, right here, right now." Her mouth opened as she pressed her lips to mine.

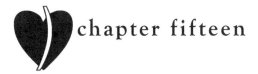 **chapter fifteen**

asked Ann, actually begged her, to spend the night with me but she was resolute. She said doing that would have to wait until I had come to terms with Angie's death and was ready to not feel guilty when I was with her—ready to move on with my life.

"How long do you suppose that will take?" I asked.

"I have no idea but if you need me to put a number on it, I'd say at least six months, maybe a year."

"But we'll see each other during that time, right?"

"I don't know. Perhaps we should just talk on the phone from time to time and leave it at that for a while. If we see each other, you know what'll happen. I'm not that strong and neither are you."

I smiled and squeezed her hand. "You're sure as hell right about that." I stood up and gently gave her a hand up. We were standing face to face. I put my arms around her and she responded with a light kiss.

"Okay then," I said. "That's the plan. I'll take off for LA in a week or so and start looking for a place to live and a job."

Ann said, "Why a week or so? Why not tomorrow?"

I had to think about that one. Why indeed? The truth was I really didn't think I was ready to trade the peace and serenity of

Monterey for the hustle and bustle of Los Angeles. "I don't think I'm ready just yet to face the reality of city living, not to mention the stress and responsibility flying a plane full of people. Besides, I have to deal with Frontier and get that squared away so they'll give me a good recommendation."

Ann cut in, "Okay, okay. I get it and you're right. I guess you really shouldn't leave here until you get your emotions under control. So take your time and call me anytime you need to talk, you know, about how you're feeling or just anything at all. I'll be there to help whenever you need me...okay?"

I allowed myself a big grin. "You're okay, in fact you're one swell gal...the best. I think you and I are going be fine." I took her hand as we walked away from our perfect Shangri-La toward Ann's car.

She stopped and looked back. "Do you think you and I will ever come back to this place?"

Without a moment's hesitation I replied, "Absolutely."

We drove back to the boarding house, kissed goodbye and she was gone. I stood by the side of the road and watched her until all I could see was a tiny green speck.

I hung around Monterey for another month taking little side trips on the bike almost every day. Sometimes I'd go north as far as Santa Cruz or inland to places like Soledad, Greenfield and King City. One morning I left Monterey early in the morning and rode down to Cambria and dropped in on Emmett and Edna. Emmett was outside his house under the hood of an old Hudson when I drove in. I pulled up next to the car and killed the engine.

Emmett laid down the screwdriver he'd been using, wiped his hands on a shop towel and shook my hand. "Well, my boy," he said, glancing at the odometer, "looks like you've been doing some runnin' around since you were here. Anything interesting along the way?"

"Sure thing." I grinned. "Nothing but one exciting day after another."

Emmett removed his cap and wiped his forehead with his sleeve. "Is that right. Well, I'm all ears so lay it on me, why dontcha."

I laughed. "What? Right here, right now? Can't do that. What will Edna say when she finds out she's missed out on all the juicy details of my wild and wicked adventure?"

Emmett chuckled. "I reckon you got a point there, son, so let's go inside and have a beer and you can weave your magic on both of us."

And I did, albeit leaving out huge hunks of the Ann story, other than to say I saw her and spent the day—emphasizing "day"—with her. They invited me to stay for dinner which once again was a simple but delicious meal. They pressed me for more details about Ann which was my fault—without thinking, I had brought her name up several times, including seeing her in Monterey. That brought on more questions from Edna, which I was able to duck thanks to Emmett who suggested to his wife that it was, after all, none of their business. After breakfast the next morning, Emmett said I should change the oil and take care of some other maintenance on the bike.

We worked on the bike together and while waiting for the oil to drain, Emmett turned to me and said, "Listen, son, I know it ain't none my binness, an' you kin tell me to button my lip if ya want but what's the real story on that gal?" He looked over the top or his reading glasses and gave me a questioning look. "I see the way ya look and how ya kinda light up when ya talk 'bout her. There's somethin' goin' on betwixt you and her, am I right?"

I screwed the drain plug in and tightened it with a half inch open end wrench. I was sitting on a little box and looked up at him. In a pleasant voice I answered, "You're right. It's none of your business unless I want to make it your *binness.*"

"You makin' fun of the way I talk?"

"Yep. What about it?" I stood.

"I reckon yer smart 'nuff ta know I could knock yer block off if I had a mind ta."

"Oh," I said playfully, "Really? Why don't you try it and see what happens."

Emmett laughed and grabbed me in a bear hug. That guy was strong as a bear. He popped the wind right out of me. He let go. "Ya see what I mean? You wouldn't stand a chance in Hell if I wuz ta git serious." He moved to the bike. "Let's quit fartin' 'round and get this bike done. I reckon you'll tell me 'bout the girl whenever yer ready and it 'pears as tho you ain't nowhere near ready." He sat on the box and went to work on the spark plugs.

I hovered over him. He looked up and asked, "Now what?"

I let out a breath. "Okay, you win. Ann and I just might get serious."

"Serious? What the hell does that mean?"

"It means that she wants me to take some time to get over my loss, you know, my wife, and when I feel I can deal with it, what she calls mourning over my wife and accepting the fact that she's gone, then I can get on with my life and maybe have a relationship with someone."

"Someone bein' her."

"That's right. And that's what I'm going to do. I think I'll be ready to face the world pretty soon and go down to LA and get a job. I miss flying and I want to get back to it. It'll be good."

"Well, by golly, I think you be on the right track and you're gonna be alright." He stood with the two plugs in his hand. "I think it'd be best ta replace these instead of jes' cleanin' 'em."

Emmett showed me the two fouled spark plugs. "I've got some new ones like these in the garage. I'll jes' go git 'em."

Emmett walked off and as he did I realized the man had a lot more savvy than I had given him credit for. He knew when to push and when to back off. In the end he seemed to always get the answers he was looking for.

I spent the rest of the day and night there and in the morning I headed back to Monterey. I cruised along at a modest speed, taking in the sights and smells of the countryside, making a few stops here and there. I realized during the run up north that my mind wasn't dogging me as it had in the past. I could enjoy the ride as I hadn't the last time I took that trip.

At a gas station with a phone booth, I checked the Frontier Airlines business card Matt Dumbrowski had given me. He had told me to take all the time I needed, that my job would be secure. This was going to be tough. Frontier had been good to me and Angie. Somehow quitting made me feel like a traitor and I didn't like the feeling. It was against everything I valued about loyalty and appreciation for what people had done for me. And yet, it was exactly what I needed to do.

I bought some gas and asked the filling station guy to give me five dollars' worth of quarters so I could make a long distance call. I entered the phone booth and stacked the quarters on the shelf under the phone. I picked up the hand set and dialed zero for the operator. When she came on the line, I hung up, realizing that I had better rehearse what I would tell Matt. I leaned against the glass booth and thought.

Eventually, I came up with an idea. I'd tell Matt how much I enjoyed working for the company, how much I respected the people, especially the pilots I had flown with, and let him know I wasn't leaving because I got a better, higher paying job. In fact, I'd tell him I had no job and hadn't even looked for one yet. I'd say that, when he and I talked at the funeral, I had no idea how traumatic Angie's death would be for me and I sure wasn't over the sting of it yet and therefore I had no business flying a plane... any plane. That's what I'd tell him. I was sure he'd be okay with it. I had another thought. I'd offer to return any salary they had paid me while I was on leave. Yes, that definitely would be the right thing to do, plus it would ease my guilt for taking money from them without having earned it.

I dialed zero, asked for the long distance operator and gave her the number. I deposited the quarters she asked for which bought me three minutes. A Frontier office girl answered the phone. Matt was on another line, but could call me back. I gave her the number. Then I took one of the quarters into the gas station and bought a pack of filtered Parliaments. I opened the pack, pulled out a cigarette, picked up a book of matches from a box on the counter and lit up. I took a drag and started coughing.

"Smoke much?" the teen-age attendant snickered.

I took another puff, coughed a couple of times, threw the cigarette down and stomped on it. I walked over to the phone booth and waited. Five minutes later the phone rang. I grabbed the handset and put it to my ear.

"Richard?"

"Yes, it's me. How are you, Matt?"

"Never mind how I'm doing. How are you?"

"I'm okay, I guess."

"You guess? Does that mean you're not okay?"

"What I mean is that I'm not totally okay, at least not yet."

"Okay, it's okay. Tell me about it," Matt said, his tone quiet and concerned.

I went into my long spiel hitting most of the points I'd rehearsed. Matt didn't say anything although he'd interject "huh,

I understand, sure, of course" and similar comments. When I told him I would return any money they had paid me during my absence he told me that there wouldn't be any money if I left. I said that made good sense. The conversation ended with Matt wishing me the best of luck and saying that I should not hesitate to ask him for references which he would be more than happen to supply. And that was that. I was now officially unemployed.

I got on the bike, kicked the starter and headed for Monterey. It was time to get my ass in gear and get my life—my real life—going again.

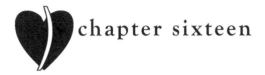 chapter sixteen

O n April 14th I said good bye to Monterey and once again was on Highway 1 or the PCH (as the folks in LA called it) heading south toward Los Angeles. I stopped briefly at Emmett's house, assuring him and Edna that I'd be seeing them again as soon as I had a job lined up and some time off. Passing Route 41, the road to Atascadero, without turning in to spend a little time with Ann was the hardest part of the entire trip. I consoled myself by thinking that she probably wouldn't have been there anyway.

Checking my road map, it looked like it was about three hundred miles to Los Angles and I'd be getting there right in the middle of all of the rush hour traffic. Not knowing exactly where I was going when I got there, I decided to stop somewhere around Santa Barbara, get up early the next morning and arrive in LA around ten when it would be a lot safer to be on a motorcycle. I had heard about the crazy way people drove in LA and didn't want to end up being another motorcycle statistic.

Isla Vista, a little north of Santa Barbara, looked like an okay place to spend the night. I cruised the area for a while and settled on a small tourist court near Goleta Beach. I was bone tired and lay down on the bed as soon as I got in my room. The next thing I knew, it was dark. I felt for the table lamp next to the bed, found it and turned it on. Several rather large bugs scurried across the floor and disappeared through cracks in the wall. Okay, you get what you pay for and all that, and I only paid two dollars. I walked down the beach toward a blinking neon light proclaiming, "EATS." It was rather late, about nine-thirty. As I slid onto a stool at the counter, the only other customer was at the register where an attractive waitress in a green uniform with white cuffs and collar was taking his money.

"G'night, Bert," she said.

"See ya tomorrow, Shirley. Good night." The man turned toward the door, acknowledged me with a nod and pushed the screen door open. It snapped closed behind him with a bang.

I glanced at the specials on a large chalk board on the wall.

"I was just about to close up for the night," Shirley said. "The cook's already left." She moved from the cash register and stood across the counter from me. I was getting ready to leave when she placed both hands on the counter top, leaned in and stared for an uncomfortable few seconds before speaking. "Tell ya what. If ya order somethin' that ain't too fancy, I'll go ahead and fix it for ya 'cause there ain't no other place open near here."

"Well, Shirley," I said. She smiled at the mention of her name. "That would be mighty nice of you and if what you make is good, why there just might be a dollar tip lying on the counter when I leave."

Shirley laughed. "That's rich. Okay, I'll make sure it's good... better than good. Now, what would ya like?"

"Make it easy on yourself. I'll eat whatever you put in front of me."

A mischievous look lit Shirley's face. "You might be surprised what I might put in front of you." She laughed as she walked in the kitchen. "Help yourself to the coffee. The cups are under the counter."

I walked behind the counter past the cash register, thinking, *Damn, she sure is trusting.* I got a mug and the coffee pot and sat back down. The coffee was strong enough to bend a spoon but it was hot. I loaded it with sugar and slowly sipped it.

Shirley came out with a dinner plate in one hand and some silverware in the other. She put the plate down in front of me and said, "There you go. Dig in."

Two small chops covered with cream gravy, French fried potatoes and green beans filled the plate. "Smells good, looks good." I cut a slice of meat and popped it in my mouth. "And damn if it doesn't taste good."

Shirley came around the counter and took a seat next to me.

Still chewing, I asked, "What's the meat?"

"Those, my friend are veal cutlets. Pretty good, huh?"

I was pretty hungry and the food was great so I just nodded as I chewed away.

Shirley watched me eat for a couple of minutes then went back to the kitchen. A moment later, she stuck her head out the pick-up window and asked if I wanted some pudding. I declined, telling her I was plumb full. She came out and took my plate and began cleaning up. I had a chance to look at her, all of her, and came to the conclusion that she was probably in her early thirties, about five foot six or seven, with a trim figure and soft brownish hair. She was a very nice looking woman. I stood up and said, "That was a first class dinner and I sure do thank you for making it. What's the tab?"

"I guess two-fifty will do it. Veal is expensive...close to a buck a pound." She walked over to the register and pushed two keys and $2.50 popped up in the window.

I reached in my pocket, pulled out some bills, selected a five and handed it to her. "Here you go. Keep the change."

She blushed slightly. "Gee, that's the biggest tip I've gotten since I started working here. Most of 'em leave ten to twenty-five cents. Thanks. That's real nice of you." She put the bill in the register, took out two dollar bills and a fifty cent coin which she put in her apron pocket. She reached behind her and turned off a switch. The neon sign went black. "Listen, you in any hurry to go back to that flea bag where you're stayin'?

I was surprised by her question but answered, "No, not really. Why do you ask?"

"I'll be straight with you," she said earnestly. "I never get a chance to just sit down with someone," she frowned, "someone who might be capable of holding an intelligent conversation."

"And you think I'm someone who could do that?"

Shirley smiled. "Come sit down with me and we'll find out."

She turned out the lights leaving just the glow of one light above the cash register and slid into a booth. I took the seat opposite. She asked, "Do you smoke?"

"Not really, but I've got a pack and some matches if you want one." I withdrew the almost full pack of Parliaments from my jacket pocket. "Here, you can have them."

She fished out a cigarette and guided my hand when I lit the match. She inhaled deeply, turned her head and blew smoke.

"What's your name?"

I told her.

"And what brings you to this burg?"

I gave her a synopsis of my motorcycle trip down from Monterey.

"And you drove it all the way from Monterey. Boy, that's some ride." She took another drag on the cigarette.

"Actually," I told her, "I drove the thing all the way from Colorado."

"Really? My husband borrowed a motorcycle from a friend one time and darn near killed himself on it. I told him I never wanted to see him on one of those damn contraptions again." She paused and seemed to be lost in thought. A wistful look came over her as she said, "And then he goes and gets himself killed in Korea."

I thought she might cry but she held it together. I reached across the table and put my hand on hers. "I'm sorry, really. I know what that's like, losing someone you love. My wife died in an auto accident last December and I'm a long way from being over it."

Shirley looked up, her eyes glistening. "I'm sorry. Are you doing okay now?"

"Yeah, I guess so but every now and then I..."

Shirley sighed, crushed her cigarette in the ashtray, and said, "Sure. I know just what you're saying. That feeling of loneliness comes over me sometimes and, and I can hardly take it. I just want to run out into that water and keep going, if you know what I mean."

I wanted to get off the subject but couldn't help saying, "I was in Korea, World War Two as well. Lost a lot of good friends. I've come to terms with all of that but I guess I haven't quite come to terms with loosing Angie. Maybe I never will."

"Sure you will." Shirley said. "Eventually you'll find someone else to love and your pain will fade and a new life will begin." Shirley slid out of the booth and I joined her. We stood face to face and I put my arms around her and held her for a while.

"Thanks," she whispered. "I needed that."

"So did I." I kissed her cheek, said goodnight and walked into the black night.

I awoke around six the next morning, took a shower and shaved off my beard. I checked the result in the mirror. *I need to do something with this hair. Nobody's going to hire a hippie.* I would find a barber after breakfast and get a neat haircut. I packed my stuff in the sleeping bag and saddlebags and left them on the bed. In the motel office, I picked up a detailed map of the Los Angeles area and walked down to the café.

I looked around the place but didn't see Shirley. An older lady, wearing the same kind of uniform that Shirley had on, greeted me, guided me to a booth and offered a menu. Waving off the menu, I asked her for two fried eggs over easy, bacon, spuds and a biscuit. After turning in my order she returned with a pot of coffee and a mug. I opened the map and studied it until my breakfast arrived. After polishing off the food and refilling my mug, I again spread open the LA city map. My best bet was just to stay on the PCH all the way past Santa Monica right to LAX.

I folded the map, stuck it in my jacket pocket and walked back to my room. I stowed my gear on the bike and took off. At a barber shop in Oxnard I struck up a conversation with the barber. I told him where I was going and asked for any suggestions on my route. It turns out he had never been to LAX or anywhere near it. But he did say that staying on the One was safer than traveling the freeways where cars traveled at, as he said, "breakneck speeds."

Eventually I made it to the airport and spent an hour or more just trying to find the United office. The gal there said I needed to go to another place and the other place told me to go to another place which came close to being what I was looking for. After a short wait, a man came into the waiting room, introduced himself as John Whatley and invited me to follow him into his office. I told him I was looking for a pilot's job and handed him a two page typed résumé that I had written while in Monterey.

He glanced briefly at the pages and then looked at me as if he were trying to size me up.

I leaned across the desk pointing at the pages. "As you can see, I've checked out in—"

Whatley held up his hand. "Just a minute, Mr. Elkins. You can give us that information on a formal application form, but before you invest a lot of time and trouble, I have to tell you that there is no way, even if you have more hours and are better qualified than any pilot in our system, that you can get on as a pilot with United."

I sat back. I'm sure Whatley recognized the surprised look on my face.

"I can see that you were not expecting that." He put his elbows on the desk and leaned in. "Let me lay it out for you. First of all, this airline, as well as all the other major carriers, have a very strict seniority system. Obviously, you'd be given a number at the bottom of the list. We'd send you to Denver to get your Flight Engineer ticket on a DC6 or 7. After you successfully checked out as an F/E, you'd be assigned to wherever you were needed in the system. You need to understand that LA is a very senior base and you would have to build a lot of seniority before you could hope to be assigned here." He paused to let that information sink in.

At that point, I just wanted to get out of there. I had no idea...

Whatley interrupted my thoughts. He sat back and eyed me carefully. "But that's not all. Here's the rest of the picture: So off you go to some base needs an F/E, even one with no seniority, and you'd work as a flight engineer for maybe five years or so before moving into the right seat on a DC-6 or a B-737." He looked away for a moment, then returned his attention to me. "I was just thinking that in five years the DC-6 will be history so you'd probably be assigned to a low weight jet. Your salary would be around $1,500 a month."

"If you were to make an educated guess," I asked, "about how long would it be before I made captain?"

Whatley chuckled. "Good question. I don't know if this is a good answer but I'm going to say ten years, maybe more." He smiled when he saw the incredulous look that shadowed my face. "No kidding, it definitely could take ten years. I'm not horsing you around. I'm telling you this because I don't think at your age which I'm guessing is around thirty-five..."

"Thirty-seven."

"Okay, add ten years to make captain and you're forty-seven years old which still leaves you," he made the calculation in his head, "sixteen years if your medicals are clean. Personally, at your age and with your experience," he studied my resume, nodding his head as he glanced through the lines, "ten or more years is a long time to wait for the big money. Am I right?"

"Absolutely," I said. My dejection must have been palpable. "To tell the truth, I had no idea what the drill would be."

"I had a hunch that with your experience and given your age, you wouldn't be interested in starting at the bottom when you've been flying left seat all these years."

I sat there saying nothing but feeling washed out. This certainly threw a monkey wrench in my plans. I stood and we shook hands. "Thanks a lot for laying it out for me. I appreciate it that you didn't try to sugar coat it." As an afterthought I muttered, "I guess I should have stayed with Frontier. If I'd been smart enough to find out about how you folks operate, I would have stayed with them."

"Maybe they'll take you back. Why wouldn't they? Frontier is a growing airline and I can't see them letting go of an experienced pilot like you."

"I'd feel like a jerk asking them for the job I just quit. Anyway, that's not your problem. Again, thanks for talking to me and setting me straight." I turned to leave and was just opening his office door when he hurried out of his chair and came over to me.

"Wait a minute, I've got an idea you might be interested in." He pointed to a couch and said, "Sit down." He sat beside me. "Did you ever think about flying for a company in General Aviation? There are a lot of big corporations who have their own equipment or lease all kinds, from single engine Cessnas and twin engine Beechcrafts to four engine military bombers refitted for cargo hauling. With your experience, I'm sure you could sign on as captain, right off the bat. I've heard the pay is darn good, sometimes better than the commercials. A lot of guys don't go for it because of the unpredictable schedules and constant layovers away from home—tough on the married guys."

I immediately brightened. "Sure, I could do that. I could be based anywhere and I have no wife, so layovers and weird hours wouldn't bother me."

Whatley stood and tapped my shoulder. "There you go. I'll check around and find out who may be looking for a pilot and let you know. How can I get in touch with you?"

"You can't right now but how about you give me your number and I'll call you once in a while."

"Sounds okay. How about getting back to me around the middle of next week? Maybe I'll have something for you. You never know."

Whatley walked me the door. "I'll be expecting your call, right?"

"Absolutely. And thanks a million, Mr. Whatley, for taking an interest in me."

"Hey, buddy," he said shaking my hand again, "I read your

résumé. You served in both wars. I was a Navy pilot in Korea and us old-timers need to help each other out, right?"

"Right."

He opened the door and I walked out feeling a whole lot better about my prospects than I had just minutes before.

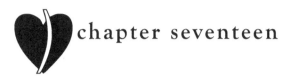

chapter seventeen

I t was on the second day after arriving in LA that I found a studio apartment in a newly built apartment house located a block off of Santa Monica Boulevard. The building was unique, situated as it was on a street of small single family homes which they called bungalows. The next day, I bought a used Chevy pickup for $600, reasoning that I needed something more than a motorcycle for day-to-day travel. I bought some furniture, dishes, pots and pans and got my little place habitable. On the third day I called Ann and told her about my situation and promised to give her my phone number as soon as I got a telephone. We made no plans to meet. After getting myself squared away, I began to look for a job in earnest.

A week later, I was sitting at an airport bar feeling a little down, ruminating about my job prospects. I had talked to Whatley several times, but so far he hadn't lined up a single interview. Of course, I knew he had other things to do. I had made a number of calls to corporate flight departments. At the time, most of the big companies owned or leased aircraft and kept a crew of pilots to fly their top execs around.

So, there I was on a balmy day in early May wondering what my next step should be when I spotted a guy in what looked to be a pilot's uniform, although I didn't recognize the insignia on his coat or cap. He looked around and saw the empty stool next to mine and sat down.

I turned toward him and said, "Excuse me, but I was just wondering about that badge. What airline is that?"

He gave me a broad smile. "It's not exactly an airline. I fly for USS–United States Steel."

"Oh. You like the job?"

"Hell yeah. We fly all over the place, including some South American cities. It's a lot more exciting than flying commercial. A hell of a lot more fun, too. Never know where the hell you'll be going next or when."

"That sounds interesting," I said wistfully. "And something I'd sure like to do."

He seemed to size me up. "You a pilot?"

"Yes. Flew left seat for Frontier for over five years–or rather, left seat the last three. Sorry, my name's Richard Elkins." I offered my hand.

He shook my hand and said, "Ron Schmidt. Pleased to meetcha."

I signaled the bartender. "I'd like another bourbon and ginger ale and whatever my friend here wants."

"Make it a beer–Schlitz."

When the drinks arrived, Ron lifted his bottle."Thanks."

We did the obligatory clink of glass.

"I'm guessing, Richard...It's Richard, right?"

I nodded, "Most people call me Rick."

"As I said, I'm guessing, but I'd say you spent some time in the military. Is that where you got your training?"

"That'd be a good guess. I was a Navy pilot. Fighters during Korea and then transports."

He blew air through closed lips. "I'll bet you've filled a bunch of log books."

I laughed. "I've probably got more hours than Carter has pills."

We moved to a table, ordered another round and got to know each other a little. He asked if I was married and I said no. He told me he was a bachelor. He said although quite a few of the corporate pilots were married, it could be hard being away so much and the long layovers could be a problem for the married guys. I told him I had heard that. He asked if I had flown any of the larger aircraft and I said I had flown left seat on the R5D.

"Wow," he exclaimed. "So ya think you might be interested in flying corporate?"

"Are you kidding me? Hell yes. I'd love it."

"Let me see what I can do." He stood and we shook hands. He took out a small notebook and pulled a good-looking Parker pen from his shirt pocket. "What's your phone number?" I told him I didn't have a phone yet. "Okay," he said. "Here's mine." He wrote the number down and tore the sheet from the notebook. "Give me call and say, if you'd like to go to dinner sometime..."

"Sure. I'd like to learn more about flying corporate—"

Ron laughed as he broke in. "I was thinking more along the lines that I'd invite a couple of very lovely ladies to join us and make a night of it." He paused and gave me a thoughtful look, "I mean, if you're up for that sort of thing."

"Hey man, I don't know a soul in town, so you bet, I'd definitely would like to do that. A dinner is almost always better with a little female companionship."

The telephone company installed my phone a few days later and I called both Ron and Mr. Whatley. I left my number on Ron's answering machine and with Whatley's secretary. That evening I was heating up some canned pork and beans and about to toss a pork chop in the frying pan when my new phone rang. I picked up the handset. It was John Whatley.

"Mr. Whatley, good to hear from you. Have you anything good to tell me?"

"First, let's drop the Mr. Whatley crap—it's John and yes, I've lined up an interview with Charlie Borden. He's ops manager for Esso—Standard Oil. They are going to update their fleet with either the Lockheed Jetstar or the North American Saberliner. So they're looking for experienced pilots with a shit pot full of hours who would be willing to take the time and get checked out on the new equipment. I told Charley I thought you'd be perfect for the job."

After getting the details, I thanked him and promised I would call him after the interview.

Charlie Borden was a large, overweight man in his sixties who dressed casually—no tie—and his office was pretty casual as well. As I stepped through the door, I couldn't stop myself from glancing around and taking it all in. Photographs lined the walls of a much younger Charlie standing beside a variety of planes. There was more aviation history in his office than in a museum.

"I see that those pictures have your attention, so while I'm reviewing your history that John sent over, help yourself to a look around."

It was absolutely fascinating. One picture showed Borden standing next a Pan-Am four engine flying boat. They called them "Clippers." I remember as a kid seeing a movie about the China Clipper and the struggle to bring it on line.

I turned back to the desk. "Did you fly one of those clippers?"

"Sure did," Charlie said, a broad grin spreading across his face. "I was one of the first to fly left seat. God, what a thrill! It was all manual and you had to really work hard. At the end of each leg, you'd be exhausted from wrestling that monster." He gestured to a chair. "Okay. Sit down and we'll get on with it."

Over the next hour or so Charlie laid it out for me. He said that they were about to take delivery of two new Jetstars and while the company assigned the pilots based on seniority, they made exceptions from time to time. In my case, he said, I had more hours on more equipment than most of their pilots and since the Jetstar was new, he thought I should have a shot at checking out in it.

"I've got four pilots who I think would be a good fit for this plane and it might be that you'd be in the right seat for a while. Would that be a problem, since you were a captain with Frontier?"

"No, sir...I'd be happy to co-pilot on that plane. And don't worry, I'm sure I'd have no trouble checking out in it."

Charlie stood and I stood. He said, "Okay. You'll be hearing from me in a week or less. I've got to run it through channels. Oh, by the way, you never asked what the pay might be."

"To tell you the truth, I'd be willing to pay you just to get my hands on that plane."

chapter eighteen

hinking back on it, it probably wasn't such a good idea, calling Ann and leaving my phone number on her answering machine. But nothing I could do about it now. Sure enough, Ann called and we had a pleasant enough conversation without any sexual innuendo. I took that as a good sign. I told her about my job prospects, my little apartment, while she told me that she had left her job and found another with a very prestigious company.

"So, do you have any plans for this weekend?" she asked.

"No, not really."

"How about this idea? I'll come over to your place after work Friday and we'll go to a really nice place for dinner. Then on Saturday we could ride the bikes someplace fun."

"On Saturday? Does that mean you'd be going back to your place Friday night and returning Saturday or..."

Ann laughed long and loud. It was contagious. I couldn't stop myself from laughing as well. Gasping for air, she said. "Boy, oh boy, you are too funny. Are you sure you're not a teen-ager?" Without waiting for an answer she said, "Of course I'd go home Friday night. What do you take me for...some floozy? I know the rules, self-imposed though they might be. I haven't forgotten one word of what we talked about in Monterey."

Feeling relieved, I said, "Okay then. Good. That's good. 'Cause right now I'm in pretty good shape mentally and I want to stay focused on this new job, if I get it. You know what I mean?"

"Of course. And I certainly agree with you." A long pause then Ann added, "Anyway, back to my original question. Dinner Friday?"

"Love to." And I meant it.

Late in the afternoon on Friday, Ann called to tell me she would pick me around six and I should be wearing a coat and tie to comply with the "required attire" rule of the fancy restaurant we were going to. I had given most of my clothes away when I left Durango but I did keep a sports coat, a white shirt, a pair of wool dress pants and a few ties. I took a shower, shaved, slicked up my hair and got into my civilian "dress blues." I checked out the look in the bathroom mirror. Not bad. I hadn't been this dressed up since Angie's funeral.

Angie! There she was again, overpowering me with thoughts of her and how it had been with us. I almost broke into tears but pushed hard to move her back to the far recesses of my brain. I quickly walked to the kitchen, pulled the cork from a bottle of Old Forrester and took a generous slug right from the bottle. There, that was better. Ann was right on when she said I was a long way from being over Angie. Thinking about that and how she handled the situation on the phone, I was satisfied that tonight would be okay. We'd have a nice dinner, a couple of drinks. Not too much. Not so much as to push away inhibitions. No, it would be okay, as the kids say—we'd be cool.

My doorbell rang a little after six and when I opened it, there she was. My God! She was beautiful and dressed up like a movie star. A huge smile spread across her face as she moved toward me, arms wide. I moved into her embrace.

Kissing my cheek, she gasped, "You have no idea how much I've waited for this moment." She took a step back to check me out. "You look terrific. Really." She hugged me again. "You are one handsome son of a gun."

I closed the door, took her hand and walked her into the living area. "You know what?" I said. "There are very few, if any, movie stars who look as beautiful as you do at this moment. I'm at a loss for words." I peered at her. "Something's different." I let my eye travel from her shoes to her cute little hat. "Ah, you've cut your hair, right?"

With a little cry of delight, she said, "You are so sweet. Yes, I cut it. Do you like it?"

I gave her a ferocious hug, lifting her off her feet. "I love it. Take off the hat so I can see it all." I let her down and when her feet touched the floor she removed the hat with a flourish and a bow.

"Excellent," I exclaimed, then I glanced at the clock on the stove. "What time is our reservation? And where are we going?"

"Seven. And as to the venue, that's a surprise." She looked at the tiny gold watch on her left wrist. "We'd better get going. Are you ready?"

I opened the door and we walked hand in hand to her car, a recent model Oldsmobile convertible, bright red with a white top.

"My goodness, this is some car," I commented as I held her door open. "Is it yours?"

Ann laughed as she slid in and put a key in the ignition. "Of course. I told you I had a very good job."

I was captivated by how well Ann navigated the busy streets, jumping off the main roads to take some obscure side road that obviously avoided bottlenecks, traffic lights and the press of cars that clogged the main roads. I looked her lovely profile and said, "Man o' man. You sure know your way around. I'm impressed."

"I should since we're heading for my home ground." She turned her head and smiled. "We'll be there in a couple of minutes."

We were driving through a pretty classy neighborhood when I spotted a bronze sign. I turned to Ann, "Beverly Hills, eh? Isn't this where the rich and famous live?" She nodded. "What in the world are we doing here?"

"We're here because I'm rich and you're going to be famous. How's that?"

I laughed. "Hey, that's fine with me. Why should I have thought otherwise?" Ann turned into a circular drive and pulled up under the portico of the Beverly Hills Hotel.

"So this is it? I've heard of this place but I never in a million years thought I'd actually be inside of it."

Ann grinned. "Now you'll have something to tell your grandchildren."

A uniformed doorman opened Ann's door while another opened mine. "Good evening and welcome to the Beverly Hills Hotel," the doorman said, handing Ann the ticket. "Have you been a guest of ours before?"

"Many times. What's the matter, Paul?" Ann reproached him playfully. "You don't remember me?"

"Oh. I am sorry Mrs. Silbert." He gave her a careful look. "It's just that you look a little different tonight," he said as he held open the door. "Have a wonderful evening."

"Come along, Rick. We're going to have cocktails and dinner in the famous Polo Lounge."

"I'm sure it's famous but I've never heard of it." I was gawking around like a tourist from Japan. The place was magnificent. I thought, *This is where the movie stars come. And the shakers and movers of industry.* Ann gave my hand a gentle tug.

At the entrance to the Polo Lounge, a tuxedoed maître d' greeted us. "Good evening, Mrs. Silbert. So nice to see you again. It's been a while, hasn't it?" He glanced momentarily at me as if to say, who is this guy?

Ann gave him a dismissive smile. "Yes, yes it has. I've been away—traveling abroad."

After we were seated and huge menus had been placed before us, a bright young man asked if we would care for a cocktail. Ann ordered a very dry martini with just one olive. I asked for an Old Forrester with ginger ale. The waiter gave me an odd look. I think he found my choice of drink to be rather plebian.

I let my eyes take in the room. I guess super elegant would describe it. I saw Gregory Peck, Jean Arthur, Tyrone Power, Ann Southern and at least a half a dozen other movie stars.

"Rick," Ann cautioned, "let's not play the gawking movie fan, okay?"

"Take it easy, I'm trying to get a handle on all this. I've got to say it's a bit awe-inspiring if you know what I mean." Nevertheless, I returned my eyes to her for a moment. "By the way, speaking of gawking, I noticed a lot of people looking our way and I'm sure it wasn't me they were looking at. What I'm saying is, there isn't another woman in this room as beautiful as you."

Ann laid her hand on mine. "That's so sweet and you're too kind, or maybe..." Her mouth formed a faint smile. "Anyway, that's very nice of you to say. But, here's my take on it; if you look around—no don't look now—I can tell you that a number of gals are giving you the once over. Do you know why?"

"No, but I'm excited to find out."

"Because, my darling, you are not one of the most attractive men in this room. No. You *are* the most attractive and handsome man in this room."

I laughed aloud. "And you are the best bull-slinger anywhere."

Our cocktails arrived and as we sipped we opened the menus. I was flabbergasted! The price of a meal could buy the average family food for a week. Ann saw my mouth drop as I read through the offerings.

"Yes, it's expensive, but you'll find the food is worth every penny they charge. Furthermore, this is my treat so you order anything and everything that appeals to you, okay?"

I shot her a curious look. "Tell me, is this going to be charged to Mr. Silbert? I'm assuming he has an account here."

"And I, too, have an account here," Ann said. There was a distinct bite to her words. "Actually," she continued, her voice softening, "I have an account here because I frequently bring clients here for lunch. So please, let's not get all goofy. I want tonight to be fun, something we'll remember for a long time." She looked around the room and sighed. "It's going to take a while, I'm afraid, for people to stop calling me Mrs. Silbert. As a matter of fact, I should have set them straight as soon as we got here." Ann's lips formed into a pout. "Come on. Let's eat, drink and be merry, alright?" Ann motioned to a waiter. "Please bring us a wine list."

Ann handed her ticket to the doorman who handed it to a kid who ran off to get the car. Turning to me, she said, "It looked like you enjoyed your dinner. That was some huge steak and you ate every bite. Very impressive!"

A big sheepish grin lit up my face. "Yes, I did...every damn bit of it. I've never tasted anything like it." I shook my head, "I'm telling you, that was unbelievable. And, all that other stuff was top of the line as well, but the steak...I don't suppose I'll ever have another like that."

Ann laughed, her green eyes dancing. "What do you mean? Of course you'll have another steak like that...lots of them."

I was about to reply when the car pulled up. The boy jumped out to hold the door for Ann who slipped him some bills. The doorman opened the passenger door and I got in. He walked around to the driver's side. Ann rolled down the window, the doorman said something to her and she thanked him and handed him a bill.

We drove along in silence for a while. I was just reliving the last two hours and relishing the thought of all that wonderful food—and wine. "Damn, that was a great bottle of wine. Never had any wine like that before."

Ann smiled, as a mother might smile at her little boy. "That was a '59 Lafite Rothschild Bordeaux. Yes, it was excellent."

I said, "I hate to think what that dinner cost you, but just let me say thank you very much. It was an experience not to be forgotten, although not to be repeated."

Ann snapped her head around in surprise. "And why is it not to be repeated, especially since you enjoyed it so much?"

"For one thing, I sure as hell can't afford dinners like that or even close to that. This job I'm trying to land would pay no more than $1,200 a month, probably less. People making $15,000 a year don't eat at the Polo Lounge."

"No, they don't but—"

I cut her off. "No, they sure as hell don't. Now you may think this is square but the way I've operated since I was old enough to date works like this: the guy pays and the girl says thank you. And so while I am grateful for your generosity, maybe benevolence is a better word, it's not something that'll happen again, at least not in the foreseeable future."

Ann laughed and slapped the wheel. "So, I am to play fair maiden to your knight in shining armor, is that it?" She shot me a look of exasperation. "This is not the nineteen-thirties for God sake. The old fashioned concepts of chivalry have given way to a much different society. Women can and do buy things for their husbands and, yes, for their boyfriends as well. I see nothing wrong with it—in fact, I got a lot of pleasure just watching you enjoy yourself. You think about that, mister, before you get all righteous with me." She took a deep breath before continuing. "But if it makes you uncomfortable for me to do things for you, things, by the way, I can well afford, then fine. You can take me to one of those nineteen-cent hamburger places and I'll be perfectly happy because, and this is the important part, I'll be with you. End of speech."

I sat back saying nothing as she parked the car in front my place. I got out and walked to the other side to open the door for her, but she was already out of the car.

"You see," she said in a mocking tone of voice, "I'm perfectly capable of opening a car door. Now, are you going to invite me in?"

Feeling a bit overwhelmed and not sure of my next move, I replied, "Of course." I unlocked the door and we walked in. I turned on the kitchen light, took off my jacket and hung it on a kitchen chair. Ann removed her wrap and her cute little hat and placed both on the kitchen counter. Leaning back against the counter, hands on her hips, she gave my little apartment a good going over, sometimes nodding, sometimes shaking her head in disapproval.

I watched her for a moment, then asked, "Is this an inspection or were you wondering how a person could live with such meager amenities?"

Ann strolled around the apartment, making little comments

as she went. "You need help, my friend, and I'm the perfect person to help you whip this place into shape."

"Really? And what exactly do you mean by shape?"

"I'm talking about making your little home comfortable and attractive. More furniture, some lamps. Curtains, definitely. Maybe a picture or two on the wall...that sort of thing. So, here's my plan: tomorrow I'll come over about ten and we'll take your pickup and go shopping. If you don't have the money right now I'll lend you some and you can pay me back when you start working."

I took her in my arms and gave her a hug. "You're too much. But I'm not broke. Actually I'm in pretty good shape after selling the Durango house and there's the insurance money...But wait a minute. So you're really not planning on spending the night here?

"Of course not," she vehemently replied. "If I had even thought about spending the night here, I would have brought some clothes to wear tomorrow. I can just see me in the second hand furniture stores in these duds." Ann gestured to her elegant dress. "No, darling, I never intended to spend the night. Remember our vows to abstain until the time was right?"

She stood close and reached up, putting her arms around my neck. Our lips locked in a long, long kiss. I was about to drag her to the bed but stopped short. She was right. We should end the evening right now before things got out of hand.

Ann broke away and retrieved her shawl and hat from the counter. We walked to the door where she kissed me again. I opened her car door and she slid in, saying, "See you tomorrow. Goodnight." She smiled sweetly. "And thanks for a wonderful evening. Best date I've been on in years."

"No, thank *you* for, well, everything. It was special, that's for sure." I touched her cheek lightly. "But the next dinner is my treat. See you tomorrow." I stood by the curb and watched as her taillights faded in the dark.

Ann's knock came a little before ten. We hugged and she gave me a perfunctory kiss. "Ready to transform this place," she said with a sweep of her arm, "from a sorry bachelor pad into a bright and comfortable home?"

My face broke into a large grin. "I guess so, but I'm wondering, is this about me? What I mean is, I find the place okay as-is." I gave her a questioning look, "Or, is this about you wanting to spend more time here in, shall we say, a more hospitable environment?"

Her response held mock disbelief. "Where did you ever get the idea that I wanted to spend more time in this place? How audacious!" She threw her arms around me and pulled me down until we were face to face. "You big lug," she said through a laugh, "I could love a guy like you." She gave me a peck on my cheek. "Oh, don't frown. I said I *could* love a guy like you. So don't get all a-twitter." Ann took my hand and led me to the door. "Okay, let's get in that rattle trap truck of yours and get going."

"It's not a rattle trap. It's a damn nice Chevy and..."

Ann punched my shoulder. "Of course it is. Maybe you're the rattle trap."

Ann seemed to know exactly where she would find whatever she thought I needed to turn my place into a home. We spent most of day shopping and buying and when we got back that afternoon the bed of my truck was filled. By the time we placed the little couch, the two chairs, the lamps and the countless other gewgaws, the place looked much improved and quite nice.

She looked at her watch. "I'll see you tomorrow morning. We

can have breakfast together and then I'll sort out all of this," she said motioning toward the pile of stuff in the middle of the floor. "Then I'll do the curtains and other trappings."

I'll admit I was a little confused. "You're leaving? I thought we'd go to dinner and maybe a movie in Westwood."

"Can't darling, not tonight. I've got other plans, but I'll see you tomorrow morning." She gave me a quick kiss and was gone.

I stood in the open doorway scratching my head and thinking, *What the hell just happened here? Other plans? What the hell does that mean? Is she going out on a date?* Suddenly, I became irritated. I wondered what kind of a game she was playing. Underneath her socially appropriate demeanor, was she in fact the party girl I'd seen in the New Year's Eve movie? I heard Angie's voice repeating, *Do you want to be with a whore?* No, no! I didn't want to, could never be with a whore. And yet, something told me not to go overboard and shut her out of my life until I find out what is going on because there was no doubt in my mind that Ann was up to something.

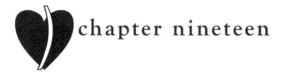# chapter nineteen

I poured some bourbon over a couple of ice cubes, found Ron Schmidt's phone number and dialed.

"Hello."

"Ron, it's Rick Elkins. How's it going?"

"Good, good. Man, I'm glad it's you and not flight ops calling to tell me I have to fly tonight. So, what have you been doing?"

I told him about my interview with Esso and the possibility that I might be hired and trained in the Jetstar. He was impressed and said so.

"I've been checking around here and think I'll be able to get you an interview, although you won't be flying anything like a Jetstar, more likely a G-2 Turbo-prop. I'd definitely take the Esso job if they offer it."

"Yes, that certainly would be the way to go but if it doesn't happen I sure would appreciate interviewing with your outfit. Give me a call if anything comes up." I gave him my phone number and was about to hang up when he asked, "Say, are you doing anything for dinner this evening?"

"No. I have nothing planned. I was..."

"How about having dinner with me and a friend, a girl?"

"That's nice of you to ask but you don't need a fifth wheel to..."

"No, listen. Marilyn has a roommate, Cindy. I'll find out if she's free tonight and if she wants to go on a blind date. I'm sure she'll say yes after I tell her you're another Tyrone Power. What do you say?"

"Ah, well, I guess that'd be fine but don't build me up too much. We don't want the girl to go running away screaming when she gets a load of me."

Ron laughed. "Don't worry, pal, she'll be tickled pink. I'll call you back in a few minutes."

I finished my drink and put the empty glass in the sink. I looked around the room, looked at all the stuff we'd bought, and began to wonder how it would be in the morning when Ann came back. I was sure it would be awkward, at least for me, but I had to find out what was going on with her. Where was she heading and why?

The phone rang. I picked up the handset.

"Rick? It's all set for tonight. Let's see, what time is it now?"

I glanced at the clock on the stove. "About four-thirty."

"Okay, we'll pick you up around six-thirty."

I gave Ron the directions, poured a small bourbon, and got in the shower. The phone was ringing when I stepped out of the shower. I grabbed a towel and hurried to pick up the phone, thinking it was Ron calling to tell me the date had been cancelled. "Hello."

"Richard, my boy, it's Bud Schultz. How have you been?"

"Fine, and you?"

"Excellent. However I'm somewhat irritated with you. Didn't you promise you'd call me at least once a week? What happened about that? I finally was able to get your phone number from information. Anyway it doesn't matter now."

"Why's that?"

"Because my boy, I got you a settlement check from the insurance company for—want to guess?"

"Geeze, Bud, no, I don't want to guess. Why don't you just tell me?"

"Okay, ready? One hundred-eighty thousand bucks. Huh? How about that?"

Astonished almost speechless, I said, "Holy smokes, Bud, you must be a hell of a lot better lawyer than I thought you were. That's great!"

"Richard, you should have heard me plead that case. Honest to God, I even amazed myself." Bud broke into a laugh. "You should have been there. I swear to God, half those jurors had tears in their eyes by the time I finished my summation." Bud broke into prolonged laughter again. "It was wonderful, possibly one of the best days of my life, really."

"Okay, okay. Don't break your arm patting yourself on the back, but hell yes, I'm proud of you. So, what happens next?"

"Next? Why you take out your First National checkbook and write in a deposit of $176,112 on April 26. The difference is my fee and other expenses."

"You did all that for four thousand dollars?" I asked.

"Do you think that was too much? You know I've been working this case for—"

"I know you've put a hell of a lot of time and effort into it. No, I was thinking you weren't charging enough. How many hours did you spend on it?"

"Hell, Richard, I don't know. Who keeps track of hours? I figure out what I need to do and about how long it'll take and come up with a fee. Can you imagine lawyers charging by the hour? That'd be ridiculous."

"Yeah, I suppose so. Still you've done a great job for me,

much more than I expected. I sure do appreciate it and I would be happy to throw in a couple thousand more."

"Richard, my boy. I'm fine. I'm satisfied I charged you a fair price so let's drop it. Next time you're in Durango, you can take me and the wife out to dinner or something."

We said our goodbyes and I sat down in one of the new chairs. It was very comfortable. *A hundred and seventy...what did he say the number was? I should have written it down. I'm rich! Yes, I'm rich but I paid a terrible price for it.* I stood and walked around the room. *So next time we go to the Polo Lounge, I'll be the one who pays for dinner.*

"Ha," I muttered aloud. "I doubt there ever will be a next time."

When Ron arrived, he spied the stuff on the floor. "What the hell happened here?"

"I went shopping for stuff for the apartment. Haven't had time to put it all away yet." I put on my sports coat, straightened my tie and said, "Okay. Let's go."

Ron led the way to his green and white 1962 Pontiac Chieftain station wagon. He opened a back door and I slid in. "Rick, this is Cindy and the lovely lady up front is Marilyn."

Cindy offered her hand. "Ron was telling Marilyn and me about you on the way over here." She smiled and added, "I reckon he didn't lie nor embellish, did he, Marilyn?"

Marilyn looked back at us with a warm smile. "No, he didn't."

On the way to wherever we were going, I said to Cindy, "I detect a British accent. Are you two from England?"

"Yes. My home is in Slough. It's a smallish town a bit west of London. Marilyn lives in Cirencester in the Cotswolds. It's a wonderfully charming area."

"I'm going to guess," I said, "but I have a hunch you two work for an airline."

Marilyn laughed. "Brilliant! How ever did you sort that out? Yes, we are both stewardesses for BOAC." Marilyn pointed out the window. "Ron, there's the car park, just there."

Ron pulled into a parking lot adjacent to a restaurant whose illuminated sign read "Ben's Place—Fine Steaks, Seafood, Full Bar." The four of us went inside and were seated at a booth. I had my first chance to have a good look at the two girls. Marilyn was quite tall, about five foot nine, while Cindy was perhaps a couple of inches shorter. Marilyn was wearing a solid colored sleeveless dress, while Cindy wore a print dress. I'm not sure what the material was but she looked very cute. Her wavy brown hair was short and I'd say stylish. At first blush I guess you'd call her pretty. She had a very animated manner and I fell in love with her accent and her quaint British expressions.

We ordered several cocktails. Both girls drank gin with what they called "quinine water." Ron drank Pabst beer and I had my usual 100 proof bourbon. By the time our food arrived, we were pretty relaxed. Ron suggested we go to a movie after dinner. "That new James Bond movie, *From Russia with Love* with Sean Connery, is supposed to very good."

Cindy said, "I'd love to see *Charade* (she pronounced it, shar-aahd) with Cary Grant and Audrey Hepburn. He's a fellow Brit, you know."

We discussed various options but in the end the girls wanted to go back to Ron's place and relax.

Ron looked at me. "That okay with you?"

"Sure, if that's what the girls want to do."

We declined dessert but opted for another drink, and finally, we left Ben's Place and headed for Ron's home in Westwood, which turned out to be a little bungalow similar to the ones near

121

my place. It was fixed up really nice, very comfortable, which I thought was a bit unusual for a bachelor pad, but I later learned that Ron had lived with a girl for over a year and it was she who had added all the amenities. Within minutes I saw Ron lead Marilyn to the bedroom or maybe it was Marilyn who led Ron. In any case, Cindy and I were left alone.

Ron had a wonderful stereo system and an incredible number of records. He had placed a stack of records on the turntable spindle. The first song was *Blue Velvet* sung by Bobbie Vinton.

Cindy jumped up and playfully said, "Come along, Rick. Let's have a bit of dance." She kicked off her shoes, grabbed my hand and pulled me up and the next thing I knew, we were dancing. She was delightful, jabbering away as we danced around the living room. I remember how she snuggled up to me as we danced to Frank Sinatra singing *Close to You*.

"You are a brilliant dancer," she said. "Some of your moves are spot on."

"I don't consider myself any kind of a dancer but with you, it just seems easy." I pulled her to me in a hug. We stood motionless for a long moment. She turned her face up and I kissed her. Her lips remained closed. I kissed her again and her lips parted ever so slightly.

"Oh, Rick," she moaned, "perhaps we better cool down and not let this get—"

I pulled her into my arms and kissed her again. Her arms encircled me and her mouth opened and I felt her tongue searching for mine. At that moment I had a thought, not about whether I'd end up in bed with Cindy but the word *retribution* sprang into my consciousness. *So, Ann, how do you like it? I, too, can play games.*

Cindy released her hold and stepped back. "What is it?

Suddenly you seemed to be somewhere else. Is it something I did?"

"No, not at all. You're perfect, really. It's just that I get these flashbacks and they just take over...I mean just momentarily." I took her hand and led her to the couch. We sat there for a long moment simply looking at each other. It was obvious Cindy was upset and I needed to set it straight. "Okay, here's the thing. Last December, just before Christmas, my wife was killed in a terrible auto accident."

Cindy put her hand to her mouth and gasped, "Oh my God. How awful."

"It's just that I haven't come to terms with it although I thought I was making good progress. Just now, dancing with you, holding you, kissing you was wonderful. I truly do miss being loved and loving someone. And you felt so good in my arms, I thought if you were willing...But it's obvious I'm not ready yet. But if and when I can overcome this guilty feeling, I'd love to be with you. You are adorable and I certainly hope that we will see each other again."

Cindy squeezed my hand and gave me an earnest look. "Then, it's a good job there is only one bedroom in this house." She stood and pulled me up. "Come along," she said, guiding me toward the kitchen. "Shall we see if we can sort out some tea and a kettle? I should think a proper cup of tea would be a satisfactory antidote to all this."

Mocking her accent, I said, "Right you are, mate. You find the tea and I'll search for a kettle. It's tea and crumpets and long live the Queen."

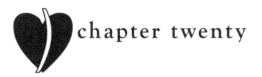 chapter twenty

It was after two in the morning when Ron dropped me off at my place, with the parting comment that we should go out again the next time the girls had a layover in LA.

I was still asleep when the doorbell rang. I checked my watch—it was 9:15. *Holy smokes,* I thought, *who in the hell?* I pulled on a bathrobe and padded to the door. The bell rang again just as I opened the door. There was Ann with her finger on the button. She was dressed in her biker outfit—leather jacket, leather pants, the whole deal. A look of surprise lit her face as she gave me the once over.

"What the hell happened to you? You look like you were hit by a truck." She laughed and slapped her thigh as she pushed her way in. "Are you just getting up? Oh, I see," she snickered. "Are we a little hung over?" She pulled off her jacket and threw it on a chair. "Ricky, Ricky, Ricky. What am I going to do with you?"

I spun around and headed for the bathroom. "Make yourself a cup of coffee. I'm going to take a shower."

About twenty minutes later I presented myself. She was sitting at the table. "Ah, there you are and looking a hell of a lot better. What did you do last night besides getting drunk?"

"Okay, you're right about getting drunk, although not falling down drunk by any means. But my question to you is, what did *you* do last night? You told me you had plans, but you didn't say what those plans were."

"Oh, for Christ' sake," Ann said with disgust. "I had dinner with Royce. We had some issues that needed to be resolved, one of which, you'll be happy to learn, was his turning over all the movies I was in. As long as he had those movies—"

I interjected, "He could blackmail you or use them to get back at you."

"Exactly. But I have leverage as well and he knows it so, we agreed that I'd get all the films. All of them. I know how many there are. And I agreed that as far as anyone knew, we were married but got a quiet divorce several months ago, and that's the story we'd both put out."

When she finished speaking, I didn't know what to say. To tell the truth I felt like a dimwit. Here I was all upset with her for going out on a date when she actually was taking care of business. I took a deep breath and exhaled slowly. "I'm sorry, Ann. I don't know what's the matter with me. I mean, if you had gone out with some guy, maybe even slept with him, it's none of my business. I have no proprietary rights. We've made no commitment to be," I made quotation marks in the air, "*true* to one another."

Ann nodded silently.

"As a matter of fact, I did go out to dinner with a friend of mine and his girlfriend and they brought along the girlfriend's roommate."

"As your date."

"Well, yes. I guess you could say that. Maybe more like a dinner companion."

"Sure it was. Nonetheless let's call it what it was, a date."

"Okay it was a date. The two girls are stews with British

Overseas—very nice, respectable ladies. And that's that." I didn't feel the need to say more.

Ann got up from her chair and put her empty coffee mug in the sink. "All right then. We've both come clean as to our whereabouts last night and as you say, that's that. No harm done, all's right with the world. I just want to say, anytime you want to go out with someone, do it. You don't need to feel guilty about it and you sure as hell don't need permission from me. I'm not your wife. I'm not even your girlfriend. I'm a friend who hopes someday to be more."

She came over to me and gave me a hug and peck on the cheek. "Now go put your boots on because you and I are going motorcycle riding today. It's a beautiful day for a ride and getting out on the bikes is the best therapy there is for clearing your head and your heart. Am I right?"

I took her in my arms and kissed her. "Damn straight."

"Funny, I never heard your bike when you drove in," I said as I pushed the Harley out of the carport.

Ann said, "That's because the Honda is a civilized bike, refined and quiet, not at all like that monster you're so in love with."

I laughed. "So, where are we going?"

"I was thinking we'd go down the coast to Oceanside. Maybe have lunch there. Find a quiet beach and sit in the sun for a while. Maybe even talk to each other—you know, things like that. What do you think?"

"Sounds good. I don't care where I go as long as I'm with you and this bike," I said, patting the tank. "How far is it to Oceanside?"

"I'm guessing about a hundred miles, something like that."

"Okay, then. Let's go. You lead," I said as I kicked the start pedal.

It was one of those blue sky days with very little smog. Sunday morning traffic was light, and Ann set the pace at around sixty-five, slowing down every now and then to admire the spectacular scenery. She pulled off the highway at Seal Beach and drove up to a drive-in.

I pulled alongside. "What's up?"

"I just realized you haven't had anything to eat. You must be starving. Get some coffee and a hamburger to tide you over 'til lunch." Ann swung a leg over her bike and took a seat at one of the outdoor tables.

I went inside and ordered two nineteen-cent hamburgers, some French fries and two milkshakes. The bill came to ninety-eight cents. I handed the clerk a dollar bill and said, "Keep the change." He gave me a wry look. I laughed, fished out a quarter from my pocket and handed it to him.

"Thanks a lot, mister." He looked at the quarter and then said, "Do you want change?"

I took the tray of food to the table.

"I don't need anything," Ann said as I handed her the milkshake and hamburger.

"Go ahead and eat it. Hell, there isn't enough meat in that thing to plug up an ant's ass."

Laughing, Ann said, "Where do you come up with all those sayings? Plug up an ant's ass, that's rich."

I was famished and gobbled up the food and milkshake in no time. When Ann finished we fired up the bikes and headed down the road. When we reached Oceanside, Ann pulled into a beach parking lot and then we walked hand in hand toward the water. There were only a few people on the beach plus a couple of surfers on surfboards looking for a wave. We took off our jackets and lay down on them.

I sighed, "This is more like it. The ocean, the blue sky, the warm breeze. Nice."

"You forgot the other ingredient...me."

I smiled. "Yes, you. You very definitely are the most important part of this scene."

Ann rolled onto her side, propped her head in her hand. "Tell me about your date last night."

I sat up. I hadn't been expecting that question. "What do you mean? I already told you."

"No, you didn't. You didn't say anything about where you ate or what you did after dinner or describe the girl you were with. What was she like? What was her name? C'mon. I'm just curious, that's all."

"First of all this is not going to be a confession or anything like it. There's nothing to confess and nothing happened last night that I would be ashamed to tell you." I went on with a synopsis of the events of the previous evening, including the dancing. I described Cindy as best I could. Ann wanted to know what she wore, how she looked.

"Was she pretty?" she asked.

I said yes, I thought she was pretty, very pretty, but I emphasized that she was "not a beautiful girl like you, but pretty and bright." I watched Ann's face as I talked. "She could not hold a candle to you in any way."

Ann planted a kiss on my lips. "You may be a liar but I'll have to admit, you're sweet and you do tell a very convincing tale. Regardless, I'm glad that you had a nice time. Besides, you should go out on dates, me included, of course. But if we ever do get together I need you to know that you picked the right girl. So get out there and see what's available."

We ate at a lovely little restaurant with a view of the ocean and, after strolling along the beach for a while, we donned our jackets, fired up the bikes and took off for Santa Monica, arriving at my place around five.

"Okay, we've got to get this stuff off the floor and tidy up before I leave," Ann said. "Then I've got to go."

Surprised, I asked, "Then you don't want to have dinner with me later?"

"Of course I want to, but I've got a big day tomorrow and I've got to prepare for it. Oh, don't look so glum, for God's sake. We'll get together for dinner during the week."

After we'd dispatched a fair amount of wrapping paper and cardboard boxes, Ann was satisfied. "Okay, now this place looks more like a home." She put on her jacket, gave me a kiss and opened the door.

I grabbed her arm and pulled her to me with a hug. "You be careful going home on that bike. I mean it. Keep your eyes open and take it slow, okay?" I looked deep into those marvelous green eyes. "I couldn't stand it if anything happened to you. That'd be the end of me for sure so—"

Ann stopped me with a deep kiss. "You're too sweet. Don't worry, I'll be extremely careful. We have a lot of unfinished business to take care of and I plan to remain in your life until it's finished—one way or another."

I stood in the doorway and watched as she piloted the Honda down the driveway.

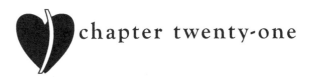 chapter twenty-one

On Wednesday the following week I received a call from Charlie Borden, the flight ops manager at Esso. If I was still interested in training in the Jetstar, he had cleared it with the brass. Standard Oil would hire me and send me to the Lockheed training center in Marietta, Georgia. The initial course would take about six weeks. After initial training, I would go to proficiency training and checks. After that I'd get simulator training at a pilot training company in Atlanta. After receiving my certification, I would be sent to the Lockheed plant in Georgia.

Since Lockheed's main offices and facilities were in Burbank, California, there was also the possibility that the company would accept delivery of the new planes there and those of us in the Jetstar training program would spend some time flying the plane and take our final checks there. All of this training and then some, before we'd be flying any company big-wigs around. At that time, many corporate executives were actually afraid of flying and the flight department had to be especially careful who they picked to pilot an entirely new aircraft and the first jet in their fleet.

Three other Esso pilots would train for the Jetstar. Two of them were the company's most senior pilots. Terry Halverson was a sixty year old ex-bomber pilot, ex-Capitol Airlines captain who had been flying left seat for Esso for nearly a decade; he was the pilot the company president and senior execs wanted at the controls when they flew in company planes. The other senior pilot was Alvin Conley, a fifty-six year old Marine fighter pilot. Eugene Parrino, a forty-nine year old ex-TWA captain was the third trainee. And that left me, a thirty-seven year old with no seniority but with a hell of a lot of hours in a variety of aircraft. Since the mandatory retirement age was sixty-five, I think they were thinking they had better train a younger man and, apparently, I was that man.

I called Ann and told her I would be off training for quite a while but that I would check in with her from time to time. She said she was happy that I was so excited about my new job and the upcoming training, but at the same time she confessed that she would miss seeing me. Truthfully, I was so damn excited about flying the Jetstar that Ann's confession blew right by. I hadn't been this passionate about flying since I took my first ride in the Corsair fighter.

In 1963 there were major events taking place throughout the country, events that in my little world, and with my obsession with what I was doing, had a minimal impact. Lee Harvey Oswald killed John F. Kennedy, Lyndon Johnson became president, Kennedy's assassin, and Jack Ruby killed Lee Harvey Oswald. All of these huge events captivated the country. Then there were the civil rights marches, the two-hundred-thousand-people march on Washington in support of civil rights, the famous King "I have a dream" speech, and much more. But I, Rick Elkins, was only interested in one thing: learning how to fly the Lockheed Jetstar. Nothing else, no one else mattered. I was consumed with it. When I began training, I made up my mind that I'd be the best damn Jetstar pilot ever. That's right. I wouldn't settle for less. No, sir. I'd be the best!

Terry Halverson and I began our training around the middle of May. The other two pilots slated to take the course would begin their training after Terry and I had completed our certification. The training wasn't easy by any means and some students might have found it daunting, but Terry and I were seasoned pilots and, although we had to work hard at it, particularly the transition from traditional engines to jet propulsion, we did just fine. After simulator training, we got down to business in the cockpit of the living plane. My first ride at the controls was certainly an eye-opener.

Without getting too technical, let me tell you about that plane: With its four Garrett AiResearch jet engines, it cruised at 500 miles an hour, had a range of 3,000 miles, a service ceiling of 43,000 feet and a 4,150 feet per minute rate of climb. You could take off and be at a cruising altitude of 40,000 feet in less than ten minutes. By way of comparison, the DC-3 I flew for Frontier Airlines had a cruising speed of 200 mph, a rate of climb of 1,100 feet per min and a service ceiling of 23,000 feet. It would take about 20 minutes to get to a cruising altitude of only 23,000 feet. You can see what a huge leap forward this was. It was not only about performance, but it was also about the avionics and other high tech features of this plane. It was something to get excited about and believe me, I was excited.

chapter twenty-two

I got a long weekend off from training and flew from the Lockheed factory in Marietta to LA, arriving in the early afternoon on Friday. I had called Ann and she agreed—actually seemed quite eager—to spend the weekend with me.

I asked, "By that, do you mean stay with me at my place?"

There was a long pause and I think I heard a sigh. "Richard, I'd be willing to sleep with you for the rest of my life. The question you have to answer is, are you ready to move this relationship to the next level?"

"I think the answer is obvious. I wouldn't be asking if I wasn't emotionally ready."

"And you think you are emotionally ready to take on the responsibilities of an intimate relationship?"

All of a sudden my mind exploded in a jumble of thoughts.

"Rick, are you still there?"

"Yes, of course, I was just—"

"Listen," Ann said, "I'll come over after work and we'll go to dinner. Afterward, we'll just play it by ear and see what happens. Okay? Meanwhile, take a nap, have a drink and try not to get all crazy. Remember there isn't anything you have to do other than relax and have a nice time."

"Of course. You're right, as usual. I'll see you later. Oh, any place special you'd like to go?"

"If you're there, anyplace is fine. Bye."

Ann rang the doorbell a little before seven. I opened the door to the most beautiful girl in LA. She was wearing what I assumed was her business attire. The jacket was a light tan or beige and the pleated skirt was a dark brown. A light pink scarf with a fancy tie artfully adorned her neck and disappeared into the front of the jacket. Sheer stockings led to low heel pumps. She had a very healthy glow about her—she had obviously spent some time in the sun while I was away.

I took the whole thing in and gushed as I took her into my arms, "You are a vision, you know that? You're just too darn pretty to be real."

"Are you going to just stand there gawking or are you going to kiss me right now?" she said, throwing her arms around my neck and planting a hungry kiss on my mouth. And then another. And another. Then she pushed me away and gave me a thorough looking over. "You've bought a new suit, haven't you? Very smart looking and I like the tie as well. I'm glad to see you're taking an interest in how you look."

"I bought it and several more at a place in Atlanta."

Ann smiled, "What happened, did your great aunt Matilda die and leave you her fortune?"

I blinked and unthinkingly muttered, "No, my wife died and I got the insurance money."

Ann put her hand to mouth, "Oh, darling, I'm so sorry. That was very crude of me. I'm sorry. It was meant as a joke." She hugged me and kissed my cheek. "Please forgive me."

"It's okay. I shouldn't have responded the way I did. So, let's forget it and go have a nice dinner."

I had planned to take her back to the Polo Lounge but couldn't get a reservation. However, I was able to get a reservation for eight-thirty at Lowry's Prime Rib in Beverly Hills. Arriving about a half hour early, we went into the bar, found a table and Ann ordered a dry Martini. I was about to order my usual bourbon but on second thought I told the waiter to bring me the same with an olive. The drinks arrived in stemmed cocktail glasses.

"So, this is an extraordinary moment in your life, your first martini. It is a first, isn't it?" Ann asked.

I shot a broad smile in her direction as I raised the glass, "Yes, it is. In fact, I don't think I've ever had any kind of a gin drink. Anyway, one must expand his social horizons. So I raise my glass to you, my sweet and beautiful Annette. May we always be happy together." As an afterthought, I added, "No matter what." We clinked glasses and I ended up spilling some of my drink. I took a long swallow of the Martini and damn near choked. "Jesus, this stuff is awful! How the hell do you manage to drink it?"

Ann doubled up laughing and managed to blurt out, "You call yourself a man? You're a big sissy." Several patrons turned in our direction but Ann could not stop laughing. Eventually she had me laughing as well. "I'm sorry, I should have warned you. You have to acquire a taste for the dry Martini."

"No kidding. I don't think I'll live long enough to accomplish that." I hailed a waiter. "Bring me an Old Forrester and ginger ale please. Make it the bonded."

We entered the dining room and took our seats at a table for two by a wall. It really was an amazing place with every table occupied. There was a steady din of conversation throughout the room, but it wasn't overpowering.

Ann leaned toward me. "This is a very lovely place. I've heard of it but have never been here. They say the food is as good as it gets."

"And we're about to find out," I said. "Ah, here's our waiter now." A gray-haired gentleman in a tuxedo asked if we would like to start with a cocktail. "Of course," I said smoothly. "The lady will have a dry Martini with an olive and I'll have a bonded Old Forrester with ginger ale please."

Ann chirped up, "What, you aren't having a Martini?"

I smiled politely saying, "You know I'd love to, darling, but the olives are very fattening and I'm watching my weight." To the waiter I said, "I'll stick with the bourbon and ginger ale."

"Very well sir," he said with a slight bow. "I'll bring your cocktails and menus in a moment."

Looking across the room an elderly gentleman in a tuxedo was approaching a very large grand piano. He took a seat at the keyboard and began to play *Stardust,* one of the old standards that so many of the patrons, like myself, had grown up with. Soon couples were heading for the small dance floor.

I turned to Ann, "Care to trip the light fantastic with an amateur?" I asked.

Ann grinned. "Nothing would please me more," she whispered.

I stepped behind her chair and helped her up, then I guided her to the floor and we danced. She felt so good in my arms I didn't let go even when the song ended. Most of the people returned to their tables but we stood there swaying to the subtle rhythm and then dancing to *You'll Never Know,* followed by *We'll Be Together Again.*

Ann whispered, "Look around. People are staring at us."

"Not us. You! Are you not the most beautiful, most desirable woman in this room? Of course they're staring. The men all wish they were me."

Ann looked up at me, her eyes dancing, "You big dope." She broke away and led me back to our table. Suddenly someone started clapping, then several more people joined in, until finally most of the people in the room were looking at us and applauding.

I took Ann's hand and said, "There you are. There's your proof. Okay, one, two, three, bow." And so we did, to the delight of the crowd.

The waiter returned with our drinks and menus. "That was quite wonderful," he gushed. "I think you two had these people quite captivated."

I saw some red creep into Ann's cheeks. "Thank you," she said, giving the waiter a generous smile. "We weren't expecting anything like that to happen. But there you go."

"Just so," the waiter said. "Now please take your time ordering. We are noted for our prime rib but whatever you select for dinner this evening will be delicious." Another slight bow and he backed away.

The waiter was quite right. The prime rib dinners were out of this world. The piece of beef was huge, at least a pound. I was surprised by how much of it Ann ate. We passed on dessert but ordered sherry, Ann's idea. We sipped the wine and chatted. The pianist returned to the piano and began to play.

"Ready for another dance?" I asked.

"No, we'd better not," she said, eyeing the pianist. "I don't want to end up betraying our new-found celebrity. Let's quit while we're ahead." Her lovely green eyes grew moist, "No matter what happens with you and me, I'll never forget this night." She brushed away a tear with her finger. "For the first time in my life, I now think I know what love is." She smiled bravely, "And truthfully, it scares the hell out of me."

139

Ann parked the car on the street near my place and we walked hand in hand to my door. I unlocked and opened it and started to walk in, but Ann stopped me.

"Are you sure you want me to come in?"

I turned and faced her. "What?"

Ann repeated, "Are you sure you want me to come in? Wait, think about it."

I pulled her into my arms and hugged her. "What's there to think about? I want you to spend the night with me. You'll be in control all the way. We'll go no further than you want to."

"Really? You and I will be in bed, probably nude and we'll go no further than *I* want to?" Ann patted my cheek. "You poor, naive boy. Obviously you don't recall how things worked out the last time we got in bed together."

"I know, but this is different. We're different now...on a different level," I said, pulling her into the room and closing the door. "Anyway, we're, or maybe it's just me, over-thinking this whole thing." Suddenly a thought burst forth. *Maybe this isn't such a good idea. Maybe I'm not ready for this. Maybe the whole thing will blow up and then what?*

Ann scrutinized my face. "You're thinking twice about this aren't you"? She stepped away.

"No, not at all I..."

"I don't care what you say, I can tell you're hesitant and I better go home...now!" She moved toward the door.

I took hold of her arm. "Ann, I'm begging you. Please stay, even for a little while. I don't want our perfect night to end like this. I need to hold you, feel you close to me. It may be a month or more before I finish training and I probably won't be able to come back until I've flown the plane and checked out. What do you say?"

Ann's look told me she was torn between what she thought

was the right thing to do and emotionally what she wanted to do. She sat down on the couch, put her elbows on her knees and laid her head in her hands.

"Okay," she murmured. "You win. You know I can't refuse you." She patted the cushion, "Sit down and hold me. Tell me how much you love me and..." she lifted her head and smiled, "and other lies."

I put my arm around her and drew her to me. Ann laid her head on my shoulder. Neither of us spoke. I must have fallen asleep because I awoke with a start some time later and Ann was gone.

"It was meant to be," Ann said. "Otherwise the evening would have turned out differently. You see that, don't you? When you're ready, I'll be ready. Meanwhile, as you said last night, let's not over-think it."

My doorbell rang. "Wait a sec," I said into the phone. "Someone's at the door."

"Okay. Call me back, I'll be here." She hung up.

The doorbell rang again. I opened the door and the landlady's daughter who lived in the apartment above mine said, "Sorry to bother you, Mr. Elkins, but I was wondering if you could give me a jump start. The battery's gone dead on my van. I've got cables."

I smiled, "Of course. It's Nancy, right?" Nancy, I guessed, was about twenty. She was a pretty girl with a cute little body and marvelous blue eyes that almost seemed to be purple. She wore her short black hair in a fashionable style although fashionable would not be the word I'd use to describe her clothes. But that's how college kids dressed those days. Her mother had told me that Nancy was a student at UCLA.

Nancy nodded. "That's right."

"I'll get my keys and we'll see what we can do."

We walked to the carport behind the building and I fired up my truck and backed out. Nancy's van was a decrepit old VW bus. The windows were plastered with stickers from just about everywhere including some foreign countries.

I pointed to the windows and said, "Surely you haven't been to all those places."

Nancy laughed. "Hell no, but my grandfather has. This was his bus. I took it over after he died." She entered the bus and returned with the cable jumpers, opened the engine hatch in back and attached the cables to the battery.

Looking over her shoulder, I said, "Looks like you've done this before."

"Plenty of times," she replied. "Drive your truck up close and we'll hook up."

I started to get my pickup but stopped and said to Nancy. "Wait a minute. That's a six volt battery and my battery is twelve volts. I don't think that'll work."

"Don't worry. When the motor starts, pull the cables off right away."

Nancy got in the bus, I hooked the cables to my battery, she started the engine and it fired off right away. I yanked the cables off. Nancy came around and slammed the hatch shut.

"Thanks a lot, Mr. Elkins. I appreciate the help. Sorry to have bothered you but I had to get going."

"Hey, I'm glad I could help you out." I had an afterthought. "Listen, I'm going to be gone for, I'm not sure how long...probably a month or more. Tell you what; I'll leave the keys to the pickup on the kitchen counter and if you need to use it, help yourself. And, if you don't mind, check my apartment once in a while to make sure everything's okay. Want to do that?"

"Sounds great. Thanks." Nancy got in that old VW and took off.

I walked back inside thinking, *Did I just tell that kid she could use my pickup? What the hell was I thinking?* I picked up the phone and called Ann. "Hi. It was the landlady's daughter needing a jump for her dead battery. Anyway, how about we get together for lunch? My plane leaves for Atlanta at 4:20 so we'd have time."

"Sure," Ann replied, "I'll pick you up around noon and after lunch I'll take you the airport, so bring your bags."

We had finished lunch and were sipping coffee. I said, "Sorry about last night...falling asleep, I mean. That wasn't very..."

"Cool?" Ann took my hand. "It was fine. I told you, last night, the dinner, the dancing, the people clapping, just being with you...it was wonderful."

"I'd certainly agree—it *was* wonderful—*you* were wonderful. You were the most beautiful girl in the room. I'm just sorry we didn't end it properly, the way I thought we would."

She squeezed my hand. "It ended as it was meant to end. Now please put it out of your mind."

Changing the subject, I said, "I'm not sure how long the simulator training will take but I'm thinking it's going to be at least three weeks or more. Then there'll be check flights with a Lockheed test pilot. I'm sure I won't have any trouble checking out, but I'm just saying it could be quite a while before I'm back."

"Don't fret about it. Go to the bank and get a ten dollar roll of quarters and call me as often as you can."

I got up and lifted her from her chair. Holding her close, I whispered in her ear, "I'll probably use up all the quarters on the first call." Some people nearby looked at us and smiled. For a moment I thought they were going to applaud.

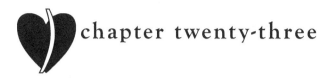 **chapter twenty-three**

I saw Terry Halverson at the airport. He had booked the same flight to Atlanta to begin simulator training at Flight Safety. Terry had a seat next to a gal and I asked her to trade seats with me so I could sit next to Terry.

After I had sat down and buckled up, Terry gave me sardonic look. "That little trade sure as hell didn't work out to my advantage." He leaned close and whispered. "She's a lot better looking and probably a lot more interesting to talk to than you."

During the trip I got to know more about Terry, his past experiences as a pilot, his wartime stories and I also had a glimpse into the personality of the man. This was my kind of straight up guy. He struck me as the kind of man who says what's on his mind and doesn't pull his punches. At his request, I gave him a brief bio with emphasis on where and what I've done in airplanes.

Terry said, "You know, at first I wondered why the hell they'd put some guy without a day of seniority into the Jetstar program. But after they showed me your ticket and what you've just told me, I can see the logic in it."

I thanked him and added, "It sure looks like we'll be spending a lot of time together."

He looked at me and smiled, "Yeah, I guess so. Just don't try to kill me so you can get in the left seat."

Terry and I finished our simulator training at Flight Safety. We both received our FAA ratings in the simulator and technically were qualified to fly the Jetstar; however, Charlie Borden wanted us to take additional training at the plant in Marietta, flying the plane with a Lockheed test pilot. Actually, he told us, the "brass" insisted on it, being, as he said, "Nervous Nellies" when it came to flying, especially in a new aircraft piloted by newly trained pilots. I was perfectly fine with taking the additional training, but Terry wasn't.

"What the hell," he groused. "We're ready to fly the plane, we've got our ratings and I'm anxious to pick up the plane and get going. We can always do a few touch and goes with a factory guy. I'd be okay with that and maybe spend an hour in the air with him."

"I know what you're sayin'," I replied, "but Charlie is probably getting pressured so what's the harm spending a little more time? You never know, even *you* might learn something. Besides we've got to go to the factory to pick up the plane anyway."

In the end, Terry got over it. Frankly, I don't think he really objected to the extra training. It was an ego thing and when it came to piloting airplanes, Terry definitely had an ego as big as a DC-8. Nonetheless we went to Marietta, took the addition training from a Lockheed test pilot, which even Charlie admitted was well worth the time, and flew our new plane, a Jetstar II with four AiResearch TFE-731 turbofan engines, to LAX, taking turns with take-offs and landings. The truth is, as I mentioned earlier, that plane was a pure pleasure to fly and without passengers on board, we made the most of that trip, meaning we had a lot of fun developing our skills flying an unconventional route to LAX.

I returned to LA around the middle of May. When I got to my apartment, I checked the answering machine. Among the messages, mostly from Ann, were two from Ron Schmidt asking if I was available to go to dinner with the two gals from BOAC. Both of his messages concluded with him saying that Cindy was, as she put it, "quite keen to see me again."

Ann's messages apparently were recorded between the times when I had called her from Georgia. Mostly they included phrases like, "can't wait to see you, I miss you so much, when you get back I'm going to...." and so on. To tell the truth, I was particularly interested to find out just what she was going to do when I got back. I dialed her number and got the answering machine. I asked her to call me. The next call was to Ron. He, too, was out but I left a message telling him that I'd love to go to dinner the next time the girls had a layover in LA.

I removed my stuff from the two suitcases, bundled up the dirty clothes and headed for the laundry room. The two washing machines were busy and Nancy was pulling clothes from a dryer. She looked over her shoulder when I walked in.

"Hey. You're back," she said brightly. "You've been gone quite a while but I've been checking your place and everything's fine." Nancy laid the hamper of dry clothes on a table and started folding. "How did the training go?"

"Just great," I replied, "It was a lot of fun and now I'm a certified Lockheed Jetstar pilot."

"Never heard of it. It's some kind of a jet, right?"

I laughed, "Yeah. Some kind all right. It's one hot airplane and a real kick to drive."

Obviously, Nancy wasn't interested in hearing more about

147

the plane. "I started your pickup a few times to keep the battery charged but I didn't use it. I ended up buying a new battery for the VW and it's been starting just fine." Nancy looked at her watch. "I'm fixing a lamb stew with barley. It'll be ready in about an hour. Want to have dinner with me?"

That invitation caught me by surprise. "Sure. That'd be nice. What can I bring?"

Nancy thought for a moment. "Have ya got any good red wine?"

"I think so. What would you prefer?"

Nancy pursed her lips and let her purple eyes drift toward the ceiling. Presently she said, "How 'bout a nice French Bordeaux or Burgundy? Either one would go good with lamb."

"Okay," I said, "Anything else? Maybe a French bread or baguette?"

"Yeah, sure, that'd be perfect."

I dropped my bag of clothes on the floor. "Can I leave these here? I'll do them after dinner."

"Sure." She gave me a big smile. "I'll toss 'em in the washer for you." She looked at her watch again. "How 'bout you come up at 6:30? Will that work?"

"Perfect. I'll see you then," I said and left the room.

When I returned to my apartment, I called Ann. The machine answered again. I picked up my truck keys and walked out to the carport. With a couple pumps of the gas pedal and a liberal dose of the choke, the Chevy started on the third try. I drove to a wine store in Westwood and picked up a bottle of imported French Burgundy and a bottle of Bordeaux. Both, the clerk assured me, were excellent choices. They'd better be, I thought. One was eight dollars and change, the other ten plus. Most French red wines were priced below five dollars. Two doors down from the wine store was an excellent little bakery that I had visited many times before. The baguette I purchased was still warm.

I'll say one thing, Nancy sure could cook. Her lamb stew was out of this world. Along with the stew, the two of us actually consumed both bottles of what turned out to be excellent wine. I think we were a little snockered by the time we were half way through the second bottle.

Nancy said, "So, tell me about that redhead who drives that cool Olds convertible. I've seen her several times. Is she your girlfriend or..."

I shot Nancy a look and said, "What? You've been spying on me?"

"When I'm here, I always keep an eye who comes and goes. We had some things stolen from the carport last year and—"

"I'm just kidding. The redhead is kind of a girlfriend, I mean she's a girl and a friend—a good friend."

"Where did you meet her?"

"I was riding my motorcycle up the PCH last January and Ann, that's her name, and a bunch of other bikers were at a gas station. I met her there." I went on with the story, albeit a very abbreviated—and sanitized—version.

Nancy poured herself another glass of wine and added the last of the bottle to my glass. "From what I've seen of her, I'd say good for you. She's really pretty, maybe even glamorous. When I first saw her I thought she might be a movie actress." Nancy wagged a finger, "Is she?"

"No, 'fraid not. She's a financial consultant."

Nancy smirked, "You gotta be kidding. Financial consultants don't look and dress like that!"

I had to laugh, remembering the night Ann and I went to the Polo Lounge. Ann really did look like a movie star. I recalled how the people stared at her when we danced, how they clapped. That was some night.

"No, really. She's a financial planner with a very prestigious firm here in LA. But when she gets all dressed up, I'm sure people think she is in the movies."

"Are you two serious? I mean are you guys sleeping together?"

I must have given her a shocked look.

"What? Geeze, I didn't mean to embarrass you."

I put down my wine glass and, in what I thought was a very firm tone, said, "You don't ask people things like that, for gosh sake. Are you sleeping together. What the hell is that? I'm not one of your school chums."

"Geeze," Nancy exclaimed, "Don't get all weird. Okay, maybe I shouldn't have asked but why not? It's no big deal if you are sleeping with her. Hell, if I was a guy, I'd be all over her like white on rice!"

I couldn't help myself. I began to laugh and couldn't stop. Maybe it was because of all the wine. Here was this kid interrogating me about my love life and I was getting all righteous about it. It was absurd.

Nancy began laughing too. She stood and came over to where I was sitting. Still laughing, she suddenly threw her arms around my neck and planted a wet kiss on my lips. Pulling back she said, "If I was that redhead, I'd get you in bed and wouldn't let you up for a week."

I quickly stood and looked down at her. "Okay, that's enough of that. We're not going to play any games. I appreciate the dinner and the lively company but it's time for me to go."

"Oh, give me a break will ya," Nancy barked. "I was just screwing with you. Hell, you don't need to get all bent out of

joint. C'mon, I'll make you some coffee and I promise I won't
try to rape you."

I thought about it for a moment. She was just a kid and kids
seemed to have a whole different set of standards than people of
my generation. I flashed a smile. "You're right. I'm sorry to have
reacted that way but people my age—"

"Yeah, I know. People your age are too uptight. You don't
know how to relax, have fun. And you get embarrassed when
people talk about sex...right?"

I nodded, "Yeah, I guess so."

Warming to her subject, Nancy went on, "Nowadays, people,
I'm talking about unmarried people, are having sex all the time.
Hell, if you were to interview the students at UCLA I bet you'd
find that seventy-five percent of them are having sex."

I started to laugh again. "Having sex?"

Nancy's brow furrowed. "What's so funny? I thought we were
having a serious conversation."

I throttled back my laughter. "It's the way you use the word
'sex.' I mean, you use it as a noun. I might say, having intercourse
while you say having sex."

"So? What's your point?"

"The word sex is a noun and refers to whether a person or
animal is male or female. You use the word as a substitute of
the word intercourse." I waved my hand. "It's no big deal, as you
would say. It's just that I find it amusing when you say, 'he was
having sex with her.' It just sounds odd—as if you're saying 'he
was having gender with her'."

Nancy gave me a dismissing look, "You know what? That's
totally dumb and how did we get so far off the subject?"

"My fault. So to answer your question, no, Ann and I haven't
had sex." I had to smile even as I said it. "And for all I know we
may never have sex, at least not until we are married, if we ever

marry. Okay, now that you have that bit of information you can rest easy and I can go home and go to bed. I'm tired." I gave Nancy a peck on her forehead and left.

The light on the answering machine was flashing. It was from Ann who asked me to call her even if I got home late. It was a little after ten. I picked up the phone and dialed her number. We talked for at least half an hour. We agreed she would come over to my place after work and we'd have dinner.

I drove to LAX the next morning and met with Terry at Charlie Borden's office. We gave Charlie the run down on our training, told him what a great plane the Jetstar was and so on.

Terry said, "You need to fly that plane, Charlie. You'll love the way she handles and man, when you push those throttles, that bird takes off like a rocket, no kidding."

"Yeah, yeah, I know. But that's not my job, it's your job and the kid's." Charlie glanced in my direction and saw the look of surprise on my face. Apologetically he said to me, "Not that you're a kid, I mean you're the new guy—new kid on the block—ya know."

Terry and I laughed. I said, "Hey Charlie, I don't mind being a kid even at thirty-seven. After all, what pilot isn't a kid at heart?"

"You got that right," Terry muttered.

Charlie leaned forward, elbows on the desk, "I want you to take Alvin and Gene up today. They'll be starting their training in about a week or so and they're anxious to see what the ship can do. Also, a couple of the division guys want to check out the plane, so they'll go with you. Do your pre-flight and be ready to light the fuse at 1300."

Terry asked, "How long do you want us to stay up?"

Charlie thought a moment. "File a flight plan to Victorville.

Land there, give control to Rick and come on back. That should do it for those guys. Any questions?"

"Wilco," Terry said. "Ask the passengers to be at the apron by 12:30 so then, if they have any questions, we can show them around before takeoff."

The demo flight went off smooth as silk. Terry had the leg down, I had the leg back. It was fun and our passengers were properly impressed with the spaciousness of the cabin (room for ten passengers), and when we cranked her up to 520 mph and showed them a very hot rate of climb, that blew them away.

Landing back at LAX, I shut down the plane and made sure the ground crew took care of the hanger details while Terry closed our flight plan.

"What are you doing for dinner?" Terry asked.

"Got a date with a beautiful redhead," I replied.

"Beautiful?"

"That's right. Beautiful as in movie star beautiful," I said boastfully.

"Redhead?"

"Yep."

Terry gave me a look. "Beautiful redhead. Pretty as a movie star?"

"That's right," I repeated.

Terry punched me hard on the shoulder. "You lying bastard. In your dreams that's your date."

I grabbed Terry's arm. "Tell you what. Get yourself a date and we'll go to dinner and you can see for yourself if I'm lying. This girl is a knockout and smart as a whip, real intelligent, so don't be bringing some bimbo date or she'll get lost in the dust."

"Okay, wise ass. I'll just do that. What say we go next Sunday, if we're not flying?"

"You're on, sport. Better get started right away finding a date…"

"Don't you worry. I've got lots of girls who'd be tickled pink to go with me."

In the parking lot I got in my truck.

Terry motioned for me to roll down the window. "Let me ask you a serious question, Rick. You're certainly not going to be taking this movie star redheaded beauty to dinner in this pile of shit, are you? I'm assuming you'll be using your Cadillac."

"Well, Captain," I answered in my most deferential tone of voice, "no, I won't be using this pickup. Actually, we'll probably use her new Olds convertible. Although she is not the type of girl who would object to going in this pickup. She's not a snob. In fact, like me, she also rides a motorcycle." I gave Terry an enormous smile, started the engine, leaned out the window and said, "Goodnight. Better get right home and start searching for your dinner date."

Ann showed up at my place a little after six. Dressed in her financial adviser's outfit, a pale blue skirt and matching jacket, white blouse with a long-peak collar that extended over the lapels of her coat, a single strand of pearls around her neck and pearl studs in her ears, she was the epitome of the quintessential successful woman executive and, not so incidentally, amazingly beautiful. I wondered how it was that each time I saw her, she seemed even lovelier than the last time. Or was it something else? Was it that I was actually in love with her and with each new encounter, was the love I felt opening my eyes to see her anew, to witness some new and wonderful aspect of her as if I was seeing her for the first time? This thought ran through my brain in a flash and yet it was as flawless and clear as if I had pondered it for an hour.

Ann tossed her purse on a chair. "Hi, darling. It's been a while, hasn't it?"

I wrapped my arms around her and we kissed. It was a long, hungry kiss and then another. I held her tightly, my mouth close to her ear. I whispered, "I love you."

Ann pushed me back. "What?" She looked deeply into my eyes. "What did you just say?"

I held both of her hands in mine and murmured, "I said, 'I love you.' I assume you know what that means."

"It can mean all sorts of things," Ann replied, "but I think it means that you have finally realized that I am, after all, the girl you were meant to be with."

"No, it's more than that. You are the girl I want to marry."

Suddenly, Ann's eyes filled with tears and she began to cry. "I'm sorry," she blubbered using the back of her hand to stem the flow of tears. "But this is so unexpected. I mean, I always felt you'd come around to this some day but you caught me completely off guard just now."

"I know, I know." I pulled a handkerchief from my pocket and wiped her tear-streaked face. "Honestly, I hadn't planned to say anything tonight, but when I saw you," I gestured with my hands, "I couldn't help myself. I knew it just had to be you and this was the right moment."

Ann allowed a smile to slowly spread across her lips. "Did I hear you say that I was the girl you want to marry?

"Yes. You heard right. That's what I said."

Ann's expression became pensive. "I'm all for it." She considered me for a moment. "But let's not be in a big hurry to actually do the deed. We need more time to explore each other and I want to stick with the one-year rule we talked about in Monterey. I don't want either of us to be unsure in any way." She paused and searched my face for an answer.

155

I nodded. "I can live with that. I agree. There's no need to hurry. We'll take our time and if it's meant to be, then it'll happen. But just between you and me, I'm pretty sure it's going to happen because I know you, and only you are the one I want to spend the rest of my life with." I added facetiously, "Do you think there is another beautiful redhead anywhere in this world who can ride a motorcycle, who can excite me, who can..."

Ann put her hand over my mouth. "Please, please stop talking." Taking my hand she led me to the bedroom. Pushing me back onto the bed, she laid on top of me. "The time for talking is over. Now, show me how much you love me."

Ann, wearing my bathrobe, ambled into the kitchen.

"How about some scrambled eggs and bacon?" I asked.

"Great. I'll make the coffee and toast." Ann opened the refrigerator and fished out the ingredients.

We ate our meal in virtual silence but both of us couldn't help smiling, knowing what each of us was thinking but not wanting to articulate. The love making was not frantic the way it had been that first time so long ago. It was tender and sometimes tentative but so satisfying that when at last we spoke, we spoke the words in unison. "I love you." Neither of us would ever forget this night.

Terry and I flew two company execs to a meeting in Newark, New Jersey on Friday. The trip covered about 2,500 miles and took us a little over five hours from wheels up to the gate. The two passengers were impressed not only with the speed of the plane but with the comfort of the cabin and the amenities we provided. Arriving at EWR (Newark Liberty International Airport) around noon, the two passengers took a cab to their meeting. After closing our flight plan and taking care of business, Terry and I walked over to the General Aviation building for lunch.

We placed our orders and got a pot of coffee. I filled Terry's cup and mine and took a careful sip. I laid the mug down and asked, "Did you manage to dig up a date for our Sunday evening dinner?" You might think we would have discussed this during the flight but I think you will find this interesting—Terry and I had agreed during our first trip in the Jetstar that flight deck talk would be limited to matters concerning the flight. In other words, small talk, chitchat and the like would not be a part of our cockpit conversation. I think some of that came from our military backgrounds but more than that, Terry was a professional and he definitely played the part and, I mean, played it to the hilt.

"Yes, I did," Terry emphatically exclaimed. "And a very smart and pretty girl she is."

"Good for you. Anyone I know?"

"Maybe. She's Hank Wheeler's secretary."

I furrowed my brow. "Hank Wheeler? Why does that name sound familiar?"

"He runs maintenance. You must have talked to him at some time and you probably saw Emily when you were there."

I thought about it. "I don't think I met Emily, but I'm sure she's a lovely gal."

"Damn straight she is. Anyway, you'll see."

Later, we sat in the cabin's comfortable leather swivel chairs waiting for our passengers to return. Terry immediately fell asleep. That guy could fall asleep darn near anytime he wanted to, maybe even standing up. No doubt another residual of flying long trips during the war. I pulled an Esquire magazine from the rack and was flipping through the pages when the radio squawked our tail number. I picked up the mike and answered.

The message was from our guys who advised they should be ready to go by 1630. We did our pre-flight checks and when the two men arrived, we buttoned up the plane and lit the fuse.

Terry contacted the tower and when we were cleared to taxi he asked me, "Want to drive?"

"Why? You want to finish your nap?"

Terry looked at me over the top of his sunglasses which told me I'd better behave.

"Aye, aye, Captain. I have control of the aircraft," I said and released the brake and pushed the four throttles forward.

On Sunday, as arranged, Ann and I met Terry and Emily at a very nice restaurant in the valley. I had asked Ann not to dress up too fancy as I didn't want Emily to feel uncomfortable in case she wasn't knowledgeable about fashion. Ann, therefore, was attired in a dark blue sleeveless dress, no hat or gloves, medium heel black pumps, and a colorful scarf which she had artfully fashioned around her neck. Other than her watch, I don't recall that she wore any jewelry.

"So, what do you think?" she had asked when she picked me up at my place. "Don't think I'll be any kind of a fashion horse in this outfit." She did a model-like stance then slowly turned around so that I could take it all in. "Any comments, criticisms, or..."

"Okay. You've made your point and I think your outfit is just perfect for this occasion, however..."

"However? What? What's wrong?" Ann thrust her chin forward as if to say, *I dare you.*

I raised my hands in self-defense, "Easy, take it easy. I was just going to say something about your face and hair."

She glared. "What's the matter with my face and hair?"

"Your hair looks wonderful but your face is, well, it's just too

158

damn pretty. I'm afraid you're going to intimidate the poor girl and Terry will ruin his tie by drooling all over it."

Ann hit my shoulder with the flat of her hand. "You damn goofball," she bawled through a laugh. She took a step back and gave me the once over. "And what about you? Is that another new sport coat and pants? When Emily gets a load of you, she'll dump Terry and be all over you and then you're going to have a real problem." She grabbed her purse. "Come on, we're going to be late."

As it turned out, Emily was just fine and, as they say, well turned out. She also had a big smile and a mellow voice. She had light brown curly hair, big brown eyes over which she wore rimless glasses. I judged her to be about five-foot-five or -six, with a nice figure that bordered on being just a little overweight. I wasn't sure about her age but thought she could be anywhere from late thirties to early forties. Ann and Emily hit it off at once and chatted throughout the lunch. After the meal, the two girls excused themselves and headed for the ladies' room.

I said to Terry, "Okay, Captain, I'm impressed. Emily is one hell of a nice girl. She's pretty, she's fun, she's just exactly what I'd expect given your excellent and discerning taste in women."

Terry raised his wine glass and we clinked. He said, "And I gotta tell ya, I don't know how you did it and I'll be damned if I know what she sees in you, but that is one amazing lady you brought to lunch. You sure didn't lie when you said she's movie-star beautiful."

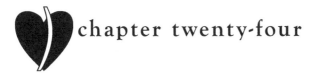 chapter twenty-four

flying corporate can be a lot of fun, and for me, it usually was. Unlike commercial pilots who fly established routes over and over again, we never knew where we'd be going or for how long or at what time of day or night. We were at the beck and call of the Company and that, as promised, did present some problems, especially with my social life.

Ann and I would have something planned like a dinner date or a long motorcycle ride or a day at the beach and I'd get a call from Flight Ops telling me to be ready to take off at whatever time. I'd have to call Ann and cancel whatever it was we had planned. She took it with good grace—most of the time—but there were times when she'd get exasperated with me and ask if this was going to go on forever. I explained that when Al and Gene got certified and picked up their plane, it would take a little of the load off of Terry and me. The problem was that the top honchos in the company didn't want to fly in one of the older prop planes. They wanted to fly in the new jet which was so much faster and way more comfortable. I also suspect, being about half afraid of flying, they wanted to fly with their best pilots and that would be Terry and me. I was sure things would get better as more pilots got certified to fly the Jetstar. Meanwhile, however, my flying schedule was raising hell with my romance schedule.

Having said that, and I sure hope it didn't sound like bellyaching, I was having the time of my aviator life. And, I'd have to admit, the most important part of my day-to-day life. Yes, believe it or not, more important than my spend-time-with-Ann-life. Yeah, I know; it's crazy but that was the reality.

I'll give you some examples of what my life was like back then. We'd been flying the plane pretty steadily throughout most of the summer. On-duty time was limited to sixteen hours a day and the FAA limit of one thousand hours a year works out to around ninety hours a month, assuming a month off for vacation. We'd get a call to leave at 0300 on a Monday. The plan might call for a stop in Mexico City where our passengers would have a meeting that might last all day, meaning we'd overnight there and fly back the following day unless the meeting lasted two or three days, in which case Terry and I would be eating lots of belly-busting chow but unable to wash it down with a cold Corona (rules about drinking twenty-four hours before flying) unless we knew for sure we'd not be flying the next day—but that was something we rarely knew because our guys frequently didn't know either.

How about this one: Ann and I had made plans for a four day bike trip up the California coast. Had it all worked out—where we'd stay, what we'd do, the whole nine yards. Two days before our trip I get a call from Flight Ops.

"Good news," the disembodied voice says. "You're taking the head guy and four of his assistants to—ready for this? Iran! You think you and Halverson will be able to find it?"

That's right, across the ocean, over unfamiliar territory all the way to Iran. Seems that our head honcho needed to speak face to face with Shah Mohammad Reza Pahlavi about developing some more oil fields out there in the desert and, of course, he would be traveling in his newest airplane with his most knowledgeable and trustworthy pilots.

Flying west over the Pacific, it is 7,600 air miles to Tehran, Iran. Commercial flights take about 16 hours. Flying east over the Atlantic is roughly 9,000 miles. Commercial flights from Los Angeles take 19 hours. The problem with flying west is getting clearances to fly over a whole bunch of countries that wouldn't allow some private plane that could actually be a CIA spy plane to invade their air space. On the other hand, flying over parts of France, Italy, Greece and Turkey was something the company had done many times so getting clearances was no problem.

The cabin of our plane was refitted for the flight and the tiny galley was enlarged so that hot food could be prepared. It was hurry up and get there and hurry up and get back. I have to admit that Terry and I enjoyed the trip immensely, mostly because of the navigation challenge and the opportunity to fly over some beautiful country and land at different airports. Another perk was our chance to meet and spend time with the president of the company. But for Ann, all the trip meant was that I was away for a week and making plans to be together was going to be a continuing problem.

It wasn't all bad. With my on-duty time limited, I did have lots of time off. The problem was that sometimes my "off duty" time was invaded by the need for me to fly some exec who insisted on having Terry and me at the wheel.

During one of my off times, Ann had to take a business trip to San Francisco for a few days and I was left with nothing special to do. I decided to get on the old bike and take a ride up the PCH to Cambria and have a visit with Emmett and Edna. That afternoon I had finished checking out the bike and was packing the saddlebags for the trip the following day when the phone rang.

"Hey Rick, it's Ron. How ya doin', buddy?"

"Good. How about you?"

"I heard you flew that bird to Iran. Is that right?"

"You heard right. It was quite the trip."

"You got to tell me all about it. All I've been doing this past month is milk runs," he said. "Anyway, here's why I'm calling. The two Brit stews, Marilyn and Cindy, are here and they called, asking if you and me would be their guests for dinner tonight."

"They want to take us to dinner?"

"That's what they said. Want to go? If so I need to call 'em right back and let 'em know."

I thought about it. *How would Ann react to my going out with someone? But it's just dinner, not a real date or anything like a date. Well, yes, it is a date. But it's just a dinner...*

Ron became impatient, "So, what about it? You want to go or not?"

"Sure, okay," I said.

"Okay. I'll call you back and let you know what time we'll pick you up." He hung up.

I had finished packing my saddlebags when Ron called to say they'd pick me up around six. I took a shower, got dressed up in one of my new suits, then watched TV and drank bourbon until they arrived. I guess I had several drinks worrying about what Ann would think if she found out I was having dinner with another girl. But there was nothing I could about it now. I'd just have to watch my Ps and Qs and make sure everything stayed under control. Switching off the TV, I walked outside to catch a little fresh air when Nancy came rumbling up the drive in her VW bus. She parked in her usual spot and walked up to me.

"Well, well, well," Nancy said with a smirk. "You're all dressed up and looking pretty damn good. Got a date with that redheaded goddess?"

"Maybe or maybe not," I said. "Why? You writing a book?"

"Ha, maybe I am. You two would make good subjects for a sexy novel." Nancy pretended to concentrate. "Hmmm. Let's see. I think the title could be *Flying High*, the story of an aviator and his mysterious girlfriend." She held up her hand, "No, no. This is even better: *Love at Thirty Thousand Feet–Their Love Took Wings*." Nancy was still laughing as she entered the building. At the door she turned and bawled, "Don't do anything I wouldn't do!" She took a few steps toward me and in a stage whisper added, "And that leaves you lots of freedom to do just about anything."

Ron arrived with the two girls. As I approached the car, the back door opened and Cindy piled out, threw her arms around me and planted a kiss on my lips.

"Rick, it's so good to see you again," she gushed. Stepping back she looked me over. I guess she was admiring my new suit. She nodded. "You look very smart indeed, very up-market."

I was a little embarrassed, "And you look as delicious as always." And in fact she did look delicious in a very pretty dress that did nothing to hide her lovely curves.

"Right, then," said Marilyn from the front seat. "Shall we be off? Do get in the car, you lot. The mutual admiration society can continue once we're underway."

We started our dinner with a couple rounds of cocktails and a lot of chit chat. I asked the girls what equipment they were flying and they responded in unison.

"VC-10." Marilyn added, "It's a lovely plane, the Vickers. We also crew on 707s at odd times."

"And you're still flying the Lockheed jet, right?" Cindy asked me.

Ron said, "He recently flew that little plane to Iran. Can you believe it? That's one hell of a trip."

I gave Ron a fierce look. "Hey, it's not exactly a Cessna 172. That baby has four—"

Cindy broke in, "Iran? That's brilliant! Do tell us about it."

I gave them a thumbnail sketch of the adventure. They wanted to know more about the Shah of Iran and what Saudi Arabia was like—we flew there before returning to the States—until that subject was as exhausted as I was talking about it. I asked Ron, "Did US Steel get those G-2s to replace the Viscounts?"

Ron's reply was enthusiastic. "This month sometime. I'm going to Atlanta for simulator training."

"That's great. They tell me the G-2 is an excellent ship. You'll have a lot of fun flying it."

Ron was about to respond but Cindy held up her hand. "That's enough shop talk for one evening. May we please get on with something a bit more entertaining?"

After dinner, which included two bottles of wine and a couple more cocktails, we went to Ron's apartment and after a respectable time, Ron and Marilyn retired to the bedroom.

"They must be tired," Cindy said. "I imagine they'll be wanting a bit of a nap." She paused and gave me a smile. With eyes half closed she added in a husky voice, "Actually, I wouldn't mind a lie down as well." She walked over to the couch, kicked off her shoes and lay down on the couch. "Come along, Rick, do lie here with me. It's jolly comfortable, hmmm?"

I hesitated momentarily but thought, *Oh, what the hell, we're certainly not going to do anything right here in Ron's living room, especially with Ron and Marilyn in the next room.* I took off my shoes, removed my suit jacket and laid it carefully on the back of a chair, loosened my tie and lay down next to Cindy who had turned on her side to make room for me. It was a tight fit.

"Mmm. This is quite nice," Cindy whispered. She raised her head and before I could make a defensive move—I will be honest, not that I really wanted to—she planted a full-on open mouth kiss.

"Come on," she said, "That was rubbish. You can do better than that." She rolled on top of me and kissed me again. This time her tongue came into play and without thinking about it, I returned the favor. Now she was pressing her pelvis into my groin and making little whimpering noises.

I put my hands on her ass and pressed her tightly against my rising erection. Suddenly, she rose up on her knees, reached behind, unzipped the zipper and let her dress fall away. Reaching back again she unhooked her bra and let it, too, fall. I gawked. Her breasts were magnificent. Without a spare thought or a moment's hesitation, I reached up and took them in my hands. She bent down and kissed me, a long, passionate kiss that said, *I'm yours for the taking, so take me.* Cindy began unbuttoning my shirt with an urgency that suddenly moved me to action.

"Hold it. Take it easy. We're not going to have intercourse on the floor."

"Why not? I don't mind and I want you to do it."

I pushed her off and sat up. "I'm sorry, Cindy, but we can't do this. It's not right. Besides, I'm not prepared. I don't have any..."

She became annoyed. "Well, I do. But never mind. The moment's passed." She put on the bra and pulled up the dress from around her waist and zipped it up.

I babbled on. "I have a girlfriend. She's actually more than a girlfriend—we're more or less engaged. I'm sorry, I should have said something but I never thought we'd..."

"You never thought? Exactly. You never thought. I must say, it's bloody embarrassing but—"

"I know and I'm truly sorry. I like you a lot and were it not for...well, I mean I certainly could go for you. Really!"

Cindy whirled around, hands on her hips, a scowl on her face, and cried, "Oh, just bugger off! Do us both a favor and leave."

Just then Ron entered. "What the hell's going on here?"

"It's okay," I said. "Cindy and I just had a little disagreement. It's over and I'm going home. I'll catch a cab." I put on my shoes and jacket and walked out the door.

I walked around for half an hour before finding an empty cab prowling the deserted streets. Sitting in the back of the cab, unmindful of the cabby's inane conversation, I made up my mind that as long as I was with Ann, and that could be forever, there would be no more screwing around with anyone else. Period!

chapter twenty-five

arl Rosenberg was a frequent passenger. I can't remember his title but he was responsible for the overall management of quite a few properties in the States, in Mexico, and in several South American countries. Terry and I frequently had dinner with him while we were on off-base layovers and the conversations were always lively and, at times, very interesting. I learned a lot about the oil business from Carl. This time, in late September, we were on our way home from Chile and I had gone back to see if Carl needed anything.

I was about to return to the cockpit when Carl called me. "Hey, Rick, I wanted to ask you something."

I returned and took a seat next to him. "What can I do for you?"

Carl said, "I'm going to be taking my wife to the Big Apple for a long weekend to celebrate our fifth anniversary. I've cleared it for you and Terry to take me in this plane."

Frankly, I was surprised and said so. "Private trip in a company plane—the jet, no less. I'm impressed."

"Yeah, I know but to tell the truth, it was their idea. I didn't ask for it—hell, I haven't the balls to ask for something like that. No, it was offered, maybe in lieu of a bonus, and I accepted."

"Good for you. And it's a layover in New York for Terry and me?"

"Sure is. Pretty nice, huh?"

"You bet it is."

Carl leaned close and in a conspiratorial tone said, "And here's the best part. I'm inviting you and Captain Halverson to bring your girlfriends along. There's plenty of room and it won't cost the company a penny more to fly a couple of extra passengers, right?"

Carl knew that neither Terry nor I were married and he had heard us talk about Ann and Emily, who Terry was now dating rather consistently.

Carl asked, "So, check with your girlfriends, see if they want to go. We'll leave Friday around noon and return Sunday evening."

The PA came alive. "First Officer Elkins please return to the flight deck. I'd like to relieve myself and I would prefer to use the head."

Carl and I laughed. I said, "I better get up there. And thanks a lot. Ann is going to love it."

I returned to the cockpit, sat down, buckled up and said, "Wait 'til you hear what Carl just told me." I took hold of the yoke, feet on the pedals, did a quick scan of the instruments and said, "Okay, I've got control of the aircraft."

When I told Ann about Carl's offer of a trip to New York, she let out a scream.

"Are you kidding? You better not be kidding or I'll kick your ass."

"No, it's for real. You and Emily will be flying in our private jet with one of the company big shots and his wife."

"What's his name and his wife's name?"

"His name is Carl. I have no idea what his wife's name is."

The plane was ready to go at noon on Friday. Emily and Ann had been in the cabin for about an hour while Terry and I did our preflight routine, and now I was in the cabin chatting with the girls. Terry was standing at the bottom of the aircraft steps when Carl's limo pulled up. I looked out the window. Carl got out and held out a hand for his wife. She stepped out of the car and I'm guessing that Terry had the same reaction I did. Carl's wife was a knock-out, beautiful blonde who I guessed was at least ten to fifteen years younger than Carl.

Terry said something, shook the wife's hand and motioned for them to enter the plane. The limo driver handed Terry two suitcases which he stowed in the luggage locker. I was standing in the isle. Emily and Ann were seated behind me as Carl's wife entered the cabin. Close behind, Carl said, "Rick, I'd like you to meet my wife Charlotte." To his wife he said, "Honey, this is our first officer, Richard Elkins."

I took her hand, released it, turned and took hold of Ann's outstretched hand. Ann stood and looked at Carl and Charlotte. Her eyes widened, her mouth went slack and all color drained from her face.

Speaking in one voice, Carl and Charlotte yelled, "GUNNER!"

Charlotte pushed past me to hug and kiss Ann. "My God, you're about the last person I expected to see on this plane. This is great! We are going to have such a super time this weekend."

Now Carl eased past his wife to hug Ann. "I agree. What an unexpected pleasure to see you again. Geeze, how long has it been? I heard you and Royce got divorced but I never thought I'd see you, particularly as the girlfriend of one of our pilots." Carl gave Ann another huge hug. "This is terrific."

Taking note of Emily he said, "Oh, I'm so sorry," realizing

she had been overlooked in all the excitement. "I'm Carl and this is my wife, Charlotte." Addressing Terry, who had come on board, Carl said, "Gunner, I mean Annette, we used to call her Gunner, and her former husband owned a beautiful home near Atascadero. Charlotte and I spent many wonderful weekends there as their houseguests."

Charlotte nodded in agreement. "Those were some fabulous parties," she sighed.

Ann didn't say a word initially but soon found her tongue and took up the conversation with Charlotte.

Carl turned to Terry. "Sorry about the holdup, Captain. We'll take our seats and you can take us all for a ride." He sat down next to Emily.

I said, "If you will all buckle your seat belts for takeoff, I'll explain the safety features of this aircraft and we can get going." I went through the required talk, secured the door and took my seat up front.

Terry didn't say a word but gave me the oddest look as if to say *What the fuck was that all about?* I forced myself to put all thoughts of what had just happened out of my head and concentrate on getting the plane in the air. Terry had control and I did my thing. When we hit our assigned altitude, Terry went to auto-pilot, loosened his tie and furiously scratched his head.

"I guess you'd better tell me what's going on, otherwise this trip could turn into something other than the fun weekend as advertised. And don't tell me there's nothing going on because when Ann saw Carl and his wife, she turned pale. I mean, she looked like she'd seen a ghost."

I thought about it and replied. "To tell you the truth, I believe she did see a ghost. The Ghost of New Year's Past."

Terry left the cockpit shaking his head. "I'd better see how it's going back there. You got it?"

"I have control." I had control of the plane but little control of anything else. My brain was on fire. *Carl and Charlotte had to be swingers who had partied with Royce and Ann–Gunner. She was a "gunner" alright. Thinking about the movie I watched, I began to believe that the girl who had her arms around Ann in that first scene was Charlotte. Who was the guy? The guy she...hell, it certainly could have been Carl. Jesus, is all this going to be dragged up again? I suppose they'll want Ann and me to party with them. That'd be something, wouldn't it? Me fucking the boss' wife while he did the same to my girlfriend! That's not going to happen, that'd be crazy. Carl's not stupid, he'd never make a play for...Or would he?*

Terry returned. "They all seem to be happy as a bunch of clams." He sat in the left seat, buckled his harness and scanned the instruments. "Still on auto?"

"Yes. So everyone is happy in back?"

"I guess so. Emily is a little out of it but the rest of 'em seem like they're trying to keep her in the conversation." Terry laid his head back. "I'm going to take a nap. Wake me if you forget how to fly this thing."

The trip from LAX to Teterboro Airport (12 miles from midtown Manhattan) is about 2,500 miles. Since our plane had a range of 3,000 miles, we were not required to take on more fuel en-route. Cruising at 500 mph, the trip, with the help of a 12 mph tail wind, took a little over five hours gate to gate.

We taxied to our assigned parking and shut her down. Before disembarking, Charlotte asked Ann to call her later to make plans for the next day. Carl and his wife took a limo to the prestigious Pierre Hotel on Fifth Avenue. The company had reserved a double room for Terry and me at the Taft Hotel on West 51st Street. We took care of getting the plane secured and refueled, then took a cab to the Taft. After acquiring another room on the same floor, the four of us went to our rooms, having agreed to meet for dinner at eight.

"God," Ann groaned throwing herself on the bed. "I thought that trip would never end." She raised herself up on her elbows, "Rick, I'm so sorry about what happened. I know you hated it but who would have ever thought I'd be on your plane with people I knew from the past? It's too bizarre—too unbelievable. And of all the people I ever partied with...those two!"

I sat on the edge of the bed. "What about those two?"

"They were always after me, both of them but especially Charlotte. She's not a lesbian, she's 'bi' but I know that she would rather play with women than with men." Ann sat up and grabbed my arm. "Listen, you've got to tell Carl that you don't think it would be a good idea for the six of us to go out together. It's their anniversary and just the two of them should go out and celebrate. Tell him not to worry about us, we'll be fine and we'll see them Sunday at the airport." Ann laid her head on the pillow and covered her eyes with her arm. "How the hell did this happen?" she wailed. She sat up again and said, "What if Carl or Charlotte were insulted? Do you think that would affect your job?"

I shook my head. "Hell, I wouldn't think so, but what about this: Suppose Carl takes me aside and says that Charlotte would love to have just the four of us get together for some fun and games—like they did in the good old days at your house. Should I say, 'Sure boss, whatever you want'?"

"God damn it, Rick, quit screwing around. This is serious."

"Really?"

"You may be jacking around but let me tell you something. That little scenario you just suggested, don't think for a minute that couldn't actually happen. I know those people and they are not the least bit bashful when it comes to this stuff. And I'll tell you another thing—I know Charlotte well enough to know she'd love to get her hands on you. Her mouth, too." Ann observed my wide-eyed expression. "Oh, don't look so shocked."

"Did I look shocked? Maybe. But look, you're blowing this up into a crisis. Do you really think that one of the major executives of Esso is going to expose himself to anything like what you're talking about? I know this guy and the way he thinks and I'm telling you, regardless of what his wife may want to do, he'll never go for it. He's not stupid or crazy, so quit worrying."

Ann shook her head, bit her lower lip, and dropped her head back down on the pillow.

I got up and paced the floor beside the bed for a moment. Then I turned and leaned in close to her. "Aside from all of that, what is really important in this whole lash up—what I really *hate* about this situation is, it dredges up all of the old memories I have of you at those parties—all those images that I've tried so hard to put out of my head."

Ann sat up and looked at me. With tears welling up and spilling onto her cheeks, she murmured, "Oh God..."

I went on, "And now here they are, back again." An image of Angie popped into my consciousness. *What is she saying? Ah, I hear it now. "Do you want to be with a whore?"*

The phone rang. I hesitated but then picked up. It was Terry saying he was tired and asking if we could just have dinner here at the hotel. I relayed the message to Ann who shook her head no.

"Ann's got a bad headache and I'm still in my uniform so we'll just order from room service. Let's meet for breakfast at nine in the coffee shop—how's that?"

"Sounds good to me. We'll see you then. Good night."

Ann got off the bed and headed for the bathroom.

"I'm calling room service. What would you like for dinner?"

Ann said, "I'm not hungry. Get yourself something, though."

"Come on, honey, you need to eat." I took her arm and pulled her to me. She laid her head on my chest and cried and cried. I just held her, saying nothing.

Ann kept murmuring, "I'm sorry, I'm sorry," over and over.

I took her head in my hands and kissed each tear-drenched eye. "There isn't anything that you need to be sorry for. What happened today was an..." I tried to think of the right word. "An anomaly, a fluke, an event no one could predict. If you think about it, why should this even matter? You saw two people you used to know who know things about you, things that perhaps embarrass you now. But it isn't as if these were deep-dark hidden secrets that I know nothing about. The fact is that I do know all about the partying and what you did at those parties. Sure, I hated it at first but I'm over it and we've got on with our lives. Now, suddenly and without warning, I've come face to face with real live people, people with whom you partied. But you had no control over it. Like I said, it was a fluke."

"I know, I know," Ann sobbed. "But it did happen and it opened a wound and now you'll have to start the healing process all over again." She looked into my eyes. "You didn't need to be reminded about what a stupid sex addict...whore I was. Yes, whore! Your Angie was right."

"Shush, you're not a whore. Angie is wrong. She doesn't know the real you. She just knows Gunner in the movie. Movies aren't for real, you know that."

A faint smile passed her lips and gave way to a pout. "It was real, very real and you know it."

"Okay, I'll admit facing it again is disconcerting in a way...but I'll get over it. I'm over it right now. Everyone has done something in their lives that they're not very proud of. I know I have." I held her at arm's length and gazed into her moist green eyes.

Ann returned the gaze, unblinking. "I love you and would never do anything to hurt you. You know that, right?"

I kissed her mouth and held her tightly for a long time. "Right? And I love you no matter what. You understand? No matter what."

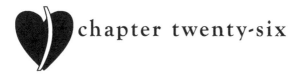

chapter twenty-six

mily had never been to New York or for that matter anywhere east of Arizona, so at breakfast, she chattered happily about seeing the sights of Manhattan. So we decided that Ann— qualified to act as tour guide by virtue of many trips to New York—set the itinerary for sightseeing. For Ann's part, she was willing to do anything that would keep her away from Charlotte. When we returned to our room, I saw the message light blinking so I called the operator who informed me that a Mrs. Rosenberg had called and asked that Ann call her as soon as possible. I relayed the message to Ann.

"I was afraid of that," Ann said. "What am I going to tell her?"

"Tell her the truth. Tell her you've made plans to take us all sightseeing today. Remind her that none of us has ever been here before and we want to see the places that everyone talks about."

Ann called Charlotte and explained the situation. Charlotte didn't comment one way or another but she did say that Carl wanted us to join them this evening for the big anniversary dinner at the Tavern on the Green in Central Park.

I heard Ann say, "By us, you do mean the four of us, right?" Long pause. "I'm sorry, no, we can't do that." Pause. "No, that wouldn't be right. Listen, Charlotte, it's your special night. You and Carl don't need any company on your anniversary. Have a fantastic dinner, which I'm sure it will be at the Tavern, and we'll see you at the plane tomorrow." Ann listened patiently for the next few minutes. "Charlotte, the boys can't afford to... They certainly wouldn't expect Carl to buy the four of us a terribly expensive dinner." Long pause. "I know that. Exactly. Look, you and I can get together in LA for lunch sometime and have..." Pause. "Okay then. You and Carl have a wonderful evening together and we'll see you at the plane." Ann covered the mouthpiece with her hand and asked me what time we leave. I told her two o'clock. "It's two o'clock. Have a wonderful time tonight. See you tomorrow. Bye." Ann laid the phone down and sighed. "Geeze, I hope Carl is good with this."

"Hell, he'll be fine with it. Besides, he's going to save the price of four dinners," I said.

Ann added, "And at the Tavern on the Green, that could easily amount to four hundred dollars or more."

We spent a delightful day checking out the sights, the sounds and the tastes of Manhattan. After returning to the Taft and cleaning up, we went to Danny's Hideaway for dinner. It was spectacular and expensive as hell but as Terry observed, "Hey, every once in a while you got to live it up." Because we were flying the next day, Terry and I didn't do any drinking, which probably saved us a bunch but the girls made up for it.

We checked out of the hotel and took a cab to the airport around noon. We ate lunch, I picked up some sandwiches and soft drinks to serve on the trip and returned to the plane, did our pre-flight check, filed a flight plan and waited for Carl and Charlotte to show up. Around two thirty I began to worry. Terry told me to go inside and telephone the hotel to see if they'd checked out. The desk clerk said that they'd checked out a little after two. I was walking back to the plane when a Checker Cab rolled up and Carl and Charlotte got out. The cabby pulled their luggage from the trunk and set the bags down next to the plane. Carl paid the driver, who tipped his cap and left.

"Did you have fun last night?" I asked.

Carl gave me a woeful look. "Yeah, maybe too much fun. You guys ready to roll?"

"Yes, sir. Soon as you two get aboard."

They climbed the steps, acknowledged Ann and Emily with a nod, sat down and buckled up. I stowed the luggage, secured the door, entered the cockpit, got in my seat and buckled the harness. "Okay. We're good to go."

About two hours into the trip I went back to the cabin to offer refreshments but everyone was asleep. I took a good look at Charlotte and believe me, she didn't look anything at all like the young sprite who had boarded the plane on Friday. As a friend of mine used to say, "She looked like she was rode hard and put away wet." I returned to the cockpit.

Terry asked, "How're they doing back there?"

"All asleep. Charlotte looks rough. They must have had some night."

"We had a good time. As far as I'm concerned, this trip was one of the better ones." After a long silence passed, Terry said, "I've got something to tell you."

"Okay."

"I'm going to stop flying, probably by the end of the month."

That caught me by surprise and I said so. "I know sixty is the retirement age but as long as you can pass the medical, I think they'll let you fly 'til you're sixty-five."

"That's just it," Terry said with a hint of remorse. "I won't pass the medical—at least that's what my doctor tells me."

"Why not? What's wrong?"

Terry didn't answer right away. He glanced out the windscreen, scanned the instruments, then fiddled with the radio until finally he looked at me and I don't think I'll ever forget that look. "He told me I've got pancreatic cancer." I thought he was going to cry as he said it.

At first, I was speechless, then I rushed in with denials. "Wait a minute. Has that diagnosis been confirmed? Did they do a biopsy and all the other stuff?"

"Yeah, I'm afraid so." Terry unbuckled and slipped out of his seat. "I'm going to the head. Be right back. You have control."

I guess I was in shock or something like it. Pancreatic cancer? Man, that was the worst—you don't survive pancreatic cancer! I stared out the windscreen into the darkness, watching the light from our beacon bouncing off the glass. I was simply unable to process the magnitude of this unexpected news.

Terry returned, slipped into his seat, buckled up and put on his phones. "I'd appreciate it if we don't talk about it right now and don't say anything to Emily or Ann. Let me deal with this my way, at least for now."

"Okay. Whatever you say, but just remember, you want to talk or if you need anything, I'm your guy."

Terry looked at me, nodded and smiled.

After landing the plane at LAX, we taxied to our parking spot and shut her down. Carl and Charlotte thanked us and we in turn thanked them profusely for allowing the girls to come along. Charlotte took Ann aside and had a brief conversation with her. A limo showed up and Carl and Charlotte were gone. Emily and Ann went into the pilots' lounge while Terry and I secured the plane, ordered fuel and took care of the required paper work. We walked to the parking lot, said our goodbyes, got in our vehicles and left.

Ann said, "You're being very quiet. Something wrong?"

"No...well yes, but I can't talk about it now. It has nothing to do with you and me. All I can tell you is that Terry has decided to retire and ahh...it's sad because I know he loves his job so much and he's—"

"Does that mean you'll make captain?"

"Probably. But that's not the point. I love flying with that guy. Honest to God, he's the best. What he doesn't know about driving an airplane isn't worth knowing." I needed to get off of that subject. "What was it Charlotte said to you before she left?"

Ann chuckled. "You don't want to know but I'll bet you can guess."

"She wants us to get together for a swap party...right?"

"You got it!"

"And what did you say?" I asked.

She smiled, mischief in her green eyes. "I said, 'That's entirely up to Rick.'"

Terry, a half dozen pilots, a gal and three guys, execs from the Flight Department, and I were gathered in Charlie Borden's office in early November. Charlie made my promotion to captain official, complete with a certificate and a short speech. Everyone shook my hand and offered congratulations. I thanked all those present for being supportive, of overlooking my lack of seniority which had allowed me to fly right seat with the best damn airplane driver in the business. Terry actually blushed when I heaped the accolades on him but truthfully, he deserved every word.

On that day Terry looked pretty grim—he had lost a lot of weight and his skin was the color of clay. Before the end of February, he was dead. I'd have to say that aside from Angie's death, Terry's was the most gut-wrenching experience of my life and I had a hard time getting over it. He was my mentor and my friend. One of a kind. And I knew I'd never again fly with anyone who could match his skill.

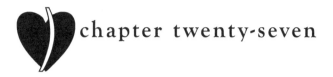

chapter twenty-seven

I exceeded my on-duty hours and had to take at least a couple of weeks off. I asked Ann if she would like to go with me on a motorcycle ride up the Pacific Coast Highway. We'd just take our time, stop at interesting places, no hurry, just take in the sights, the sounds, the people and most of all, enjoy being with each other every day and night.

"So, it would almost be like being married?" Ann suggested. "And, if we're still talking to each other by the end of the trip, would that be like an omen that we possibly could stand the strain of marriage?"

"Ah, gee. I hadn't thought of it quite like that. It's not going to be a test, you know. It's a bike ride, for gosh sake."

Ann gave me a peck on the cheek. "Okay, okay. Relax. Don't get all nervous and jerky about it. I'll see if I can take the time off. Actually, it shouldn't be a problem; I'm long overdue for a vacation."

Ann called to tell me the trip was a go and asked me to come over to her place to check out her bike and help her pack. You can't carry a whole lot of stuff on a motorcycle so it's important to pack only what you need and what you can secure on the bike. I drove over, changed the oil and worked on her bike until I was satisfied it was ready to go. Then I went inside. She had all the things she wanted to take laid on her bed…way too much stuff.

"You're not going to need a sleeping bag," I said. "Sleeping on the beach sounds romantic and all that but on this trip, we'll skip the sand fleas and bird crap and enjoy the luxury of hot showers and a bed in a motel." I noticed a snub-nosed .38 revolver. I picked it up and popped open the cylinder—it was loaded. "Planning on killing some folks along the way?" I let a few bullets fall into my hand. "Hollow points. You don't fool around, do you? I'm impressed."

Ann gave me a righteous look. "No, I don't. The guy I took shooting lessons from said I should never point a gun at someone unless I was prepared to kill him."

"Whoa!" I exclaimed. Then I thought about it. "Actually, that's really good advice. You don't want him to end up taking the gun away and using it on you."

Ann responded, "That's right. My instructor said, and these are his exact words—no kidding—'Aim your first three or four shots at his chest. That'll knock him down. Get close and put your last bullet in his head. You want to be sure he's dead because that last thing you want is for him to show up in a courtroom.'"

I put the bullets back in the gun, snapped the cylinder closed and laid the gun down. "Okay, Annie Oakley, I do believe your man gave you some damn good advice."

"So I take the gun along?"

"Absolutely."

I put all of Ann's things in my truck and she rode to my place on her bike. Nancy was on her porch overlooking the driveway when Ann and I drove in. I was hanging the saddlebags and lashing the rest of Ann's kit on her bike when Nancy walked into the carport.

"What are you 'Easy Riders' up to?" she asked.

Ann said, "We're going to take a long ride north tomorrow. Just getting everything ready so we can get an early start."

I added, "We'll probably be gone for a couple of weeks, so would you keep an eye on my place?"

"Sure, no problem." Nancy looked as though she had something more to say. She looked first at Ann, then at me, and then back to Ann again.

"Something on your mind?" I asked.

Nancy put her hand to her mouth and fiddled with her lips. "Naw, well, I just wanted to ask you something but it can wait 'til you come back, I guess." With that, she turned and walked back into the building. Over her shoulder she yelled, "Have a good time but be careful. Motorcycles can be dangerous."

Ann and I looked at each other.

"What the hell was that all about?" Ann asked.

I raised both hands, palms up. "Damned if I know."

After getting all set for an early departure, we went to a local restaurant for dinner. Upon our return I asked, "Want a nightcap? I'm going to have some port."

"Go ahead. I'm going to bed. We've got a big day tomorrow and if we're really going to leave around five, we'd better get some sleep."

"I'll be joining you in a minute," I said. I sipped the port as I walked into my little office and pulled open the bottom desk drawer. Resting where it had been since I put it there was my Colt .45 pistol in its shoulder holster. I decided I had better take it along just in case Ann needed some back-up.

I awoke the next morning to the sound of water running. It was dark as pitch outside. I walked in the bathroom, took off my tee shirt, pulled back the shower curtain and stepped in. Ann was bent over washing the shampoo from her hair. I stepped behind her and pressed against her adorable butt. She jumped, let out a little yelp and whirled around.

"You goofball. You scared the crap out of me." A slow smile crossed her face. "But, as long as you're here..." She pressed against me, shoving me hard into the wall, "We may as well do something and soon before the hot water runs out."

Presently, the water turned cold and we jumped out of the shower. I wrapped her in a beach towel and rubbed her dry. She did the same for me.

"Too bad," she whimpered, "the hot water ran out just as I was about—"

"Oh, that is too bad. How very frustrating," I said, my voice dripping with compassion. "Something must be done at once, before you develop the hives or something equally annoying." I picked her up, letting the towel drop to the floor and carried her to the bed where I laid her on her back. I lay between her legs. "Let's see, what would be the appropriate action to remedy your distress?"

"You definitely are a goofball, but an excellent lover," she squealed as she took my head between her hands and pulled me into her. "Emmm. There, right there. Yes, that's it."

In spite of the unscheduled delay, we still were able to be on our way by daybreak. Traffic was light and we were on the PCH heading north in good time. An hour later, we stopped at Oxnard for breakfast.

I looked at my riding companion sitting across the table, sipping coffee from a heavy china mug. She looked radiant. "Riding certainly agrees with you. You'd make a terrific cover model for a motorcycle magazine. Really! There's a glow about you...you're absolutely beautiful."

Ann set her mug down, lowered her sun glasses and peering

over the top of the frame, those green, green eyes sparkling, said, "You are too sweet, but perhaps just a little overcome by exhaust fumes. This glow to which you refer," she patted her cheek, "is the result of two things: one, your ability to satisfy me as no other man can, and two, having the cold wind hit my face at seventy miles an hour." She pushed her glasses back up and gave me a bright smile. "Regardless of all other considerations, I'll just say thank you for the compliment." She raised her coffee mug in a salute, drank the last of it and stood. "C'mon. Let's hit the bathroom and get on up the highway."

We stopped at Pismo Beach for gas and a look around. Like most of the little beachfront towns along the coast, Pismo was, as Ann put it, "charming."

"When I retire," I said, "we should buy a place somewhere along the coast in one of these little towns."

"Oh," Ann replied, "I see. You're assuming that we'll still be together and presumably married when you retire."

"Of course. How could we not be together? You are the love of my life and now that I've made captain, I believe I'm in a position to be able to keep you in the lifestyle to which you've become accustomed."

Ann grabbed my arms with both hands and brought her face close to mine. "Wait a minute. Was that some kind of a lopsided marriage proposal?"

I stuttered a reply. "I, ah, well, yes, I guess you...What do you mean, lopsided? It's not lopsided at all." Suddenly and without having given it much thought, at least not at that particular moment, I dropped on one knee in front of her. Taking both of her hands in mine I looked up at her astonished face and said, "My sweet, darling, adorable Annette, will you marry me?"

"Oh my God," she blurted out. "You just proposed...Is that what that was?"

"Hell yes. That's exactly what it was. Are you going to give me an answer?" I stood and wrapped her in my arms, lifting her off of her feet. "Well?"

"In a word, yes! And thank you for asking. I've been waiting for a long time for you to pop the question, but I can't believe you just did it...I mean here in Pismo of all places, and now? You are too much—a genuine goofball but I love you and oh darling..." Suddenly Ann began to cry. "I love you and I'll be a good wife."

I kissed her forehead. "You'll be a great wife."

Before leaving Pismo Beach, we agreed that we would stop in Cambria and have a visit with Edna and Emmett Walker. Ann was eager to meet them. It was early afternoon when we turned off the highway and took the road to Emmett's place. The sound of our engines brought Edna out of the house onto her front porch. We pulled up, cut the engines and as we were getting off the bikes, I saw Emmett slowly walking out of the shop. *Is he limping? What the hell is going on? His left arm is in a sling and his face looks like he walked into a brick wall.* I got off my bike and hurried over to him.

"Emmett, what the hell happened here?" I called out, then I looked toward the house and saw Edna hurrying toward us, while Ann caught up with us all. I trotted up to Emmett. "What's going on? Were you in an accident?"

"You might say that," he croaked, his voice all gravely and unfamiliar. "Had a little altercation with a couple o' guys and come out second best..." He chuckled. "Truth is, they beat the crap out o' me. I reckon you can see that."

"Hell yes, I can see that. Looks like you got busted up pretty good."

Edna, a little out of breath, exclaimed, "Look what they done to my poor husband, will ya? God damned animals jest pulled into the yard and raised six shades o' hell."

Emmett added, "That's about the size of it. I jes' thought they was looking ta get their old pickup repaired—it was a beat up ole Dodge—so I come out o' the shop an assed 'em could I hep 'em. They wanted ta know if'n I wuz the onliest one here an' I said yes, that it was my place, when they upped and pulled a gun on me. I done tole 'em, hell boys, I ain't got nothin' worth stealin' ifn that's what yer up ta. The one guy, the one with the bald head and the beard give me a push, knocked me flat on my ass. Well, as ya kin imagine, I didn't much go fer that. But, I waited in the dirt ta see what they wuz gonna do. They walked inta the shop and wuz lookin' aroun', ya know. I crawled aroun' the side fixin' ta get my 12 gauge from the house but one them buzzards spotted me an' grabbed a shovel and hit me 'cross the back." Emmett blew a stream of air through his lips, "knocked me down on my face. Nex' thing I knew he was working me over with that damn shovel."

Ann gasped. "Oh my God."

Edna looked at her, the question obvious.

I took Ann's arm. "I know this is a hell of time, but this is my girlfriend...actually my fiancée, Annette." I addressed Edna. "Were you in the house when all this was going on?"

"No, I had gone ta the grocery. I wish ta hell I'd a bin here. I'd a blown a hole in those two bastards big enough to drive a truck thru. They must a jest left when I come back 'cause I seen Emmett laying out in front of the shop. I darn near had a heart attack whenever I seen him. He wuz beat up somethin' awful. I checked him an' run in the house and called the fire station ta send an ambulance."

Ann stood very close to me just shaking her head in sympathy. Then she walked up to Emmett and gently put her arms about him. "I'm so sorry we had to meet like this," she said gently. "But if there's anything we can do, or anything you need, just ask. And don't be bashful."

I added, "That's right. We've got no place we need to be so whatever you need, we'll do it."

Edna said, "Let's go in the house. Emmett needs ta sit down fer a while."

We walked inside and took seats in the parlor.

I asked, "So, when did this happen?"

"Day before yestaday," Edna answered. She stood. "I'm gonna make a pot o' coffee less y'all rather have a beer or somethin' cold." She walked over to Emmett and leaned over. "Ya want somethin', honey?"

"Beer sounds mighty good."

"I'll git it fer ya. Jes' take it easy now. Y'all want a cold beer too?" she asked Ann and me. We did.

I turned to Emmett, "So what was it they wanted? I mean, did they steal anything or break up stuff?"

Emmett shook his head slowly. "Yeah. They loaded my good air compressor. Hell, it wuz only a year ole. An' they took a lot o' my hand tools, a floor jack, some tires an' my ole Indian bike. God damned bastards would a loaded up my Indian Scout too, but they wasn't any room fer it." Emmett let out a deep sigh. "I tell ya what. If I ever lay eyes on them two agin, I god-damn guarantee ya they'll be sorry they ever set their eyes on me."

Ann and I drank our beer and chatted some more with them. Ann asked, "I'll bet you've got some chores Rick and I could do for you. Just tell us what you need and we're on it. Or do you need anything from the store? We'll go get it. How about that?"

"We're fine, honey," Edna replied. She thought a moment. "But we sure would like fer ya ta have dinner with us. Can ya stay?"

"Of course we can," I said, "but we'll fix the dinner and you two can just take it easy. If you'll just loan us your pickup, we'll run into town and get some stuff. After dinner, we'll go to town, spend the night at a motel and come back tomorrow morning and give you a hand with whatever you need." I glanced at Ann for affirmation and she was quick to give it with a nod. And that's what we did.

The next morning, Edna prepared breakfast, complete with her delicious baking powder biscuits. Over a second cup of coffee, I asked Emmett for more information about the two guys. He told me they were driving an older black Dodge half-ton pickup. He wasn't sure, but he thought the license plates were not from California. One guy had a shaved head or was bald. He had a heavy black beard, was about 5'-10" tall, thin, wearing beat-up tan work boots, blue jeans and a faded denim shirt with snaps, not buttons. The other guy was shorter, heavier, maybe Mexican, wearing blue jeans, plaid shirt, and a baseball cap with something written on the front. He was wearing dirty white tennis shoes and his belt buckle was a large silver cowboy type with some animal on it...maybe a horse or a cow.

I said, "Damn, Emmett, those are great descriptions. Did you give the sheriff the same information?"

"The sheriff?" he asked with a look of surprise. "No, I never talked to any police 'bout it."

"You didn't? Why not?"

"Never thought of it." He made a wry face. "Damn, I shoulda talked to 'em while I was in the hospital." He brightened a little, "I'll call the sheriff right away and give 'em the low-down."

Ann remarked, "You'd think the hospital would have called the authorities when they brought Emmett in with all those wounds. It seems like they'd have sent a deputy out to question him."

"That's what I was thinking too, but we're out in the sticks. I guess they do things differently than they do in LA." As an afterthought, I added, "Too bad, though. If they would have had the intel, they might have been able to catch those guys. Now, there probably isn't a chance of ever finding them."

Emmett called the sheriff's office and told them about the robbery and the attack. Within an hour, a uniformed deputy and a plain clothes detective arrived to take Emmett's formal statement. They looked around the place and talked to Emmett and Edna for quite a while. They wanted to know who we were and what we were doing there. We answered their questions and they took down our names and addresses. They also included in their report the make, model, and license plate number of each of our motorcycles. Before leaving, the detective said that the information would be in the hands of various law enforcement agencies up and down the coast as well as some of the inland communities.

There wasn't much else we could do at that point. Besides, Emmett and Edna insisted that we get on with our vacation... that they were fine and perhaps we could stop by again on our way back to LA. We promised to do that, and Ann told them we would be on the lookout for the black pickup and the two thugs.

Emmett groused, "Not much chance you'll see 'em. Hell, they're prob'ly half way to Timbuktu by now."

We said our good-byes. Ann gave them both a hug and I hugged Edna. When I gave Emmett a pseudo-hug, damned if he didn't give me a big hug back as he said, "Sure do appreciate the hep. Y'all be careful now."

It was close to noon by the time we were back on the highway and an hour later we arrived at Big Sur where we gassed up and ate lunch. The conversation centered on the events of the past few days. Ann said we should be on the lookout for the Dodge pickup as we traveled north. I laughed at the suggestion. I agreed with Emmett—those guys were long gone and probably in Mexico, where they could peddle the stuff without having to answer a lot of questions about ownership.

Ann made a wry face. "You're probably right." Then she brightened. "Are we going to spend some time in Monterey?" In a little voice she added, "I'd love to stay there for a while."

We were only 30 miles or so away. "You bet we are. It's a special place for you and me, remember?"

Ann smiled and nodded. "Do I remember? I'll never forget that day. You broke my heart and yet, within an hour, somehow you managed to mend it. Or perhaps you gave me hope that in time it would mend." She gazed softly into my eyes. "That little cove you discovered is a magical place." Her eyes were glowing like liquid emeralds. "We must go there again."

I got caught up in the moment and wrapped her in my arms. I couldn't believe how much I loved her. The overpowering feelings I had for this girl amazed me. "We will go back to that cove and finish what we left undone the last time."

"Yes," Ann whispered. "Yes, we surely will."

Lightening the tone, I told her, "I called Bea, the landlady at the place where you and I had that," I made a quotation sign with my fingers, "'life-altering talk.' She's holding her nicest room on the second floor for us. I told her we'd be there for at least a week."

"See?" Ann cried. "I knew it—I knew you'd have something up your sleeve to bowl me over with, just like you have so many times before. That's why I love you...that's why I'll always love you!" Ann pulled on her helmet and hopped on her Honda, shouting, "Let's get this show on the road."

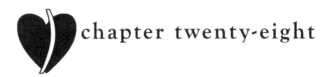

chapter twenty-eight

ea must have heard the bikes coming up the road—she was standing on the porch when we pulled into her yard. We off-loaded the bikes and lugged our stuff up the front steps.

"Glad to see ya made it okay," Bea said. "I'm also glad that this time it's gonna be a happy occasion, right?"

Ann dropped her kit and gave Bea a hug. "Much happier. Actually, Rick and I are engaged so I guess you could call this our pre-honeymoon."

Bea smiled broadly. "Oh, that's great. I'm sure pleased you're gonna spend it with me."

I gave Bea a peck on her cheek. "And, if it works out, I'll give this incredible redhead a great big diamond." I looked around. "Still looks the same and that's good. And how've you been?"

"Still chugging along," Bea said with a toss of her hand. "Business is a little slow but now that you two are here, I'll be back in the chips in no time." She turned to Ann. "Here, let me help you with your stuff." She opened the screen door, held it open with her foot, picked up the two saddlebags and went inside. "Come along, your rooms are upstairs. I decided to give you the mini-suite. It's got a little sitting room and a king size bedroom. I think you'll like it."

At the top of the stairs, we turned left down a short hallway that led to a white paneled door. Bea set the bags down and retrieved a key from her apron pocket. She opened the door and motioned for us to step inside. Ann dropped her bag on the floor and let out a little squeal of delight.

"This is charming," she said. "It's like a fairytale place."

And it was indeed. The woodwork was painted bright white enamel. The walls were covered with an old-fashioned flowered wall paper. Sheer white curtains covered the two windows and on top was a valance of dark blue velvet. The lamps, the furniture, in fact, everything made you think of an early American farm house. Even the fixtures in the bathroom complimented the setting and enhanced the feeling of Ann's "fairytale place." I was fascinated by the many pictures in what appeared to be antique frames. Many were prints of Norman Rockwell's *Saturday Evening Post* covers. I smiled as I remembered each one from my childhood. Hanging in little groups were old magazine ads of 1920-1930 era automobiles. I remembered these as well—the Hupmobile, Hudson Terriplane, Pierce Arrow, Stutz, Chrysler Air-Flow, and more.

Ann brought me back to earth with a call from the adjoining room, "Rick, come and see the sitting room."

Reluctantly, I left my nostalgic browsing and walked into the other room. It, too, was like a movie set from an early thirties Western. I know you must think I'm nuts—a man talking about this stuff. But I have to say it was just about as perfect a venue for a honeymoon, or in our case, a pre-honeymoon, as one could wish for. As for Ann, she was just bubbling, and Bea was obviously glowing with pride. No doubt, she had put a lot of thought and effort into creating this unique, two-room Paradise and now, Ann and I were the beneficiaries of her labors.

During the following five days, Ann and I wandered and explored the incredibly beautiful Monterey Peninsula and surrounding area. We ate seafood until we thought we'd grow gills, we drove our bikes up and down the coast visiting nearby towns and hamlets, eating in quaint seaside cafes, diners and restaurants. We gawked at people and places—the Royal Presidio Chapel dating back to the 1790s, the Custom House built by the Spanish around 1800. Our day trips took us to Carmel-by-the-Sea and Pebble Beach. We drove around Pacific Grove to Asilomar beach and enjoyed seeing the many old Victorian homes, some recently refurbished. We explored Carmel Valley and visited tiny Arroyo Seco. We stopped at a wharf and bought fish just caught by a grizzled old man who claimed he use to ride a motorcycle. He said he'd trade the fish if I'd let him ride my bike for, "jes' a couple of minutes." I opted to just pay for the fish.

We stayed busy every day and decided that a person could spend a lifetime in that part of California and never begin to see it all. Again I told Ann that this was where we should end up after we retired. Ann agreed it would be "something to consider" which I interpreted as *maybe, we'll see.*

The sixth day of our Monterey stay was a Saturday. I said to Ann, "Let's take a ride up to Salinas after breakfast. I read something in the newspaper I want to check out."

Ann set her coffee mug down. "Salinas? What's in Salinas you want to see?"

"There's a guy there by the name of Handleman who I read has a very interesting shop with lots of unusual merchandise. I think it would be fun to take a look. Besides, we haven't been to Salinas, and I'd like to see it—wouldn't you?"

"Sure. We could see your guy, have lunch there and maybe run over to see that mission at San Juan Bautista."

I set my napkin aside and stood up. "Sounds like a plan. Let's go."

An hour later we parked our bikes at a shopping center and set off a-foot. I had read a newspaper ad touting that Handleman's Fine Jewelry was having a big diamond sale with "deep discounts on every diamond." I had to go see what that was all about, especially since I had proposed but had failed to cement the deal with the obligatory diamond ring.

I stopped abruptly and said, "Ah, here we are."

Puzzled, Ann looked around and then saw the sign. She made a fist and punched my shoulder. "You goofball. This is the Handleman you had to see?"

"Yep. This is the guy. Let's go in and see if I can make an honest woman of you."

"Are you kidding?" Ann said. "You're not thinking of buying me—"

"Yep, that is exactly what I'm thinking." I laughed, took her arm and propelled her into the store.

Mr. Handleman himself waited on us. "We have some outstanding engagement rings."

"Something really nice," I said, "with at least a one karat stone."

Handleman brought out a tray with a dozen diamond rings. One of the rings caught my eye at once. "Let's see that one," I said pointing my finger.

"Wait a minute," Ann said, "No, I don't think so. That's a little over the top. Let's have a look at that one." She pointed to a ring with a smaller center diamond.

Handleman looked at me for direction.

"It's okay. Bring out the first one." I gave Ann a stern look. "Listen, lady, this is my deal. I'm sorry but you don't get to vote. The only reason I brought you along is so I could get the ring sized to fit your third finger, left hand. Okay? Now, let me handle this...please."

Ann took a step back. "I'm sorry. You're right. This is your deal, so proceed. I'll go sit over there," she pointed to a row of chairs behind us. She strolled over to them and sat down.

Mr. Handleman, holding the ring I had picked, said in a half whisper, "This is a platinum setting. The diamond is a one point eight karat, very high quality blue-white stone and these six little side diamonds equal about one karat."

"Yes, this is a beautiful ring, no doubt," I said in a low voice. "What about it? Is there something I'm not seeing, something wrong with it?"

"No, sir. Not at all. It's exactly as I have said and I have the certificate to authenticate it. It's a perfect diamond. Here, use this jeweler's glass." He looked over at Ann as I inspected the diamond. In a quiet voice he said, "This ring is priced at $7,998. That's the sale price. The regular price was $10,998."

"I see." I turned toward Ann and said, "Look at that lady sitting over there. Is she not one of the most beautiful women you have ever laid eyes on?" I had to smile as I said it. Ann was wearing Levi's, a leather motorcycle jacket, heavy boots and a cap over unkempt hair. "Well?"

"Yes, sir. I'd have to say she is very beautiful."

I pushed on, "So is it not incumbent upon me, her fiancé, to match her beauty with a ring that is also an outstanding beauty?" I held up a hand. "No need to answer. The answer is obvious. So unless the lady refuses to wear this ring, I think you can consider it sold."

Mr. Handleman beamed as I beckoned Ann to come over. To Ann I said most solemnly, "My darling, I have selected this particular ring as an appropriate statement of my love and devotion for you. Will you accept it?"

"Quit goofing around. Of course I will. Put it on my finger and the deed will be done."

Mr. Handleman gave me the ring. In spite of her bravado, her hand was shaking as I slid the ring on.

It was a little large. Nonetheless, I said in a stentorian tone, "I now pronounce us to be officially engaged." With that, I scooped her up and planted a major kiss on her open mouth. Mr. Handleman clapped as did two other women who had entered the store a few moments earlier.

"How long will it take for you to resize it?" I asked.

"I can have it for you in an hour." He opened a drawer and pulled out a set of measurement rings and when he found the correct size he said, "Very well. Now about payment. How did you want to handle that as the ring must be paid for before I resize it."

"You're in luck," I said. "Thinking I was probably going to buy a ring today, I brought along a check."

"It's Saturday—the bank won't be open today so I can't verify your account. Do you have a Diners Club card or one of those new American Express credit cards?"

"No," I replied, "I don't use them. But I assure you, you'll have no trouble cashing my check."

Mr. Handleman had a pained look about him. "I'm sure it will be fine but could you come back Monday? Write the check and I'll call the bank Monday morning and verify the amount and then I'll resize the ring and you can pick it up by noon."

I sighed deeply. "I suppose I—"

Ann broke in. Reaching inside her jacket pocket she pulled out a small wallet from which she extracted an American Express credit card. She handed it to Handleman. "Oh, for God's sake, just charge it on this card, go ahead and resize it and we'll come back in an hour or so and pick it up. How's that?"

I couldn't help but break down laughing. "There you go," I said to Handleman. "Did I not tell you she is a beautiful, one-of-a-kind lady? Not only that, she's got a damn American Express card and can—and just did—buy her own engagement ring."

Ann gave me the expected punch on the shoulder. "I didn't buy anything. What I did do is float you a loan. This is what is known as *financial planning* and I'm sure you remember that is what I do, so just make out the check to me. We're not leaving this town without that ring on my finger."

"Thanks for coming to my rescue," I told Ann as we walked out of the store. Feigning anger I added, "Can you imagine that guy not taking my check? I'm insulted! I've a mind to go back there and tell him to forget it and keep his damn ring."

"Oh no, you don't. No way are you not giving me that ring now that you've made the commitment and got my juices flowing," she said. Grabbing my arm, she propelled me down the street toward the place where we had parked the bikes. "I think I saw a restaurant in the shopping center. Let's have lunch, go back and pick up the ring then hurry back to our lovely suite, take a shower and make love the rest of the afternoon."

"Lady," I said, putting my arm around her waist, "I love the way you think."

"There it is," Ann pointed. "There's the restaurant over there." We were heading through the parking lot toward the restaurant when suddenly Ann pulled up short. "Oh my God!" she said in a lowered voice. "Quick, look over there."

I followed her gaze. "Holly crap! I see it. It's the black truck with Emmett's bike in back. I'll be damned. Who would have thought..."

"Never mind. What can we do?"

We watched as the pickup pulled into a parking space not far from our bikes.

Ann said, "We need to find a policeman right away."

I watched as two men got out of the pickup. No doubt about it, these were the guys that beat up Emmett. The tall, thin man was no longer wearing a beard. He looked around and said something, then the two of them walked toward the line of shops.

"Okay, I'll keep an eye on them, see where they go. If possible, I'll try to disable their truck. You find a telephone and call the Monterey County Sheriff's Department. You have change for the phone?"

Ann checked her pockets, she had change. She started to leave. I stopped her. "Wait a minute. I'll ease over there and get the license number in case they leave before the cops get here." I walked around the line of cars, until I got a bead on the pickup. It was a New Mexico license plate. I pulled a ball point pen from my shirt pocket and wrote the number down on the back of my hand. I hurried back to Ann who wrote the number on the back of the American Express receipt. "Okay, now get to a phone quick as you can." Ann hurried off.

I wanted to get to the truck and open the distributor cap and pull off the rotor but I was afraid they might come back and see the hood raised up and I'd end up being their next victim. I wasn't keen on that idea. I looked back toward the shops but didn't see them so I moved to different spot where I could keep them in sight if they came out of one of the stores.

The door of the hardware store opened and my two guys walked out. They glanced both right and left, then walked to the restaurant and went in. I moved in closer and through the large window I could see them sitting down in a booth about half way back. Time to make my move. I hurried over to the pickup and searched for a latch to open the hood but couldn't find one. The release must be inside. I tried the doors. Both were locked. Now what? Tires. I took out my pen knife, pushed down on the air valve and let the air out of the left tire. It was a slow process but in a couple of minutes the tire was flat. I sneaked around behind the truck, stood up and looked toward the restaurant. All clear. I let the air out of the other front tire and carefully made my way back to the place where I had first seen them. I could see the front of the restaurant and glanced at it every few minutes but aside from a man and a woman, no one else came out.

Ann returned. "I talked to the sheriff," she said through ragged breaths. "He said he saw the bulletin and would dispatch a couple of deputies at once. He said it wouldn't take but a few minutes for them to get here. I suggested that they not use sirens so as not to scare the crooks away." Ann smiled, "It was funny because after I made the suggestion about the sirens all he said was, 'Yes, ma'am.'" Ann glanced around the lot. "So, do you know where they are?"

I glanced back at the restaurant and thrust my chin in that direction, "They went in there about ten minutes ago. I let the air out of both front tires so if they do try to leave before the cops get here, I don't think they'll get very far." As I said that, the restaurant door opened and our two men walked out, holding paper bags. Apparently they had ordered their food to go.

"That's them, right?" Ann asked.

"Yep. Damn, I didn't think they'd be out so soon." I looked toward the entrance to the parking area but no police car appeared. "Where the hell are those cops?"

"They should be here any second now," Ann said. "Maybe we should just go over to our bikes and get on like we're about to leave. And maybe we should leave, in case there's any trouble—

you know, they might pull out guns when they see the cops. I sure as hell don't want to be around if bullets start flying."

From our vantage point, I watched the men go to the pickup, get in and start the engine. They began to back up just as a sherriff's patrol car came rolling into the parking lot. The pickup was now out in the aisle and I could see the driver having a hard time turning the steering wheel. The pickup began to move forward just as the patrol car made the turn at the end of the aisle and headed directly toward them. The officers must have recognized the pickup as the one Ann had described and so they turned on their flashing red lights. The bad guys jumped out and ran between the rows of cars. I lost sight of them but the cops were out of their car and running.

"Oh, my God," Ann yelled. "Where did they go?" Just then the two deputies came into view. They were in the next aisle looking right and left.

One of them shouted to the other, "Get back to the car and call for backup."

I looked in the direction of their car. All I could see was the top and the red lights flashing. Suddenly, the lights began to move. The patrol car backed up, made the turn at the end of the aisle and took off out of the parking lot. The deputy came running out of a row of cars yelling at his partner, "They got the car! They took the car!"

Ann looked around, wild-eyed, "What the heck happened? What's that deputy saying?"

"Those guys took their patrol car."

"What? How could they do that?"

"I don't know but my guess is the deputies saw the pickup, turned on their lights and jumped out without turning off the engine. The bad boys must have circled back, saw the car was running and took off in it."

"What the hell!" Ann exclaimed, "This is crazy. What are we dealing with here, the Keystone Cops?"

"At least we got the pickup and Emmett's bike and air compressor." I took hold of Ann's hand and walked her toward the restaurant. "I'm hungry. Let's get some lunch then we'll call the sheriff and Emmett and they can work out what happens next."

"What about those two crooks?" Ann asked.

"How far do you think they'll get in a patrol car that every cop in the county will be looking for?"

Using the pay phone in the restaurant, I made the two calls and got everything squared away. "Thanks a lot for your help, Sheriff. Oh, by the way, did you locate your stolen patrol car yet?"

"I just got a call from one our deputies—they saw the car south of Santa Rita, gave chase and those damned fools ran the car off the road and hit a tree. The driver was pretty banged up but the other guy took off on foot."

"Did they catch him?" I asked.

"No, apparently not. I haven't got the details on that yet. Something must have gone wrong."

"I guess so. Thanks again for helping Emmett—Mr. Walker."

"Listen, fella, thanks for your help. Glad you had your eyes open and spotted those guys. Goodbye."

I joined Ann at our table and told her about my conversations. "You should have heard Emmett. He couldn't believe you spotted that pickup and got some of his stuff back. And the sheriff thanked us too."

"But, they let the one guy get away? How did that happen?" She thought about it for a moment. "Oh, I remember, they're Keystone Cops. They're not supposed to catch the crooks."

I chuckled. "I guess not. Now, let's forget about them and get something to eat. After lunch we'll go to the jewelry store, get your ring and ride back, as you said, to our little paradise and make love. All things considered, I think this has been a pretty busy day so far and I'm looking forward to some diversion before we see what the rest of the day has in store."

The lunch was okay, the ring fit Ann's finger perfectly and the ride back to our little paradise on the beach was uneventful. When I opened the door to our suite, Ann stepped in, looked around and turning back to me said, "Ah. This is more like it." Throwing her arms around my neck, she pulled my head down so that we were face to face. "Now, take my clothes off and carry me to the shower and clean my body so that you can make love to it—all of it."

I started to unbutton her shirt while she was unbuttoning mine. "Stop," she suddenly said, holding up her left hand to admire her new ring, then turned her hand so that the ring was in my view. "Is this not the most beautiful diamond ring you've ever seen?"

I gently took her hand and kissed it. "Yes, milady, it is. And art thou not the most beautiful woman on the face of the earth who deserveth such a ring as this?"

"Yea, verily and forsooth I am and thus, as my knight, thou must have thy way with me and without further delay." Ann slipped from my grasp and tore her clothes off and sprinted toward the bathroom. "Do hasten, my good man. There is much to be done."

chapter twenty-nine

nn described the love-making that afternoon as *delicious.*
That's probably not the way I would have characterized it but
who cares? I think *delicious* sums it up very well. Afterward,
well truthfully, I don't remember afterward because I fell asleep.
When I awoke, I glanced out the window and saw the sun was
low in the sky. I sprang out of bed and pulled on a pair of chinos
and a tee shirt. Ann was in the sitting room reading a book. She
was wearing shorts and a cotton blouse.

"Ah, you're alive. You were sleeping so soundly I didn't want
to wake you," Ann said.

"You wore me out. But never mind, come on, I want to show
you something outside." I pulled her out of the chair, hurried her
down the steps and out the back door onto the beach. Near the
water's edge I commanded, "Sit down." I sat down next to her.
"Look out toward the horizon."

Ann mumbled, "What's this all—"

I put a finger over her lips. "Shhhhh. Just look out over the
water and be patient. No talking." I put my arm around her
shoulders and gently pulled her close.

Soon the sun began its inevitable decent to the sea
accompanied by the most spectacular array of orange and red
and yellow lights. Others on the beach had stopped to watch

the majestic show of light and color. Aside from the sound of the surf, it became very quiet except for the occasional "ewoo," "ahhh," and the like. Ann, too, joined the chorus. The sun appeared to dip into the water and extinguish itself and suddenly the show was over.

Now, in the twilight Ann turned to me.

"You are something, my magical lover. First you propose at a most unlikely place at a most unlikely time, totally without preamble, taking me completely by surprise. Then the ring today—another total surprise. And now this magical moment on the beach, feeling you close to me, knowing your love for me is genuine and will stand the test of time." Her eyes became misty and there was a quiver in her voice as she added, "I just don't know what to say—except I love you."

"There's nothing more you need to say. You said it all and quite eloquently." I kissed her lightly on the lips. "And you need not ever worry. I will always be your lover, your friend, your most ardent admirer, your protector, your personal pilot and most of all, your devoted husband."

Ann smiled bravely, doing her best to hold back tears. "And I'll always be your devoted and loving wife."

Back in our room, I mixed a couple of cocktails—Martini with an olive for Ann and a bourbon and ginger ale for me. I held up my glass. "I propose a toast and I ask you to join me in it."

"All right. Let's hear your toast." She raised her glass.

I touched it with mine, and then I raised mine high above my head, "Goodbye, Gunner. Hello, Annette, soon to be Mrs. Richard Elkins." I brought my glass down, clinked Ann's' glass again and drank.

"I'll definitely drink to that," said Ann, downing about half her Martini in one gulp.

We had dinner that evening at a beachfront café, dining on lobster tails and other good stuff. The subject of a wedding date came up and we tentatively decided on sometime in either April or May but couldn't agree on a venue. I thought being married aboard ship while taking a cruise would be fun. Ann was ambivalent about that idea but didn't have a precise idea of her own.

I asked her about her family and whether she'd want them involved. She wasn't sure. I realized that I knew very little about her background, and this seemed the right time to ask. She was born in Memphis, but later on her dad got a job with the government—he was an attorney—and they moved to Washington, D.C. Her mother got a job with the Commerce Department and Annette and her younger sister Sophie spent a lot of time with housekeepers and babysitters. Both girls were good students and were able to get into first-rate colleges. Annette took her undergraduate and graduate courses at Stanford, while Sophie attended Brown. Sophie dropped out of school in her junior year and married one of her classmates, and Ann hadn't heard from her in years. Ann's parents, both retired, lived on the Big Island in Hawaii. Ann said she hadn't seen her parents in over five years but they wrote or called fairly regularly. When I mentioned Hawaii as a possible wedding venue with her parents attending, Ann thought that was a possibility but she really didn't warm to the idea.

"Tell ya what," I said, "for starters, we'll check our schedules for April and May and see what works out best for both of us and I'm sure that by early April we can decide on where we want the deed to take place and all the rest of the fuzzy details."

"Sure," Ann replied. She took a sip of wine and looking over the rim of the wine glass added, "You do want to do this, right?"

"What?" I said it so loud that several people at nearby tables looked our way. I lowered my voice. "What are you talking about?" I reached for her left hand and held it up. "I believe this is an engagement ring. Don't tell me you're getting cold feet all of a sudden?"

"No, of course not." Ann pulled her hand from my grasp, refilled her wine glass and said, "Let's drop it for now and talk about something else."

I hailed our waitress and ordered a bourbon. Frankly, I was a bit puzzled about Ann's remarks, especially after everything that had happened today that was so positive. I decided not to push it and started a conversation about where we should travel next.

Ann's mood definitely brightened. "But I do hate to leave here and our lovely little suite. I just love it!" Ann put her elbows on the table and cupped her chin in her hands. "This week has been the best week of my life and I hate for it to end."

I leaned toward her and in a low voice I said, "Heck, we don't have to go. I just thought you'd like to get on the road and check out some more country before we head back. But if you want to stay here another week, it's fine with me. I love it here as much as you do."

"Really?" Ann said. There was a renewed energy in her voice. "You know there are many places we can visit right from here, places we haven't seen. There are lots of things to do and most important, we don't have to leave our little dream home."

"Okay, then. It's settled. We'll stay right here until it's time to go back. I'll call ops on Monday morning and see what's going on. What about you? Do you definitely have to be back at work a week from Monday?"

Ann opened her purse and removed a lipstick. "I'm afraid so." She skillfully applied lipstick, bit down on a piece of tissue, and, wide-eyed, asked, "How's that?"

"Which part, the look of your lips or you having to be back at work?"

Ann laughed, "Nothing we can do about work. I really do have to be back. I've got appointments scheduled. As for the lips, if they look tempting, why don't you just lean over and kiss them?"

The next day I went to the store before Ann woke up and bought some picnic items. Returning, I found her in the bathroom fixing her hair—not that it was broken. Her hair always looked good whether she had just come from a beauty parlor or had just woken in bed. The red hair was natural; she didn't have it dyed although every now and then she threatened to become a blonde. I pleaded with her to never, ever do that. The combination of her red hair, pale white skin (sometimes tanned) and vivid green eyes was, in my opinion, the perfect look, and I suggested that I would be much put out were she to change it.

Turning from the mirror, Ann asked, "Where have you been?"

"To the store. Got us some food and wine to take with us so we can have a little picnic lunch."

"We're going on a picnic? That sounds like fun. Where are we going or is this going to be another big surprise?"

"We'll just head up the coast and look for a good spot." I patted her butt and pushed her toward the door. "But right now I'm kind of hungry so let's dig up some breakfast."

Around noon, having packed our lunch in my saddlebags, we took off. We hadn't gone very far before I turned off the road and stopped.

Ann hopped off her bike, looked around and let out a little cry of delight. "It's our place, isn't it?" She looked around some more and then wasn't sure. "This is the place you and I came to before I left. Or is it?"

I stepped behind her and put my arms around her chest. I located the zipper and zipped open the leather jacket and laid my hands lightly on her breasts. I bent down and kissed the back of her neck. "This is the place, darling. I just came in a different way. Let's get the picnic and we'll walk out to the spot where you and I said a sad and tearful goodbye."

Ann turned around. "Driving home that afternoon I didn't know if I'd ever see you again." She paused and gave me the saddest look. "Do you know that I cried all the way to LA?"

"We're not saying goodbye this time, are we? So come on, let's see a big smile."

Ann forced a smile but there remained a sadness in her demeanor. She fixed me with her gaze for a long moment, saying nothing.

I returned the intent look with one of my own. "What's going on?" I asked.

Ann shook her head.

"No," I said. "Something is bothering you. It started at breakfast." I took hold of her shoulders and brought my face level with hers. I looked deeply into her eyes and said in a measured voice, "You're having doubts about getting married, aren't you? You're scared that something will go wrong and—"

"No, no," Ann insisted. "It's something else, I don't know, I don't understand it myself. It's an uneasy feeling. But no, I'm not afraid...But maybe something could go wrong."

"Like what?"

"Like..." Ann turned and walked off a little way. She turned back and faced me. There was a distance between us and she raised her voice, "I'm afraid of Angie. There, I said it. I'm afraid I'll always have to deal with Angie—she'll always be in the back of your mind."

I ran up to her and wrapped my arms around her. "Angie? What are you talking about? She's gone. She can't hurt you."

Ann pulled back and yelled, "But she can hurt you, she can turn you against me!" She lowered her voice. "She can remind you of the past and what I did."

"Ann, be sensible. You're letting your emotions and imagination get the best of you. Angie is a memory now, that's all. You are the one I love and want to be with."

"Really?" Ann spat out the words, "Do you want to be with a whore?" Ann broke away and ran toward a grove of trees by the water's edge.

I stood, transfixed by her words. It was true—Angie's words would still come to me once in a while but I never mentioned it to Ann, Never! But, now I understood that Ann, too, was haunted by Angie's agonizing question: *Do you want to be with a whore?* But I was well over it. Ann was never a whore, for God's sake. Sure she was promiscuous and definitely out of the mainstream of social behavior, but I put it down to pressure from Royce and the influence of drugs that seemed to be a part of the swinging scene. Still, I had to admit she did love the sex act and was very familiar with it in all of its forms and variations which she had employed so well at the house in Atascadero.

I walked slowly up to the grove of trees. It came to me that I never had analyzed my feelings before. Her love-making with me since Atascadero had never been as wild and uninhibited as it was then. It now dawned on me why. Of course, she was trying to erase from my memory, as if she ever could, her past behavior. In order to do that, she thought she must act like the moral, upstanding person she thought I was. And basically I was a moral person—maybe even a bit too high-minded. Were it not for that, I never would have been so incensed and disappointed by what I saw in that movie.

These thoughts were still running around my brain when I came upon her sitting on a large rock she and I shared the last time we were here.

Ann looked up and gave me a faint smile. "I'm sorry, Rick, truly I am. I'm such a moron. I know you love me and I'm sure you are comfortable...well, maybe not *comfortable* but okay with the past. In your dreams Angie's words and your memories may still haunt you, but I know you'll find a way to deal with it. At any rate, I don't think you would let it hurt me or our marriage." She gave me a questioning look. "Would it?"

I sat down next to her and thought about what I would say. I sighed, letting the air out slowly. "You don't get it, do you? I love you; you are the love of my life. Do you remember me telling you that?"

"Yes, many times."

"What does that mean? I'll tell you. It means in all my life— mind you, I said *all* of my life—you are my love. Does that mean you take the place of Angie or that I'll forget her? No, but it does mean that in the world of the living (and we are in that world, Angie is not), you are my one and only love and we are going to get married and live happily ever after. That's right, happily ever after."

I paused to let those words sink in. "If you want to talk about what you did or didn't do in the past, fine. We can have that discussion. If you never want to mention it again, that's fine, too. I know what you did, there are no secrets about it, and I swear to you, I'm okay with it. You've never been a whore, although you may have been somewhat immoral, but it no longer matters. Maybe it never really mattered." I took her hands in mine and asked, "Do you remember my toast last night?"

Ann's brow wrinkled. "A toast?" Ann put a finger to her lips and thought about it, "Of course, I remember it. You said,

'Goodbye, Gunner, hello, Annette.'" Her eyebrows lifted and her eyes widened. Under her breath, she repeated, "*Goodbye, Gunner, hello, Annette.* Oh my God, I missed the meaning of it, what you were trying to tell me, what you wanted me to understand." Ann kissed me and her face lit up with a wide smile. "Of course. You were trying to tell me something very important to our future relationship and I totally missed it." Ann slapped her forehead with the palm of her hand. "I told you I was a moron."

Ann jumped up, cupped my head between her hands and kissed my forehead. "Thank you so much, darling, for being patient with me. I know it must be difficult for you at times but I promise I'll try hard to do better in the future." Ann released her grip. "Now that we finally have that issue laid to rest, I can relax and enjoy the rest of our time here." She took my hand and pulled me up. In a cheery voice she said, "Come on, let's go get the picnic stuff and find that little place where we *almost* made love the last time we were here."

 chapter thirty

nn stretched and pulled the covers up to her chin. She turned on her side and whispered, "Are you awake?"
I kept my eyes closed and answered, "No."

She jiggled my shoulder. "I'm cold. You need to warm me up." She leaned over and lightly laid her lips on mine. "Don't you want to warm me up?"

I kept my eyes shut tight. "I can't right now."

"Why not?"

"Because I'm asleep. You wore me out last night and now I'm still tired and that is why I'm asleep."

I was ready for it when it came.

Ann punched me on the shoulder, "You goofball, quit screwing around."

"That's just the point, isn't it? We're not screwing around because I'm sleeping. Got it?"

Ann rolled on top of me. "I've got it alright," she jeered. She turned her head toward the window, "Look, it's raining...hard. We can't ride, can't walk on the beach. We have to stay inside." She put her hands on my chest and pushed herself up. "Oh dear me, what shall we do...what can we do when it's cold and rainy like this?" She bent down and planted a hickey on my neck.

"Hey, what the hell? That hurt."

"Oh dear, did I hurt the little boy? I'm sorry, but what can I do? He won't wake up and take care of me even after I told him I'm cold and need his warmth."

I opened my eyes and scrutinized her face. "Really? You want to do this?"

"Of course. Don't you?" A look of disappointment etched the corners of her eyes and mouth.

"Oh, for God's sake, don't pout." I said lightheartedly. "I need to go to the bathroom, then we'll take a nice hot shower, after which or possibly during, I'll do my best to warm you up." I had to laugh. This girl didn't need to be warmed up, she was already much too hot to begin with.

Returning to the bed all warmed up and smelling like a couple of lilies from the French milled soap, we played and napped and played some more. It must have been close to noon or maybe later when Ann whispered in my ear.

"I'm hungry. I need to eat something."

I was tempted to reply with a sexually explicit yet obvious suggestion, but thought better of it and instead said, "Me, too. Let's get moving,"

Bea was standing at the bottom of the steps as we came down. She gave us a bright and cheerful, "Good morning, or should I say good afternoon? You two been in bed all this time?"

Ann's face showed a trace of color. "No. No. We were reading and waiting for the rain to stop but it kept coming down."

Bea held back a smile. "A'huh. I hope it was a good book. What are you reading?"

Ann gave Bea a blank look. "What is the title? It's book by ah..."

I jumped in, "It's a book by a doctor named Kinsey. Very interesting book, maybe a little too technical for—"

Bea interrupted with a smile. "Yeah, I know. Besides I really don't care." She looked out the window at the rain which had stopped but started coming down again. "I'm not going anywhere this afternoon, so why don't you use my car and go someplace? You could have lunch and see a movie in Salinas."

Ann and I exchanged glances. I said, "That be great if you're sure you don't need the car." I turned to Ann. "Want to do that—go to a movie?"

"Sure. That sounds like fun."

Bea left and came back with the Sunday paper and the keys to her car. "Grab a couple of umbrellas on your way out, you'll need 'em." She stopped Ann. "Wait a minute. Let me see that ring again." Ann held out her hand, Bea took it and examined the ring closely. She looked up at Ann. "Ain't that a beaut?" she said. "Yep, that's the real McCoy alright. You don't find one like this in a Cracker Jack box."

"Rick gets the credit. He's the one who picked it out," Ann exclaimed as we headed out the door to dash to Bea's car, a '58 Buick Special two-door sedan.

The rain let up to a light drizzle as we drove toward Salinas on Route 68. Ann flipped through the newspaper. "There are two movies playing. *Hud* with Paul Newman, and *To Russia with Love* with Sean Connery. Which one would you prefer?"

"I don't care. I imagine they're both good. You pick."

Ann thought about it. "I love Paul Newman. Let's see *Hud*."

We had something to eat then walked over to the movie theater, just a block away. The four o'clock showing had already started. The usher used her little flashlight to show us to a couple of seats near the back of the theater. After the feature film, there was a newsreel followed by a short Walt Disney animated comedy featuring Daffy Duck.

"Seen enough?" I whispered to Ann. She nodded. "Okay, let's get out of here."

We walked up the aisle and pushed open the door the led to the main lobby. There were a number of patrons waiting for the next show. I looked at my watch, 6:20. Ann was walking in front of me, maneuvering through the crowd, when suddenly she stopped, turned around and faced me.

"Rick, I think that guy is here. He's standing by the wall over there," Ann cocked her head to the left and rolled her eyes in that direction.

"What guy?" As I said it, I looked to my left and scanned the far wall. "Geeze! That can't be him. You mean the tall one with the green cap who's talking to that girl?"

"Yes, I'm sure that's him. Don't stare at him. Let's go before he spots us." She headed for the exit. When we were outside Ann asked. "What should we do, call the police or the sheriff?"

I took her arm and walked her further away. "Do you think he's waiting to get into the show or—"

"I don't know." There was urgency in Ann's voice. "But we need to do something right away."

I looked up and down the road but didn't see a phone booth. "Okay, let's go back to the restaurant; they'll have a phone there." I started walking in that direction but Ann grabbed my arm.

"We better not both go. I'll phone the sheriff. You stay here in case he leaves the theater. Maybe you can follow him and see where he goes or get a license plate number if he gets into a car."

"Good idea. If I'm not here when you get back, wait at the restaurant and I'll meet you there. Now, get going." I walked back to the theater and stood by the side of the ticket booth where I could see into the lobby. I scanned the wall where we had last seen our man but he wasn't there. Suddenly, people were streaming into the lobby from the theater and exiting out the doors. I got swallowed up in the jabbering crowd that more or less carried me along to the sidewalk in front of the building. Quickly, I scanned the crowd looking for that tell-tale green cap. But nothing. No sight of him or the girl he was talking to.

The crowd was thinning in front of the movie house as I took up a position in an adjacent storefront. I swept the area with my eyes once again but no luck. I looked up the street toward the restaurant, hoping to see Ann coming back but the pedestrian traffic made it difficult to see. I looked back toward the theater and as I did, the lobby door opened and out walked our man and the girl.

They were holding hands and talking. They turned right and continued down the street. I walked behind them at a discreet distance. The girl dropped the guy's hand, stepped off the curb behind a green car and opened the driver's side door. The man got in the other side. I stopped in front of a store window and pretended to be looking at the display. The car engine came to life, the lights came on and the green car—an older Nash sedan—pulled into the street. I tried to read the California license plate, but all I retained were the last three numbers, 319.

I hurried back to the movie theater and as I approached, I saw Ann. "Did you get a hold of the sheriff?" I asked.

She had run all the way from the restaurant. "Yeah." She caught her breath. "Fortunately, I talked to a deputy who remembered the case and said he'd call the sheriff right away and also inform the Salinas police. He also said that we were to do nothing if we saw the crook. Just wait for the police and give them the information."

Minutes later a police car pulled up in front of the theater and two uniformed officers got out. They looked around and spotted us. We approached them.

"Are you Ann?" one of the policemen asked.

"Yes. I'm the one who called."

"Yes, ma'am. We understand you saw the man in question here a little while ago. Do you know if he's he still inside? Or has he left?"

"I'm Richard Elkins. I stayed here and kept an eye on the guy while Ann called the sheriff."

The other officer asked, "So, is he still inside?"

"No. He and the girl he was with came out about fifteen minutes ago, got in a car and took off." I gave the policemen a description of the car and the last three numbers of the plate. One of the cops hurried over to the police car and radioed the information while the other asked us some more questions. We gave him a description of the man, what he was wearing, etc., and the same for the girl.

After the police left, we got into Bea's car. "Can you believe it?" I said. "That's twice we've spotted that crook and he's got away both times. I mean, what are the chances of that? To have seen him the first time was strange enough, but to see him again, in a movie theater of all places, is beyond belief."

"You're right. This whole thing is starting to look like a B detective movie." A look of concern crossed Ann's face. "He didn't see you, did he?"

"No, I'm sure of that. When they came out of the theater, the two of them were talking and holding hands all the way to their car. He never looked back. Besides, I was being very careful."

"So, now what?"

"Oh, let's see." I put my forefinger against the side of my nose, feigning deep thought. "We could go for a cup of coffee or maybe over to the hotel for a drink. What's your pleasure?"

Ann said, "No, I wasn't talking about what to do now. I meant, what's going to happen with that guy?"

I took my hands off the wheel and held them palms up. "I have no idea. The cops will catch him some day and he'll serve time and that's that. Now, about my other question: coffee or cocktail?"

Ann pursed her lips. She was obviously not happy with my analysis of the situation. "Oh, let's just go home. All this excitement has made me tired."

I started the Buick and backed out of the parking space, then I shifted into first and said, "Home it is, then."

Ann gave me a hopeful look. "I wish it was our home. I love it there."

I looked at her and with a smile said, "Someday, my sweet. Someday."

chapter thirty-one

he sky had cleared and the moon was rising as we drove into the yard. I got out of the car and walked to the other side and opened the door for Ann. "C'mon," I said, helping her out with my hand. "Let's take a walk on the beach."

"Okay, but not too long. It's getting cold," she said.

We walked hand in hand around the side of the house and down to the beach. The moon's light reflecting off the shimmering waves was awesome.

Ann said, "That is one beautiful sight. The waves seem to be lit up from inside." She turned toward me and said in a soft voice, "I am going to miss this so much when we leave."

"Me, too, but there's a good side to it, you know."

"What's that?"

"When we leave Monterey this time, we'll be together and that's the best part of this whole trip."

Ann put her arms around my neck, rose up on tiptoes and kissed me long and hard. "You're right, being together is the best part." She signed contentedly. "And leaving together this time is a dream I've had for a long time." She kissed me again and said, "Oh, and one other thing just in case you've forgotten, I love you, you goofy aviator."

I called flight operations Monday morning and checked my schedule. The following Monday they had me flying to Bartlesville, Oklahoma with T/O at 0800, then to Odessa, Texas, overnighting there. Tuesday morning, 0700 to Houma, Louisiana, then TBD Tuesday afternoon back to LAX. Eugene Parrino was listed as co-pilot. We'd be carrying eight passengers, so Carlotta Menzalora would come along as the cabin gal.

I knew Gene—he and Alvin Conley had checked out on the Jetstar after Terry and I, but I'd never flown with him, so I had no idea about his skills. However, having earned his Navy wings in World War II, he probably was a first-class aviator. He was my senior by at least ten years so I couldn't help but wonder why he wasn't a captain since he had flown left seat on the Convairs. Well, I thought, this will be an interesting first trip as captain.

Ann and I spent the next two days on our motorcycles exploring more of the surrounding countryside. The weather was a little on the cold side but it was sunny and it didn't rain so we were okay on the road.

We decided that we would leave Monterey Friday morning, run down to Cambria and visit Edna and Emmett, stay overnight in Cambria, which both Ann and I found a charming and quite beautiful town, and leave Saturday morning for LA with a possible stop or two in between. On Thursday afternoon, using the phone in Bea's little office, I called the Walkers to make sure they would be home when we arrived Friday.

Edna answered. "Hello."

"Hi, Edna, it's Rick. How're you guys doing?"

"We're fine."

There was something in the clipped tone of her voice that made me think maybe she wasn't fine. Besides that, when I'd talked to her on the phone before, she was always very talkative.

I asked again, "Edna, has something happened to Emmett? You don't sound right." There was a long pause. I thought I heard someone say something. "Edna, are you there?"

"Yeah, I'm sorry. I, ah, but what was it you wanted?"

That definitely didn't sound like Edna. I was puzzled. "I called to tell you that Ann and I are returning to LA tomorrow and we thought we'd stop by and spend a little time with you two. We'll leave Saturday morning."

"No, no...Don't come...ah...Me and Emmett will be..." Pause. "We won't be here. Ga-bye."

"Edna? What's going on?" There was no answer, just a dial tone. I ran up the stairs to our suite and burst into the room. "I just talked to Edna. Something's wrong down there."

Ann, startled, put her book down and brought her rocking chair to a halt. "Something's wrong? What do you mean?"

"Something screwy is going on at their house. I told Edna we were coming down there and she said we shouldn't come because they're going to be away. It's not so much what she said but the way she said it that tells me something isn't right. She didn't ask if I wanted to speak to Emmett or how you were. She just said they won't be there and that was it. She hung up."

Ann was equally puzzled. She began rocking. "You don't think—"

"Yes, I do. I think Green Cap has gone down there to either hide out or, hell, I don't know. The guy's probably a psycho—who knows what he's thinking or what he'll do."

I paced the floor trying to think of something we could do while Ann sat in the chair rocking furiously and mumbling to herself. I stopped my pacing in front of her and took hold of the rocker. "Got any ideas?"

Ann looked up. "If we call the sheriff and tell him what we

think may be happening, he'd probably send an army of cops down there and..."

I broke in, "Green cap would either kill Edna and Emmett or hold them as hostages."

"Exactly what I was thinking," Ann said. "So that's out?"

I walked to the window and looked out. "Not sure, but maybe the sheriff could be persuaded to do some kind of covert thing—try to trick Green somehow." I rubbed my chin with thumb and forefinger. "Nah, they'd probably botch it and get Edna and Emmett killed."

Ann came over to the window, glanced at the scene below momentarily, then brightly said, "Why don't we figure out some cloak and dagger plan? We both have guns, we could—"

I laughed a big laugh. Still laughing, I blurted out, "Why sure, we could storm the place, guns blazing and kill the bad guy and rescue the hostages."

Ann couldn't help but laugh as well. "Yeah, that was dumb. We don't even know if Green is alone. He may have brought that girl or he may have some other guys with him and they're probably armed to the teeth."

I turned from the window and looked at her. "The girl!" I paused and thought about it. "Maybe she could be the key player in this deal—that is, if she's with him. The problem with any plan is how we keep Edna and Emmett from getting killed."

"Right. That has got to be our number one concern."

"Maybe that should be our number two concern."

She asked, "Number two? What would be number one then?"

"Our number one concern has got to be how we keep ourselves from getting killed."

Good sense prevailed. I called the Monterey County sheriff and told him about our suspicions that the fugitive might be at the Walker home near Cambria. He told me the fugitive's name was Arnold Dykes but that Cambria was not in his jurisdiction—it was in San Luis Obispo County. He said he would call Sheriff Harbough, give him my name and phone number and ask him to call me right away. I gave him Bea's number.

The sheriff said, "I'm sure they know about this case. We sent an all-points *Fugitive from Justice* bulletin and his department was included. So, just tell him what you know and what you suspect and I'm sure he'll be able to help you out. If it turns out that Dykes is there, we sure want a piece of that guy."

Early Friday morning, Ann and I packed some clothes, our two guns and a pair of binoculars and took off for Cambria in Bea's Buick. We told Bea what we planned to do and she agreed the rationale for not taking the bikes was obvious. I told her if anything happened to her car, I'd buy her a new one. That secured the deal.

As we approached Cambria, I kept an eye open for the entrance to the winery which I remembered was located both behind and adjacent to Emmett's place. Ann saw the sign and read it aloud: "CAMBRIA ESTATES WINERY AND VINEYARD - TASTING ROOM - VISITORS WELCOME. ENTRANCE 500 FEET AHEAD."

We turned on to the gravel road, drove about three hundred yards to a parking lot. The tasting room and winery were nearby in an attractive stone building.

In the tasting room, the girl behind the counter suggested several wines and we drank small samples of three reds.

I said to the counter girl, "I'll take a couple bottles of that second one we tasted."

The girl carefully wrapped the two bottles and put them in

a bag. I paid the eight dollars and change and said "My wife has never been to a vineyard before. Would it be all right if we just walked around a bit?"

"Of course," the girl exclaimed. "We love to have people enjoy themselves when they visit us. Just over that little hill," she pointed, "by the other parking lot, is a little picnic area and you're welcome to use it any time." She smiled broadly. "Of course, any picnic lunch is always better with a bottle of Cambria Estates wine."

Ann said, "Hey, that's a great idea. We're staying in the area for a few days, maybe we'll bring a picnic lunch tomorrow."

"That sounds like fun," I said. "We'll probably see you tomorrow." I picked up the wine and we strolled over to the car. When we were out of earshot, I said, "Okay, this works perfectly. Emmett's house and shop are right over there."

Ann followed my look.

"If we cut across one of those rows, we would come out behind the house. He's got a lot of junk back there which should make pretty good cover if the cops want to scout around." I started the engine and backed out. "Right now I'll drive down to that other parking lot and we'll take a stroll through the rows of grapes like good tourists."

We parked and walked over to the picnic pavilion which was nothing more than a concrete slab about fourteen foot square, with a four-sided roof. What was good about was that it gave us a vantage point from which we could see Emmett's house and back yard.

"You were right about the junk. What's he do with all that crap?" Ann asked.

"He makes stuff with it. Anyway, who cares? Do you see what I mean about making good cover?"

"Do you think the sheriff's guys can pull it off?"

"When he called me, he told me he's got some good men in what he called his 'Special Unit,' whatever that is. Now that I see what we've got here, I need to call him back and give him the lowdown. He's going to send the men after he hears from me."

Ann said, "On the way out, we should stop and take a look in front of the house, see what's going on there."

We drove slowly down the drive toward the road but couldn't see much of Emmett's front yard. When we reached the road, I turned left and drove slowly past Emmett's drive and continued on about fifty yards and then stopped. "Hand me those binoculars on the back seat." I scanned the area in front of the shop, then I handed the binoculars to Ann. "Take a look just inside the shop and to the right."

Ann adjusted the focus and scanned the shop building. "It's a green car. Is it—"

"It's the Nash they got away in. It obviously was the girl's car. She was the one driving it the other night." I pondered that thought for a moment. "So, did Dykes steal the car or is she with him, or what?"

Ann reached around and laid the binoculars on the back seat. "I guess we won't know until we flush Mr. Dykes out of the house and I have my gun pointed at his head."

We checked in at a motel in town and I called Sheriff Harbough in San Luis Obispo, about forty miles south of Cambria. I told him what we saw from the vineyard, including the Nash. However, I told him that we didn't see any signs of life.

Sheriff Harbough replied, "Okay. You're right. The car is proof enough that Dykes is there or somewhere nearby. I told you about our team and they're on standby so I'm going to dispatch them now. They'll be in an unmarked black Ford. Where would be a good place to meet you?"

I thought about it. "I was going to say the vineyard but..."

"No. Don't think so. People around..."

"Yeah, that's what I was thinking so let's make it the Sunset Lodge in Cambria, corner of Stafford Street and Seabreeze, room 108. The phone number is 805-471-4777."

Harbough repeated the information back and added, "Look for my men in about an hour. If anything changes, call me right away."

The four man "Special Unit" arrived at our motel in less than an hour. They were well equipped with high powered automatic weapons. One of the men was a sniper. He had some kind of special rifle with a very high powered scope.

I laid it out for them. "Here's what we know: There's an elderly man and woman—I think they're in the house but I can't be sure. They could be tied up in the shop. These are the people we need to save so be careful who you aim your weapons at. I'm guessing, because I don't know for sure, that the bad guy is Arnold Dykes, the guy the Monterey Sheriff has been trying to find for the past week. Dykes is tall, I'd say six-two, very thin, I think he's bald, at least he was when we saw him at the shopping center in Salinas the day he and his buddy stole and crashed a police car. The last time we," I nodded toward Ann, "saw him, was at a movie theater in Salinas last Saturday, he was wearing a green baseball cap, a lighter colored shirt, a leather vest, black or dark brown, blue jeans and work shoes, light tan. He was with a shorter girl, with brown or dirty blonde hair. She was wearing slacks, a blouse or shirt with a tan jacket. I followed them when they left the theater and saw them get in and drive off in a green four-door Nash, probably four or five years old. The girl was driving. I'm guessing it's her car. We saw that same car tonight in the shop next to the house but I don't know if the girl is with him or not. I also don't know if there is anyone else with him."

There was a flurry of questions which I answered after which I described what we knew of the lay of the land.

"Here's my plan, subject to your approval. The Walkers know that Ann and I are riding motorcycles. So when I pull up to the house in a car, they won't know it's me. I'll step out of the car like I was a customer—Mr. Walker does auto repair—and knock on the door. If either Emmett or Edna, the Walkers, answers the door, I'll say that I've got something wrong with the car, the engine is running ragged, and ask if it can be fixed while I wait. I'm counting on them to play along and not do something stupid. However, my guess is that neither of the Walkers will open the door. I'm thinking it will either be Dykes or the girl if she's with him. Or it could be that nobody will answer the door. If it's Dykes, then the sniper should take him out. I'll try to position myself so he can get a clean shot."

The guys in the squad broke into laughter.

"Whoa, cowboy," the lieutenant in charge said after regaining his composure, "We can't just shoot someone like that. Have you never heard of due process of law? If he came to the door with a gun in his hand and it appeared as though he might harm you, then we'd probably be okay to take him down before he killed or injured you. But without some sort of menacing on his part, we'd be in deep shit." He turned to Ann, "Sorry for the language ma'am. What I meant was, we'd be in serious trouble—legal trouble if we just up and shot the guy."

The lieutenant turned to the other men who were still chuckling and talking, "Hey pipe down. Let's give this man some credit. At least he's given it some serious thought and has tried to come up with a plan." He looked at me, "Sorry about the outbreak but you see what the problem is, don't you? We can't let civilians participate in something like a hostage rescue. Hell, we'd be crucified if we pulled a trick like that. And think what would happen if something bad happened to you. Jesus!"

Again he turned to Ann and motioned with his hands that the word had slipped out. Then he continued, "I'm going to get us a room and we'll pow-wow and see if we can come up with a workable plan that won't get anyone, including Dykes, killed. I'll call the Sheriff and run it by him and get his okay to proceed. He may decide to ask for a special unit from LA County that does this hostage stuff. We'll see. Right now, from what you told us, we could maneuver from the vineyard down to the back of the house using all that scrap you say would provide cover and we could probably work our way around the back, maybe to the south side of the shop where that car is. Okay, have I got it right?"

I felt a little foolish that my plan was so damn juvenile. I was hoping my face didn't show my embarrassment as I answered, "Yes, sir. That's it."

The four men left.

I closed the door behind them. "So, what do you think?"

Ann shook her head. "I don't know. I'm not very hopeful they'll be able to do anything. What can they do? They can't storm the house and risk getting the Walkers killed. They have to be able to get what's-his-name—"

"Dykes."

"Right, Dykes. They have to get him alone, maybe promise his freedom in return for letting the Walkers go. Something like that." Ann came to me. "What I need now is a hug and a drink."

About an hour later, the lieutenant knocked on our door. "Just so you know what's going on, we're going to wait 'til dark and then, as you suggested, we'll go over to the vineyard and enter the back of the Walkers' property from there. I've cleared it with the winery folks—they lock the gate at six but they'll have someone there to let us in. We'll get as close as we can to the house and using a high sensitivity listening device, we'll try to pick up any sounds, conversations and so forth. If we do hear talking, then at least we'll know they're in there. Other than maintain surveillance throughout the night, there's nothing more we would do—too tricky in the dark. However, there is a possibility that someone may come out. Maybe Dykes needs something from the car or if he has the Walkers tied up in the shop, he would probably come out to give 'em food or check on them. You know what I mean? Of course, if he or the girl or anyone does come out, we'll grab 'em. And no, they won't make a sound. Don't worry, we're good. "

Ann said, "That sounds like a great plan. Let's hope someone does come out. Anyway, thanks for telling us about it and good luck."

I patted the lieutenant on the shoulder as he exited the room. "Good luck," I whispered.

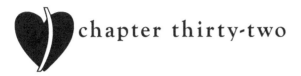

chapter thirty-two

nn sat on the edge of the bed and kicked off her shoes. "I'm
a tired." She lay back, swung her legs onto the bed, cupped
her hands under her head and stared at the ceiling. "What
do you think we should do from this point?"

I sat on the bed and looked down at her. She did look tired,
her forehead wrinkled with worry. "There's nothing we can do
tonight, but I'd like to be out there tomorrow around daybreak,
get to that parking lot by the picnic place and have a look down
at the house. If anything happens, we should be able to see it
and if they get a hold of Dykes, we can get right down there and
check on Edna and Emmett."

"Sounds like a plan, but it's so frustrating being this close
and not being able to do anything right now." She swung her legs
over the edge of the bed and stood. "I'm really hungry, let's grab
something to eat, and I still need that drink. After dinner, let's
get right to bed so we're rested up for tomorrow. Better call the
desk now and leave a wakeup call for—"

"Five? We can be at the vineyard before six, okay?"

"Okay." Ann reached for the phone on the nightstand and
handed it to me. "Call the desk."

Ann and I were wide awake even before the wakeup call. We

washed up and got dressed in a rush. Ann was slipping into her leather jacket and was about to open the door. I said, "Wait a sec. What do you think about the guns? Should we take them?"

Ann turned around and made a face. "I don't know. Would it be legal?"

"I thought you told me that after you took those lessons, the instructor issued you a permit or something. Was it a permit to carry a concealed weapon?"

Ann looked perplexed. She obviously was trying to remember what she did with the permit. "Wait a sec." She reached in her purse and pulled out her wallet. "Here it is. Anyway, that doesn't matter in this situation. If something happens and we have to defend ourselves, I don't think these guys would give us a hard time. Would they?"

"I don't know, but you have the permit although you brought up a good point—if we have to defend ourselves, that's the key." I opened a suitcase and took out the two pistols and a box of ammunition. I loaded Ann's gun with five bullets, closed the cylinder and handed it over. I said, "Put that in your right jacket pocket and see if it fits."

Ann slipped the snub nosed piece in her pocket. "That works." She took some bullets from the box and put them in her left pocket. I gave her a look. "What?" she asked. "It's okay to have loose bullets in my pocket, isn't it?"

"Yes, but I was just thinking, if you can't get the job done with five shots, better not use it."

Ann shot back, "You know, my instructor said something like that." She walked to the door. "Let's go."

I buckled up the shoulder holster, slipped a loaded clip in the gun, holstered it, put on my leather jacket, grabbed the car keys, and together, we walked to the car.

Before getting in the Buick, Ann gave me a long look. "This is going to be okay, isn't it?"

The winery gate was closed but the chain lock was hanging down.

"They must have left it unlocked so the cops could get in and out," Ann observed. She got out of the car and opened the gate, closing it after I drove through.

I turned off the headlights and slowly proceeded up to the further parking lot. I parked and cut the engine. Pocketing the key, I said, "I'm not going to make the same mistake those deputies did in the parking lot and let Dykes get away in this car. Don't think Bea would like that."

"Very funny," Ann countered without humor. She reached back and took the binoculars off the back seat, opened her door then closed it quietly. She walked toward the first row of vines. I walked up behind her. "Should we go through this row or go down a little farther?" she asked.

"This is okay. When we come out, don't walk to the brow of the hill in case one of the cops or even Dykes is looking this way. We need to get down low as we come out of the grapes and take a look through the glasses before we go further."

"Okay. Lead the way."

I entered between two rows of vines and slowly worked my way to the end. I looked to my left and saw the sun was coming up. I whispered, "It's going to be light real soon so get on your belly, stay low and we'll crawl to the edge of the hill and have a look. No talking."

We looked down and scanned the area in back and in front of the house and shop.

Ann put her mouth close to my ear and whispered, "See anything?"

I shook my head. I looked through the binoculars and very slowly checked out the junk-filled area behind the house. I thought I saw a figure lying behind a rusty vintage tractor. I watched for several minutes but I didn't see any movement. If it was one of the cops, he sure was good.

Ann motioned for the glasses. She adjusted the focus and aimed at the side of the house. There were six windows on the north side. As I recalled the layout of the interior, there were two windows on the north wall of the living room, one in the bath room, between the living room and the bedroom, two in the bedroom and one in the little room in back where I had slept. Ann stifled a little cry with her hand.

"What? Did you see something?" I asked in a loud whisper.

She handed the glasses to me. "I think I saw movement in the window, the third one from the right."

"That should be the bathroom." I focused on the window. "Oh! I see a light, might be a flashlight."

"Shhhh," Ann whispered as she stared at the window.

"It is a flashlight... It's bobbing around. Wait a minute, the light went out. What the... The window is being opened...it's open. Someone is coming out head first. Geeze, it's a girl, long hair...can't be Dykes."

Excited and forgetting to whisper, Ann reached for the binoculars, "Give me those..."

I pushed her away with my elbow. "No, I don't want to lose sight of her. Okay, she wiggled through and fell on the ground. She's on the ground. Okay, she's up and running this way. Looks like she hurt her leg, she's limping."

Someone came running out of the shadows and grabbed the girl. I couldn't believe it. *Where the hell did he come from?* We heard a muffled shriek that stopped instantly.

Ann was pulling on my arm. She could see the action below. "Is that one of our guys who grabbed her?"

"Yeah. He's carrying her around the back of the house. No, he's heading for that piece of junk, back over there." I pointed and handed over the glasses.

"There's another guy there," Ann reported. "He's got the girl now. That's gotta be the girl we saw at the movie." She handed the glasses back to me. "So where do you suppose—"

Just then, I saw a figure running up the hill toward the vineyard on a slanting path east of our position. "Jesus Christ, it's Dykes! Where the hell did he come from?" I trained the binoculars on the running man. No doubt about it, it was Dykes and he was carrying a weapon of some sort. I took a good look and recognized it. It was an AK-47 with a long curved clip attached.

I reached in my pocket and took hold of the car keys. "Here, take the keys, run up there, get in the car and drive away."

"Out of the vineyard?"

" Yes, of course. Now move it!"

"What about you? You aren't going to do something crazy, are you?" Ann was insistent. "You'd better go with me. Let the cops handle this."

"Don't worry, I'll be fine. I need to run down there and tell them where Dykes is heading."

Ann pleaded, "Please, Rick, come with me, please?"

Some motion from below caught my eye I turned and saw two of the cops heading for us, guns at the ready.

Ann screamed, "Oh my God."

"Don't move." I slowly stood, put my hands over my head and waved them back and forth. I yelled, "It's Rick and Ann, take it easy and watch where you're pointing those guns."

The two men stopped. They immediately recognized us and

lowered their weapons. "Did you see him? He was running this way," one of them said.

"Yeah, we saw him—he's headed toward the vineyard. Better watch out when you get to the top of the hill. There's a lot of cover for him in all those grapes and he's got an AK-47 with a big clip."

One of the men pulled a walkie-talkie from a belt clip and told the other team members what was going on. I saw the black Ford come roaring down the drive and come to a skidding stop in front of the house. It was the lieutenant. He went running up the steps and when he realized the door was locked, lifted his leg and gave a mighty kick. The door came apart and the officer ran in.

I said to Ann, "Come on, we need to get in there and see if they're all right."

We bolted down the hill, ran across the yard and entered the house.

"Lieutenant," I yelled. "Where are you?"

"In here, the room in back. The Walkers are in here," he shouted back.

We hurried to the back of the house and entered the room. Emmett and Edna were sitting in kitchen chairs, their hands and legs tied to the chairs. Both of them were gagged with dish towels.

The lieutenant was untying Edna. "Good that you two are here. Can you take care of the Walkers? I gotta get on up to the vineyard and help the squad."

"Sure," I said, "go ahead. We'll take care of them. And watch out—he's got an AK-47." I undid Edna's gag and then pulled off the one on Emmett. Both of them started talking at once.

Edna moaned, "Glory be ta God, am I glad ta see you."

Emmett said, "Tell ya what. I thought it was gonna be over

for us." As soon as both were free, they stood, holding each other up as they embraced.

Ann came over to me and we too hugged each other. She had tears in her eyes as she murmured, "I didn't think it would end this well." She took hold of Emmett and Edna's hands saying, "But you two are okay now. That guy thinks he'll get away but they'll get him one way or another."

Emmett added, "I hope they kill the son of a bitch."

I asked, "Tell us about that girl. We saw her climb out the window and start to run but one of the cops grabbed her right away."

Ann added, "Was she his girlfriend?"

"Hell no," Edna and Emmett said in unison. Edna explained, "I reckon they met someplace up north—"

"Salinas," Emmett added.

"Thas right, Salinas," Edna said, "Anyways, we think he made her drive him down here—"

Emmett broke in, "That's her car, the Nash—I think they hid it in the shop. She was plumb 'fraid to death of that guy. He kep' her tied up in a chair mos' of the time—"

"'Cept when he wanted her," Edna said, "Then he'd pull her into the bedroom and we could hear her crying and screaming. When he brought her back, she'd be all messed up with bruises on her face and arms. It was pit'full."

Emmett shook his head and looked at the floor, "Sure was. Early this mornin' she said she had ta go to the toilet and he untied her an' took her in there. I'll bet thas the winder she got outa."

"Yes, it was," I said.

"Speaking of bathroom," Ann said, "I sure could use one. I've had to go for the last hour. I about lost it when I saw those two cops running toward us with their guns aimed our way. I'll be right back." Ann left but came back at once. "That toilet is all plugged up."

"I know, I shudda tole ya," Emmett said. "I don't know what they put in there but thas what we've had ta deal with—"

Edna interrupted. "They's a toilet out in the shop. It's the door right past the sink on the left side. Use that one."

Ann grabbed her purse and hurried out. I heard the sound of her boots as she ran down the porch steps.

We wandered into the kitchen. Edna said, "Land O' Goshen, look at the mess that man made." She opened a cupboard and took out a can of coffee, washed out the coffee pot and filled it with water. Emmett and I were just taking seats at the kitchen table when we heard a noise behind us.

"Hold it right there. Don't anybody make a God-damn move. You, lady, sit down."

I slowly turned my head in the direction of the voice. Of course, I knew who it had to be but how the hell did he get away?

As if reading my mind, Dykes growled, "Them fuckin' cops think they're so fuckin' smart. Well, who's the smart one now?" He waved his weapon around. "It sure ain't none of you."

I looked at Dykes and he stared back. "Who the hell are you? You a cop?" He aimed the weapon at me.

Emmett shouted, "He ain't no cop—he's a friend o' ours come by ta see us, thas all."

Dykes spat out the words. "Shut the fuck up, ole man. If I want any shit outa you, I'll knock it outa you." Dykes turned back to me, "So you're just a friend. Well, friend, you and me is gonna take a little walk out to my car and if your cop buddies show up you better tell 'em to lay off or you're a dead man—savvy? Now, get them hands up high an' keep 'em up. Get up and walk out that door nice and slow." He addressed the Walkers, "You two make a move and your *friend* will get a back-full of lead. Got it?"

I stood and walked through the front door. I went down the steps and turned left and continued walking very slowly toward the shop. I said in a rather loud voice, "Listen, Dykes, why don't you just give yourself up? The cops have seen your car. How far do you think you'll get?"

Dykes hissed, "You just shut the hell up and walk."

We walked past the north end of the shop. The Nash was parked inside near the south wall. Suddenly, a deafening shot rang out. I heard a cry from Dykes and spun around. Dykes was on his knees, the gun was lying on the ground next to him. He reached for it.

I pulled my gun from the shoulder holster under my jacket and aimed it at him. "Don't touch that gun," I yelled.

Ann came out of the shop, pistol in hand. Without a moment's hesitation she walked up to Dykes, aimed her gun at his head and fired. He fell on his side and was still. She looked at me and said, "We won't be seeing him in court."

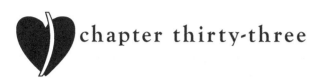 chapter thirty-three

e dna and Emmett came running out of the house, but slowed down to approach cautiously when they saw the body lying at our feet.

"Holy Mother of God!" Emmett exclaimed. "What the hell happened here?"

Edna, with her hand to her mouth and a horrified look on her face, was speechless. Dykes' head did not present a pretty picture.

Ann still had the gun in her hand.

I said, "Better let me have that." I put the gun in my jacket pocket, took her arm and said, "Let's move away from here." We walked to the house and I sat down on the porch steps. The others did the same.

Emmett asked me for details and I told him exactly what happened, including pulling my gun after Ann had fired the first shot and Dykes was on his knees trying to grab his gun.

"So where is your gun now?" Emmett asked.

I pulled back my jacket revealing the shoulder holster. "Right here."

Emmett said, "Take that damn thing off and give it ta me. Them deputies don't need ta know you was armed."

I hesitated but Emmett insisted. "Use yer head, fer God's

sake. If they know you had him in your sights before Ann killed him, then she might be in trouble. Ya unnerstan'? You wouldn't have been in danger and she had no cause to kill 'em. So, give me that gun and I'll take care of it."

I took off my jacket, removed the shoulder holster and handed it to him. Emmett went at once into the shop where I presume he hid it.

Ann was shivering. The enormity of what had happened was finally hitting her. I sat beside her and held her tightly. "It's okay, baby, you saved my life. You did the right thing. If he'd got his gun up and pulled the trigger—that's an automatic, like a machine gun. He wouldn't need to aim. If he just pointed in my direction and fired, at least one of the bullets would have found me. Believe me, you did the right thing."

Ann murmured, "I hope so."

Edna added, "Of course ya did, honey. Nobody's gonna fault ya fer pertecting yer man."

Emmett rejoined us and took a seat. "Did them deputies ever see you with that gun?"

"No. I just put it on this morning before we left the motel."

"All right then. You don't have a gun, not here anyways, and that's that." Emmett stood. "Here they come. 'Bout time too."

The cops arrived and stood around the inert body of the late Arnold Dykes. One of the deputies rolled the body over and took a good look at the entry wound in Dykes left side. The lieutenant stood next to him observing, then came over to where we were sitting.

"Okay, then. Our man is dead and I don't imagine anyone's particularly sad about that. So, who is going to provide the details?"

"I guess I will," I said. I began the story from the point where the lieutenant left us in the house with Emmett and Edna. I told him about Ann going to the toilet in the shop and us being at the kitchen table when Dykes snuck up and pointed his AK-47 at us. I paused and watched as two deputies worked Dykes into a body bag. They carried him into the shop.

The lieutenant also watched. When the deputies came out of the shop, he said to me, "Okay, Dykes had the gun on you, then what'd he do?"

"He told Edna to sit down—she was standing at the counter—and he asked Emmett who I was and Emmett said I was a friend. Dykes didn't believe it; he thought I was a cop. He warned the Walkers not to move away from the table, then he told me to put my hands up and walk out the front door. He said that he was going to get the car and make a run for it. I knew Ann was in the shop and had probably heard what was going on in the house. As we walked by the shop I told Dykes to give up—that he wouldn't get very far. I said it in a loud voice so that Ann would hear it. I knew Ann had her pistol with her and—"

"How'd you know that?"

"Because we discussed whether she should take it before we left the motel. I loaded it and gave it to her. She took lessons and has a permit, so yeah, I thought it be a good idea for her to have it so she could protect herself if something happened."

"Okay, so Dykes is behind you with his AK-47, Ann is in the shop, sees you two walk by, then what?"

"Next thing I knew, I heard a shot, heard Dykes scream. I turned around and he was on his knees holding his side with his left hand. He looked at me and started to pick up his gun when Ann came out of the shop, saw that Dykes was raising his gun. She got close and shot him in the head."

The lieutenant asked, "That's it?"

I looked at him, "What do you mean, that's it? What else is there? The man is dead, period."

The lieutenant addressed Ann. "Is that about the way it went down?"

Ann nodded her head and simply said, "Yes."

"I see. In other words, if I understand your actions," he said, "You saw Dykes raise his gun and aim it at Mr. Elkins and thinking he would shoot and kill him, you decided on the spur of the moment without really thinking about, to shoot Dykes before he could shoot Elkins . Is that about the size of it?"

Ann looked at him with just a hint of surprise. "Yes, that's exactly what happened."

"And that's the way you'll tell it when you make a statement for the record?"

"Yes, sir," Ann replied. "I'll tell it just like you just said."

I couldn't help but smile but only for a second. What the lieutenant had just done was create a scenario that would no doubt become evidence that would justify Ann's actions and forestall the possibility of her being accused of manslaughter. I was thinking he was as anxious as we were to close this case with a straightforward set of answers about how and why Dykes was killed.

A deputy informed the lieutenant that a team was on the way and the coroner's office had dispatched an ambulance to retrieve the body.

The lieutenant turned to Ann, "I'll need your pistol. It'll be returned to you after all the paperwork has been completed."

I took Ann's gun from my pocket. "I took it from her after the—"

"That's fine." He called to one of the deputies to bring an evidence bag.

When the bag arrived, I dropped the gun in and the bag was sealed.

"I can't say for sure, but I think it will be necessary for both of you to appear at the coroner's inquest. However, this is a pretty straightforward case with no loose ends that I can think of, but you never know. The deputy will take down all your personal information and then you're free to go. I want to thank you very much for all your help on this case. I didn't expect it to end this way, but I have to say, I'm not unhappy about the outcome." He shook my hand, then Ann's. "Goodbye and good luck to the both of you."

He walked over to the Walkers. "We'll need you two to come down to the station in San Luis Obispo and give us the whole story of your imprisonment and everything else that happened from the time Dykes first arrived at your home until now. Would you like us to provide transportation?"

Emmett said, "No, we kin manage ta git down there. Jes draw us a little map an' we'll find it. I suppose you want us ta come on down now."

"That would be best," the lieutenant said. "While everything is fresh in your mind. By the way, did either of you actually see Ann shoot Dykes?"

Edna answered, "Naw, he was on the ground and I guess dead whenever we come outta the house."

"Thas right," Emmett answered. "Tell ya what. If the girl hadn't a shot the bastard, I sure as hell woulda. He was a no good, mis'ble son of a bitch."

The lieutenant allowed a smile to spread across his face as he walked with one of the deputies to his car and drove off. The other deputies remained, waiting for the coroner's people to show up.

Back inside, Edna filled the coffee pot and lit a front burner on the stove with a stick match. The four of us sat down at the kitchen table.

Suddenly, Emmett jumped up and hurried out of the room. We all jumped.

Ann cried, "Now what?"

Emmett came back with his 12 gauge double barrel shot gun. He sat down at the table with the gun lying across his lap. "The next uninvited guy ta come inta this house is gonna git his se'f an ass full a buckshot."

Emmett unplugged the toilet in the bathroom. "That was a God-awful mess," he exclaimed as he exited the back door with a bucket, plunger and mop. He returned a few minutes later and said, "As things turned out, we're damn lucky that commode was plugged up."

"How's that?" I asked.

"Well, jes think about it." Emmett gave me a look that suggested I actually think about it. He realized no answer was forthcoming, so he provided it. "Purdy simple. If that toilet had been workin', Ann wouldn't have had ta use the one in the shop and that woulda changed everything." He puffed up his chest like he'd just let us in on the meaning of life. "If Annie Oakley here wasn't right there ta where she could get a bead on that guy, I'm thinkin' you'd be dead fer sure and maybe the rest of us to boot. Ya never know what some little thing will do ta change yer life."

Edna clapped her hands. "I say amen ta that. By golly, honey, you done figured that one out jest perfec."

"Wow! By God, Emmett, you're exactly right." I shook my head in wonder. "A little thing like a plugged up toilet changed the entire course of today's events."

The Walkers cleaned up and put on their Sunday best for the trip to San Luis Obispo. Before leaving, Edna gave Ann a huge hug. "You saved our lives taday an' don't you be worryin' none 'bout killing that man. He deserved it. If you'd been shy or even stopped fer a second ta think 'bout it, he probably woulda killed both you and Rick. So jes promise me ya won't worry yer purdy little head 'bout none o' what happened today. It all come out jes fine 'cause you did what ya hadda do. God bless ya and I know he's gonna forgive ya too."

Emmett shook my hand and hugged Ann. "Edna's got it right. You did what you hadda do. Don't fret 'bout it. An' remember we love ya." Emmett turned to me, "You gonna head back up north taday?"

"Yes sir. We got to get on our bikes and get back to LA. I got a trip on Monday morning and I don't dare miss it, if I want to keep my job."

Ann chimed in, "I've got to be at work Monday morning, too, or I'm going to have a lot people mad at me, and after all that's happened, I sure don't need that. Don't worry. Next time Rick and I have some time off, we'll head up here again and we'll all have a good time. Okay?"

The Walkers headed for their pickup in the shop and we went in the opposite direction, climbing the hill and walking through the rows of grapes to Bea's car.

I backed out of the parking space and drove slowly toward the vineyard entrance. When I stopped at the road, Ann looked back toward the Walkers' house then turned to me. "I don't ever want to come back here again, ever."

I pulled onto the road, shifted into second and glanced her way. "You mean the winery?"

"No. I don't ever want to come back to this area, especially Walkers' place. I just couldn't deal with it."

I shifted into third gear, reached over and squeezed Ann's hand. "I understand."

I drove to our motel in Cambria, where we packed up, I paid the bill and we took off for Monterey. Our idyllic vacation was definitely over.

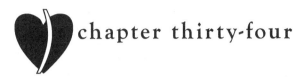
chapter thirty-four

killing Arnold Dykes had a profound effect on Ann. I certainly could understand it. When she took the second shot that blew out a part of Dykes' skull, I remember how she just stood there looking at him after he tumbled over on his side. It really was a horrible sight and one I'll never forget. But for Ann, it was more than that. It was, I think, the realization that she had killed a human being whether she'd been justified or not. That and the visual, which she later told me recurred in her nightmares, was intense. I noticed a gradual change in her personality. She didn't seem to be the happy, light-hearted girl she had been before our trip to Monterey. I suggested she seek counseling. She told me she was seeing a therapist but I wasn't really sure she was.

We were called upon to testify at a coroner's inquest a couple weeks after the incident. Ann was terribly worried that she would, as she put it, "mess it up." However, at the hearing she did fine, telling it just as the lieutenant had expressed it. But driving back to LA, she couldn't stop weeping.

I didn't know what to do or say when she said that she was having a rough time at work and might have to quit before she got fired. I told her again and again, as we all had the day it happened, that she'd had no choice, she did the right thing, she saved my life and probably her life and the lives of the Walkers. But none of these rationales persuaded her to let it go.

Meanwhile, I had my life to deal with and that included taking on the responsibilities of being a captain, the left seat pilot of a very powerful airplane. I was responsible for the lives of many others, and flying a high tech plane like the Jetstar required a great deal of concentration. A pilot can't have his mind on other things and maintain the vigilance that piloting an airplane demands.

My first trip as captain was on the Monday morning after our return to LA. I was worried sick about Ann but simply had to put it out of my mind as co-pilot Gene Parrino and I did the required walk around and went through the startup check list. I had been out of the cockpit for over two weeks, plus being in the left seat was a bit of a struggle but I said and did all the right things and Gene gave the correct replies and made all the correct settings and the stewardess, Carlotta Menzalora, did her thing. After the passengers got on board, the door was secured, the tower gave us clearance to taxi and we moved to the runway.

I said to Gene, "I guess this is the first of many trips you and I are going to take."

"Yeah, I guess so. Probably be a long time before there's another left seat vacant."

"Oh, you never know..." Ground control called our number. I released the brakes and off we went into the wild blue yonder. Would you believe it? That's what popped into my head until Gene called rotate speed. I eased back on the yoke and we were airborne. On course and at altitude, I gave control to Gene. I put on my cap and said, "I'll check on the passengers. Be right back."

Our eight passengers were chatting away as I entered the cabin. All conversation ceased as they looked in my direction.

"Good morning," I said in a cheery voice. "I'm Captain Richard Elkins, your driver. Eugene Parrino is the co-pilot—I think he's driving the plane now." I looked out a window. "The plane seems to be level so I guess he's doing okay. The lovely lady sitting in the back is here to provide you with whatever you need, be it a drink, a snack or her recipe for great cannoli. Her name is Carlotta Menzalora."

Several passengers turned their heads and gave Carlotta a smile.

"The weather ahead looks pretty good so I think the ride will be a smooth one. Nonetheless, as I'm sure you already know, it's a good idea to keep your seat belt fastened. You're on a Lockheed Jetstar, the fastest and most advanced plane in the Standard Oil fleet." I glanced out the window again. "From the look of it, I'd say we're doing about 440 knots, that's about 500 miles an hour." That remark generated a few raised eyebrows. "The trip to Bartlesville should take us a little under three hours, so enjoy the ride." I tipped my cap to a smattering of applause and returned to the cockpit.

"Everybody happy back there?" Gene asked as I took off my cap and slid into the seat.

"Seem to be. The stew is a gal I've seen before but never had her on a trip."

"Yeah. Carlotta. She's the sister of Mario Menzalora—he's on the ramp crew—crew chief."

"Right," I replied. "I thought I recognized the name. It's not a name you hear a lot."

"Their father is an ex Air Corps flyer. He was born in Italy. His parents came to America when he was just a kid but he still has an accent. He always calls Mario, Marriano. He's got some crazy nickname for Carlotta but I can't remember what it is."

ATC called our number and advised they were handing us

off. Gene acknowledged, I made the course adjustments and Gene resumed his patter. It was one question after another while I was trying to get used to flying the left seat. It was disconcerting, especially after having flown with Terry, who was the antithesis of Gene when it came to cockpit chat.

Carlotta came in and asked if we'd like something to drink and eat. Funny or weird, I'm not sure which, I had a flash back to my days flying for Frontier Airlines—the Denver-Durango route and a stewardess who asked if we'd like some coffee. That stewardess was Angie who later became my wife. That sudden recall triggered an emotion that I thought was buried deep in my consciousness and I'll admit it, my eyes suddenly filled with tears.

Gene said, "Hi, Carly. Just some coffee, please. So, how are you, and how's your dad these days?"

"I'm fine and Dad's the same as ever, just older," she replied then addressed me, "What about you, Captain? Can I bring you something?"

Without looking at her, I asked for coffee and a Danish.

"Coming right up," she said and returned to the cabin.

Gene said, "She's a sweet girl, nice family, twin girls. They must be around six or seven by now. Her ex-husband flies right seat for U.S. Steel."

The trip to Bartlesville was uneventful. By the time we landed, I was feeling fairly comfortable in the left seat. One of the men, John something-or-other, was in charge of the passenger group. He advised that I should be ready to leave at four. The passengers disembarked and got into a couple of cars waiting on the tarmac and off they went. Gene arranged for the fuel truck, I went into the GA office to take care of the paperwork and Carlotta busied herself tidying up the cabin. When these chores were completed, the three of us walked over to the airport terminal building and had lunch.

My two companions, who obviously had known each other for some time, kept up a lively conversation. I learned, for example, that Gene had flown commercial with Carlotta's father, Anthony, years ago. They were great friends with Gene, who was a frequent visitor to the Menzalora home. I mostly listened and observed. Carlotta was very animated when she spoke, moving her hands actively as many Italians do. I guessed her to be in her mid-thirties. She was small but certainly not petite, five foot five, with black hair, large brown eyes, a smallish nose, nice mouth and full figure that was attractive—some might say, sexy. Her best features were her quick smile that produced large dimples, her lilting laugh, and the timbre of her voice, which was a little unusual yet very pleasant to the ear.

Gene Parrino, on the other hand, was perhaps the antithesis of his friend's daughter. As I said, he was at least ten years my senior, which would make him close to fifty. He wasn't really overweight, but he was rotund with a bit of a belly, and he was only 5'-6." Gene's head was large or so it seemed, and one might have guessed he was a wrestler when he was younger. Gene was quick to laugh and equally quick to scowl. All in all, an interesting kind of guy, and from what I observed during our three-hour flight, he knew his way around a cockpit, no doubt about that.

"I'm sorry, Captain," Carlotta said. "Seems that Gene and I have hogged the conversation. Would you mind sharing your background with us?"

I looked at her smiling face. Was this a beautiful face? Beautiful like Ann? No, but a pretty face. Maybe cute was a better word. She was cute and bright.

"Captain?" she repeated. "Do you mind telling us about yourself?"

I think I might have blushed. "Sorry, my mind drifted off. By the way, call me Rick."

Carlotta said, "Okay, but only if you call me Carly."

"Sounds like a deal. So, let's see," I pulled back my shirt sleeve and looked at my watch. "Yes, we have time to hear my life's story."

Gene and Carlotta laughed and then I commenced to give them a thumbnail sketch of my history, going all the way back to my Navy days and ending with my engagement the previous week in Monterey. I didn't say a thing about what happened at Cambria. The whole deal didn't take more than ten minutes.

Gene said, "So you and your girlfriend ride motorcycles all over the place? That's sounds like fun."

"It is fun. I can't explain it exactly, but when you're on a bike, it's a lot different than riding in a car. Everything is more intense, the sights, the smells, the feeling of motion, wind, and every little bump, it's..." I laughed. "Sorry, but I get carried away. I guess you have to experience it to appreciate what I'm talking about."

Carlotta said, "My brother Mario rides a motorcycle, has for years. When he was a kid he kept pestering my parents for one but they said it was too dangerous and wouldn't let him have one or even ride on the back of one."

Gene joined in, "I remember Tony telling Mario, 'If you want to kill yourself, get a gun and shoot yourself, it's quicker and less painful than going down on a motorcycle.' His mother, Carmella, felt the same way."

The words *get a gun and shoot* made me shudder. I mean I physically shook for a second or two as I had immediate recall of Dykes lying on the ground with part of his head gone.

Gene and Carlotta noticed my sudden movement. Carlotta

touched my arm and said, "Something wrong? Are you all right?"

I smiled as I shook off the feeling. "Sure, I'm fine—just a weird response to something Gene said. Never mind, I'm fine."

Gene and Carlotta exchanged glances but said nothing.

We were ready to "light the fuse" when the first car returned. About ten minutes later, the second car pulled up, the passengers boarded and we rolled to the taxiway. I asked Gene, "Want to fly this leg?"

"Sure. Thanks."

Gene greased the landing at Houma, Louisiana.

I looked over at him as he taxied to our parking spot. "Nice job. You've got the touch."

The passengers off-loaded, we secured the plane and hopped a cab for town. I should mention that usually when we only had a few passengers, especially if they were some of the top execs, they would invite the pilots to join them for dinner. In this case the passengers were field guys whose job it was to fix things or get on-site information.

We checked into the motel the Transportation Department had arranged for us—we each had our own room—having agreed we'd meet in the lobby in an hour. This gave us plenty of time to change out of our uniforms, shower and get dressed in civvies. It also gave me time to call Ann. The phone rang for quite a while. I was about to hang up when she answered in a low, tired sounding voice.

"Hello."

"Hi, darling," I said brightly, "How are you?"

"Okay, I guess."

"You sound funny."

"I just woke up...I took a nap. Where are you?"

"Houma, Louisiana. We just got here about an hour ago."

"Did the trip go all right?" Her voice rose an octave. "Oh, and how was it sitting in the left seat, El Cap-e-tan Ricardo?"

I laughed, "Good. It was very good. No problems. And how was your day?"

There was a long period of silence before Ann answered. "I woke up this morning and just wasn't feeling good so I didn't go to work."

My response was tentative. "You weren't feeling good? What's the matter?"

"I don't know. I didn't sleep very well and I woke up with a terrible headache..."

"Did you take something for it?"

"Yes, but it didn't do much good and so I made coffee and a scrambled egg." Silence. "I don't know what's wrong with me but I don't seem to have any energy and..." More silence.

"And you're thinking about what happened at Walkers', right?"

"I'm trying not to think about that. I keep telling myself it wasn't my fault. I had to do it. He would have killed you."

"That's exactly right. You had to do it and by doing it you saved all of our lives. Think of yourself as a hero because that's what you are—everybody says so."

"I know, I know," she said wearily. "But you and I know different, don't we?"

"No, we don't," I replied in a stern voice. "No! You did what you had to do to save me and yourself. It's what anyone in that same position would have done." I paused and thought about it before articulating it. "Listen, Ann, you did exactly what your shooting teacher said you should do—remember?"

"Of course I remember." I heard her whimper, "I never should have listened to him. I could have just shot him in the arm so he'd drop the gun and—"

I broke in. "And you would have seen him in court and likely you'd be charged with something and sent to jail. You think that would have been a better outcome? Hell no. Besides you don't know he would have dropped the gun, he might have swung it around and put a dozen bullets in you."

"Rick, I know you're right." Silence, then a deep inhale. "I know it but I can't seem to be able to convince myself. But, darling, I'm sure that eventually, I'll be okay and we can get back to where we were in Monterey. Right?"

"Right. Now, have you had anything else to eat today besides that egg?"

"No, but I was thinking of going over to that Chinese place and getting something."

"Okay, do that. I'm going to dinner with the crew but I'll call you when I get back, okay?"

"Sure. Have a nice dinner. Don't worry about me—I'll be fine. Call me later. I love you."

"I love you, too. I'll call you later. Goodbye." I hung up the phone and sat there thinking about our conversation. It was depressing and I hated the feeling. A knock on my door pulled me out of my reverie.

"Hey. Rick, ready to go down?" It was Gene.

I thought, *Go down? Hell, I was already down.*

chapter thirty-five

he December 1963 holidays found me flying the Esso big-wigs here, there and yonder not for business reasons so much as for holiday fun. While it's true they almost always invited Ann to come along—there were always plenty of extra seats—it still wasn't what we needed for our relationship. And frequently, Ann turned down the chance to go along. Before Dykes (we referred to it as "B. D."), she would have jumped at the chance to travel with me but now she was ambivalent not only about taking trips, but about almost everything. We would go to a nice place for dinner and we hardly spoke, she picked at her food, or she would drink too much and then I couldn't shut her up. It was wearing me down. Yet at times she seemed her old self and we'd talk and make love and I'd be fooled into thinking she was getting better. On the few trips she did take with me on the airplane, we had a good time. I think the change of venue and scenery pushed her bad thoughts back a bit. But it was a roller coaster ride and I never knew for sure how each episode was going to play out.

Because of all the hours I racked up during the holidays, I took a week off in early January. I went over to Ann's place for dinner one evening—we were still living in two locations—and Ann had prepared a very nice dinner of prime rib and several side dishes. We were just finishing the main course when I smelled something burning. Ann smelled it too and jumped up, ran into the kitchen. She yelled, "God damn it!"

I jumped up and ran into the kitchen. The smoke was pouring from the oven. Ann grabbed a pot holder, yanked open the door, and slid out the oven rack. We both stared down at a pie plate and a blackened mess that I assumed was a really over-done fruit pie.

"Shit, son of a bitch," she shrieked. She opened a drawer, pulled out another pot holder, got a hold of the pie plate and threw it in the sink. When she turned on the water, the thing smoked up the room. Ann threw the pot holders across the room, sank down in a chair and began to wail.

I quickly knelt down beside her chair and put my arm around her. "It's okay, honey. It's okay. Come on, it's no big deal."

She turned her head and buried it in my chest. "It's no good. I can't do anything right anymore." Sob. "It's just..." Sob. "It's just too much." She looked up at me with tear-filled eyes. "What's wrong with me?" Her crying increased to jolting sobs. She was having trouble catching her breath.

I took hold of her and pulled her out of the chair. "Take it easy. Let's just walk a little. Take a breath, come on, breathe." We walked into the living room. I put my arms around her and gave her a quick but fairly hard squeeze. She gulped air and began rapid breathing. I walked her to the bedroom and was about to pick her up and lay her on the bed when she began retching. I got her into the bathroom and over to the toilet just as she threw up.

I spent the night in bed with her and early the next morning I made some hot tea with lemon and honey and insisted that she drink it. We were sitting at the kitchen table. She was sipping the hot tea, and I sat there watching her.

Ann set the cup down, turned to me with no trace of sparkle in those wonderful green eyes and said, "I'm so sorry, Rick. I know I'm making your life miserable and you don't need that." She twisted the engagement ring off of her finger and handed to me. "I'm setting you free. There'll be no marriage. You don't need to be married to a lunatic—"

"Wait a minute, you're no—"

She held up her hand, "Shhh. Don't say anything. You've said it all in the past and it just doesn't work. I'm checking myself in to a psychiatric facility. My doctor says it's probably the only way I'm ever going to get my mind back."

I sat back, speechless. I hated the idea but at the same time I knew I had to embrace it. Ann couldn't go on like this without help—real, professional help. I told her so. She seemed relieved that I wasn't giving her an argument.

She called the doctor who said he would take care of everything. He told her to get her life organized today and be at the facility at nine the next morning. I stayed with her all day. We even went to dinner and she seemed more relaxed, more like her old self. I shared her bed that night and held her close.

I drove her to the facility. I carried her suitcase to the door, set it down and kissed her. I reached in my pocket and pulled out her diamond ring, took her left hand and slid the ring on her finger. "You don't ever want to be without this. I love you, you love me, and when you're better, we are going to be married just like we planned."

Ann gave me a weak smile. "You may be a goofball, but you're a good guy and I love you."

I opened the door, she picked up her suitcase and disappeared inside. I looked through the window and gazed down the long empty hallway wondering if the old Ann would ever walk out.

chapter thirty-six

egardless of what was going on in my little world, the world beyond was spinning away, and 1963, the year just ended, had its share of apocalyptic events. I suppose bad news is tempered by how it touches you personally. The Kennedy assassination, while a national tragedy, didn't impact my life nearly so much as did the killing of Arnold Dykes.

1964 rolled around and more of the same. Our forces attacked North Vietnam, which changed the dynamic of that war and affected thousands of young men—and the entire country—but I was too busy worrying about Ann and flying an airplane to be much concerned with any of it.

The escalation of the war and the demands of the military certainly had an impact on the oil industry. We were not only flying the execs all over the place, but frequently we'd be ferrying technicians and field people to various oil field locations in which Esso had an interest. During the summer and fall of 1964, we were all busy.

In late May, all the pilots, along with the ancillary departments, were called to a meeting with the heads of the Flight Department and several company execs. We needed to retire some of the older planes and replace them with aircraft that could operate out of locations with short runways and primitive facilities.

One of the pilots asked, "Are you talking about unpaved runways?"

"Possibly, and maybe not as long as you are comfortable with," was the response. "That's why we've asked you pilots, maintenance folks, and others who would be involved, to this meeting. We need your expertise to learn how best to accomplish what we need to do, that is get into locations that are something less than ideal."

There was a lot of murmuring among the pilots. The exec continued, "The Flight Department will set up another meeting with you people in the near future. I want you pilots to come to that meeting with recommendations for new aircraft that will fit the bill. With short runways, we'll obviously need aircraft with lower landing speeds and shorter take-off distances. You other folks should be prepared to bring ideas and suggestions about what we will need to do to make these outlying fields...air facilities, operational. I think you know what I'm talking about. Now, do any of you have questions?"

There certainly were questions from all of the departments. The pilots mainly wanted to know what the maximum loads might be if planes were configured for freight and, if for passengers, how many seats.

Gene Parrino asked, "Will we be flying into any areas where an armed conflict is taking place or is likely to erupt?"

His question was answered with just two words, "Absolutely not!" The sighs of relief were palpable. The meeting adjourned and we commenced doing our homework.

Throughout the summer and fall when I wasn't actually in the air, I was doing research with all the aircraft manufacturers, trying to learn as much as I could about what they were offering now or, if in development, when the plane would be certified. It certainly didn't give me much time to think about anything else;

however, I saw Ann every chance I could, which sadly wasn't all that often.

During some visits she seemed a little better, but on others, maybe not. On the days when we'd just sit together with Ann saying very little, I'd leave the hospital terribly depressed. Lying in bed at night, I'd feel so lonely and desperate to have her by my side. When I was flying, I tried hard not to think about her and concentrate on what I was doing. Talking with the co-pilot, usually Gene, about the type of new equipment we'd recommend kept my mind off of Ann and that helped. But I couldn't help but wonder if the love of my life, my motorcycle buddy, my lover, my companion, my friend would ever return.

At the company meeting in September, the plane most favored by the group was the Grumman Gulfstream G-159, usually called the G1. Powered by Rolls Royce Dart twin turbo-prop engines, this aircraft was less expensive to operate and maintain, had lower landing speeds, and could take off and land on dirt-packed runways. Typically, the plane carried eight to twelve passengers and two crew, it cruised at 350 mph (not nearly so fast as the Jetstar), had a range of 2,500 miles, a 33,600 foot ceiling and a rate of climb of 1,900 ft/min.

Alvin Conley, another Jetstar captain, and I were directed to fly to the Grumman factory in Bethpage, New York, and check it out. After flying with one of Grumman's pilots and making a number of landings and take-offs, Al and I decided the G1 was certainly a plane the company should consider, and we so reported at a meeting in December. There was some talk about three other pilots and I taking G1 simulator certification but for the moment, the moment being mid-February, nothing was done. Frankly, even though the G1 was a dandy ship and fun to fly, I really didn't want any part of that program because, in addition to the time away from LA to train, I knew that pilots flying that plane would be spending a lot of time away from California.

I had to take some time off and, even though it was unusually cold for California, I decided I'd take the bike for a run up to Cambria to see how Edna and Emmett were doing. Before I left, I visited with Ann but didn't say anything to her about going to Cambria. I also took that opportunity to have a chat with Dr. Wilhelm, the doctor in charge of her care.

While what he told me was supposed to be encouraging, in truth it wasn't all that great. He said they needed some sort of a "breakthrough" therapy or an event that would "let her understand that killing Dykes, while not okay per se, was in fact a necessary act given the circumstances, and should not be an event that required remorse or self-recrimination."

"Suppose, Doctor," I proposed, "I was to take her, perhaps with you or one her therapists, back to the place where the shooting took place. She would see the two other people whose lives she saved living a normal life. She would see the place where the shooting took place is nothing more than a field—obviously with no sign of what happened—just a field of grass and weeds, and everything and everybody connected to that incident was going about their normal lives without remorse or problems. So if everyone involved is fine, there's no reason for her not to be." I paused and gave him a questioning look. "I'm not trying to play doctor, but what about it? Could something like that help her, or is that too simplistic?"

Dr. Wilhelm smiled and made a most important point. "Everyone, as you say, is not the shooter. Only Ann holds that position. However, you pose a good question, Mr. Elkins. I need to think about it and talk it over with staff." He tapped his pen on the desk and gazed for a moment into space. "Of course it could go the other way. She may look at the place where it happened and—"

I cut in, "Go nuts."

"I wouldn't put it just like that, but it could have an adverse effect. At any rate, I'm not ruling it out. I'll let you know. How's that?"

"Perfect. I'm going to go to Cambria tomorrow and see how everything is going with the Walkers. I guess I should make sure neither of them has gone loco over the shooting before we take Ann up there."

Dr. Wilhelm laughed. "Gone loco?"

"You know what I mean." He nodded and I continued, "I'll be back Sunday afternoon. You can call me at my home number—your office has it. If I'm not there, leave a message and I'll get back to you."

Saturday I got up early, ate some breakfast, packed a few items of clothing in my saddlebags, and stepped out into a bright and windless morning. I was walking to the carport when I heard Nancy calling from her second floor balcony.

"Wait a minute, will ya? I'll be right down."

I secured the saddlebags to the Harley and was pushing it out of the carport when she arrived.

"Where ya goin'?"

"Up north—Cambria. Want to jump on and go along?"

"Are you kiddin' me? I wouldn't go from here to the corner on that thing."

"Humppf. Very well then, you can't go." I got on the bike and kicked the start pedal. It didn't start.

Nancy put her hand on my arm. "Wait a minute. I need to ask you something."

I turned off the ignition. "Okay. Ask away."

Nancy said, "I've got this friend...well, he isn't exactly a friend, he's the guy that keeps me in weed."

"Marijuana," I corrected.

"Okay, fine, marijuana. If you want to get technical, it's *cannabis*. Anyway, can we stay on the subject, please?"

"I thought marijuana—*cannabis*—was the subject," I said through a laugh.

Nancy gave me a look of exasperation. "Come on, Rick. Will you just listen and not interrupt please?"

I held up my hands and Nancy said, "Good. Like I was saying, this guy, Malcolm, is a dealer but he's a good guy just tryin' to make a living. Anyway, I was telling him you're a pilot with some big company and he got all interested and asked if I would ask you for a favor—"

I could see where this was heading. "A favor? Don't tell me. Let's see, he wants you to ask me to deliver a little package for him or maybe pick up a package the next time I fly down to Mexico or Chile or Columbia. Am I close?"

"Sort of, but that's not exactly the deal. See—"

"Yeah, I see, but look, even if I wanted to, I can't take drugs on the plane. Our security guys look through everything we take on board," I lied. "So tell your friend no way can I do anything for him or you. Sorry."

Nancy looked disappointed and I'm sure she was, but no way in hell was I going to be a drug courier. I kicked the starter again and the engine fired up. "I have to go. See you later," I said and took off.

Morning traffic wasn't too bad, and soon I was rolling up the good old Pacific Coast Highway. As I think I mentioned before, when you're riding a motorcycle at highway speeds, you need to pay attention to what's going on all around you, including what's in front and in back and on either side. Other than that, there's not much else to do except think about stuff. On this particular ride, I was thinking about my first ride up the PCH and realizing how much things had changed in just a little over a year. I vividly recalled stopping at that gas station where I saw all those bikers; how Ann came up to me, introducing herself as Gunner, handing me her card when I got mad and left. "Call me," she had said. And I thought about how that one call had started a chain of events that hadn't ended yet. No doubt about it, you have plenty of time to think when you take a road trip on a motorcycle.

I stopped once for gas and a visit to the outhouse, and arrived at the Walkers' place around noon. They heard the bike coming down the drive and both of them were standing on the porch when I pulled up. They were all over me when I got off the bike, asking questions faster than I could answer them.

"Come on in," Edna said. "We jes' fixin' ta set down ta lunch. Got plenty, so come on."

"Thanks." We walked to the house but just before entering, I looked over to the shop and the place in front of it where...

Emmett noticed me looking over there and interrupted my thought with, "Yeah, I do the same dern thing. It's hard ta shake something' like what happened there outa yer mind."

"I know. For Ann, well, she still has nightmares about it. It's a real bad deal."

Washing up in the bathroom, I had a sobering flash of the girl climbing out that window. I looked out at the hill from where Ann and I used binoculars to watch her escape. I dried my hands, hung the towel back on its hook, took a deep breath and joined the others.

As soon as I was seated, Edna asked, "Tell me, how's our little Annie?"

"Not that good. I just don't know how it's going to end."

Emmett snapped his head in my direction. "What you talkin' 'bout...howzit gonna end?"

I held up my hand as if to say *take it easy*. "What I meant was, I don't know if there is going to be a happy ending. Will she be able to deal with what happened and get on with her life? Or is this depression and feeling of terrible guilt going to stay with her indefinitely? We just don't know."

Edna and Emmett both shook their heads but said nothing.

"I saw her doctor yesterday and we had a long discussion about her condition. They're doing all sorts of things, but nothing is working so far, although the medication she's taking is helping, I guess."

Edna asked, "Is there anythin' we can do ta hep?"

Emmett added, "Ya know, ya jes have ta tell us what we could do an' we'd be on it. Anythin' at all."

I told them about the idea I'd run by Dr. Wilhelm. "He hasn't agreed yet, but if he does, can I count on you to just act normally, as if everything was fine? I think we need to show Ann that you folks are leading the same life you did before Dykes showed up, and that you understand what she must be going through and sympathize and all that, but remind her that what she really did was save your lives, and you're grateful. In other words, she's the hero, not the villain."

Emmett nodded. "That Dykes feller—he was the villain."

"So, do you two think you could pull that off and make it work?"

"Course we kin. The thing is not ta overdo it. Jes' keep it simple, quiet, so's she knows we're okay and that she can be okay, too."

I gave Emmett a pat on his shoulder. "That's the ticket. You got it just right. If the docs say it's okay, I'll call you and set up a time that works for you." I said to Edna, "Maybe you could prepare some soup and your baking powder biscuits, and we could all sit here at the table. That might be good for Ann. Doing things we used to do to show her it's alright, we're alright and she's alright. What we won't do, unless the doctor says to do it, is take a walk out by the front of the shop."

"No, don't want ta go there...no point to that," Emmett said.

To change the subject, I said, "Hey, Emmett, you suppose you can take a look at the bike? It was starting to run a little rough just before I got here. Plugs may be fouled."

"Sure thing, right after we eat."

After lunch we rolled the bike into the shop and Emmett pulled the plugs. "What about yer gun?" he asked. "You want it?"

"Sure, unless you want to keep it for protection."

"Hell, I don't need it. I got plenty of fire power." He chuckled and added, "The key is having the firepower plumb handy so's you kin use it before someone gets the drop on ya."

I laughed. "You sure got that right. So do you?"

"Do I what?"

"Jesus, Emmett. Do you have firepower handy like you said?"

"Damn right. When you go back in, take a look around."

I spent the rest of the day with the Walkers. Emmett got my bike running like an eight-day clock and after one of the best dinners I'd had in quite a while, I bid the Walkers goodbye, rode into town, and stayed overnight in a motel. In the morning, I rode back to Santa Monica. Dr. Wilhelm had left a message saying he had discussed my plan with his staff and, while most thought it might be a good idea to take Ann back up to the Walkers' home, they all agreed that now was not the right time. They wanted to try some new therapies and different drugs to see if they could get Ann to reveal more of herself to them. They also suggested that I not visit Ann for a while, as she seemed agitated and unwilling to talk to them after my visits.

I called Dr. Wilhelm and after the usual greetings, I got right to the point. "How long would I need to stay away?"

"I'm not sure. It would depend on what progress she is able to make. I'd say a few weeks, maybe a month, but that's a guess."

"A month?" I thought, *What the heck are they going to do to her for a month? That's a long time. I can't believe that she wouldn't want to see me...*

"More or less," he said. "Oh, by the way, there's something I need to ask you. Does the name Angie mean anything to you?"

I stiffened. "What? Angie? She talked about Angie?"

"Yes, she did. Obviously you are familiar with the name. Do you know this Angie?"

I rubbed my cheeks with thumb and forefinger somewhat dumbfounded. After a pause, I said almost inaudibly, "Angie was my wife. She was killed over a year ago when her car was struck by a drunk driver."

Dr. Wilhelm's tone changed. "I don't understand. Did Ann know your wife—Angie?"

"No, I met Ann afterward. The only thing she knew about Angie was what I told her."

Wilhelm said, "I'm confused. I'm trying to understand the connection..."

I cut him off. "There is a connection, believe me, but I don't think I want to tell you about it because it might do more harm than good if you question her about things she hasn't told you herself. You told me that before, right?"

"Absolutely. You're right. We need to let her tell us about Angie and whatever incident was associated with Angie."

I said, "But I will give you some information that may assist you. You'll want to know about her former boyfriend, Royce. You might say the word *Gunner*, a nickname she had at that time, and see if that gets her talking about her and Royce and their lifestyle."

Dr. Wilhelm replied, "Wait a minute. I need to take some notes." After a moment, he returned to the phone. "Okay, I've got it. Now, you were saying..."

"If you can get her to talk about Royce, Ann may talk about the 'scene.' If she does, she'll be referring to the swing scene she and Royce participated in. You know what I'm talking about?"

"I think so. Are you talking about couples swapping partners, typically at parties?"

"That's exactly what I'm talking about. And they took movies at these parties and Ann was in those movies doing everything, if you know what I mean."

Wilhelm was obviously surprised. "A-huh. I get the picture. May I ask, were you part of all this?"

"No. But I did see one of the movies..." I choked up a bit and rubbed the back of my hand across my mouth. I cleared my throat. "I saw one of the movies and frankly I was horrified and ran. At that point I never wanted to see her again. I knew Angie would not have approved of me being with someone like that." I swallowed. "I think maybe I've said too much. Anyway, that's the Angie connection. Believe me, it's important. I'm starting to think that it's part of a bigger picture, and the Dykes killing is just one piece of the puzzle. Hopefully you'll be able to get her to acknowledge all of it and then she may understand it's not her fault."

Dr. Wilhelm said, "Hold on a minute 'til I get this all down."

After a minute he said, "All right then. This new information will be very helpful—we may be able to make substantial progress with this. Anyway, let's hope so."

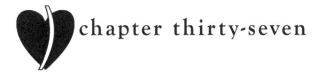

chapter thirty-seven

he company decided to go with the Grumman Gulfstream and ordered two. They also took steps to upgrade and re-configure two of our Super DC-3s for cargo service but with seating for four passengers. These planes are very sturdy and extremely reliable aircraft which was why they were preferred for the new tasks, meaning flying in and out of those "less than ideal" locations. One of the DC-3s was the plane the company president and CEO had used before we acquired the Jetstars.

Another proposal was that Richard Elkins, since he had a pot-load of experience flying DC-3s both in the Navy and for Frontier Airlines, should fly captain until such time as some of the other pilots could be checked out in the aircraft. When the idea was presented to me, I was not happy and told them so. My argument was that anybody who could fly a Cessna, Beechcraft or any twin could master the DC-3 in a matter of hours. It was, even with the upgrades added since the '40s, a simple plane to fly. They insisted that wasn't the point and they stroked me good on this one. Here's how they did it—of course I'm paraphrasing.

"You see, Rick," they said, "it's not the flying. It's the landings and take-offs–the flying in and out of short dirt strips with lots of tall trees all around that may present a challenge. And it's the navigation. You're not going to pick up a beacon to lead you to some remote strip. You'll have to find it! And until some of these pilots have flown right seat with a guy who knows how to do it... We need you and maybe Parrino and Conley to hold their hands until they get comfortable with it. It won't be for long and the bonus pay should help mollify your ego. You'll be back in the jets before you know it. So, what do you say?"

And what could I say? The only other choice was "I quit!"

Meanwhile, although I had agreed not to visit Ann until I received permission from Dr. Wilhelm, I did get updates on her progress from him every week. He told me that in a recent session, Ann had said that Royce had "made her do things" although she wasn't specific about what "things" meant. Wilhelm felt that he had established some sort of breakthrough when he asked her, "Who is Gunner?" and she replied, "Gunner is a bad person—she's a whore." Dr. Wilhelm asked her why she thought so and she replied that, "Angie said it. Angie said Gunner was a whore."

When I spoke with Dr. Wilhelm a week later and asked him if Ann had told him anything else about Gunner or Angie, he told me that in two other sessions when he asked her about Angie, all she said was, "Angie is dead but Richard still loves her. He'll always love her." Wilhelm said that he tried to get Ann to expand on that statement but she went off-subject. He said that when he mentioned Gunner, Ann got belligerent saying, "I hate Gunner. She's a whore."

Throughout that spring and summer, I flew execs, engineers and other company personnel around the states, and down into Mexico and countries in South America. Whenever we used the Jetstar with more than four passengers, and the trip required layovers, a stewardess would be added to the crew. On one ten-day trip with eight passengers to Brazil and several other South American countries, Alvin Conley was co-pilot and Carly Menzalora was the stew. We flew to Guarulhos (GRU) Airport near São Paulo, Brazil. I had never been there and was surprised and pleased that it was a modern, well equipped facility with a nice terminal. The ground personnel did a first-class job handling the plane. The city was a busy place. People of many races dressed in colorful clothing filled the streets, shops and restaurants. Fresh fruit juice vendors were everywhere and the tropical flavors were delicious. I couldn't get enough of the guava juice.

We remained in town for three days and nights while the company folks took off to various destinations by car. Our rooms were on the fifth floor of the Hotel Trianon Paulista, a very nice property next to the park. There wasn't anything we had to do, other than see to the fueling and security of our plane, so the three of us explored the city. Obviously, none of us spoke a word of Portuguese, so communication was tedious, especially when we ate at little off-beat cafes and restaurants where none of the employees spoke English. Carly had a working knowledge of Spanish; unfortunately very few waiters understood it. Regardless, we had some pretty interesting meals, some good, some not so good. One night we went to a movie, *Zorba the Greek*. It was in English with sub-titles in Portuguese. That was a switch. Mostly, we hung out in bars or nightclubs taking in the local color and listening to singers murder American songs, which they usually tried to sing in English. The patrons scowled at us when we'd laugh at their performers but nobody offered to fight us.

The second night, Alvin wasn't feeling very well. Something he'd eaten at lunch apparently upset his stomach, so he begged off going to dinner. Carly and I ate at an upscale restaurant and when the waiter handed me the check, Carly made a grab for it. I told her it was my treat and she reluctantly accepted with many thanks. We had managed to drink a bottle of a pretty good red wine at dinner, plus we had several tequila drinks at a bar afterwards. Returning to the hotel, I walked her to her room and was about to say goodnight, when she surprised me.

As she opened the door, she smiled over her shoulder at me. "It's early yet. Come in and..." She threw her arms around my neck and pulled me down so that we were face to face. "You need this and so do I," she purred as she planted a long and rather intense kiss on my mouth.

I was surprised, but not unreceptive. Her lips were so soft, her need obvious, I didn't resist. It felt so good and it had been so long since... She took my hand and led me into the room and locked the door. I started to speak but she shushed me. "We don't need to have a discussion about this. I know your circumstances and you know mine so please, let's just do this. I'll say it again, I need it and so do you."

Carly pulled down the bedspread and covers, then she went into the bathroom, saying, "Just be in that bed when I come back."

I had enough alcohol in me to put aside my inhibitions, although I thought about what we were about to do and considered running away. And yet I didn't. When Carly returned a few minutes later, I was in the bed and my clothes were on the chair. She stood naked by the side of the bed for a moment then lay down next to me. She felt warm and soft, and nervous. I could feel her body trembling a little. I wrapped her in my arms and kissed her. "God and Ann forgive me," I whispered, "but Carly, you're right. I do need you."

I stayed in her bed that night.

In the morning we cuddled, but did nothing more.

As we lay there, Carly murmured into my shoulder, "I just

want to thank you for helping me out. It's been such a long time..."

"The feeling is mutual," I said, hugging her. "So I thank you, too."

The phone broke us apart, and Carly answered. It was Alvin wanting to know if she was going to go to breakfast with him.

Giving me a wink, Carly asked, "Is Rick coming along?"

I could hear him answer that he didn't know where Rick was, that he had called him and knocked on his door but apparently Rick had left the hotel early.

Carly faked a yawn and said, "I just got up. Give me forty-five minutes and I'll meet you in the lobby. Okay, see you then. Oh, Al, if you see Rick, tell him where we're going. Okay, see you in a bit."

I grinned. "Very good." Then I jumped out of the bed and started to dress. Carly came up behind me, and laid her hands on my shoulders. I turned around and looked at her naked body and muttered, "That was nice last night. Maybe we'll have to do it again, or at least, something like it."

Carly smiled sweetly, gave me peck on the cheek and replied, "We'll see," and trotted off to the bathroom.

During the late afternoon I was in the lobby when some of the Esso group returned to the hotel. Mr. Trujillo, one of the engineers, invited the flight crew to join them for dinner, and so at seven we all met in the hotel dining room to enjoy a very nice dinner—although, with an early departure planned for the next morning, the flight crew could not participate in the enthusiastic toasting and "hail fellow well met" drinking. We left that mostly inebriated crowd early. Our pre-flight at was set for 6:00 a.m. Plus, we would be flying over new territory to an airport I'd never seen, at Valdivia, Chile. We slept alone in our rooms that night.

Between Al and me, we managed to find Pichoy Airport, which was located about twenty-five miles northeast of Valdivia. Our passengers left for town in a couple of cabs while we secured the plane, took care of the paperwork and all the usual required rigmarole. Then we also took a taxi to town. Valdivia is a charming town right on the ocean. From the balcony of my third-floor hotel room, I took some time to enjoy the spectacular view. I guess you could say that my job was fun, I thought, watching the busy street below and the light glinting on the Pacific. Didn't I get to see many new places, use my skills as a pilot and navigator and get paid a great salary for doing it? How could that not be fun?

And how could spending another night in Carly's bed not also be fun? Oddly enough, I was feeling no guilt or remorse. I wasn't *making love* to Carly, I wasn't *in love* with Carly, my constant thoughts were not of Carly, no! As the kids might say, *I was just having sex with Carly.* Just having sex didn't count, did it?

Our next stop was Iquitos, Peru, a fairly large city on the banks of the Amazon, where we spent the afternoon and night and took off the next afternoon for the Yucatán Peninsula, landing at the airport in Cancun around 5:00. There were several limousines waiting on the tarmac, but when Carly opened the cabin door, much to my surprise, only Mr. Trujillo exited the plane. From the cockpit, I saw him walk up to one of the limos, a rear window opened, and Mr. Trujillo bent down to speak to someone inside. He turned and beckoned to Carly, who was still standing on the top step, to send the others. Then several men in dark suits got out of the limos and held doors open for our group. I left the cockpit, hurried down the stairs and walked over to the limos.

I tapped Mr. Trujillo's arm and led him a short distance away. "What's going on?" I asked.

"A good friend of mine—and a friend of the company—has

invited us out to his villa near the town of Playa del Carmen. It's forty miles, an hour's drive from here."

I gave him a questioning look. "You're going to someone's house? Excuse me, but the info I was given states that your party were to–"

Trujillo cut in, "Yes, but something came up and the plan was changed. You see, my friend Mr. Antiago is very well connected to certain government people who are involved with issuing drilling permits—that sort of thing. As you no doubt realize, obtaining new locations and getting the governments of these countries to allow us to explore and eventually move in equipment is what this trip's about. They do things differently down here, and conventional methods of acquiring drilling rights typically don't get the job done. You understand?"

"Sure. I wasn't trying to butt into your deal but I'm responsible, I think, to get you back home safely. You understand what *I'm* saying? I'd feel pretty foolish if for some reason you folks don't return to the plane and I have to explain it to the execs at Esso."

"Yes, yes, I understand." Mr. Trujillo rested his hand lightly on my shoulder. "Of course you are exactly right. I appreciate your concern."

I said, "So, when should I expect you to return? My schedule lists T/O by no later than noon tomorrow. It also lists the crew and all of you scheduled to stay at the Belleview Beach Hotel in Cancun tonight."

A man stepped out of one of the limos. Trujillo held up a finger to signal he'd be just a minute, but the man came up to us and spoke urgently to Trujillo in Spanish. "I must go," Trujillo said as he turned to leave with the man. "We will probably return to the hotel tonight but if we're invited to stay overnight at the villa, we'll be back in the morning." He hurried over to the limo, got in and the cars took off.

289

We secured the plane and took a cab to town. On the way to the hotel, Al asked what the confab with Trujillo was all about.

"That's kind of weird isn't it?" Al said when I told him.

Carly chimed in, "How come we weren't invited?"

"Hey, I don't know any more about than you do. I'm captain of the airplane. I don't have any authority over what these people do or don't do. But I agree, there's something about this deal that doesn't feel quite right. It seems to me someone either here or at the office would have radioed something about it."

"I gotta agree with you, Rick," Al said. "I've never had anything like this happen on any of my trips, and I've been down here over a dozen times, and with some of those same people."

"Was Trujillo ever on one of those trips?" I asked.

"No."

Carly said, "Hey, maybe there's nothing to it. This rich friend of Trujillo's is just inviting them out for dinner. You know, people with lots of money do that, right? Why worry about it? I'm sure I'll hear plenty of talk about it in the cabin tomorrow on the way to LA, and I'll let you know." Sitting between Al and me, she turned first to Al, then to me, and added, "I don't know about you guys, but I've had a swell time on this trip. The food's been great, the hotels and other places we went to were great. I mean, it's been like a first class vacation, don't you think?"

Al said, "You don't see me complaining, do you? If you're a commercial pilot, this kind of flying is about as good as it gets." Al gave me a sly smile, "Right?"

I grinned back. "Right!" I touched Carly's arm with my elbow and said, "I agree, it's about as good as it gets."

That night I slept with Carly. Was it as good as it gets? No, but it was very nice. Of course I was spoiled. I had made love with Ann. It doesn't get any better than that.

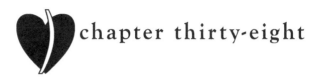 chapter thirty-eight

he three of us were having breakfast in the hotel coffee shop when a page came walking through calling my name. I raised my hand and the page handed me a note: "Call me as soon as you get this message. T. Trujillo." There was a phone number listed below his name.

I showed the note to Al and Carly, then headed for the lobby, found a phone and gave the operator the number. Someone answered in Spanish and I said, "*Señor Trujillo, por favor.*" (Well, I knew that much Spanish anyway.)

Trujillo came on the phone.

I said, "Good morning. I got your message to call. Where are you?"

Trujillo replied, "We're still at Antiago's villa. I called the company this morning and talked to...let's just say I talked to the person in charge of this expedition and told him about some very interesting information that I learned from Señor Antiago last night. After he heard about it, he instructed me to make some changes in our plans. Basically, we won't be heading back to LA today because he wants me to check out this information before we leave."

Somewhat confused, I said, "So, we're not going back today?"

"That is correct. However," he added, "we will be flying to Ecuador as soon as we can get to the airport, which shouldn't be more than a couple of hours from now."

I checked the time. "It's 8:10 now, so you want to leave by, say, 10:30?"

"Or sooner, if we can get there by then. How much time do you need to get the plane ready?"

"If we check out of the hotel right away, I suppose we can be ready to fly by ten or a little after."

"Good. We'll see you at the airport."

"Wait a minute. What about clearances, filing a flight plan? I assume we'll land at Quito. But we have to have permission from the Ecuadorian authorities to—"

Trujillo cut me off. "They're taking care of all of that right now. You will pick up a Telex at the airport operations office with all the information including navigation. If you have questions call flight operations in LA and sort it out."

"Excuse me for saying it, but I've got to tell you that this sounds crazy to me. I'd better call LA and get confirmation that we're cleared to fly into Ecuador and land at Quito. And I'll definitely need to file a flight plan."

When Trujillo and his party arrived at the airport, we had the plane ready to go, but because of paperwork problems we couldn't get clearance to depart. I took Trujillo aside and said, "Okay, are you going to tell me what the hell is going on and why all of a sudden we need to go to Ecuador?"

"All right, Captain, here's the picture." Trujillo pulled out a pack of cigarettes and offered me one which I refused. He lit one, took a deep drag and began talking while smoke filtered out his mouth and nose. "First of all a little history. This year, actually just months ago, Texaco discovered oil in the remote northern region of the Ecuadorian Amazon, known as the *Oriente*. It is in a rainforest that covers about a hundred square miles. In other words, we are talking about a huge patch that theoretically could support hundreds of wells." Trujillo took another couple of long drags on his cigarette, blew out smoke and continued, "They've done most of the geological and other prelim work and, believe it or not, they convinced the Ecuadorian government to go along with it. Pretty soon they'll be building roads through the forest, putting down drilling pads, installing the equipment, the works. I'm told they plan to build a town there for the oil workers and they hope to begin operations by 1967."

He checked to make sure he still had my attention. He did. He dropped the cigarette and ground it out with his boot. "There are five indigenous tribes in that area."

I asked, "Are these small, scattered tribes?"

"They tell me that there are at least thirty thousand people living in the *Oriente* and I'm guessing that these tribes have no idea what to expect or how to prepare for what will take place over the next half dozen years when all those oil workers move into their backyard and build a town. But probably that won't bother them half as much as the noise. Plus, there'll be all the mess from the actual drilling, which I expect Texaco will just dump into the rivers and streams."

I asked, "What do you mean 'all the mess'?"

"It takes a lot of water, millions of gallons of what we call formation waters, a byproduct of the drilling process. This water is toxic and highly saline. What do suppose they'll do with all the used formation water?"

"They'll dump it in the rivers?"

"You bet they will. That's a lot cheaper than having to deal with it like they do in the U.S. So, yes, I'm sure it will end up in the water and eventually become a disaster for those natives."

"You'd think the government would monitor the operation to protect—"

Trujillo stopped me. "I feel quite certain that the Ecuadorian government has no clue about this. No one has ever successfully drilled for oil in the Amazon rainforest."

"Excuse me, this is all very interesting," I said. I'm sure I sounded impatient. "And I'll admit disturbing those native tribes bothers me, but again I have to ask, what the hell does all that have to do with us? That isn't a Standard Oil deal, it's Texaco."

Trujillo gave me a knowing look. "Is it? Maybe Texaco doesn't understand what they are getting into. This is uncharted territory. Maybe someone at Standard thinks Texaco may need help with this monster. Hmm?"

I raised my eyebrows and nodded. "Ahh. And you're going out to the rainforest oil patch to find out how much help they may need." I chuckled. "Damn, the machinations of corporate America are beyond the comprehension of us poor folk who just pull into an Esso gas station to buy gasoline. The part that bothers me in all of this is what happens to those poor native bastards when they get overrun by oil workers? Or maybe what happens to those poor oil worker bastards if the natives get pissed off and set out to run them off?"

"Good point, Captain." Then he shrugged. "But enough of that. My sources tell me that they've built some sort of an airstrip out there. If that's true and we can pinpoint exactly where it is, I need you to fly me there."

"What? Fly you to some unknown little strip in God knows where? In what? A balloon?"

"The company brains say they will find out where this strip is, and by that I mean, be able to tell you how to get there. We will rent a small plane that can do the job. That's the plan."

I began to laugh, I mean really laugh. The whole idea was so ridiculous I couldn't stop laughing.

Trujillo watched silently.

Catching my breath, I blurted out, "I'm going to fly a little rental plane—a plane I know nothing about, rented from an outfit in an almost third-world country—to an unknown and unlisted spot somewhere in the Ecuadorian rainforest without any knowledge of the conditions or even if a landing strip exists. Wonderful!"

Al came over to us. "We're good to go. I borrowed a Jeppesen SA manual and Quito has a page but it looks pretty primitive, and the tower isn't manned full time. What kind of a flight plan are you going to file? I'm thinking straight southeast across the water, over Panama, then skirt the west coast to Quito. If we don't like the look of it or the weather becomes a problem we can jump up to Bogota. I've been there. It's okay."

I looked at Trujillo. "Since just you and I are going jungle jumping...that is, if I agree to go, which will depend on how good the intel is on the location and verification that there actually is a usable landing strip there... By the way, why are you taking your whole crew with us to Ecuador? They could stay right here in Cancun and we could pick them up when we go back to the States."

"That's a good point," Trujillo said, "but it's not what they told me to do. They'll stay in Quito while we're gone. If I need help, these guys are experts and I may need to consult with them."

Al had been listening to this exchange and said, "Excuse me, Mr. Trujillo." He said to me, "I've been looking at the maps and there's a mountain range with some 19K peaks. That could be a problem."

I said, "We'll need a good road map, because I think the only way we can be sure of finding the place is to follow the road in. There has to be one, doesn't there? They would have needed it for the getting their exploratory trucks in and out."

Trujillo agreed to work on that. I hoped they'd have a good road map we could use.

We filed a flight plan and took off from Cancun, landing in Quito about three hours later. The tower was unmanned but we did make radio contact. There were people on the ground to guide us to parking. It was all pretty primitive. I looked at the line of private planes tied down to a steel cable that ran along the ground and decided to tie our plane down, too—just in case. In the office, I had Carly ask the man at the desk in Spanish if any of the aircraft parked outside was available to rent. He told her that the owner of the Beechcraft Bonanza sometimes rented it, although he usually flew it himself. He had the phone number and offered to place the call.

The Bonanza owner told Carly he'd be at the airport in half an hour. Meanwhile Al found out that there was no jet fuel available, which wasn't a particular problem as we had plenty of fuel to get us to someplace that would have it. The owner, Bill Prickett, showed up—he turned out to be an American who lived part time near Quito. I told him what we wanted to do. He said that while he had no doubt that I could manage his plane, he would rather pilot it himself. At that point, I got Trujillo involved in the conversation.

"I'm sorry, Mr. Prickett," Trujillo said. "Company rules require that I fly only with a company pilot."

Prickett wasn't too receptive to the idea of me taking his plane, especially when he found out where we were going.

"How about this," Prickett said. "I'll rent the plane if I go as pilot. The captain here," he nodded in my direction, "can fly right seat, and you," he addressed Trujillo, "will sit in back."

I said to Trujillo, "That works for me. The Bonanza is a four-seater so you won't be sitting in the luggage space." I asked Prickett if he'd ever flown over or near that rainforest. He had but he didn't know about any oil company landing strip up there.

Trujillo questioned Prickett some more and then agreed to the plan. Pricket and I went to check out the Bonanza. An hour later I was flying it, making a couple of touch and go landings and enjoying myself. The plane was in very good shape, the engine was steady and strong, the avionics were everything you'd want and I felt we'd be okay to take the trip to the Texaco facility. Since all pilots used road maps to guide them in the interior of most South American countries, following a road to the oil patch would not be a novelty for Prickett, who told us he had been flying his plane all over South America for the past four years.

We took off at daybreak the next morning, eventually found the road we were looking for and followed it into the rainforest, where the dense foliage canopy made it more difficult to see. Several times we lost sight of the road and had to backtrack, pick up the road and try again, flying as low over the trees as was reasonably safe. Prickett did a good job flying while Trujillo and I used high powered binoculars to focus on the road. Around 0800, I spotted the strip and Prickett headed for it, ran out some flap, dropped the gear and put that baby on the ground slick as you please. I was impressed.

"Hell," he said, "I've landed in worse places than this one."

He taxied up to the end of the runway, turned around and cut the engine. A man came running over to the plane as the three of us got out.

"Hey, Thad," one of the men called out as he approached. "I heard you were coming but didn't expect to see you this soon." Trujillo jumped down and the two shook hands.

"Good to see you, Jack," Trujillo said. "Where can my crew go while we talk?"

Jack escorted us to a crude wooden building where comfortable chairs, a small kitchen, and two sets of bunk beds were available. "Make yourself at home," he said. "There are food and drinks in the frig and coffee if you like." At our nods, he reached up to a shelf and pulled down a Mr. Coffee machine, added water from a large bottle on the counter and filled the basket with ground coffee. When he plugged the coffee maker in, I could hear an electric generator somewhere nearby go from idle to full speed. "You want something, Thad?" Jack asked.

"I'll have some coffee when it's ready, and maybe a sandwich later," Trujillo said.

Jack said, "Okay. Come on into my office and let's see what we can do."

Prickett and I made baloney sandwiches, washed them down with some of the worst coffee I've ever tasted and lay down on the bunk beds.

It was close to four when the two men emerged from Jack's office. Trujillo was carrying a large manila envelope.

"Okay, gents," Trujillo said. "Time to head back. But first, I could use a sandwich and a cup of coffee."

Jack slapped together a baloney sandwich and poured a cup of coffee from the pot we had made earlier. Trujillo took a sip and declared, "Good God! Do you actually drink this stuff?" Leaving the coffee but keeping the sandwich, Trujillo moved to the door. "C'mon boys, let's go."

Jack shook hands with Prickett and me and handed each of

us a small package. "Here's a little souvenir for you. Don't open it now—wait 'til you get back home. I think you'll enjoy it."

We spent the night at a hotel in Quito. Carly had asked me if she thought it would be prudent (her word) to spend the night together and I said that I didn't think so.

The next morning we flew to San Salvador, loaded jet fuel, some food and drinks and continued on to Los Angles, arriving at five. As the passengers collected their luggage, I took Trujillo aside and asked, "So, how did it go up there with Jack? You sure didn't say much flying back to Quito."

"I couldn't discuss it with Prickett there. Besides, it was so God damn noisy in that plane you couldn't hear anything except the motor."

I said, "That's true. But did you accomplish what you set out to do?"

"Yes, I think so. We'll see what the boss thinks about it. Regardless, I want to thank you and the crew for doing a great job on this trip. Will you tell them?"

"I sure will." We shook hands. "And that trip up to the rainforest is one that I'll not soon forget. That guy, Prickett, is a hell of a stick handler."

I went into the ops office, closed the flight plan, brought my log book up to date, and filed the usual trip report while Al took care of securing the plane.

When I left the office, Carly was waiting for me outside.

"I was just wondering," she said, "What about us, I mean from this point on?"

"I don't know...I actually hadn't thought about it, to tell you the truth."

"I have, and I don't want it to end. I want to keep seeing you and spend time with you." She looked up at me, her dark eyes shining, "I'm afraid I've...I like you—a lot. I don't want it to end just like that."

"Boy, you kind of caught me off guard," I stammered. I picked up her suitcase, took her arm and led her out to the parking lot. "Where's your car?" She pointed and we walked in that direction.

"You know how much I've enjoyed being with you," I said. "Both in and out of bed. Really, it's been great. Obviously we've made some sort of connection both physically and emotionally."

At her car, she unlocked the door and I handed her the suitcase which she threw on the back seat. She faced me and said, "You're dancing around my question."

"Which is?"

Slightly exasperated, she asked, "Are we going to continue seeing each other or is this the end of the road?"

"Yes, I want to continue seeing you, of course. That's what I meant when I said we have made a connection. You're a special person and we need to let this play out and see where it goes. Don't you agree?"

"Of course I agree. Isn't that what I've been saying?" She pulled me to her and kissed me hard on the mouth. "Besides, I love your kisses and I'd miss them terribly if suddenly they were no longer available." She slipped into the driver's seat and started the car. "Good night. And call me—soon. We'll go to dinner or I can come to your place, if you like. My mother is always available for babysitting my kids. Anyway, don't wait too long to call, please?"

She backed out of the space, turned and drove off. I stood there for a long time wondering what I had just done. I did tell her we'd let it play out. That wasn't a long term commitment, was it?

It was dark by the time I got to my place and I was hungry. I pulled off my jacket and the small package that Jack had given me fell on the floor. Curious, I took my pocket knife and slit open the brown paper wrapping, exposing an envelope which I opened. Inside was something that looked like dried weeds. My first thought was it must be some kind of exotic spice, but why would Jack give me spice? Then it hit me: weed! Damn, I just did the thing I told Nancy I definitely would never do.

There wasn't anything in the ice box I wanted to eat so I heated up a can of chicken noodle soup and a small can of pork and beans. Ruefully thinking about the great meals we'd enjoyed on the trip, I opened a can of Spam, cut a couple of thick slices and put them in a pan to fry. The message light was blinking so I listened. One was from Nancy asking me to call her. There were several from my buddy, Ron Schmidt, wondering where I was and asking me to call. There was a message from Dr. Wilhelm in which he said that Ann was doing better and perhaps I should pay her a visit but to call him first.

I punched the stop button, walked to the stove to turn the spam over and stir the beans and soup, and sat down at the kitchen table. I thought about Ann and decided that regardless of circumstances, I had made a commitment to her. I had asked her to marry me. I felt that should be a commitment I had to honor.

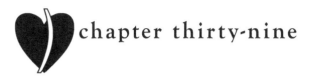
chapter thirty-nine

d
r. Wilhelm stood when I entered his office and offered his hand. "Good to see you again, Mr. Elkins." He motioned to the chair next to his desk. "Do sit down. Will you have some coffee or water or..."

I shook my head, "No, thanks. Well, maybe some water."

Dr. Wilhelm picked up his phone. "Mary, would you please bring Mr. Elkins a glass of water?" He addressed me, "I'm happy that you could come here this morning. I've been calling you—have you been away?"

"Yes. I flew a trip to several South American countries. We were gone for over a week. Just got back last night."

Mary came in with the water. I thanked her, took a drink and asked the doctor, "So tell me, how's Ann doing?"

"I think we made some real progress this past week. She told us about her relationship with Royce, she alluded to but did not go into detail about their parties. When she mentioned them she'd say, 'I'm not proud of it but.' She must have used that phrase a dozen times or more. Now, you have to understand that this was significant. First of all, admitting that she had done what she called 'bad things' without saying 'Angie said I'm a whore,' as she has in the past, makes me believe she's getting her mind around the problem and starting to look at it from a more reasonable perspective. Furthermore, she is articulating other things that happened to her prior to the shooting. This also is evidence that she is accepting the realities of her life and dealing with them in a more rational, that is, less histrionic way." He looked at me intently. "You understand what I'm telling you?"

I leaned forward, hands on my knees, and said, "Yes, absolutely. This is certainly good news." Reluctantly, I asked, "Does she ever mention me or our relationship?"

"Yes, and more frequently. It appears to be very positive. I think that is also a good sign."

I thought for a moment. "Has anything about the shooting come up yet?"

"No, Ann hasn't said anything about it and so we haven't broached that subject yet. I'm hoping that she will volunteer something about it. That would be best but if she doesn't, we're still thinking about your suggestion of taking her to where it happened to trigger a positive reaction. And I would define 'positive' as having her remember the shooting and be willing to talk about it and come to terms with it. We want to move her to understand and accept herself as a hero who saved not only her own life but the lives of three other people. That should be our goal and, by definition, her goal as well. Ann as hero, not Ann as killer."

"That's exactly what I'm hoping for, too." I was enthusiastic, but also getting anxious. I wanted to see and talk to Ann. "So, what do you think? May I see her today?"

"Yes. I think that would be all right. I would want you to keep the conversation very neutral. Talk about things you've done since you saw her last. Show an interest in anything she may talk about, which may have nothing to do with what we're after but that's okay. If you find she's getting nervous or fidgety, or if she becomes silent, say goodbye and leave."

"Okay, I'll do as you say. Should I check back with you afterward?"

"No, that won't be necessary. We'll be monitoring your visit so we'll know what was said. I hope you don't mind but you never know what little gem may be forthcoming when patients speak with their family or friends. Sometimes those little innocuous remarks provide clues that we can successfully use in our treatment regimen." He stood. "I'll take you to Ann's room now." He led me down a hall to a stairway. "She's on the second floor," he said.

We walked up the steps and continued to her room. He knocked quietly and opened the door. "I've got Rick with me, Ann. Want him to stay a while and visit?"

Ann smiled at me. "Yes, of course."

"Hi, darling." I said, stepping toward her. "How are you?"

She came to me, put her arms around my neck and whispered, "A lot better now that you're here."

I kissed her lightly on the lips. She responded aggressively.

Dr. Wilhelm quietly left the room, closing the door behind him.

It was a very nice room, bright and cheery, and hardly institutional. There were a table with chairs, a couple of easy chairs, a small couch and, of course, a bed and other furniture. The walls were a very light yellow and the printed curtains lent a nice touch. Ann led me to the couch and we sat holding hands.

She started the conversation with, "Where have you been? It's seems like a long time since you were here last. Has it been a long time or am I confused?"

"No, you're right. It's been a while. The company sent me down to South America and I was down there for a while. That's why I haven't been able to come here and see you. But I've got time off now so I can see you a lot more, if you want to see me."

"You goofball, of course I want to see you. I love you, remember?"

I darn near broke down and cried. She'd called me "goofball." She'd said, "I love you." This was the old Ann talking, and talking is exactly what we did for the next hour. She wanted to know what I had done in South America, what towns and cities I visited and what they were like. She talked about her treatment, the sessions with the doctors and therapists. She said they were giving her pills, although not so many as before. She almost seemed normal, except occasionally she'd drift off subject.

I was telling her about flying low over the rainforest jungle canopy when she broke in. "I used to do bad things, you know, but that doesn't make me a bad person."

I nodded, then continued to describe the jungle. Several times, she interrupted me again and say something like, "I'm not a bad person, you know." Or, "I used to do bad things but that doesn't make me a bad person." Or, "People do things they shouldn't do sometimes, but then they stop and they're okay, right?"

I had been with Ann for over an hour when Dr. Wilhelm returned. "I'm sorry, Ann," he said, "but you have a session with Margaret in a few minutes so I'm afraid Rick will have to leave. But I'm sure he'll be back real soon."

Standing at the door, I hugged her tightly for a moment and kissed her mouth. "I love you even if I am the world's greatest goofball."

Ann laughed. "I know and I love you, too." She squeezed my hand tightly. "Come back and talk to me some more real soon, okay?"

"Don't worry. I'll probably see you tomorrow." I glanced at

Dr. Wilhelm who nodded approval. "Okay, darling. I'm leaving but I'll see you tomorrow." I kissed her and left.

Dr. Wilhelm caught up with me as I got to the bottom of the steps. "What do you think? Do you see signs of improvement?" he asked.

"It was great! She darn near seemed like her old self."

Wilhelm said, "What I thought was most interesting was how she interjected those remarks about being a bad person as if she was looking for confirmation from you that even a bad person is redeemable. Did you get that?"

"Yes, but I didn't comment when she said those things, because I didn't want her to dwell on it and besides, I might have said the wrong thing and..."

"No, you handled it perfectly. If she wants you to participate when she articulates those thoughts, I think she will let you know. Other than that, better to leave it alone for the time being. The best thing to come out of that meeting was how she related to you. Frankly, I wasn't expecting that but I'm pleased that you brought out all those good emotions from her. Let's hope that continues with your next visit."

I said, "I'll come back tomorrow. Is that really okay?"

"Yes, indeed," he replied. "That would be very good. I may have some questions prepared for you to ask her. Would you feel comfortable doing that?"

"I guess it depends on the questions, but sure I can do that."

"Very well then. See you tomorrow."

I drove back home feeling pretty good about my visit with Ann. She definitely was making progress, she certainly looked a lot better than she did the last time I saw her and she was talking about things mostly normally except for those few times, but she seemed to be rational, and when she said she loved me and called me a goofball, I knew she must be getting back on track.

Nancy was getting in her VW bus as I pulled in the driveway and parked under the carport. She came running over to my pickup. "Hey, Ricky, when did you get back?"

"Yesterday. Why, did you miss me?"

"Yeah, I missed you but next time I'll take better aim." She laughed.

I flashed a smile, "Very funny. So what have you been up to while I was gone?" I started walking to my door and she followed.

"School mostly. Saw a couple of concerts, nothing very exciting. Where have you been?"

"South America." I opened the door and walked in. Though uninvited, Nancy followed me. I turned to face her. "Did you want something?" I asked.

"No, just being neighborly."

"Say, I just remembered. I brought you a present all the way from the Amazon rainforests of Ecuador. I'll get it." I walked over to my desk and took the envelope of weed out of the bottom drawer. I strode up to Nancy and handed it to her. "Here you go. This is the real deal."

Nancy carefully opened the envelope and then put it up to her nose and took a deep sniff. She looked up at me, her eyes aglow and said, "Wow. Really? What a great present. Did you try it?"

"No, I didn't try it," I replied with mock disgust. "I don't do that."

"You don't know what you're missing." Nancy headed for the door.

"Hey, where you going?"

"Upstairs to get some papers. I gotta try this shit out. You wanna try a joint?"

I waved my hand for her to go. "No, you go ahead, but don't bring it down here, okay?"

I had to laugh as Nancy ran out the door and headed for the stairway to her apartment. *Ah,* I thought. *Must be nice to be young and carefree with an envelope full of excellent weed.* Then I worried that perhaps I shouldn't have given it to her. Hopefully she wouldn't smoke too much of it.

That thought elicited another. *I'll bet Ann smoked marijuana when she was Nancy's age...probably did other drugs too. When she met Royce with all his money to support his crazy lifestyle, she probably found it terribly exciting, hard to resist. I can see that happening. It starts out slow, just take a few drags then smoke a whole joint and another and then maybe something stronger, mix it with lots of booze, loud music, fun people, lots of laughs...a girl takes off her blouse, gets up on a coffee table and dances around, the bra comes off, she's lifting up her skirt showing everybody what she's got... Other girls join in, encouraged by their boyfriends and husbands... Here, try this pill, it'll make you feel real good, real relaxed. What? You want do what? In front of everybody? That's crazy.* "Come on, Gunner," someone yells, "do it." *Soon a chorus of women is screaming,* "Do it, do it." "Hell, I'll do it," *some girl says, slithering out of her clothes, lying down and pulling a man down on top of her.* "Come on, Gunner, give us a show...do it do it do it." *And then it becomes part of her lifestyle and she's doing it, doing it until one day someone comes along who says,* don't do it. *It's wrong, it's cheap, it's all going to blow up in your face and you'll be sorry. You're no better than a whore. YOU ARE A WHORE! You don't deserve to marry a decent man and now what have you done? You killed a man. I told you it would all blow up in your face. You're a whore and a killer! You need to get away, you need to hide.*

Finally, I thought, *I may have the whole picture of Ann's reasoning. It made me relieved and unspeakably sad at the same time.*

I visited Ann the following day armed with some questions Dr. Wilhelm had given me. He said I should only ask them if I felt Ann might be in a frame of mind to answer. She and I were sitting on the couch again, holding hands and chatting, when much to my surprise she asked about the Walkers.

"Have you talked to Edna and Emmett since I've been here?" she asked.

This was one of the things Dr. Wilhelm had asked me to mention. I decided to just tell the truth. "Yes, as a matter of fact. I went up there about a month ago to see how they were getting along."

Ann didn't give any sign that my answer bothered her. She asked, "And how are they?"

"They're fine, about the same as always."

"Did they ask about me? Did you tell them about my breakdown and coming here?"

I was a little put off by those questions. Was she really ready to talk about what happened up there? Again, I decided to just tell her the truth. "Of course they asked about you. They wanted me to assure you that they were just fine but were concerned about you. They said they hoped that you'd be better soon and perhaps come up for a visit. They'd love to see you."

"I'd like to see them, too, but I don't think the docs would approve of me going up there, especially since that's where..." Ann suddenly stopped in mid-sentence and looked at me. "I'm not a bad person. I did a bad thing but I had to. It wasn't my fault, was it?"

I took her in my arms and whispered in her ear, "Of course not, darling. You saved my life. You saved the lives of Edna and

Emmett. You're not a bad person—you are a hero! That's right. You are a hero!"

"Do you think so, really?" Her stare was intent.

"Darling, everyone knows you did the right thing... everyone."

"I don't know. I keep having these bad thoughts and it frightens me. I did all those bad things before I met you, and Angie..." Ann started to cry. She blubbered, "Angie hates me. You know that."

"Ann, listen. Angie is dead. Angie doesn't even know who you are. Don't think about Angie because Angie doesn't exist— she's dead. She died long before I ever met you. Angie doesn't exist and you must let go of her just as I have."

The pitch of her sobbing increased.

The door opened and Dr. Wilhelm and a nurse carrying a small tray came in. "I'm sorry, Ann, but Rick has to go now, don't you Rick?"

I stood. "Yes, I have to leave now, honey, but I'll be back again real soon. Meanwhile just relax. Everything is fine, and you're doing fine."

"Yes, she is," Dr. Wilhelm said. To Ann he said, "Here's Margaret—she has some hot tea for you."

Ann hugged and kissed me. "You still love me, don't you?"

"Of course, more than ever." I kissed her lips. "I've got to go, but I'll see you real soon. Bye." I walked out of the room with Dr. Wilhelm.

Wilhelm was excited. "That was fantastic. You did a great job in there. Great! I think Ann will be ready to take that trip to Cambria pretty soon."

The phone began to ring as I opened my door. I hurried to pick it up.

311

"It's Carly. Got a minute?"

I thought about my answer for a second or two and decided to bite the bullet. "Sure. What's up?"

"I was wondering if you'd like to have dinner with me tonight, my treat."

"Dinner? Tonight? Ah..." Damn, what was I going to tell her? "Sure. Where would you like to eat?"

Carly replied, "I really don't care where...anyplace you like is fine with me. Tell you what. I'll come by around six and pick you up. Is that okay with you?"

"I can pick you up, that's no problem. Tell me where you live."

"No, this is my treat. I'll pick you up at six," she said.

I let out a long sigh which I hoped she hadn't heard. "Fine. Six it is. See you then." I laid the handset on its cradle and grabbed a Carling's Ale from the ice box. As I searched for the bottle opener I wondered how she knew where I lived. Finding the opener, I popped the cap, took a long drink and plunked myself down on an easy chair. For some reason, I pictured Laurel and Hardy. *A fine kettle of fish you've got us into now.*

By the time Carly knocked on my door, I had already put away a half dozen bottles of ale and was sipping straight Bourbon from a water glass. I was a little wobbly. In fact, when I had finished my shower and stepped over the rim of the bathtub, I damn near fell on my face. Right now I was thinking that preparing for Carly's visit with alcohol probably wasn't such a good idea after all. So, what did I do? I offered her a drink which she readily accepted. We sat at the kitchen table.

Carly asked, "Are you okay Rick? You look a little—"

I blurted out, "Drunk?"

"I wasn't going to say that but it's obvious you have been drinking—maybe quite a bit."

"Yeah, maybe I have."

"Why? You knew I was coming over and we were going out, so why did you feel the need to, to...emmm... fortify yourself?"

I looked at her a moment and then just let it out. "You scare the hell out of me!"

Wide-eyed she said, "What are you talking about? What do you mean?"

"Just what I said. When you're around I look at your cute little body, those lovely breasts, that sweet smile and I just want you." I waved my hands in front of me. "It's an animal thing—I can't explain it. And then when we do make love, it's nice but somehow I get the feeling you're holding back, you're not into it as much as I am or as much as I'd like you to be." Carly seemed puzzled. "Have you any idea what I'm talking about?" I asked.

"Not really, but I want to understand it. I need to understand what it is you want from me and why you think I'm holding back." Carly fixed me with her gaze and held it for a long time.

Now I felt uncomfortable. This whole scenario wasn't going at all the way I had envisioned. But then, I really hadn't envisioned anything. What the hell was I thinking, starting this whole line of conversation? I blinked and looked away. "Gee, I'm sorry, Carly. This was stupid. I don't know why I drank so much." I swallowed. "Well yes, I do. Like I said, you scare me. You know I'm committed to Ann and desperately want her to get her mind back to where it used to be. I'm praying she'll be all right and soon. Meanwhile you're here and available and I really do love being in bed with you. I'm just screwed up, I guess. I don't know what the hell I want. I guess I want it all."

Carly walked behind my chair, leaned down and kissed the top of my head. Her voice husky, she whispered, "I want you to have it all. I want you to have your Ann, but until you do have her back, I want you to want me." She took hold of my arm and drew me out of the chair. "We are going into the bedroom now, and I will give you everything you want—everything. Don't be afraid, I won't steal your heart." Her smile was seductive. "But I will take the rest of you."

chapter forty

ach time I visited Ann, she seemed to be just a little more like her old self. There were exceptions of course, and she'd break down and rehash all the old refrains about being a bad person or how Angie hated her and so on. But the doctors and I agreed she seemed more stable and willing to confront her demons. That said, she still had not spoken Arnold Dykes' name nor had she brought up his killing. The collective wisdom of Dr. Wilhelm and the team working with Ann was that the name Dykes and what happened to him had to come from Ann without being prompted. They also felt that a trip to the scene of the incident should wait until Ann was ready to talk about what happened that fateful day.

During most of my visits with her now, Ann and I could leave the clinic, and so we'd go to lunch at nearby restaurants. Or we would visit a little espresso bar that was within walking distance. On these occasions, Ann seemed quite relaxed and comfortable being around other people, and our conversations were similar to those we'd had in the past.

One afternoon, after having lunch at a café around the corner from the clinic, she surprised me. "You know what I'd like to do one of these days?" she asked.

"Spend the night with me," I replied.

Ann smiled and said, "Well, yes, that would be nice, but that wasn't what I was going to say. What I'd like to do this fall is go up to Monterey and stay a few days at Bea's place."

"Really? I'd love to do that too. I'll ask Dr. Wilhelm about it, see what he thinks of that idea."

Ann's voice took on an edge of excitement. "On the way back from Monterey we could stop for a little while and visit with Edna and Emmett. You said they wanted to see me, right?"

"Right. That's what they said. In fact, I spoke to them on the phone last Sunday and they asked again when we were going to come up."

Ann's face lit up and those marvelous green eyes sparkled. "This will be fun, something for me to look forward to. Let's talk this over with Dr. Wilhelm when we go back, okay?"

We did discuss it with Dr. Wilhelm. He was all for it, except he asked Ann if she would be willing to visit with the Walkers on the way to Monterey. She asked him why and he said he would like to be there in case there was any problem with her seeing them.

She seemed to become confused. "Why would there be a problem? Rick and I have visited with them many times in the past—they're friends. I don't know why you think there would be any problems."

Dr. Wilhelm did a quick retreat. "I'm sorry, Ann, that was stupid of me to say that. That's not what I meant at all. I'm responsible for your care and it could be a problem for *me* if something happened while you were gone. I'd be responsible and could get in trouble. You see what I'm saying?"

Ann looked doubtful but answered, "Yes, I understand. I suppose you would need to come with us to Monterey in case something happened there."

I jumped in before things went south. "I don't think we

need to go into all that right now, do we? The company has me scheduled for several trips to South America, with the first one coming up soon. So it's going to be at least a month before I can get enough time off to go to Monterey. By that time, I'm sure we'll have all the details worked out. I don't think that by then Dr. Wilhelm will even need to go along." I gave Wilhelm a questioning look.

Wilhelm said, "I think Rick is right. I'm sure it won't be necessary for me to go with you. You've made steady progress, especially this past month or so, and by the time Rick is ready, I'm sure you'll be in good form."

Ann seemed relieved and her face showed it. Addressing Dr. Wilhelm, she said, "I think the best therapy for me now is to get away from this environment and just enjoy some quiet time with the man I love. He's the kind of therapy I need now. He's lived through all of this with me. He knows about everything that has happened in my life, good and bad. He was right there when I shot Dykes. He knows I had to do it, I had no choice."

Dr. Wilhelm gasped. I stood there staring at Ann, hardly believing what I had just heard her say. Ann looked first at me, then at Dr. Wilhelm.

Then she smiled. "You look surprised, Doctor. Did you think I just pushed that incident so far back in my mind that it wouldn't come out to haunt me? Of course you did and so did I. But I remember it—oh yes, every last little detail of it, and it gives me nightmares, as you know. But I'll be okay going up to the Walkers' place. I'm sure I'll be hesitant to walk in front of his shop and look at the place where it happened. But I will look at it, and then Rick and I will drive on to Monterey where we spent some of the happiest moments of our lives."

Gene Parrino and I were sitting in the Flight Operations office listening to the manager, Charlie Borden, explain in detail what this first trip in the refurbished and reconfigured DC-3s would involve. He said that two other pilots would be in the jump seats as observers. If we wanted to, we could use them as relief on the way back but not on the outbound leg. On the second trip, one of these pilots would fly right seat with me and the other would co-pilot with Gene. The plane cruised at 200 mph, give or take depending on the wind, and it had a range of around 2,000 miles. The cargo for this trip would weigh close to four tons.

Charlie outlined the flight plan: LA to Mexico City, 1,600 miles. Flight time, 8 hours. Take on fuel, overnight. Alternate fuel stop, depending on fuel consumption, Mazatlan. Second day: Mexico City to Cartagena, 1,700 miles. Flight time, 8½ hours. Take on fuel, overnight. Alternate fuel stop, San Salvador. Third day: Cartagena to Lima, 1,550 miles, flight time 7½ hours. Take on fuel, overnight. Fourth day: Lima to Santiago, Chile, 1,500 miles, flight time 7½ hours. Take on fuel, overnight. Perform detailed check of engines, radios, avionics, etc. Total time in air, 31½ hours. Total time including ramp time, fueling, pre and post flight inspections, etc. plus overnights, about 96 hours.

I made a mental calculation. If we made the same 6350 mile trip in the Jetstar, cruising at 512 mph, our time in the air would be about 12 ½ hours or 19 hours less than the DC-3. Plus the jet had a thousand more miles of range which meant fewer stops. Needless to say, I sure wasn't looking forward to this trip. It would be tedious.

Charley interrupted my daydreaming when he said, "Now, about the hard part. After you make sure the plane is in as good a shape as you and the local mechanics can make it, you're going to be following road maps—and I'll see that you have the best and latest—into the interior. These three destinations will have a strip that should be suitable to land a loaded DC-3 but I have to tell you, you'll be the first ones doing it. Obviously, if you don't like the look of things when you get over the strip, you'll turn around and go back to the closest alternate. That will be your call and nobody is authorized to overrule it."

Gene said, "Isn't that nice."

Charlie's voice was just a bit pithy. "It sure as hell is! Don't think we are sending you boys out on a kamikaze mission! We definitely want you and the equipment to come back in one piece. As of right now, it looks like you'll have three locations you'll have to find, but all of them have radios and beacons so they won't be as tough to find as that Texaco place you went to last month."

When the meeting concluded and we had left the ops building, Gene said, "So, Ricky my boy, what do ya think?"

"To tell the truth, this is the first time since I signed up with this outfit that I wish I was flying for an airline. What's your take on it?"

"Me? I'll tell *you* the truth, it sounds about as much fun as my last mission over Germany."

"Didn't you get shot up on that mission?"

Gene laid a wry smile on me and jawed, "Exactly."

One month later, Ann and I walked out of the clinic. I carried her little suitcase, the one she had brought with her when she checked in the previous January, almost nine months before. She said she felt good, and to me she looked good, although she had lost weight, especially during the first six months of her stay, but she had gained much of it back. There were little lines emanating from the corners of her eyes and mouth that weren't there before and her hair was quite a bit longer and darker than it was when she checked in—it looked more like it did when I'd first met her. I led her to my new car, a 1964 Ford Thunderbird.

"This is yours?" Ann asked as I opened the door for her.

"It's ours."

"I have a car, remember? And it's a very nice car, although hard to say what it'll be like after all these months of sitting in the garage," she said as she slid onto the cream colored leather seat. She patted the leather and looked around. "Very nice, very elegant, I must say, and if I know you, you paid cash for it, didn't you?"

"You know me," I replied lightheartedly. "If I don't have the dough, I just don't go." I got in, slid the steering wheel to the side, an innovation designed to facilitate entry and exit, hit the starter, put it in drive and off we went. We arrived at her place in Beverly Hills and took the elevator to her floor.

"I'm nervous," Ann said as the elevator door slid open. "Hard to say what the place will look like."

"Don't worry, I've been over here many times to bring you clothes or whatever you wanted. And I had your cleaning gal come by once a month to dust. Besides that, I started your car at least once a month, and I took it out sometimes and drove it around to keep it limber."

Ann frowned. "I guess I forgot, but anyway, thanks for doing all that. That's great."

At her door, I pulled a key from my pocket and used it. Ann paused in the entry hall and gazed around for a full minute before entering the living room. The place was very neat, clean and tidy. She smiled.

"It's good to be home after all this time." She sat in a chair and put her hands on her knees. "I want you to stay here tonight, Rick, in case...I mean if I get a little worried about being alone or have one of those damn nightmares. Can you stay?"

"Of course. I planned to stay with you right along until I have to leave for Chile."

A brief flash of panic seemed to overtake her. "What will I do while you're gone?"

"Don't worry about it. I've made arrangements for a lady to stay with you while I'm away. She'll be available starting tomorrow because I've got a trip with a layover in Miami. I may be gone for a couple of nights but the lady will be here to keep you company."

"Do you think I should go back to the clinic while you're gone?"

I could sense the rising anxiety in her tone. "No, you can stay right here in the comfort of your own home. The lady is an LPN. Her name is Irene—she'll be here later this afternoon so you can meet her. You'll like her. She's a really nice lady, and every one of her references was excellent." Ann stood and I wrapped her in my arms. "You're going to be all right, I promise. I've taken care of everything to make sure of it. Tonight, we'll go to bed and I'll hold you close so that you will know you are safe in my care and nothing can hurt you."

Ann looked up and fixed her eyes on mine. "I know I can trust you to take good care of me. Don't worry, I'll be fine and a lot more confident when I'm back to normal—whatever normal is."

The two women hit it off right from the start and I felt comfortable leaving Ann in Irene's care. When Ann and I slept together we cuddled and kissed a lot but I was afraid to try anything more than that. I was willing to wait for Ann to make the first move. I knew it would be a slow process but I didn't want to take a chance on setting her back, especially since she was doing so much better.

When it was time for me to leave on the big trip to Chile, I explained to her exactly what my mission was, how long I thought it would take, and that, aside from it being a very long and tedious ride, there was nothing for her to worry about. The DC-3 began its run, I explained, as a commercial airliner in the 1930s and probably still was the safest airliner in the sky. The plane I would be flying had been equipped with all the latest bells and whistles plus the most powerful and reliable Pratt and Whitney engines ever made. I quipped that I'd be safer in that plane than driving my car down the 405 Freeway.

The day before we were to leave for Chile, the cargo was loaded on board and well secured. In order for my co-pilot, Gene, and me to get a feel for how the plane would handle with the bigger engines and with a full load, we took a test flight. We were surprised how well the plane handled the takeoff, using somewhat less runway than I thought it would need. The landings—we each did one—were a little tricky. We needed to slow as much as possible without stalling by using full flaps and working the throttles just right. I have to say that Gene's landing was better than mine. The old bomber pilot was back in the saddle and he sure had the touch. We were happy with the plane's performance and when we checked in with Charley Borden and gave him the report, he responded with, "Nothing but the best for my boys."

I left Ann's place the next day about 5:00am and drove my pickup to the airport. I wasn't about to leave my new car in the parking lot while I was gone. Gene and I, along with our two trainee pilots, Ed Tatarsky and Harris Bullard, did the walk around and the pre-flight ritual before buckling up in our seats. None of us were wearing company uniforms except for the caps. We lit the fuse and those P & W's roared into life, belching great quantities of smoke.

I have to admit, there's nothing quite so enjoyable as listening to the sound of radial aircraft engines starting up, coughing, then smoothing out. You don't get that with jets. You set the pitch of the props and they bite into the air, moving the aircraft forward. You taxi to the runway, cant to the right so you can see the runway out the left window, wait for clearance and when you get it, you slowly advance throttles to maximum power, feet off the brakes, and then you're rolling down the runway, the tail comes up, you hit rotation speed (84 Kts), ease back on the yoke, and what do you know, you're flying. Wheels up, zero flaps and away you go.

The trip went pretty much the way Borden laid it out. We didn't have to use any of the alternate fueling places which saved us some time and hassle. Several of the airports lacked some of the amenities that even the smaller U.S. airports have and so we had to improvise—use a telephone to close flight plans and so on—but we made it to Santiago, Chile. Even though we were told not to, we gave the new guys a lot of stick time, while Gene and I took turns catching a nap with the cargo. I felt like both of them knew what they were doing.

After making sure the plane was a hundred percent ready, the four of us took off for the first oil patch, which was located about a hundred and twenty-five miles due east of Santiago. We made radio contact when we were within fifty miles and picked up the beacon shortly thereafter. From that point it was no problem finding the runway that had been carved out of a forest of very tall trees. It reminded me of the Texaco patch we landed on with the little Bonanza. But this was no Bonanza, this was a DC-3 with a loaded weight of close to 25,000 pounds.

I said to Gene, "You've got control. Come in low and circle the strip and I'll see what it looks like with the binocs." I yelled to the two guys in back to get to a window, take a good look and yell out any hazards. It looked okay as far as I could tell, except the runway seemed short although we'd been told it was 2,200 feet—plenty of runway for a DC-3 to take off. It was the trees at either end that could be a problem. I had Gene circle again and on the third pass, I said, "Come in from the south and just fly over it." Gene came in low over the trees, dropped down another five hundred feet over the strip and pulled out over the tops of the trees on the north end.

"What do you think?" he said.

I let out a long breath. I guess I'd started holding it when he flew over the trees and dropped down before climbing out. "Assuming the runway is 2,200 feet, plus it looks like they've cut the trees back another couple hundred feet at each end, I guess it's within your capabilities."

"Wait a minute," Gene yelled into his headset. "What do you mean, MY capabilities? You're the captain. It's only fair and right that you should be on the stick for this landing. Put those binoculars down and take hold of this thing and put her in there."

I looked at Gene and flipped him a finger. "Okay then, you asked for it." I was hoping the boys in back wouldn't soil their pants as I made the approach. "Drop the gear, two notches of flap." I heard the gear drop, saw it had locked. I slowed as much as I could, cleared the trees by no more than a hundred feet, let her drop, then added power, brought the nose up, cut the power and made a three point landing. When we came to a stop, we still had at least three hundred feet of packed dirt runway in front of us. I taxied to the end, turned around and cut the engines. Then I turned in my seat and yelled, "Okay, everybody breathe now."

Gene unbuckled his harness, slid out of his seat and tapped me on the shoulder. "That was one pretty three-point. Damn, where'd you learn to do that?"

"The United States Navy," I said. "If you can learn to land on a carrier, you can damn near land anywhere."

After the cargo destined for our first stop was off-loaded, we took off for number two, about a hundred and eighty miles to the northwest. Gene had control and his takeoff was smooth with plenty of runway to spare. He easily cleared the trees and we were on our way. We made radio contact with the base but were unable to pick up the beacon signal. We figured we were on a good heading. We calculated how long it should take us to get there and hoped to pick up the signal when we got closer. Meanwhile, we told the radio contact to keep an ear open for the sound of our engines. We were about an hour into the flight when the radio came alive.

"Esso one, do you read? Over."

"Esso one, five by five. Can you hear engines? Over."

He replied that he now had us in sight and gave us a heading for the strip. We were damn near on top of it before we did a visual. Gene circled the runway several times then made a low level pass at it to get a feel for the actual landing.

"I think it'll be okay," Gene said. "This one looks like it's longer and wider than the last one."

"If you're happy with it, put it in there," I said. And he did. Perfect!

The location crew off-loaded their part of the cargo and we took off without incident, the plane being much lighter, and returned to Santiago as I wanted to get down before it got dark. The next day we flew to the other location, dropped off the remaining cargo and returned to Santiago. No sweat.

Over dinner at a little café, the four of us did a re-hash of the events of the past two days. Our two jump-seat pilots, having been properly impressed by the aeronautical expertise of Gene and myself were somewhat apprehensive about piloting a full-load ship onto the kind of landing strips we had encountered.

Gene said, "This whole damn operation is stupid. Why in the hell wouldn't they load the cargo on a ship, off-load it at Valparaiso or whatever port is closest to the location and truck it in?"

Ed said, "That sure makes more sense than trying to outfit an oilfield with planes. I've been to some of their locations in Mexico and Brazil, and I know they can't load a lot of that stuff on a plane—it's way too big and heavy."

Harris spoke up. "Personally, I don't think they have it in mind to do that. I think they wanted to see what the possibilities are should they need to get a piece of equipment or some repair parts to a location in a hurry. I think they've built these fields so they can fly workers or management, whoever, to the locations and if there's some sort of an emergency, we can evacuate the personnel. What we're doing is checking the feasibility part of it and making sure we can provide a safe transport for the workers and, no doubt, some of the company big wigs."

I said, "Company big wigs are not going to fly from the States to Chile in a DC-3. They'll jet down and then use the 3 to fly to the location. But getting back to what Harris said, I think he's absolutely right. They need the planes to fly personnel and, as he said, repair parts, things like that."

Gene said, "Now, that does make sense. But as you know, there have been times when some of the things the company has done made no sense at all."

Harris said, "Maybe to you, but I'm sure Standard Oil knows what they're doing. We're just pilots working for wages, they are oilmen and, by God, they sure as hell know how to make money."

I laughed. "Very good, my lad. You hit the nail on the head. Now let's get the hell out of here and get some sleep. I'd like to be in the air by 7:00 so, let's figure on getting to the plane by 6:00."

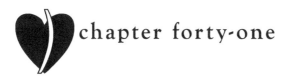

chapter forty-one

We arrived at LAX October 27 just as the sun was setting. From the cockpit, it sure was a beautiful sight, both the setting sun and the airport. As much as I loved the old DC-3, after flying it all those hours I was glad to be done with it—I hoped for a long, long time.

By the time we finished the debriefing with Charlie Borden, it was eight o'clock. I got in the pickup and drove to Beverly Hills, arriving at Ann's building around nine. Irene opened the door.

"Good evening, Mr. Elkins. Glad to see you. I'm sure Ann will be tickled. She's in her room but I don't think she's sleeping yet."

Leaving my suitcase in the hall, I walked to Ann's bedroom and tapped lightly on the door.

"Come in, Irene."

I opened the door and stuck my head in the room. "It's not Irene. It's Goofball back from the seven seas."

Ann dropped the book she'd been reading, jumped out of bed and ran into my waiting arms. We hugged and kissed and hugged some more. "Oh my God," she breathed, "What a surprise! I didn't think you'd be back until next week." She kissed me again, pulled me to the bed and we both sat on the edge. "You look tired. Was it a tough trip?"

She was looking even better than when I left. She was radiant. "It was just very long and tedious. And I guess I am tired but so what? I'm looking at you and you look terrific—really! You look just like the Ann I used to sleep with in Monterey and other places." I got up and began taking off my clothes. "I'm going to take a nice hot shower and then I'm going to sleep with the woman I love. Would that be alright with you?"

"I've got two weeks off and I'm going to spend all of it with you." We were eating in Ann's kitchen. Irene had offered to make breakfast for us but Ann insisted on doing it. She made cheese omelets, Canadian bacon, toast and coffee just to prove she could do it and do it well. She picked up the dirty dishes and headed for the sink.

"And we're going up to Monterey, right?" she replied.

I brought my empty coffee cup to the sink and rinsed it. "Right, we'll leave first thing tomorrow morning. I've made arrangements with Bea. We'll have our same little suite. It'll be great."

Ann asked, "Are we going to see the Walkers on the way up or the way back?"

"On the way back because I told Bea we'd be there tomorrow afternoon and she's holding the room."

"That's fine. Actually I think it will be better to see them after Monterey. I'll be a little more prepared for it...you know, the whole confronting-reality scene." She started wiping the table with a damp cloth.

I said, "We don't have to go there if you think it will be a problem for you. They'll understand and we can see them another time. It's up to you, but don't put yourself under pressure because there's no reason you have to, not now anyway."

"No," she said, "I think it's best to get it over with. That way I won't have to be thinking about it." She tossed the cloth in the sink, turned around and said, "I am worried about how I'll react, but I've just got to do it—and you've got to help me if I stumble, okay?"

"You'll be fine, but don't worry, I'll be right there. About the only thing you should be worried about is whether Edna will have baking powder biscuits for us to eat. You see? That's something I worry about. Other than that, it'll be just a nice visit with old friends, nothing more."

Once again, we were heading north on the Pacific Coast Highway, the good old PCH. This time, however, we were riding in comfort in my Thunderbird, its big V-8 engine purring effortlessly as we cruised along at eighty miles an hour. The radio was blaring music from an LA pop station. We sang along to *Hello Dolly*, *My Guy*, *Pretty Woman* and the Beatles' *I Want to Hold Your Hand*. The newscast reported on the Vietnam war and the attack on a U.S. destroyer, President Lyndon Johnson's war on poverty and the Warren Commission report that Lee Harvey Oswald acted alone in the assassination of President Kennedy.

As we passed Arroyo Grande, I had an idea. Pismo Beach was just a short distance further. When we got to Pismo I pulled into the same gas station we used when we rode up the PCH on our motorcycles. I stopped by a pump, the attendant came out and I asked him to fill it up with high test. I got out and went around and opened the door for Ann.

As she got out, she looked around and said, "Wait a minute. This is where we stopped for gas when we…" She looked around again, then she threw her arms around me and planted a big kiss on my mouth. "You goofball," she yelped. "This is where you asked me to marry you."

I walked her to a little open place with a view of the ocean.

The gas station guy yelled, "Want me to check under the hood, sir?"

"No," I yelled back, "it's okay." Holding Ann's hand, "You're right, this is the exact spot. And what did you say?"

"I can't remember exactly, I was too dumbstruck. I didn't have a clue you were going to pop the question, especially here at a gas station. But I know I said yes and I know you bought me this beautiful ring," she held up her left hand and admired it, "at that store in Salinas." Ann paused and looked thoughtfully out at the water. In the distance, a large freighter was sailing south, probably toward Port Hueneme. She watched it for a moment then faced me and said, "Salinas. Boy-oh-boy, we had some adventures there, didn't we?"

"We sure did." I searched her face for a clue to her thoughts. "Does it bother you to think about that time?"

"I'm not sure." She flashed a smile. "I just won't think about it right now. Maybe later I'll turn it over in my mind, but right now let's not worry about it, just enjoy the ocean, the smell of gasoline and oil..." She laughed, grabbed my hand and said, "C'mon. I can't wait to see Bea again."

I opened the passenger door for her and asked the attendant, who had just finished washing the windshield, what I owed.

He looked at the pump and replied, "Twelve gallons? That's, let's see..." He took the pencil wedged behind his ear, did some math on a small note pad and came up with $3.12. I gave him the exact change, he tipped his cap with a thank you, and we took off.

As we passed Morro Bay and Route 41, Ann glanced up the road leading to Atascadero. She turned off the radio. "That's where it all started for us. You remember? It was pretty wild and crazy that first night, wasn't it?"

"Yes it was. Looking back on it, I guess I never should have asked you how you learned to make love like that. That opened a can of worms, didn't it?"

"Sadly, I'd have to say that yes, it did, but eventually it all worked out. At least I didn't have to hide my past from you—it was all there for you to see and you saw it. I know it was hard for you to come to terms with it but you did, and now here we are, in love, engaged and on our way to a happy place and a happy life."

We stopped in Cayucos and had something to eat, then continued north. A couple hours later, we drove through Monterey and, near the outskirts of town, pulled into Bea's yard. Ann was excited. She jumped out of the car, ran up the steps, pushed open the front door and shouted, "Bea, we're back."

I followed with a suitcase in each hand. I could hear Ann and Bea jabbering away in the kitchen, so I walked up the steps to our little suite on the second floor. The room looked just like it did the last time we stayed there—nice! I was just about to head back down to the car when Bea and Ann came up the steps chatting away like a couple of magpies.

"Ah, Richard, good to see you again and your lovely wife-to-be." I stood at the top of the steps and when Bea reached me, I gave her a hug. "Did you check out your room yet?" she asked.

"Yes, I did. It looks great."

Ann ran down the hallway and entered the room. "Oh, it's just the way it was last time we were here. I love it."

Bea and I exchanged smiles. I said, "Thanks for holding the room for us. It's all Ann's been talking about since we left the city."

Bea gave me a sheepish look. "I reckon you'll find out pretty soon anyway," she said. "You're the only guests in the house. You could've rented the whole place. We don't do a lot of business in early November. Things pick up a little for Thanksgiving and Christmas but that's a ways off. Anyway, for now you have the whole place to yourselves, 'cept for me, of course."

In the room, Ann was hanging her clothes in the closet and putting things in the bathroom. She was bubbling with pleasure. "Isn't this just perfect, Rick?"

"Perfect." I repeated. "Bea just told me we have the entire house to ourselves—no other guests are here. How's that?"

Ann turned to Bea. "Is that right, no one else is staying here?"

"'Fraid so." Bea said with mock disappointment. "I reckon I'll just have to charge you folks double or triple to make up for it." She chuckled and added, "Just kidding. Now, I'll get out of here and let you two settle in. If you need anything, let me know. Oh, I don't reckon you'll be needing my car this time. That's a pretty fancy machine you have out there. What kind is it?"

"That, my dear lady, is a new Ford Thunderbird. Pretty nice, huh?"

Bea said, "Sure is. Tell ya what. I let you borrow my Buick again and I'll use your car. Would that be okay?"

"Of course," Ann said. "Anytime you want it, just let us know."

I felt it was time for me to get involved. "Hey, wait a minute, that's my car—"

"It's okay, Rick. Bea will drive it very carefully and promise not to go faster than a hundred."

I followed Bea out and headed down to get the rest of our stuff from the car. When we both got down to the first floor I said in a low voice, "She's doing really well, don't you think?" Bea said she couldn't notice any difference in Ann at all. I asked her not to mention anything that had to do with Dykes or any of the other things that had happened when we were here last.

Bea assured me she would keep the conversation away from any topic that could trigger a negative reaction from Ann.

The late afternoon was chilly but Ann and I bundled up and, holding hands, we walked to the beach to admire the sunset. For the next several days, our trip was one of absolute harmony. We ate at the places we had enjoyed previously. We drove here and there, enjoying the quaint little towns and the unusual and interesting sights they provided. We packed a picnic basket and drove over to that special cove, the place I had taken Ann the day she came searching for me. We had revealed so much to one another while we were there. This time, we sat on the rocks by the water's edge reliving that time.

Ann mused, "That's when our love affair really started. When I drove away that day, I cried. But I think down deep I had a feeling we would somehow get together." She looked down at the waves breaking over the rocks below and gave me a sideways glance, "In spite of Angie."

The mention of Angie caught me like a blow to the stomach but I managed to say, "Angie was a figment of my imagination. She wasn't real then any more than she's real now. I thought you had come to terms with that."

"I have," she said. "But back then, as you recall, Angie was very much alive in your mind and she had a huge influence on you. You knew that and I knew it too. Don't you remember? Before I left that day I said you needed time, maybe a year, to come to terms with her death."

I gazed at the rippling water, pulled my legs up and wrapped my arms around my knees. "You were right, I did need time and you gave me that time. I did finally let Angie go, at least I stopped her from getting between you and me. I'll admit it...it was hard, but when we got back together, I had no doubt that you were the girl I would marry and always love."

As if there was some unspoken signal, we both stood. I wrapped Ann in my arms and kissed her again and again. I put my lips close to her ear and whispered, "We are going to marry and I mean, soon."

She pushed back and looked into my eyes. "Soon? How soon?"

"How about tomorrow?"

We were sipping coffee and enjoying excellent Danish pastries at our favorite café. The view of the beach and ocean were somewhat obscured by a light mist that hung over the water, and the air was cold.

"So, what's the program?" Ann asked.

"Okay. Check this out and see what you think." I leaned across the table and in an intimate tone said, "I'd like to run down to Carmel."

Ann said, "I remember, we rode the bikes down there. But why?"

"I'd like us to get married there, maybe in that old church that was built a couple hundred years ago. We rode by it and you wanted to go in, but I—"

"I remember it, and I did want to go in, but you wanted to go to lunch and so—"

"Right. Well, I was hungry. I think we should run over today and see what the possibilities are of getting married there. We could get a marriage license at the county office this morning, then if we can get it together in Carmel, we could be on our honeymoon by dinner time."

Ann couldn't help herself from laughing. "You are such a goofball. You've got this all figured out, have you? I thought the bride was responsible for planning the wedding."

"Well normally, yes," I replied.

"But this is not 'normal' is that it? In other words it's abnormal."

"Come on, Annette, get serious will you?"

"Oh, Annette is it. Wow, this must be serious. Okay, let me ask you a few questions."

"Shoot!"

Ann sat back abruptly. "You meant 'go ahead,' didn't you?"

I realized that "shoot" was definitely a poor choice of words. I reached across the table and took hold of both her hands. "I'm sorry, sweetheart. That was dumb. But go ahead, please, and ask your questions."

"I shouldn't let things like that bother me. It was just a gut reaction, I guess." Ann leaned forward and allowing herself a smile, continued, "Okay. Here are the questions: Are we not inviting anyone to our wedding? What about my parents? Shouldn't I call them and see if they'd like to attend? Don't we have a few special friends who might enjoy seeing us get married? Should this be a civil or church wedding? Do you even have a wedding ring to slip on my finger at the appropriate moment? And, I believe there are some legal requirements that you have overlooked such as blood tests." She gave me a wide-eyed look.

I looked back. I was thinking how to answer when she remarked, "As much as I want to marry you, let's give it a little time to think it through so that when we do get married, we will do it right. Meanwhile, for starters, you might want to see your jewelry buddy and pick out a wedding ring."

"That guy up in Salinas?"

"Sure, that's the one. He had a wedding ring that was a match for this one." She held out her left hand and tapped her engagement ring with a finger.

"You really want to go back to Salinas?"

"Sure. Why not?"

I sighed and shook my head. "You amaze me. You know why not, but if you're okay going up there, then fine. Let's go up there this morning and at least get that part of the plan taken care of." I stood and helped Ann with her chair.

She turned around and planted a kiss on my cheek. "Don't worry. We're going to get married and it will be soon. If I had any doubts about it, would we be shopping for a wedding ring?"

We drove to Salinas and found the jewelry store. Mr. Handleman greeted us.

"Ah, you've come back," he said, shaking hands with each of us. "Don't tell me, but I'm guessing you're ready to buy that matching wedding ring." He smiled as he slipped behind the counter, opened the sliding door and pulled out the ring. "Let's see how this fits." He took hold of Ann's left hand and slid off the engagement ring. "The wedding ring is always worn first so that it is closest to the woman's heart," he said. Then he replaced the engagement ring. "That looks very nice indeed."

Ann held up her left hand to inspect the rings. "Yes, it does, but I think the wedding band is a little too loose. What do you think?"

Handleman removed the engagement ring and fiddled with the band. "Yes, you're right." He took a measurement and said, "I can have this resized in about an hour. Have you something you can do in town?"

I looked at Ann who said, "We can go to a movie."

I gave her a surprised look. "Really? You want to go to a movie—here in Salinas?"

Ann's voice revealed a hint of annoyance. She turned away from Handleman and faced me. In a lowered voice, she said, "Oh for God's sake, Rick. Quit treating me as if the slightest thing could put me back in the—"

I interrupted her. "Okay, okay. Take it easy." I addressed

Handleman. "I guess we'll take the ring. Go ahead and resize it." This time, I was prepared. I handed him a credit card without asking the price.

He wrote up the charge and handed me the receipt. "There's over a karat of diamonds on that wedding band and each one is a perfect cut which is why the price is—"

"It's fine and it's a perfect match to the other ring." I took Ann's arm. "We'll be back in a while."

When we were outside, Ann said, "That is a beautiful wedding band. Thank you so very much." Her tone brightened, "Now we have to get married if I want to wear that gorgeous ring."

We did go to a movie, *Goldfinger*, but it was not in the same theater as the previous time. Afterwards we picked up the wedding band and drove back to Monterey. After dinner, we walked on the beach holding hands and shivered—it was cold!

Bea greeted us when we returned. "Cold out there. How about some hot chocolate?"

The hot chocolate was perfect and while we drank it, we chatted with Bea. Ann asked me to show Bea the wedding band, which Bea thought was quite lovely. And who wouldn't? It was quite lovely!

When we returned to our room, Ann quickly undressed and jumped into bed. "Come on, hurry up and get in here. I'm freezing. I need you to warm me up."

And I did. The old Ann was definitely back!

I called the ops office on Thursday and learned that I was scheduled for a trip to Florida with some execs in the Jetstar on Monday. On Friday, after promising Bea that she would be invited to our wedding, we said goodbye and headed south to Cambria and the Walkers' place. Ann didn't want to stay overnight in Cambria so we decided that after our visit with

Edna and Emmett, we'd find a motel in Los Osos or one of the other little towns south of Cambria and leave Saturday morning for home. That was the plan.

I called Edna on Thursday and arranged for our visit the next day. Edna sounded warm and normal, but nevertheless I had a flashback to the time I had called her when Dykes was in the house—the memory sent a chill down my backbone.

We passed the entrance to the Cambria Estates Vineyard and Winery. Ann glanced at the sign but didn't say anything. When we pulled into the Walkers' drive, Ann remained silent, staring straight ahead.

"You okay?"

"I'm fine," she replied. "It does feel a little strange but it'll be fine."

I kept to the left of the drive and pulled up in front of the left side of the house, about as far away from the shop as I could get. Edna and Emmett came out the front door and down the steps, and waited for us to get out of the car. When Ann stepped out Edna was all over her immediately. Emmett came over and shook my hand.

"We wasn't sure that wuz you in that fancy car. Is it yours?"

"Yes, it's mine. How do you like it?"

"I'll have a look in a minute but first I gotta give yer girlfren' a hug."

Edna released Ann and Emmett took over. Edna said, "Land sakes, it's good ta see you folks again and Annie looks real good, don't she? Beautiful as ever."

Ann looked at Edna and smiled.

"Edna's right," Emmett said. "No doubt about it." He strode over to me and said, "Now, let's take a good look at that car of yours."

Edna took Ann's hand and the two went inside the house

while Emmett gave the Thunderbird a going over, including a look under the hood to check out the engine. "Boy, that's purdy. I'll bet with a big engine like that, she's a goin' Jessie."

"Oh, she can move alright," I said. I was getting a little anxious about Ann being alone with Edna. I had no idea what Edna might say to her. "Let's go see what the ladies are up to," I said as I started walking toward the house. Emmett dropped the hood and followed.

Inside, Ann was sitting at the kitchen table—*the infamous kitchen table!* Edna was at the counter doing something. I'll admit being in that kitchen again gave me a bit of a twinge. I had a momentary recall of Dykes standing there with his AK 47 pointed at me. I shrugged it off and studied Ann's face. I didn't see any sign of apprehension or discomfort. I put on a big smile. "Good to be back with you guys," I exclaimed. Looking at Ann, I said, "How you doing, honey?"

"I'm fine. Edna's fixing something for us to eat." There was something in Ann's tone of voice that sounded strange. I think she was feeling a little pressure or something—maybe feeling apprehensive.

"I got an idea," I said, "How about we run over next door to the winery and get a bottle of wine to have with lunch? It won't take but a few minutes." Without waiting for an answer, I grabbed Ann's hand, pulled her out of her chair and headed for the door. "We'll be back directly," I said as we exited the house and headed for the car.

"Rick, what's going on? What are you doing?"

"I think you needed to get out of there for a minute. I could see you were, I don't know, uncomfortable or something. Anyway, I have to say that being in that room made me feel a bit queasy. Please, get in the car. I think a couple glasses of wine will do us both good."

"I was fine, really. But I wasn't in there when he came in and surprised you. I guess it's different for you."

"Sure as hell is. I really didn't think being back here would be a problem for me—and it's not a big problem—but..." I glanced at her worried face. "Don't worry. I'm fine. It was a momentary thing and let's not make too much of it." I drove out of the Walkers' drive, turned right and then right again onto the Winery's drive and up to the tasting room.

As we headed to the tasting room, I said, "Look, if any of this turns out to be a problem for you, please tell me and we'll go, okay?"

Ann said, "Really, Rick, I'm doing fine. Don't worry. But if things get to me, I'll let you know."

We tasted several different red wines and settled on a Central Coast Pinot Noir which was quite good. I bought two bottles and we drove back to the Walkers'. When we arrived I saw that they had set up a table on the front porch.

Ann said, "These people are way ahead of us. I'm sure they understood what happened in there and they're making sure it doesn't happen again."

"You're right. They're a lot smarter than we give them credit for," I said as we left the car with the wine and walked up the steps.

"Lunch'll be right out," Edna yelled from the kitchen. "Have a seat. There's ice tea in the pitcher."

Emmett came out and set a tray of sandwiches on the table. He saw the wine and returned with four glasses and a corkscrew. Edna joined us with a large bowl of potato salad and a plate of pickles. Ann took a seat facing the hillside that led to the vineyard. I sat to her left. We looked at the hillside and I remembered that night we pushed through the vines and came down the hill while watching the girl climb out of the bathroom window.

I'm sure Ann was reliving it as well but she said nothing except, "Rick, are you going to open the wine?" She addressed Edna, "This is delicious potato salad. Before we leave, I need you to give me the recipe."

I filled the four glasses which we all raised in a toast to a good life of love and happiness. Clink!

After lunch we chatted with the Walkers for a while, got into the second bottle of wine, and then Ann said she wanted to take a little walk out to the shop and have a look around. Emmett and I exchanged surprised glances. He told Ann that everything was the same, there was nothing new to see. Ann wanted to know about the car, the green Nash, and the girl who owned it. Emmett told her the police had towed the car away and he never saw or heard anything more about the girl. Ann didn't comment or ask any further questions of Emmett. She just nodded her head from time to time as a sign of understanding.

Rising from her chair, Ann looked south toward the shop then turned her head to scan the field that led from the shop to the road. "Come on, Rick," she said, "Let's take a little walk."

I joined her, taking her left hand with my right. We walked down the steps and headed toward the shop. When we reached the north end of the shop, she stopped and looked in.

"That's where I used the bathroom," she pointed, "in there. The green car was over there, near that wall," she said pointing a finger at the south end of the shop. "I came out of the bathroom and heard you say something in a loud voice, then I saw you walk by with your hands in the air. I hid behind those oil drums." She canted her head in the direction of the oil drums.

Her voice was very calm and quiet and her face had no expression as she continued to speak. "Then Dykes came into view with his gun aimed at your back. I remember thinking that

341

his gun looked like the ones the deputies had when they met with us at the motel. Dykes was saying something to you as he walked past. Funny, I was very calm, not excited or anything, just calm. My purse was hanging from a nail by the bathroom door. I opened it and took out the gun. I stayed close to the wall and edged along it to the front of the shop. I raised my gun and aimed at his back, just the way I was taught. I slowly pulled the trigger and the gun went off. I almost dropped it. I walked toward Dykes and saw him drop to his knees. He dropped his rifle and was holding his side with his left hand. I saw you turn around and heard you yell at him. That's when he reached for his gun. I knew he would kill you if he got his gun up. I was still very calm. I walked over to him, pointed my gun at his head and fired. He fell over on his side. I was going to shoot again when you got hold of my hand and took the gun. You said he was dead. You said I saved your life. I had done a good thing."

Ann walked over to the edge of the grass, close to the spot where Dykes had died, and looked down. "I did a good thing. The police said it, too, didn't they? They said I had saved everyone's life including my own." Ann looked up at me and put her arms out, and I stepped into her embrace. She didn't cry. She just held on to me for a long while. At last she let go and gave me a smile. "I think we can go home. I've done what the doctors said I had to do. I'll be okay now."

chapter forty-two

he plane was ready to go Monday morning. I was buckled in and my co-pilot, Harris, was standing at the bottom of the steps waiting for the passengers. I looked out the window and saw a company car pull up and a uniformed girl get out. I couldn't believe it. It was Carly Menzalora holding a small suitcase. She said something to Harris and climbed the steps. I unbuckled my harness and was about to slip out of the seat when she walked into the cockpit.

"Good morning, Captain. Miss Menzalora reporting for duty."

I gave her a hard look. "What the hell is going on? There was no stewardess assigned to this trip. I only have four passengers." I think Carly was taken aback, thinking I would welcome her.

"What kind of a greeting is that, for Christ' sake?" she hissed. "I volunteered to go in return for the ride to Miami. I knew you'd be flying and thought it'd be fun." She suddenly turned and looked back at the cabin. "The passengers are coming up. I guess we'll talk later." She left the cockpit and I heard her begin to greet the passengers.

Harris stepped into the cockpit, slid into the right seat and buckled up. "Ready to light it?" he asked.

"In a minute." I walked into the cabin. Carly was locking

the door. The four passengers, two men and two women, were getting settled. I looked at them again and realized that Carl and Charlotte were on board. Carl looked up and stared at me for a moment, then yelled, "Hey, Rick, how the hell are you?" He popped open his seat belt and stood. I walked over to him and we shook hands. He turned to his wife and said, "Honey, you remember Rick, don't you? He was one of the pilots on our anniversary trip to New York."

Charlotte offered her hand. "And your girlfriend was an old friend of ours. Sure, I remember. In fact, I asked Gunner to call me when we got back to LA but she never did."

I said, "That's because there is no more Gunner. Gunner is dead."

Charlotte gasped. She put her hand to her mouth and mumbled, "Oh, I'm so sorry."

She was about to say more but I quickly said, "We've got to go. We can talk later." I walked toward the cockpit, stopped, turned around and said, "Miss Menzalora is here to see to your comfort. If you want anything, please ask her." In the cockpit, I slipped into my seat, buckled up, put on the headset and said to Harris, "Okay, start the checklist."

A couple hours into the trip, I received a radio message from Flight Ops advising that we were to fly to Bartlesville, Oklahoma Tuesday morning, pick up two company engineers, take them to Lubbock, Texas and return to LA. I rang for Carly and asked her to come up front. I told her about the change of plans and asked if she wanted to stay in Miami and fly commercial back to LA or return with us the next day. She said she would let me know after we got to Miami. I gave Harris control of the plane and went back to the cabin.

I addressed the four passengers. "I just received a message telling me that I'm to fly to Bartlesville tomorrow morning and take some engineers down to Lubbock and return to LA. You can come along if you like or remain in Miami and fly back on a commercial airline. You can talk it over and let me know later on. If you'd like to send a message back to the company, write it down and I'll radio it in." I looked at my watch, "We should be landing in Miami in about an hour."

When we parked and had shut down, the four passengers took off in a cab. Apparently they had decided not to challenge the change order. They told me that they would be staying in Miami. After refueling and securing the plane, Harris, Carly and I took a cab to our hotel where the company had reserved two rooms, one for Harris and one for me. Since Carly was listed on the manifest as a passenger, no room had been reserved for her. When she realized what the situation was she asked me what she should do. Harris was standing right there so I told her to get a room, which she did, albeit reluctantly. Later, the three of us had dinner at a nearby restaurant. The dinner dishes had been cleared and we were drinking coffee when Harris looked at his watch and said, "It's only eight—what would you guys like to do?"

As if rehearsed, Carly and I exchanged glances. I'm sure Harris noticed because he said, "If you two would rather—"

I jumped in. "There's nothing going on here. Carly and I dated a few times in the past but now that I'm engaged—"

It was Carly's turn to jump in. "Engaged? You're engaged? When did that happen?"

"A while back. You knew about it."

"But she's in the hospital and—"

"She's out now and completely fine. We just spent a week together up in Monterey. She's totally fine."

Harris looked at each of us, unsure if he should say anything.

"Listen, I'll leave you two. It's obvious you have some issues to—"

"No issues. I was just surprised, that's all, and it's settled," Carly said. She suddenly shifted gears. "I wouldn't mind going to a movie. You up for a movie, Harris? What about you, Rick?"

Harris chose to go. I opted to go back to the hotel for some sleep.

I called Ann when I got back to my room and told her about seeing Charlotte and Carl.

"Did they ask about me?" Ann asked.

"As a matter of fact, they did."

"And what did you tell them?"

"Actually Charlotte didn't ask about you. What she said was, 'How's Gunner?'"

"And what did you say?"

"I'll tell you exactly what I said. I said, 'There is no more Gunner. Gunner is dead!'"

Ann gasped. "What? You told her that I was dead?"

"No, I told her that *Gunner* was dead, and Gunner is dead! However, Annette is very much alive."

"Come on. Are you being serious?"

"As a heart attack. In any case, I don't think she'll be calling you—ever!" Taking on a more serious tone I said, "Now, about our wedding. I hope you are working on the details because I want to be married to you before the end of the month. I don't want to get married in December, okay? So get cracking on it."

Ann replied, "Okay, okay. Take it easy. Do you know when you'll be back?"

"Tomorrow evening, so get ready."

"Ready? Ready for what?"

"For me!"

"You are a goofball, you know that?"

"Yes. I know."

On the trip back to LA, Carly came in the cockpit just once to offer us something to eat and drink. Other than that, she remained by herself in the cabin. When Harris and I exited the ops office in LA, Carly was standing nearby.

Harris gave Carly a nod and kept walking. "See you guys," he said.

I shouted, "Thanks, Harris. Good job."

Carly looked at me and said, "Could we please go someplace and talk?"

"Talk about what? You know what my situation is now and—
"

"That's what I want to talk about," she insisted.

"Carly, you and I are never going to do anything again—ever! I'm getting married and I'm just old-fashioned enough to think that fidelity in a marriage is very important. To tell you the truth, I'm not real proud of myself for going to bed with you when Ann was in the hospital. But I did and that's that."

Carly didn't say anything as we started walking toward the parking lot. I headed for my pickup and she followed. I unlocked the door, opened it and got in. Carly stood there.

"I guess this is goodbye then," she said. "Don't worry, I won't bother you. If I happen to end up on a trip with you, I'll behave. Don't worry." She pursed her lips then bit down on the lower one. "I just want to say that it was nice, real nice being with you, but things are what they are and I'll move on, right?"

"Sure you will," I said. "And Carly, you know I enjoyed being with you. More than that, it was a hard time for me then and I guess I was vulnerable and you helped me." I gave her an intense look. "You know what I mean." I leaned out the door and kissed her on the lips. "You'll find someone, I know you will."

I eased back in the seat and reached for the door. I muttered, "Goodnight. Drive carefully."

She stepped back and I shut the door, started the engine and drove off. When I glanced in the rear view mirror, she was still standing there.

Ann greeted me with a hug and a delicious kiss. She followed me into the bedroom and watched me strip off my uniform and head for the bathroom.

"I'll be out in ten minutes," I said as I stepped into the shower. I was rinsing the shampoo when I felt something behind me. I jumped. Ann put her arms around me and let her hands go searching. It didn't take long for her to find what she was searching for and from then on it was "Katy, bar the door."

We were still wet when we fell onto the bed. Ann was on top of me staring down, those green eyes flashing, her breath ragged as she hissed, "And now, my friend, I'm going to show you a little trick I once learned from a very bad girl named Gunner."

I protested. "But I told you, Gunner is dead, remember?"

"I know, but I'm not Gunner and I'm very much alive!"

You might say we worked up an appetite, and it was a good thing that Ann had a pot of beef stew simmering over low heat. In the ice box (I never got use to calling it a refrigerator), she had salads plated up and a bottle of Moët Champagne. She pulled out the bubbly and the salads and asked me to open the bottle.

I poured champagne into two stem glasses and asked, "So, my little vixen, to what or who shall we toast?"

"In that context, I believe the proper word is *whom* not *who*," Ann suggested. "Regardless, I raise my glass to the success of our upcoming marriage ceremony." Her smile was impish. "Which will take place on November 25ᵗʰ at the Methodist Church in Beverly Hills, the Reverend Arthur Brawley officiating." Ann's grin grew larger and wider as we clinked glasses. Affecting a British accent, she said, "What say you to that, me lad?"

I replied, "Jolly good, old sport." I dropped the accent. "Is that for real?"

"It is. Got it all lined out and I've made a bunch of calls to invite some folks to attend. I think you'll like the guest list since it includes some of your fly-boy buddies and your little girlfriend."

My heart skipped a beat. "My little girlfriend? Who's that?"

"That kid Nancy who lives above you. She was really tickled when I called her. She's a fun gal." Ann turned serious, "Is that okay?"

"Sure it is. It's all okay. You son of a gun, you are something, you know that?"

"Yes, I am." Ann used a wooden spoon to stir the stew. "You ready to eat?"

"Yes. Say, I just realized Irene isn't here."

"I know, I told her I was okay to be alone now and I wouldn't need her to look out for me, but I did invite her to the wedding along with Bea and the Walkers. The reception will be at the church and I've got a great Beverly Hills catering company lined up. Very expensive, but don't worry, I can afford it. I think it's going to be quite the shindig." Ann, with a slight tilt of her head, gave me a self-satisfied look. Then her brow wrinkled. "What, did I miss something?"

"Well...yes and no. You've got the wedding covered and it sounds fantastic, but what about the honeymoon?"

Ann ladled stew on to the plates. "You want some bread and butter with this?"

"No thanks, this will be fine."

She sat down and put a spoonful of stew in her mouth. Chewing and talking simultaneously, she said, "Now, about the honeymoon. Here's my plan: the day after the wedding, we take the pickup, go over to your place, pack up everything you want to keep and bring it over here. You can make a list of the things you want to sell and ask your landlady if she'd like to buy the furniture so that she can rent the apartment as furnished."

I laughed. "Boy, that'll be some exciting honeymoon."

"Hmmm." She eyed me. "It could be, depending on what we do when we get back here from your place."

I gave her a look.

"Seriously, we just had a lovely week up in Monterey—it was a perfect honeymoon. Let's just relax and enjoy being together until you get some vacation time. We'll go someplace then. Meanwhile, I'm going back to work— talk to some of my old clients to start with and then, if things look right, I'm going to start my own company with just a few really good clients and see what happens."

"You've thought it all out, obviously, and I think it sounds good if that's what you want to do. But don't feel like you have to work. I'm making pretty good money and it isn't necessary for you to work."

"What would I do? Sit around and eat bonbons all day?" Ann got up and went to the stove with her plate and ladled out some more stew. "This is darned good, if I do say so myself. Want some more?"

"It's delicious, but I've had enough." As Ann slipped back onto her chair, I said, "By the way, I've been meaning to ask, what does this fancy apartment of yours cost a month?"

"Well... It is Beverly Hills and things here are more expensive than most other places."

"So, how much?"

Sheepishly Ann said, "Twelve hundred a month."

I guess my jaw dropped because Ann looked at me and began laughing. "I said it was expensive."

"Twelve hundred, that's what? That's something like fourteen thousand a year. Geeze, you could buy a pretty nice house for that kind of money."

Ann picked up my plate and put it in the sink then walked behind my chair, put her arms around me and talked into the top of my head. "Hey, that's not a bad idea. Maybe we should buy a little house." She started singing, "A cottage for two for just me and you..."

It really was a fairy tale kind of wedding. I was dressed up in a new Hickey-Freeman tailored suit and Ann wore a terrific white wedding dress. She looked sensational. Here was this thirty-one year old redhead whose beauty outshone Marilyn Monroe, Ingrid Bergman, Elizabeth Taylor and every other Hollywood star—at least as far as I was concerned, and I'll bet the people at our wedding agreed. My best man was Ron Schmidt. Ann had two lovely girls both dressed in pale green dresses, as maids of honor. I had never met either of them before the wedding but apparently they and Ann were very good longtime friends.

The reception started with a sit-down dinner followed by dancing to the music of a five piece band. It was all just spectacular. Ann had every phase of the affair perfectly arranged. I could see why she was so good at her job. Like they say, it's all in the details.

My jaw began to ache from doing so much talking and smiling that evening. And when I awoke the next morning with Ann pressed against me, I realized my life would never be the same. Here I was, married again but this time it was different—totally different. I was thirty-eight years old, an established pilot with a very good job, doing the thing I loved to do and feeling as though things just couldn't get any better. I remember being in bed the morning after the wedding, my hands under my head, gazing at the ceiling, thinking, *I'm one lucky son of a bitch.*

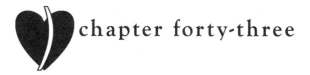

chapter forty-three

life was good—maybe too good. When you have the perfect wife, the perfect job, the perfect life—okay, maybe not perfect, but as close to it as a human being can get—I guess you get to feeling, I don't know, complacent? Yes, that's how I felt back then and for a long time thereafter—complacent, content, satisfied.

Ann's consulting business began to blossom and as it did so, her free time began to diminish. Still, whenever we could, we'd take off on our Harleys and travel someplace, any place, it didn't matter where. What mattered was we were having fun, we were riding our bikes, and most of all, we were together. As much as I enjoyed riding with my many biker buddies (mostly men), I had the most enjoyment riding with my number one buddy, Ann. She was an excellent motorcycle jock. She was a careful yet aggressive rider, which made our rides exciting.

We never seemed to run out of interesting things to talk about. I'm not going to tell you that we never had a spat or a heated discussion—sure we did. It usually was about her spending so much time at work while I had lots of time off and wanted her to ride someplace with me. We never argued about money. There was nothing to argue about. Her burgeoning business, together with my expanding salary, provided a sizeable income. And believe it or not, the insurance money I had received from the accident was still there, untouched, and with Ann's expertise, it had grown considerably.

In May, 1965, I decided to buy an airplane.

Ann had just returned from work when I popped the question. "So, how was work today?"

"Pretty good, actually. Picked up a new client who apparently is loaded."

"That's great," I said without enthusiasm, knowing that meant less time for us to have fun. Ann set her briefcase on a chair and walked to the little free-standing bar I had set up shortly after taking up residence with my new wife. I moved to her side, gave her a perfunctory kiss, then flashed a broad smile and said, "Sit down, take a load off your brains and I'll make you a drink—martini?"

Returning my smile, she said, "Sure, only make it with vodka instead of gin."

She kicked off her shoes and sat on the couch. I mixed the martini, dropped in a jalapeño stuffed olive, gave it a stir and handed it to her.

She looked up, smiled briefly and said, "Thanks. I should keep a Mason jar of martinis in my office. It can get pretty intense sometimes." She took a long sip.

"I know it can and I'm going to say it again, you need to get some help—another accountant or financial guy to help you. I get all this time off but most of the time it's wasted because you're busy working."

Ann laid her drink on the coffee table and replied in measured tones, "Yes, I am busy working which means," she raised her voice, "I'm busy making money!"

"Okay, I understand, but you've heard me say this before: You need to temper your work so that you have sufficient time to *enjoy* the money." I sat down next to her and gave her a light kiss on the cheek. "Of course, we enjoy having the money but what is the money for? It's for having fun!"

Ann looked dismayed. "Are you about to go into one of your goofball song and dance routines on how to spend money?"

I held up my index finger, signaling that I was about to say something important. "I'm going to buy a plane."

"What? A plane? You already spend most of your life sitting in a cockpit and you want to do it some more? What in the world are you thinking about?"

"I'll tell you exactly what I'm thinking: I've got my eye on a little Piper Cub. Are you familiar with it?"

Ann said, "No, should I be? And what do you mean, you've got your eye on it?"

"The one I'm interested in is a 1940 J4-E. And I can buy it for just $1,200. Wait a sec, I've got some pictures to show you." I ran into the office and brought back a folder with pictures and information about the plane.

Ann thumbed through the pictures and scanned the printed material while finishing her drink. "Here," she said, handing me the empty glass. "Make me another one, please." She returned to the pictures, "It's a cute little plane. Where is it now?"

I stirred the martini and dropped in another olive. I handed it to her and said, "That's the only bad part about this deal...it's at an airport in Willoughby, Ohio."

"Willoughby? Where the hell is that?"

"It's a little town not too far from Cleveland. I thought I'd fly commercial out there and take a look and if it's everything the owner says it is and if it checks out mechanically, of course, I'll fly it back."

Ann blew a puff of air. "Whoa, hold on. You would go without me?"

"Would you want to go? I mean, can you afford to be away for something like a week?"

"Why a week? It's not a horse and buggy is it? How long would it take to fly from Cleveland to LA?"

I laughed, I mean really, laughed.

Ann sat back and scowled. "What's so funny?"

"Honey, it's a Piper Cub. It has a seventy-five horsepower engine. The plane weighs about seven-hundred pounds—that's what my motorcycle weighs. The top speed is a hundred miles an hour; it cruises at ninety. Let's say I hit a twenty mile an hour head wind, I'll see cars on the highway passing me. Also, every three-hundred miles or so, I'll have to land and put gas in it. As I recall, the distance from LAX to CLE is 2,000 miles. Want to do the math on how long that flight will take?"

I could see from the look on her face that Ann was making a mental calculation.

"Don't strain your brain," I said, "I've already figured it out. If I average eighty miles an hour, I'll be in the air about twenty-five hours. I'll need to land seven times for gas, go to the john, get something to eat...figure an hour and a half each, that's another eleven hours, and I presume on a trip that takes thirty-six hours, I'll need some sleep, so add another ten hours. Add it up." I held up a hand. "It's okay. I already did. It's going to take at least forty-six hours, or possibly two and half days. That's about the same time as it would take in a car. Could you handle that? Would you even want to?"

Ann had begun to smile. She straightened and said, "Of course! Are you kidding? That, dear boy, sounds like a first class adventure. Go ahead and set up the trip for around the end of the month."

"You're serious?" I gave her sloppy kiss on the mouth. "That's great!"

Ann wiped her lips with the back of her hand. "You bet it is. And while we're spending all that time in that little plane, sitting side by side, you can teach me how to fly it. Does the right seat have controls?"

"Of course, darling. By golly, by the time we get to California, you'll be ready to solo and take a check ride."

Ann was caught up in it now. "On the way back, we could land near Cambria and visit the Walters. This is exciting," she said, clapping her hands. "Let's go get some dinner, drink some bubbly, then come home and make love. Would you be agreeable to that idea?"

"Sure...or we could turn it around and make love now, then have dinner."

Ann jumped up and grabbed my hand, pulling me to my feet. "I like that even better."

The little J-4 was just as the owner, Ernie Quick, described it. After I'd done a through ground inspection and had read the logs, I took it up with Ernie in the right seat. No kidding, I had the best time flying that little bird. I told him, I hadn't had this much fun flying an airplane since I took my first ride in a "Yellow Peril," the Stearman Model 75 Kaydet, the Navy's primary trainer.

Ann was waiting by the hanger when I pulled up and shut her down. I jumped out and ran over to Ann. "You are going to love flying this plane."

Ernie said, "Oh, is your wife a pilot?"

"Not now," I replied, "but she sure as hell will be by the time we land in LA."

Both he and Ann got a good laugh out of that. "No, really. I'm not kidding. She'll get plenty of stick time plus lots of practice landing and taking off."

Ann grabbed my arm. "Are you serious? You're going to let me fly it?"

I took her hand, walked to the plane and opened the right door. "Take a look." She peered into the cockpit. "Do you remember me saying that by the time you climb out of that seat in LA, you'll be ready to solo?"

"I thought you were kidding around," she said. She got in and sat in the right seat. She scanned the instruments and looked around. "Where's the steering wheel?"

Both Ernie and I laughed.

"You see that pole?" I reached in and took hold of it. "That's called the 'stick.' You move it from side to side and the plane banks. You push it forward and the nose goes down, pull it to you and the nose goes up. Those pedals under there, control the rudder...for turning right or left."

Ann put her feet on the rudder pedals and took hold of the stick and moved it around. She turned her head and gave me a huge smile. "This is going to be fun. I love it already."

Ernie said, "It's even more fun when you get it off the ground and in the air."

"So, are we buying it then?" Ann asked.

"What do you think? Should we?"

"I don't know about you, but I intend to leave here in this plane. Write the man a check."

I had done my homework. I had the course plotted with ETAs at airfields along the route. I had my Jeppesen chart in which I had marked those airfields we would use along with alternates in case we needed them. I called in our flight plan. When Ann and I climbed in the Cub at six the following morning, the plane was ready and so were we.

As we taxied out to the runway, Ann was beaming. "This is

great," she yelled over the roar of the engine which, incidentally, wasn't much of a roar compared to a 2,000 HP Pratt and Whitney engine. I kept up a running commentary, telling her what I was doing and why. I had her scan the instruments and explained what each was for. There weren't that many...just the basic stuff. "Here we go." I gave it full power and we were airborne in seconds. Ann, staring out the windscreen, had a massive smile spread across her face.

"I love it," she repeated over and over.

We slowly reached our cruise altitude of 5,000 feet and I said, "Are you ready to fly this thing?"

"Really?" She made a funny face. "Okay, what do I do?"

Four hours later, we made our first landing. Actually I did the approach and landing but I had Ann keep her hand lightly on the stick so she could get the feel of it. Again, I kept up a running commentary of what I was doing. The plane was very easy to land...it just sort of floated to the ground. Ann had control when we landed the third time and she did a pretty good job—just one bounce. She also had the stick for the take-off. The next day I had her in the left seat and she basically did most of the flying and landings. By the time we reached California, she had that Cub well under control. At our last gas stop before landing at LAX, I took back the left seat as Ann wasn't ready to deal with all the traffic and the ATC but, just as promised, she sure was ready for a check flight. As we started our decent, I looked at her. She was radiant and bubbling with cockpit jargon.

"Do you realize that you are not only an aviator now, but the most beautiful aviator in the world?"

"Do you realize how much I love you for doing this for me? It's opened a whole new world. Seeing the country from up here is beyond amazing...it's breathtaking. The view at a few thousand feet is a heck of a lot different than what you see from an airliner."

I gave her a big smile. "So, now we have two things we enjoy doing together. Riding motorcycles and flying airplanes."

Ann said, "Make that three—motorcycles, airplanes, and making love."

In 1965 the British oil rig *Sea Gem* collapsed. That sent a shock wave through the oil industry, at least for those companies that were engaged in off-shore drilling operations. I flew the president of the company and a couple of his assistants to England. The Chief Operating Officer flew in another plane. The company never allowed their top execs to travel together. I was in England for close to a week before we flew back. I asked Ann if she wanted to go as obviously there was plenty of room on the plane, but she couldn't because of business. However she did go on quite a few trips to interesting and exotic places during my time with the company.

We really had fun with our plane. In November 1965, to celebrate our first anniversary, we puddle-jumped to over a dozen California coastal towns with Ann doing most of the flying. The little unattended airports with dirt strips improved her skills as a pilot. I was so darn proud of her. I loved watching her when she was in the left seat. He face mirrored everything that was going on in her mind. When she realized I was staring at her, she would turn her head and say, "What? Did I miss something?"

"No. You're doing just fine. I'm just looking at you because I'm impressed with how quickly you've mastered this thing. You seem to always know what you are doing and more important, why you are doing it."

"Thank you. That's very kind of you to say that."

"Well, it's true. But I also keep my eye on you to..."

Ann jumped in, "To make sure I'm not screwing up."

"No. To admire you. To remind myself that I'm the luckiest guy in the world to be married to the most beautiful pilot in the world."

Ann giggled. "And I'm married to the handsomest, most skilled aviator in the world." She took hold of the stick with her left hand and with her right patted my knee. "Am I right?"

During my time off, I'd fool around with the Cub. I added some avionics, exterior navigation lights, and a really good Bendix radio. Ann was becoming jealous of all my free time and hired what turned out to be a first-class assistant. She also moved out of her office into a larger, more upscale space in Beverly Hills.

She was constantly enlarging her client base. We'd be at some airport and Ann would step out of the plane, take off her cap and run a comb through her marvelous red hair, to the delight of the mostly male onlookers, who couldn't wait to meet this gorgeous aviatrix. There are a lot of rich guys who own very expensive airplanes hanging around general aviation lounges and dining rooms. They would mostly ignore me and strike up a conversation with Ann. She would invite them to sit with us, she'd introduce me, then ask the person what make of plane he owned. Eventually, if she thought the person looked like a prospect, she'd hand him a card with a come hither look and say, "Call me if you think I could be of some help with your financial planning or investments." She picked up quite a few new clients at airports...just like that.

Once in a while, Ann would travel with me in the Jetstar. Now that she was a licensed pilot, she wanted to spend time up front. She was amazed at everything the plane had in the way of avionics, instrumentation, navigation and communication. She would ask, "How the hell can you keep track of all this stuff and at 500 miles an hour?" I think that for the first time, Ann began to understand what I did and how I did it. She was impressed!

Ann had been flying the cub for a couple of months and was all caught up in the whole flying thing. She was reading aviation magazines and constantly asking me questions—how do you do this and how do you do that? I told her I was taking one of the guys to Texas and would be flying back empty. I asked if she'd like to come along and ride up front so she could see what we were doing. She got all excited and went along on the trip.

On the way back to LA from Dallas, Ann was up front. I had a new guy, Brett, flying copilot. Ann watched everything we were doing. She asked, "Would it be okay if I sat at the controls for just a minute? I'd just like to see what it feels like."

I glanced at Brett, who returned my gaze with a questioning look of his own. I said, "Would you mind letting her sit there for a couple of minutes? I'm not going to let her fly the plane, although she probably could."

Brett unbuckled his harness, "Hey, you're the captain. If you say it's okay, then I'm cool with it, although I'm sure there's a rule that..."

"Sure there is and I wouldn't even think about it if we had passengers but, don't worry, I'll keep control."

Brett slipped out of the seat and Ann took his place. He helped her with the harness, then sat behind us.

I put on my instructor's face and tone. "Now, first thing, do a scan, check all the gauges, then the settings, switches—everything there in front of you."

"Oh, my God. How can you keep track of all this stuff?"

I replied, "It's a bit daunting at first, right, Brett?"

"That's for sure," he said.

"But," I continued, "you get to a point where you run your eyes over the panel and you have the information. What happens is, as you scan it, you're looking for anything that isn't normal... that gauge is the one that'll get your attention."

"I'm sure it will after you know what the normal reading is," Ann muttered.

"That takes time in the saddle. Most of the time, we let the plane fly itself by activating the auto-pilot, which is what we're doing now." I gave Ann a thumbs up. "Okay? I think you're ready to solo so give Brett back his seat."

Ann got up. "Do you think I could ever master flying this plane?"

"Of course you could. There are quite a few gals these days flying airliners. If they can do it, you sure can do it and do it very well."

Ann chuckled. "Sure I could—on auto-pilot."

In late May, 1967 I was told to get ready to take four execs to Yemen. Obviously I wasn't privy to the whys and wherefores of the mission but I'm sure it had to do with the trouble that had been brewing for many months between Israel and their Arab neighbors. Our government and the oil companies, with huge interests in the area, were very concerned about what might happen throughout the Middle East if there was a war. The conventional wisdom was that war between Egypt and Israel would quickly spread and compromise those oil fields. Conventional wisdom also didn't think that war was imminent. The Israelis and the Arabs had been bickering for months and it was hoped that both sides would agree to some sort of a political solution and thus avoid an armed conflict.

Our departure date was tentatively set for June 3. The final manifest listed the four men plus two of their wives. My request that Ann also go on the trip was approved. On June 2, with Al Conley in the right seat, we flew the Jetstar to New York, and the following day we took off for Jerusalem with a stop for fuel in Lisbon. The flight plan allowed for a two-day layover in Israel so that the men and their wives could have a look around. It was sort of a company perk. The plan called for us to leave Israel for Yemen on the June 5.

On June 5, Israel launched a pre-emptive strike against Egypt—the beginning of the now famous "Six Day War."

When I managed to get to the Jerusalem airport, I was prohibited from entering the hanger area where the Jetstar was parked. Furthermore, I was told that we could not depart until clearance was received from the military. So there we were, right smack dab in the middle of an honest-to-God war, and who knew how long it would last and what would happen. My first concern was for the safety of Ann, Al and our passengers. My next concern was that Egypt would bomb the airport and our plane would be destroyed. The fighting became quite intense. For a while we weren't sure if we'd survive but the Israeli troopers were quite efficient and got the job done with very little loss of civilian life. On the first day, the Israeli Air Force knocked out most of Egypt's aircraft while the planes were still on the ground and their crews were having breakfast. It really was amazing how well the Israeli battle plan was executed, resulting in a victory that was achieved in just six days. On June 11 we received permission to fly to Yemen, where we stayed for five days before returning to the States. As I said, that was one of the more interesting trips. Ann and I talked about it for weeks after returning home, and for years afterward, every time I saw Al Conley, he'd say, "Boy, how 'bout that trip to Israel?"

The year 1968 found me flying back and forth to well sites and leases all over South America. It was interesting flying, especially flying into some of those primitive back woods airports and dirt landing strips. That's the thing about flying—it's sort of like taking a road trip on a motorcycle. You're going along, the plane is working fine, the weather is fine, nothing but sky or scattered clouds in your windscreen, when suddenly you see something that shouldn't be there—maybe it's a big bird or a little private plane that inadvertently wandered into your flight path. Or you're in unfamiliar airspace and you suddenly see a mountain top that's higher than you are. That's when flying gets exciting. The adrenaline starts pumping and that's when your training plus thousands of hours of driving one of these monsters pays off. It feels like hours upon hours of boredom interspersed with seconds or minutes of sheer terror. I've been really lucky.

The pilot of an Allegheny Airlines DC-9 wasn't so lucky when the civilian pilot in a small plane wasn't paying attention and flew into the DC-9, killing everyone in both aircraft. Civilian pilots were a constant worry because, while many of them were fine pilots, others were not—they just weren't able to fly enough to become really proficient. Even the best of us, in spite of all the hours and training, sometimes had bad things happen. I was landing a DC-3 with max cargo on a dirt strip in Venezuela when a blown tire sent the plane into the trees. The crew survived but the plane didn't. I have lost engines from time to time and it can get a little exciting when that happens, but I've never lost a plane as a result of engine failure.

Several events outside my little world did catch everyone's attention in 1968. The first was the assassination of Martin Luther King. That was big! The second was the killing of Robert Kennedy when he was campaigning for president. Things were definitely changing inside this country, and the Vietnam war also changed many things and many people. But the oil business kept chugging away and it kept me in the air.

Ann and I spent many hours flying the Cub here, there and yonder. She was handling the plane very well and getting better at it all the time. Some of my best memories of her are the trips we took in the plane and on our motorcycles. Great times. Great memories.

The 70s was a good decade for Ann and me, and in some ways they were also better for the country with the end of the Vietnam war. Ann's financial consulting business was doing well. She had hired a certified public accountant and a lawyer. Later, she took on two more financial planners who helped further lighten Ann's work load so that we had a lot more time to do things together and a lot more money to pay for it.

I sold the little Piper Cub and bought a new Cessna 172 for $16,000. When I told Ann what I had done I thought she would give me some static.

I broke the news this way. "You know, honey, I think you've outgrown the Piper. You are definitely ready for something with more get-up-and-go. A real airplane, not a toy. A plane that will present more of a challenge and allow you to improve your flying skills, and yet, not too complicated...you know what I mean?"

I delivered my speech while standing by the stove stirring a pot of beans. Immediately, Ann came over and stood in front of me, hands on hips, just like she used to do when she was about to deliver a stern lecture. "Okay, okay. I know what's going on here."

"You do?"

"Damn right. You bought a plane." She was trying very hard to keep a straight face.

I just gawked at her. I thought, how the hell does she do it? I raised my hands high above my head. "I surrender—you've got me. I bought a brand new Cessna 172 with an upgraded Garmin display, auto pilot with flight director and coupled approach capability. It's a beaut. You, my darling little aviatrix, are going to love it."

She more than loved it. After I took delivery, I had it in one of the company utility hangers. We pushed it out into the daylight and Ann got in and began fiddling with the controls and scanning the instruments, switches, levers, radios and so on. Compared to the Cub, there was a lot to look at.

"Is this going to be too much plane for me to fly?" she asked. "Good God, look at all this stuff. I haven't a clue as to what half of these gauges and controls are for."

"Everything you see there has a purpose. It won't take you long to get it all sorted out. Really, it's a pretty simple plane to fly, but compared to the Cub, it's a big step up. I'll just give you a brief overview for now and then we'll take it up."

I got in the other seat and gave Ann the indoctrination speech, explaining what every instrument and control was for. The 172 was a four seat, high wing plane with 160 horse power engine, which allowed it to cruise at 140 mph. It had a range of 700 miles. "I don't think we'll have to worry about cars going faster than this plane."

In a dozen hours flying with me, Ann was ready for certification, which she passed easily. When she was flying the plane, I always felt comfortable. I can't recall but one occasion when I took control from her. She was in the left seat flying to a friend's place outside of Santa Ynez, a little town north of Santa Barbara. Our friends had a large property with a two-thousand foot dirt landing strip. Ann lined up for the approach, reduced power, set the flaps for the landing when, without warning, a strong cross wind came in. We saw the runway dirt blowing from right to left. I yelled, "I've got it. Hands and feet off—now!"

Ann raised her hands to show me she had turned over control. We were committed, too late to pick her up and make another approach. It was tricky but certainly not outside my pay grade and I put her in. When I had shut her down—the plane, not Ann—I flashed my wife a broad smile.

"How did you like that stick and rudder show?" I asked.

Sweat had beaded up on her forehead, but she returned my smile. "That was some fancy dancing, I will say. And thanks for grabbing it when you did. I couldn't have done that. No kidding, that was really something."

"That's why they pay me the big bucks. I don't smash up their equipment even when things get hairy."

I unbuckled and opened the door but Ann remained in her seat. She sighed, "I'm just thinking about it, what you did. Do you think I'll be able to pull off something like that some day?"

"Of course. You learn that stuff by putting in the time. You know, if you'd been by yourself for that landing, I'm pretty sure you would have got the plane down in one piece. Necessity, I'm told, is the father of invention."

Our friends, Bill and Shirley Sheffield, came running over as we exited the plane.

"We saw that landing," Bill said, "that was pretty."

Shirley added, "It sure was."

"Ann was flying the plane," I said, "but as I've been telling you, she's one hell of a pilot."

Ann looked my way and started to say something but I shook my head and put a finger to my lips. That evening, just before turning the bed lamp out, Ann gave me a kiss and said, "That was very nice, you telling them I landed the plane. But you know, if I'd been flying, that Cessna would be all over the ground...in pieces."

"Really? I don't think so."

She rolled on her side and kissed me. "You saved my bacon."

I smiled and kissed her nose. "Well, then, good for me because I love to eat your bacon."

The eighties, at least, most of the decade, were good years for us. We purchased an older home, close to the water, in what was then an unincorporated area known as Malibu. We spent six months or more fixing it up and furnishing it.

When I had time off, Ann went to her office in Beverly Hills, a 30 mile drive, just three days a week. She also worked at home when necessary, thanks to a new piece of office equipment known as the personal computer made by IBM. It ran on the new MS-DOS operating system (whatever the hell that means). Anyway, Ann bought one and, no surprise, quickly learned to use it. Her work schedule gave her plenty of time to ride her bike or fly the plane, which we had moved to a rented hanger at the Santa Monica airport, just 20 miles from Malibu.

As I said, most of the eighties were good years but, in 1988, that changed. I'll never forget going in for the mandatory annual flight physical and the doctor telling me that he couldn't pass me because my heart was skipping beats. On top of that, he heard the sounds of regurgitation that were later confirmed in tests. I was sixty-two—only sixty-two, for God's sake. I still had three years before I would hit mandatory retirement age. Grounded! Sure, they offered a job in the flight department and I worked at it for a year or so, but I just couldn't stand being around the planes and pilots and not being allowed to fly. It really did throw me for a loop. I was only sixty-three years old and pushed into retirement.

Think about it. That's a long time to be out of work. I tried different things, even went to work in Ann's office, but I was totally out of my element there. It wasn't as if we needed the money. Hell, Ann's business was making all kinds of money and the investments she made with my money made our combined income rather amazing.

In spite of the affluence, our home on the ocean, and all the other stuff that money allows you to do, I was bored and drinking too much. I would get on my motorcycle and ride after getting a buzz on. That was stupid, as Ann and my friends often pointed out. When Ann and I rode together (we both had the latest model Harleys), I wasn't allowed so much as beer during the ride. It's probably why I'm still alive. Left to my own devices, I'm pretty sure I would have managed to kill myself.

I spent way too much time sitting on the second floor porch of our Malibu home, a glass of bourbon by my side, gazing out at the freighters plying their tedious way, watching the wake spilling off of their bows. Then I'd daydream about my time in the Navy, but mostly I thought about some of the trips I'd flown working for good old Standard Oil.

Knowing that no one ever came up to your plane and asked to see a current pilot's license, I continued to fly the Cessna but, to my credit, never when I'd been drinking. All those years living with the rules kept me on the straight and narrow. Whenever Ann was in the plane, which was most of the time, she'd do the driving. Her skill as a pilot was incredible. I can't begin to tell you how much I loved and admired that gal. Whatever she put her hand to, be it motorcycles, airplanes, computers, or running a very lucrative business, she did an outstanding job.

Oh, I forgot to mention, making love. With Ann, it never became stale or perfunctory; it was always, as she put it, "delicious." How many men do you know who could say that about their wives after twenty-five years?

chapter forty-four

I t was one of those really nice California days in September of 1989 and Ann and I were riding our Harleys, exploring, as we frequently did, new routes with lots of twists and turns and steep hills that presented a challenging ride. We picked up the 154 (a fantastic road for a motorcycle ride) at Santa Barbara and went over the pass, continuing on to the quaint town of Solvang where we planned to have lunch. After lunch and gassing up, we headed back and were within a mile of our home when Ann pulled into a convenience store. As she turned on to the unpaved parking lot, she lost control of her bike. It went down, breaking her leg. Even though the leg mended perfectly, she never got back on a motorcycle again. I kept nagging her to ride with me after her leg healed, but she said that she was fifty-six years old and probably never would have dropped the bike if she'd been younger and more alert. She sold the Harley, and that was that. I lost my favorite riding buddy.

The nineties are little more than a blur of time as far as I'm concerned. My so-called "exciting life" was pleasant enough. I had Ann, who after all the years was still my one and only true love—that never changed. Even after she quit riding, we still enjoyed trips in our plane or car. Now and then we even got on an airliner or a large ship. We went everywhere and we always managed to have fun enjoying the sights, sounds and tastes of other countries.

In 1993, at age sixty, Ann sold her business and we traveled even more. It did fill the time in interesting ways, but I still missed flying. I'm not talking about the Cessna—I mean the Jetstar and, yes, even the old DC-3. It's hard to explain and so I won't even try, but take my word, it's a terrible thing to want to do something—something you passionately love to do—and yet not be able to do it.

To add fuel to the fire, in 1995 Ann decided that we were both too old to continue flying our plane. She insisted it wasn't safe anymore, plus she pointed out most emphatically that I no longer had a license and thus every time I flew the plane, I was breaking the law. Can you believe it? She actually laid that on me and what followed was our very first serious argument. For me, it was the last straw and I just blew up. Afterwards, I told her how sorry I was and that it would never happen again—and it didn't. The good part is that Ann understood my frustration. She felt it too. After all, she loved flying as much as I, and although she didn't articulate it as I had, nonetheless I know she hated selling the plane.

We sold our home in Malibu in 2002 and bought a very nice property in Cave Creek, Arizona, a little town north of Scottsdale. Why would we have done something like that? Two reasons: First, we wanted to be where the winters were warmer and less humid than they are on the coast, and second, because Cave Creek was not very far from the Mayo Clinic and Hospital. Ann had developed cancer and we felt that the facilities and doctors at Mayo would provide the level of care that would produce the best possible outcome. And they did...for a while. Then things took a turn for the worst and Ann refused to do all the heroic procedures the doctors recommended. Although I wanted to keep her alive for as long as possible, I nonetheless allowed her to make the decision to, as she said, "get it over with." She died in 2006 at the age of seventy-three, just a month short of our forty-second anniversary. Losing the airplane was difficult. Losing Ann was a calamity.

Ann's death left me, at age eighty, alone in a big house with no one to talk to except my dog. I had outlived any relatives I may have had—plus my dentist, my doctor and most of my friends. But I still had my many motorcycle buddies, all of whom were much younger than me. After Ann died they were very good about inviting me over for dinner or cocktails, and I'd reciprocate with a meal or cocktail party now and then, but after a while the invitations became less frequent. Or maybe it was because I was turning the invites down thinking that I was imposing on their friendship. But we still went riding several times a week. They weren't long rides as in the past, just shorter outings to lunch or to one of the nearby lakes. I guess my riding buddies figured I wasn't up for anything longer, and maybe I wasn't. At the time, I had a Harley Heritage Softail Classic, a bike that weighed 720 pounds, and it was getting harder for me to keep it upright, particularly when turning at slow speeds. Still, I only dropped it once and that was on gravel, which can be challenging for any rider.

Within a month of Ann's death, I decided that I really needed someone in the house to help me. We already had gardeners who maintained the exterior of the home, a pool guy who came once a week, and a part-time housekeeper, who came twice a week after Ann started getting weak. She was a fine woman who I think loved Ann almost as much as I did. Her name was Marcella. She and her husband Eduardo had come to the United States illegally when Marcella was in her late twenties. I asked her if she would leave her other clients and work full time for me. Her job would be to stay in the house and keep an eye on me in case something happened—I was thinking heart attack or a fall or whatever old people with bad hearts do. I told her Eduardo was welcome to stay as well. They would use the guest casita which was attached to the house.

She was reluctant at first but when I asked her how much money it would take for her to accept the full time job, she said, "I don' know. Now, I have four houses I'm doing. I charge the peoples the same like you, eighteen dollars an hour." She looked at me for a moment then added, "So I'm makin' sometimes five hundred, sometimes maybe more..."

"Let's say you worked for me six days a week and I give you and Eduardo your room and meals." I picked up a little hand calculator from the desk and entered the numbers. "Let's see," I said. "Forty-eight hours times eighteen dollars equals..." I hit the total key, "Equals eight hundred and sixty four dollars a week."

Marcella's eyes lit up. "Oh, señor, that too much money. What I have to do? Not need to clean house every day...no, it be not so much work for every day."

"Okay, then," I said. "Here's what we'll do. You look out for me if something happens...you know what I mean?"

"*Si, comprendo.*"

"And I'll pay you one thousand dollars a week but you also have to cook the meals when I am here and you may have to do the shopping for food and sometimes drive me if I'm too sick to drive. You understand?"

"One thousand a week? That is funny. You joking with me, no?"

"*No estoy bromiendo,*" I replied. "I'm not joking."

Marcella and Eduardo stayed with me until 2008 when Marcella learned that her mother was very sick and they decided to return to Mexico. But she didn't leave me in the lurch—she lined me out with one of her cousins, a forty-six year old woman named Hortensia whose soldier husband had died in Iraq. Hortensia, who preferred to be called Tensie, was an attractive lady with a sweet personality and we hit it off immediately.

Tensie came to the United States from Mexico with her parents, albeit illegally, when she was just nine years old. At age eighteen, just out of high school, she married her American boyfriend, Bert Plover. They had one child, a girl who at age four managed to crawl under a chain-link fence and drown in an irrigation canal. I know that Tensie carried a lot of grief in her heart but she never spoke of it, and when I was around, she always maintained a pleasant and light-hearted demeanor.

So, there we were, two souls each grieving but allowing nothing to be seen by the other. Tensie and I would sit for hours talking, or watching television, or walking out on the desert. She said that walking was good for me, so I walked. Not that I liked walking—I guess I wanted to please her. She wanted to sit behind me on the bike and go for a ride but I wouldn't do it. "Too risky," I'd tell her. "It's one thing for me to go out and kill myself on the bike, but I don't intend to take you with me."

She loved to hear me talk about flying and all the places I'd been during my aviation days. I'd be telling her a story and she'd sit there, totally attentive for hours. I think the stories she enjoyed most were the stories about Ann. For a long time I never told her about Gunner and her swinging parties.

I was very interested in her life as well, and I asked her to tell me about her childhood days in Mexico, about growing up as an illegal in Texas and about her married life. I avoided asking about her daughter, but one night she told me about the accident. It was heart-wrenching and I felt so sorry for her as she recounted the drama and the agony in her life afterward. I couldn't help it...I took her in my arms and hugged her for a long time. After that, I decided to avoid asking her about her husband.

One night, however, we were sitting in front of the fireplace in the kitchen (yes, we had a fireplace in the sitting room part of the kitchen) and I was talking about my first trip up the PCH and meeting Gunner at a gas station. Tensie had heard at least a dozen stories about my first wife, Angie. Recounting those days sometimes brought tears to my eyes and I'd look at Tensie and see the tears glistening in her eyes as well. But on this night, in front of the fire, I told her about seeing the video of the New Year's Eve party and what a disturbing affect it had on me. I told her about visualizing Angie speaking to me as I rode up the highway. I told her how Ann had found me and how my life changed after that. Tensie never stopped my narrative to ask a question or comment. She sat in rapt attention, soaking up every word. And when my story was over and we got up to go to our bedrooms, she put her arms around me and kissed me very tenderly on the lips.

"You're a good man and I can understand why Ann wasn't about to let you go. Maybe she did a bad thing, but who hasn't? I've done many bad things and see how God has punished me. First he takes my baby and then my husband. But God can also be kind." She held me with her eyes and allowed a small smile to brighten her face. She whispered, "So God has sent you to me." I think I saw a wisp of color spread across her cheeks as she said, "Good night," and hastily left the room.

The next morning, Tensie was sitting on a high stool at the kitchen counter sipping coffee and reading the paper when I walked in.

"Good morning, Tensie," I said. "How are you this morning?"

I was anxious to see if that kiss last night had changed anything between us. Subconsciously, I guess I was hoping it had. Realistically, I knew that was a ridiculous thought.

Tensie looked up from the newspaper and slid off the stool. "Good morning, Rick. I'm fine like always. Have a seat and I'll make you a cappuccino." She walked behind the counter and turned on the espresso machine. "What would you like for breakfast this morning?"

I took a seat at the counter, picked up the front section of the *Arizona Republic* and said, "How about some grits and a couple Jimmy Dean patties?"

"Okay," Tensie replied. "Want a glass of orange juice?"

"Ah...no, thanks." I watched as she went about the business of making my breakfast. When the cappuccino was ready she passed it over to me. She did a great job making it and I needed that jolt of caffeine first thing in the morning. My heart would frequently beat irregularly or skip beats and I think the coffee gave it a kick start because it would resume a regular rhythm after an espresso. I've had several episodes of what they call "A-fib." That's when the rhythm becomes erratic and the heart rate (pulse) jumps up and down. Not a good thing. If it doesn't correct itself, then they slap those electric paddles on you and shock your heart back into a regular (sinus) rhythm.

Tensie laid my breakfast in front of me and took a seat next to mine.

"Don't you want some toast?" she asked.

"No, thanks, this is fine." I began eating and reading the paper. I had the feeling she was staring at me so I looked at her. She immediately turned her head.

"What's up?"

Without looking at me, she answered, "Nothing."

"Really? You know what I think?" I said with a smile. "I

us.

think you're a little embarrassed about that kiss last night. Am I right?"

She sat erect and turned toward me, "No, why would I be embarrassed? I wanted to kiss you and I meant what I said about God sending you to me." Her tone was definitely defensive.

I laid my fork on the plate. "Hey, take it easy. First of all, that was a very kind gesture on your part and I do appreciate that you shared your feelings with me. Furthermore, I'm sure you know that you are more than my housekeeper—much more. You and I are kindred spirits. We've formed a connection and I have to tell you that I'm so lucky that you've come into my life, especially at this stage when I needed someone to fill that huge companionship void. I really do see you as a companion and I love it. Do you not feel the same?"

"I don't know," Tensie replied. "I mean, what is a companion? Is that like a friend? Or is a companion more than a friend but less than a lover?"

I laughed. "You're making this too complicated when it's not complicated at all. Let's just say that we've become good friends—how's that?"

"Sounds good," Tensie said. She looked at my plate. Half the food was still uneaten. "Are you going to finish that?"

"No, I've had enough. Give the sausage to the dog." I got off the stool and walked out of the room. While in the shower, I thought more about the conversation Tensie and I just had. I had said we were *good friends,* and that was true enough, but was there something more? I chided myself. What the hell was I thinking of? Someone close to eighty-three! Still, I couldn't deny I was attracted to her. She wasn't beautiful like Ann, but she was pretty. Her jet-black hair framed her face in a most provocative way and, excuse me for saying it, but she had one hell of a cute little body. Add to that, her infectious personality...I stuck my head under the water. Whoa. That's enough of that.

I had an appointment with Dr. Hasfeld at 11. I dressed, said goodbye to Tensie, and drove to Mayo. I got there almost an hour before my appointment so I went up to the second floor, checked in, picked up a magazine from the rack then took a seat in the waiting room. A few minutes after 11, I was escorted to Dr. Hasfeld's office.

After examining me and spending some time listening to my heart, he said, "I actually think it sounds a little stronger and more even than last time but it's still pretty bad. Have you changed your mind about having that operation?"

I shook my head, "No. We'll just late nature take its course. Although I have to say that I've been feeling pretty good, all things considered."

I left the clinic and before going home, I stopped at Gallagher's for some lunch and a Guinness. After eating, I ordered up another beer and settled in to watch a game on one of the TV screens.

"Rick. Hey, Rick, wake up." I opened my eyes and saw Shawna, the waitress at Gallahger's looking down at me. "Tensie called," she said, "Time for you to get on home."

I sat up against the hard back of the booth and yawned. "What time is it anyway?" I asked.

"You're wearing a watch, for gosh sakes. Look at it."

I pulled back my cuff and waited for my eyes to focus on the dial. "4:40. I better get going. What do I owe you?"

As I pulled into the garage, Harley came up to greet me with a tennis ball in his mouth. "Come on," I said, patting him on the head. "I'll play ball with you later."

I walked in the house, went to the bathroom and washed up. "*Hola*," I yelled from the hallway. "*Como esta, chica mía? Donde es usted?*"

"*La cocina*," came her reply.

I figured that was enough Spanish for today and trotted into the kitchen. Tensie was getting something from the ice box, okay, refrigerator. I scooped her up in a big hug that lifted her off her feet. "So, *chica*, want to hear the good news from Mayo?"

"Hey," she squealed, "put me down and tell me."

"Okay, but first I need a little Scotch whiskey." I glided over to the bar, put some ice in a glass and poured a generous portion of Glenlivet single malt.

Tensie stood in front of the bar and watched with interest. "I thought you only drank that stuff." She pointed to a giant size bottle of Makers Mark.

"You are very observant, my little chickadee, but now it's time for something different...hence the Scotch."

"Rick, for God's sake, quit the fooling around and tell me what happened at Mayo."

"Now, Ann would have said, 'Rick, quit being a damn goofball.' But you're not Ann—which is fine, absolutely fine." I grabbed Tensie's hand and pulled her over to the couch. "Okay, sit down and I'll tell you all about it."

Tensie sat down by my side, folded her arms across her chest and crossed her legs. "Okay, go."

"The doctor listened to my heart, felt me up, so to speak, and said everything seemed to be pretty good...not fine, but pretty good. He read me the results of the tests they had done and said it looked like I was holding my own..."

"Holding your own? What the heck does that mean?"

"I guess it means I'm not any worse. In fact he said that as far as he could tell," I deadpanned, "I was still alive."

Tensie hauled off and punched me in the upper arm and I mean, really hard. I damn near spilled my drink. Then I got to laughing.

Straight faced, Tensie yelled, "Ann was right—you are a goofball."

That was too much, I almost went convulsive with laughter. "I'm sorry," I gasped. "Are you sure you're not Ann come back to haunt me?"

I was afraid Tensie was going to get a hammer and cold-cock me, so I settled down. "I'm sorry, honey, but you reach a point where, I don't know. Anyway, it's funny and yet, I guess from your perspective, it isn't that funny, right?"

"This thing with your heart valves is not funny at all. The fact that you refuse to do anything about it makes it even worse."

"Right. I know, but we've had that discussion before and I really don't want to get into it again, not now anyway. So, let's have dinner and enjoy the rest of the evening."

The next morning, after a late breakfast, I dressed in riding clothes—boots, jeans, and a grey shirt with a Harley-Davidson logo on the back.

Tensie was running the vacuum sweeper in my office when I walked in. She took in my outfit. "You going riding?"

"Yes."

She turned off the sweeper. "Who with?"

"Nobody. Just a short ride—blow off the cobwebs."

"You shouldn't go by yourself. You know that."

"Oh, for God's sake. You're starting to sound like Ann. She always fussed about my riding alone."

"Well, Ann was right. You shouldn't ride alone. You never know when something might happen."

I reached into the closet and pulled one of my leather riding jackets off the hanger and put it on, then strode into the garage to my bike. I pulled the helmet off of the handlebar and put it on.

Tensie was right behind me. She grabbed my shoulder and turned me around.

"I thought we were friends, companions and all that other stuff you talked about. If I'm your friend, why won't you listen to me? It's not safe at your age and with your heart problems for you to ride that damn motorcycle, but if you must, then at least have the good sense to have someone ride with you. Call up Don or Carl or one of your biker buddies and ask them to go along."

She was upset and I was being an inconsiderate jackass. I took off my helmet and said, "Okay. You win. I'll find someone to go with me."

Tensie gave me a luxurious smile, put her arms around me and kissed my cheek. "That's a good boy. I know I shouldn't bug you like this, but it's just that I don't want anything to happen to you. I've had enough losses in my life. I don't think I can handle another one." She turned away but I caught a glimpse of a tear forming in the corner of her eye.

Carl said he'd be right over. When he arrived, we drove up to a biker bar called the Hideaway. On the weekends this place would have a hundred or more bikes parked around it and the place would be swarming with bikers, biker babes, biker wannabees...you name it, all of them dressed in black leather. The chrome on all of those Harleys was blinding.

Besides the large Harley eagle emblem on the back of my jacket, I had a number of rally pins and patches, my Naval Aviator's wings and a patch on my sleeve that read "World War II Veteran." In 2010 there weren't that many WW II vets still alive and I imagine that even fewer were still riding motorcycles. So I was something of a novelty to that gay band of renegades that frequented the Hideaway. Well, maybe the word *gay* is not appropriate.

I sat with Carl and three couples at a large round table outside the main building. I knew two of the couples casually. The other couple was new to me. Carl and I had a beer. The others had ordered hamburgers and had already downed a lot more beer than was prudent when you're riding. Another gal came by and greeted the others—she was tall, with unkempt hair and large blue eyes, and was dressed in leather leggings and a tank top filled with eye-popping breasts. She pulled up a chair next to me, finished off a long neck beer, ordered another, and after chatting briefly with others at the table, turned to me and asked, "So, what's your story, old man?"

I gave her a blank look and asked, "Am I supposed to have a story?"

She didn't smile. "Okay, let me put it another way." She scrutinized my jacket. "Obviously you're a biker and a vet from the Second World War and," eyeing my Navy wings, "a pilot. So I'm guessing you have a story that would take the rest of the day to tell. That is, if I was to ask you to tell it."

I sat there expressionless, returning her gaze but not speaking. Everyone at the table was quiet.

"Well?" she asked.

"Well what?" I scrutinized her face, then said, "You said *if* you asked me to tell it, which you didn't. Besides there's nothing to tell that would interest you or anyone else for that matter."

"Yeah, you're right." She stood, downed the beer and addressed the others. "Gotta go. We're riding over to Bartlett Lake. Any of you want to go?"

I looked at Carl. "Let's ride up there. I haven't been there in a long time."

"Okay, if you feel up to it," he said.

And so we joined the group of about twenty bikes and roared up to Bartlett Lake, an hour's ride from Cave Creek. It's about twenty miles from the highway down to Bartlett Lake. The road is quite steep in places and full of hairpin turns, which is no problem unless a recent rain has washed sand onto the roadway. The key is not to take those blind turns too fast because if you hit some loose sand or a rock, you can certainly lose control and go down. Of course, as you know, I'm a fairly careful biker which is why I've never had a serious accident during the sixty plus years I've been riding these hogs. But the tall girl (her name I later learned was Kitty) who, by the way, wasn't wearing a helmet, and her friends were hot shots who rolled their throttles and roared through the turns. Carl, a few others and I soon found ourselves a half mile back of the leaders. On the straightaways we'd speed up and catch up, only to fall behind again as the road became a series of sharp turns with loose sand in some of the low spots.

We were within a couple miles of the parking area above the lake. The road was all downhill and the front runners were piling on the speed. Carl and I were at the very back, at least a mile behind the leaders. We came around a bend and saw in the distance that some of the riders had stopped. A little further on, riders were getting off their bikes and running toward a sand embankment. We rode up to the parked bikes and got off.

"What's going on?" Carl yelled.

Someone yelled back, "Kitty went off the road and down that hill." A number of riders had reached the area and were looking down. "She's down here!" One of them pointed.

Carl ran to the edge and looked down. I was already out of breath by the time I reached Carl. I saw the bike lying on top of Kitty. She had been riding a 900 pound, tricked out Road King. I was panting hard by the time I got there. Carl and some of the others joined the two men who were trying to lift the bike off so they could pull her out. I had to sit down. My heart was pounding so hard I thought it might blow up.

In a few minutes they had the bike lifted high enough to pull Kitty out and then they dropped it. Carl took a close look at the girl, then walked over to where I was sitting.

"How you doing, Rick?"

Panting and wheezing, I gasped, "Not so good. What about the girl?" I couldn't see her because most of the riders were standing around her blocking my view.

"She's dead."

"Dead? You sure?"

"Trust me. She's dead. It looks like her neck snapped when the bike rolled over her head."

"Help me up." Carl gave me a hand and I stood on unsteady legs. I yelled at the group, "Has anyone called 911?" Several people had. Regaining my breath, I pushed my way through the circle of people surrounding Kitty. One of the men grabbed my arm. "Are you a doctor?"

I calmly answered, "Yes." Nobody was going to check. Carl had it right. Her neck had been broken. She would have died instantly. Some people are just lucky. If she had survived, chances are she'd have spent the rest of her life in a wheelchair.

I looked into the eyes of everyone there and lowered my voice. "Some of you should stay with the body until the police and ambulance arrive. They'll want to know what happened." I began to walk away, but then, curious, I turned back to the crowd. "Who actually saw her lose control?"

Several people raised their hands. They all told the same story. Kitty was out in front, they came through a turn and there was something on the road. One man pointed to a large hubcap just above the scene. Kitty over-corrected to avoid it and the next thing they saw was her leaving the road and running toward the hill. The bike swung to the left and Kitty was thrown off. The bike must have rolled right over the top of her, then lifted her and carried her with it as it rolled down the hill.

I said to no one in particular, "Here's this young woman dead and for no good reason." I paused and scanned the crowd. Several of the riders looked my way. I met their gaze and said, "I've been riding these bikes for over sixty years...that's right, over sixty years, and I've seen it all. I can tell you that most of the accidents that didn't involve a car happened because the bike rider wasn't paying attention or was doing something stupid. In this case, you were stupid. All of you! You were going way too fast, plus you've been drinking more than was safe."

I looked down at the lifeless body. "One of you get something to cover her up."

As we walked toward our bikes, Carl asked, "Are you okay to ride home?"

"Yeah, I'm okay now. I'll lead. If my riding gets erratic, pull up next to me and tell me to stop."

We arrived at my place without further incident. I never went faster than fifty-five. Carl went home and I went into the house.

Tensie heard the garage door slam shut and called my name.

"I'm in the office," I yelled back.

She came in and looked at me. "What's wrong?" she asked. "Something happen?"

I flung my jacket on a chair, then sat down heavily on the couch. I was exhausted. "There was an accident."

"*Madre de Dio!*" Tensie exclaimed. "Are you okay?"

"Yes. I wasn't involved. The young lady who was leading the

ride went off the road and rolled her bike. It landed on top of her and killed her."

Tensie gasped, covering her mouth with her hand.

"She was going too fast." I stretched my legs out on the couch. "They all were. God damn bunch of morons."

Tensie sat down beside me. She looked me over and said, "But you're all right? You weren't involved?"

"Carl and I were way back of the pack when it happened. They were going too fast. Hell, I wasn't about to keep up with them, stupid bastards."

"You're upset, no? Come on in the kitchen and I'll make you a cup of tea." She stood, took hold of my hands and pulled me up.

I said, "I'll be right in. I need to wash up."

We went to a Mexican restaurant for dinner, and when we came home I poured a couple glasses of port and we sat on the patio and talked. I turned on the underwater pool lights. For a while we were silent as we watched the reflected lights change from white to blue to pink. It was mesmerizing.

Without warning or preamble, Tensie said, "You have to stop riding the motorcycle. It's too dangerous and you don't have the strength anymore to ride it safely like you used to. I think you know that but you hate to admit it. You think if you stop riding, somehow your life will stop too. But it won't. It didn't stop when you had to quit flying. It didn't stop even when Ann, your best friend and lover, died—did it? And it won't stop when you give up the motorcycle. And I won't have to worry every time I hear that damn thing start up."

"Tensie, you don't have to worry about it. When I feel like I can't handle it anymore, I'll quit riding and get rid of the bike."

Tensie moved to the edge of her seat, her hands on her knees and said, "Rick, don't you understand?" Her tone was firm, yet imploring. "It's like I told you the other night—I can't lose you. You are the most important thing in my life now. My job is to take care of you, but I can't take care of you if you are riding. Don't you see that?" She stood and walked over to my chair. Standing in front of me, fixing me in her sight, she pleaded, "I need you to do this one favor for me. I won't ever ask for another."

I gazed into her soft brown eyes, and saw that they were laced with tears. I considered what she had just said. Of course she was right. I had been thinking about selling the bike for a month. But, given my deteriorating heart condition, I also thought that perhaps a motorcycle accident that killed me would give me the way out I was searching for. But that idea was fading as Tensie took on a more important role in my life. She had been so good for me, so caring, thoughtful and, yes, perhaps even loving, that I knew I owed her the favor she so desperately wanted.

I took her hands in mine and gently pulled her down next to me. Searching her face, I said, "Okay. You win. I'm done with riding, just like I'm done with everything else I ever enjoyed. I'm an old man who has lived too long—outlived the life I used to enjoy—the flying, the long road trips on bikes, the loving, the being loved, the friends, the feeling that I could do anything I wanted to do. It's sad, but it's all a consequence of living too long."

"But no. That's not so," Tensie interjected. "There are still many things you can do—fun things, interesting things. And I'm here to help you do those things. You'll see."

I thought about it. In some ways I supposed she was right.

Before I could comment, she said, "You've had a wonderful life. You're rich, you're independent, you have a fantastic housekeeper and companion who would do anything for you." She thought a moment. "Besides, even though you have a bad heart, you look and act like someone at least ten years younger. Remember the doctor telling you that you were more like a seventy year old? What about that?"

I just had to laugh. She had so much enthusiasm and courage, she simply was irresistible. I put my arms around her and kissed her on the lips. She enthusiastically returned the kiss with one of her own.

After dinner, we took a short walk, then sat on the patio sipping wine and talking. I told her I was sorry that I didn't give her an adult depiction of what happened at Mayo. I said from now on, I would take her with me when I saw a doctor so that she would have first-hand information about my condition. She was very pleased with that.

Tensie looked at her watch. "It's late. You've had a long day so you'd better get to bed." She stood and turned off the pool lights and picked up the wine glasses.

I followed her into the kitchen and watched for a minute as she straightened things up.

She turned toward me and said, "If you get bored and need something to do, why don't you write a book about all your adventures? It would make a great story."

I chuckled. "A book about me? I don't think so."

I took a shower and climbed into bed, where I lay thinking about what had happened during the last few hours. I had actually said I would give up riding. Imagine me saying that! I heard the bedroom door creak open. Tensie was standing in the dim light. I sat up. "Is something wrong?"

"Ssshh, everything is fine." She came to the side of the bed, lifted the covers and slid in next to me. Pressing her body against mine, she whispered, "Sometimes when you give up one thing, you find another thing that is even better...*Verdad?*"

the end

about the author

R.D. (Dick) Elder, born in 1927, grew up in northeast Ohio. At age seventeen, he enlisted in the Navy and trained as a Combat Aircrewman, (radioman/gunner) during WWII. Discharged in 1946, he attended The Ohio State University, graduating in 1949. In the 1950s Dick became very interested in riding, training and showing horses and in 1960 moved to Durango, Colorado and built a dude ranch which he operated for thirty-seven years. The first ten years of that part of his life is the subject of his book, *Which Way is West*.

Dude ranching, he says, "is hard on horses and hell on wives." He's been married three times. His current wife, Ginny, broke the cycle—they've been married thirty-six years.

This book is Dick's second novel. The first was *Lovers & Liars*. His book of short stories and poetry, *It Sure Beats Working*, showcases his ability as a poet. He has been a regular participant at cowboy poetry gatherings for twenty five years. The Elders, their horses and Border Collie divide their time between homes in Durango, Colorado and Cave Creek, Arizona.